P9-EJU-222

Praise for the novels of USA TODAY bestselling author Victoria Dahl

"A delightful romance between two people who struggle to discover their own self-worth."
—*RT Book Reviews* on *Bad Boys Do*

"This is one hot romance."
—*RT Book Reviews* on *Good Girls Don't*

"A hot and funny story about a woman many of us can relate to."
—*Salon.com* on *Crazy for Love*

"*Lead Me On* will have you begging for a reread even as the story ends."
—*Romance Junkies*

"[A] hands-down winner, a sensual story filled with memorable characters."
—*Booklist* on *Start Me Up*

"Dahl has spun a scorching tale about what can happen in the blink of an eye and what we can do to change our lives."
—*RT Book Reviews* on *Start Me Up*

"Dahl smartly wraps up a winning tale full of endearing oddballs, light mystery and plenty of innuendo and passion."
—*Publishers Weekly* on *Talk Me Down*

"Sassy and smokingly sexy, *Talk Me Down* is one delicious joyride of a book."
—*New York Times* bestselling author Connie Brockway

"Sparkling, special and oh so sexy— Victoria Dahl is a special treat!"
—*New York Times* bestselling author Carly Phillips on *Talk Me Down*

**Also available from
Victoria Dahl
and Harlequin HQN**

*Real Men Will
Bad Boys Do
Good Girls Don't
Crazy for Love
Lead Me On
Talk Me Down*

And coming soon

Close Enough to Touch

VICTORIA DAHL

START ME UP

HARLEQUIN®

entertain, enrich, inspire™

If you purchased this book without a cover you should be aware
that this book is stolen property. It was reported as "unsold and
destroyed" to the publisher, and neither the author nor the
publisher has received any payment for this "stripped book."

Recycling programs
for this product may
not exist in your area.

ISBN-13: 978-0-373-77751-8

START ME UP

Copyright © 2009 by Victoria Dahl

All rights reserved. Except for use in any review, the reproduction or
utilization of this work in whole or in part in any form by any electronic,
mechanical or other means, now known or hereafter invented, including
xerography, photocopying and recording, or in any information storage
or retrieval system, is forbidden without the written permission of the
publisher, Harlequin HQN, 225 Duncan Mill Road, Don Mills, Ontario
M3B 3K9, Canada.

This is a work of fiction. Names, characters, places and incidents are
either the product of the author's imagination or are used fictitiously,
and any resemblance to actual persons, living or dead, business
establishments, events or locales is entirely coincidental.

This edition published by arrangement with Harlequin Books S.A.

For questions and comments about the quality of this book
please contact us at Customer_eCare@Harlequin.ca.

® and TM are trademarks of Harlequin Enterprises Limited or its
corporate affiliates. Trademarks indicated with ® are registered in the
United States Patent and Trademark Office, the Canadian Trade Marks
Office and in other countries.

www.Harlequin.com

Printed in U.S.A.

This book is for Bill.
I'm determined to make you laugh out loud
with this one, but I'll love you even if you don't.

ACKNOWLEDGMENTS

I have to thank my family first.
Thank you so much for putting up with a writer
who's been on multiple deadlines for over a year.
I'm sorry about the messy house. It will get better
next year. I'm almost *sure* of it. You make me proud.

Thank you to my wonderful editor, Tara Parsons.
You have an appreciation for both Audis and
backhoes, and that's priceless. Thanks for
getting me. And thanks to my agent, Amy.
I couldn't have done it without you.

And to all my wonderfully supportive writer
friends—Jeri Smith-Ready, Farrah Rochon and
Kristi Astor, to name a few—your support is
invaluable. Jennifer Echols, you know how
awesome you are, but I'll tell you again. You rock.

Last, I want to thank my readers. Thank you for
making all my work worthwhile. I'm honored.

START ME UP

CHAPTER ONE

"BABY, THAT IS one fine ass."

Lori Love ignored the purring voice and gave the mounting bolt on the transmission of the old Ford one last turn, laying all her weight against the wrench.

"Oh, yeah. Work it, darlin'."

When the bolt felt tight enough, Lori wiggled the body part in question and tossed a grin over her shoulder toward the blonde behind her.

Her best friend, Molly, leered, eyebrows raised in suggestive appreciation. "Do fries go with that shake, girl?"

Lori stood and set the wrench on her tool chest. "I had no idea this look got you so hot." She smiled up at Ben Lawson, standing behind Molly and very pointedly looking at the ceiling. "You should get some coveralls, Ben. Molly likes them."

He rolled his eyes. "Are we done talking about Lori's ass yet?"

"Oo, I don't know," Molly cooed. "It's so cute and perky. Doesn't it just make you think about—"

"You," Ben interrupted, "are the strangest girlfriend I've ever had."

Lori nodded in agreement. "She's a strange girl,

all right, but then you've been sheltered in this small town. Now, Moll, did you come here just to ogle my bottom, or is there something else I can do for you today? Lube job, maybe?"

They both descended into snorting laughter while Ben resumed staring at the ceiling in disgust. He was slightly more mature than the two of them put together. Good thing, considering he was the chief of police.

"I actually stopped by for a different reason," Molly answered. "Quinn's finally acknowledged that he can't fix his backhoe. He needs help. I'm hoping you'll stop by his place."

Thinking of Molly's older brother, Lori frowned. "Quinn's an architect. Why in the world does he own a backhoe? And why would he think he can fix it himself?"

Molly waved a hand. "You know those geniuses. Think they can do anything. I told you he's building a house up on the pass, right? His backhoe won't start and he needs to finish the groundwork before winter. He'll start the real building next spring."

"Wait a minute. You mean he's building it *himself*? I assumed you meant he was *having* a house built."

"Nope. He says it helps him relax. Who the hell relaxes by building a whole house? Could he *be* more of an overachiever?" When Molly looked as though she was going to get riled up, Ben tugged a lock of her blond hair between his fingers.

"Some of us don't have your artistic abilities,

Moll." He flashed her a private smile that relaxed her immediately.

Molly wrote erotic fiction for a living, which used to cause stress between the couple, but apparently Ben had come to terms with her job. Very pleasant terms. Lori managed to hide her envy by turning away to straighten up her tool chest. Not that she was interested in Ben. She just wanted some hot sex of her own. Looking down at her striped gray coveralls, she didn't feel very hopeful about her prospects.

"I'll run up to Quinn's this week," she offered. "Where is he, exactly?"

"His driveway's right at the snow gate on the Aspen side. Turn left and the site's about a quarter mile in."

"Nice," Lori breathed. Quinn must have been doing really well with his architectural firm. Only thirty-four and building his own mountain home with the gobs of money he'd made designing mansions for billionaires.

After arranging to meet Molly at The Bar on Friday, Lori got back to work on the Ford. She enjoyed fixing cars, she really did. Her father had put her to work on an engine when she was just six years old, and she'd been doing it ever since. But she'd never planned on working in her dad's garage—*her* garage now—her whole life. No, that hadn't even been a possibility when she'd left for college at eighteen.

But now it was all hers: the garage, the tow truck, the snowplows, the old dump out back. A bounty of unwanted mechanical glory.

Lori sighed and slammed down the hood of the car. Life wasn't fair, but she was a big girl.... Well, actually she was way too short for her taste. Five-two and petite, which posed a problem when bossing around drivers and mechanics. But she was her father's daughter, stubborn and realistic and not inclined to whine. So after his accident, she'd left college, painted all the trucks lavender, and taken control of the business.

When Lori turned the key in the ignition, the Ford roared to life, bringing a sad smile to her face. This was her job now, and she was good at it, and that was that.

She backed the car out and parked it in the gravel lot, then noticed that Ben was walking toward her. Alone.

"Hey," she called as she jumped out. "Did you lose your girlfriend?"

"No, she's over at the market. I actually need to speak with you about something, but I can come back tomorrow if you like."

"No, this is fine. No problem. What's up?" Once she'd locked up the car and met his eyes, he tilted his head toward her house.

"Why don't we go inside and sit down?"

"Are you kidding?" she asked with a sharp laugh. Her dad was gone, her mom and grandparents long dead. A cousin lived somewhere in Wyoming, but if Lori was his emergency contact his life was even sadder than hers. She raised her hands in confusion.

"Did you find out about that bank I knocked over? Because that was *years* ago. Childhood high jinks."

Ben pressed his lips together and stared, so Lori just shrugged and walked toward the house. Maybe one of her mechanics had been caught stealing cars or something. When she let him through the front door, Ben gestured toward the couch.

"Oh, come on," Lori scoffed.

"I think you should sit down."

"Ben, this is ridiculous. Just spill it."

He finally gave in. "All right. I've been looking into your dad's case…"

Lori's heart flipped over and made an awkward landing. "What case?"

He glanced determinedly toward the ratty couch again, then seemed to shrug into practical mode and plowed straight ahead. "The police station wasn't run with particular efficiency ten years ago when your dad was assaulted. Though the incident report was closed out, no one sent it to records. I've been slowly going through all the old files, trying to get everything where it should be. I ran across your dad's file last week."

Wishing she were at least standing next to the couch so she could lean against it, Lori forced her mouth to work. "And?"

"And I'm not entirely sure about what happened that night."

"It was a bar fight," she said firmly. "Just a bar fight like the other dozen he'd started in his life. And bad luck he hit his head on that rock."

Ben put his fists on his hips and looked down at the scuffed linoleum for a moment before he met her gaze again. "Lori, there's a possibility it may have been deliberate. I'm going to reopen the case. Quietly."

"What? That's ridiculous. Why would you do that?"

"I'm suspicious. That parking lot wasn't exactly littered with big chunks of granite. And if someone picked up a rock and hit your dad in the head, that's assault with a deadly weapon. And now that he's gone, maybe manslaughter or…"

Murder. He didn't say it, but Lori heard it anyway. Shaking her head in slow denial, she moved into the kitchen and put her hands carefully on the counter. The cupcakes she'd made yesterday glowed bright pink in the afternoon light, mocking the slow, bad turn her day had taken.

Ben continued, and the hesitation cleared from his voice as he took on his chief of police mien. "If he had died at the time of the injury, there would've been an examination, an autopsy. Careful evidence collection. But the focus was on saving your dad's life. Still, the scene photos don't show any other rocks around. The only object that could've caused the skull fracture is that one piece of granite and we already know it had his blood on it. It seems a bit too pat to me to think he just happened to have fallen square onto that rock.

"There were no defensive wounds on his hands, no evidence of a fistfight. And he wasn't found near his truck or even near the door of the bar. The back of the parking lot is an odd place to have a fistfight. Usually people just stumble out the front door and go at it."

"I suppose," she muttered, but she shook her head all the same.

"His autopsy reports are a bit of a mess with the healed fractures and surgical scar tissue, but I'm going to send the report off to Denver to get a second opinion. Just to see if there's any confirmation of my thoughts."

Lori tried to clear the sudden tears from her throat. "What is it you think happened?"

"I'm not sure." Ben sighed. "But there's a good possibility that someone attacked your dad from behind. Maybe when he was turning away from an argument, or maybe he didn't even know someone was there. But that's not much to go on. No one at the bar admitted to seeing anything after your dad left. He didn't argue with anyone while he was there, at least not according to the notes. I'm going to have to conduct new interviews, but I'd like to keep it quiet as long as possible."

"I… Okay. What do you want me to do?"

"Nothing," Ben answered quickly. "You don't need to do anything right now. Like I said, I want to keep this quiet. I'll just be making some inquiries, trying to fit the pieces together. But I didn't want you in the dark about my suspicions."

"He's dead now," Lori murmured. "It doesn't matter."

But of course it did.

LORI COULDN'T SLEEP that night. She tossed and turned for hours. By four-thirty she felt as if she might implode, as if all the thoughts swirling through her head would finally pull her in on herself and—poof!— she'd be gone. Her father, her life, the things she'd wanted for herself...

She couldn't take it anymore, so she got up, showered and headed for the garage to change out the fuel pump on Mr. Larsen's Chevy.

The air outside was perfect and crisp, but Lori only cracked open the garage door a few inches. She didn't want to take any chances with curious bears. Especially if they were looking for breakfast.

As she worked at wrestling the old pump out, her thoughts became clearer and slightly more painful.

What if Ben Lawson was right? What if her father had been deliberately hurt? His skull fractured, his brain damaged, his life taken away long before he'd died... What if someone had done that on purpose?

She grabbed a rag and wiped sweat—or tears— off her face, then bent back to her task.

She hadn't complained about the turn her life had taken. Accidents happened. She'd given up on college and travel and dating, but she'd done it for her father, willingly. He would have done as much or more for her. So, no, she hadn't complained about what she'd given up.

But giving up something was very different than having it taken away.

Her teen years had been filled with books and hopes and a steely-eyed determination to get into the college of her dreams. And she'd done it. She'd gone off to Boston College, and her father had been so proud. Then he'd been hurt, and she'd left that behind, but she was beginning to realize she'd left behind a lot more than her education.

Her twenties had revolved around caring for her dad and keeping his business going to pay for it. Her life had been spent in coveralls and boots, T-shirts and jeans. Any love affairs had been brief and unexciting.

But lately, even before Ben's news, she'd been restless. She couldn't just leave Tumble Creek. Couldn't hop on a plane and start college again. There were simply too many bills that had piled up over the years. Caring for a semivegetative relative wasn't cheap.

So she couldn't simply walk away and start over. But she could change her life in smaller ways, and something inside her was calling on her to take action. Perhaps this was just a natural consequence of nearing thirty. But that restless feeling had rapidly grown more intense since Ben had dropped by.

Noticing that the sunlight was now bright yellow instead of pale pink, Lori glanced up at the clock. Seven-thirty. When she raised the garage door the rest of the way, the spectacular clatter echoed through the high-ceilinged garage. She strolled out into the sun and bright birdsong, but the gravel of the lot crunched and popped beneath her boots, distracting her from the beauty of the morning. She thought mournfully of the red polish she'd painted onto her toenails the night before and sighed.

Maybe she should try another fling.

Or maybe she should just order another box of books from Molly's publisher.

Either way, after she stopped by Quinn's lot tonight, she'd come home to take a bath and read a dirty story. Then maybe she'd think about going shopping for a pair of open-toed heels that would click against the ground instead of thud. She jogged back in to call Molly.

As she grabbed the phone, her thoughts were interrupted by a startling chirp from the receiver in her hand. She nearly dropped it, which would have pissed her off immensely. As it was, she'd had to replace two phones already this year. One had fallen victim to the big, clumsy hands of her least-favorite plow driver. The other had somehow gotten itself mixed up with a big tub of lube, which wasn't nearly as fun as it sounded. Not for a phone anyway.

"Love's Garage," she snapped into the phone.

"Ms. Love?"

"Yes."

"Hello! This is Christopher Tipton!" Chris always announced his name as if she'd won a prize.

Lori slumped onto a stool. "Hey, Chris." She'd known him since grade school, but she had a feeling he wasn't calling to reminisce. "What's going on?"

"I was just wondering if you've had time to think over selling that parcel of land we discussed in February."

That parcel of land, he said, as if it hadn't been everything her dad had ever dreamed of. "Look, Chris,

I'm sorry. It's only been a few mon—" Actually, that wasn't true anymore. It had been a whole year since her dad had died. Jesus. When had that happened?

"I know it's difficult to consider. And I know it hasn't been that long for you, but I think you'll find that Tipton & Tremaine has put together a very generous offer—"

"I just… I need more time."

He sighed. "I understand. Just promise you won't consider any other offers without contacting me first. I can assure you that we want to preserve the natural beauty of the place. We're not talking a big two-hundred-house development here. Just a small group of sportsmen's cottages along the river."

"Yeah, I get it," she muttered, thinking about the kind of "cottages" his firm usually built. Something more along the lines of a grand hunting lodge that could easily house seven families. Or one enormously rich one. It had always struck her as funny that rich families needed so much space for their one-point-eight children.

"I won't consider anything without calling you. Promise."

"Okay, I'll—"

"Bye." Lori hung up and kicked the steel beam in front of her, glad she wasn't wearing heels now.

JEEZ LOUISE, LORI thought as she turned onto Quinn Jennings's so-called driveway; it looked more like a dirt trail. He really was roughing it up here. She'd never have even slowed if not for the Jennings's Lot

sign tacked to a fence post. The correct placement of
the apostrophe made her smile.

Her truck scraped beneath the low branches of
lodgepole pines and stirred up the scent of the green
aspen. Even in August the air was crisp and cool in
the shade. Boy, it would be cold up here in winter.
Did he plan to stay year-round?

When she finally emerged from the trees, Lori felt
a little shock. She hadn't known what to expect, but
it hadn't been this. A tiny log cabin stood at the edge
of a meadow blooming with wildflowers. The music
of running water floated on the air, audible even over
the heavy sound of her motor. It seemed more likely
she'd find a herd of elk here than a construction site.

But when she drew closer, the backhoe appeared
behind the cabin, frozen like a strange giraffe lowering its head in defeat. Lori drove toward it, not even
noticing Quinn until she'd parked and gotten out.

He stood at a drafting table set up on the tiny back
porch of the cabin, facing the sun-drenched trees to
the east. It was no surprise that he didn't look up
when Lori slammed the door of her truck. Quinn had
a singular skill of tuning out the whole world when
he was working on something important to him. This
was clearly important.

"Hey, Quinn," she called anyway.

"Hey," he answered, without even a glance.

She smiled at his bent head, noticing the glint of
sun against his light brown hair. "I'm just going to
check out the backhoe for you."

"Sure." He frowned ferociously at something on

the big drafting sheet and began to draw. Hunched over like that, he looked shorter than his nearly six feet, but his shoulders seemed wider than she remembered. His hands… Well, his hands moved with that elegant precision she'd noticed even when she was a nerdy teenager.

Lori grinned at the sight of those hands moving over the paper. The nice thing about Quinn was that she could probably stand there for an hour watching him, and he'd never notice. Lovely man. No idle conversation to disturb her daydreaming. Still, she was going to lose her light if she didn't hurry.

After tucking a brown curl behind her ear, she climbed up into the machine. It was an old model— a strange lemon color, freckled with rust spots and complete with a small dozing shovel on the front. Quinn must have picked it up from one of his contractors for a steal. And what man *wouldn't* want to own a big ol' construction machine? Lori didn't even need one, but she was tempted to ask if she could borrow it when Quinn was done. Surely she could find some stuff to move around the junkyard behind her house.

The key was already in the ignition, so Lori turned it. There was a faint electric hum, but nothing else. She let out a breath at the sound. Good, this was probably something she could fix. If it had been a problem with the hydraulics, Quinn would've had to call in someone more expensive.

She tried again, listening more closely. It was almost certainly the starter, and hopefully this model had an electric starter and not one of those air-start systems. If it was an air-start, she'd have to refer him to a diesel specialist after all. Lori jumped down to take a look.

Half an hour later, she wiped her hands on a rag and spent a few minutes writing down part numbers and brands. She could fix this, no problem.

"Quinn, I'm going to have to order two parts, but I should have them in a couple of days. I'll be back then."

"Great," was his only response, though he followed it up with a hurried, "Thanks." The sun was still slanting across the clearing, throwing Quinn even deeper in shadow.

Lori shook her head. Not one of her other customers would say "great" without even asking the price. Then again, she didn't usually work on the Aspen side of the pass.

She allowed herself one last glance at him, watched him rub his thumb thoughtfully across his bottom lip for a few moments and then Lori headed home.

QUINN JENNINGS BLINKED from his thoughts about angles and sunlight and shadows. He glanced around in confusion, then looked down to the cell phone barely hanging on to the edge of the drafting table. Nope, no call coming in. He looked around one more time, wondering what had changed. Then he realized what had distracted him: the silence.

The backhoe stood alone, still frozen. Lori Love had been here, climbing over the machine and making a racket. She must've left at some point, and Quinn was pretty sure he hadn't even said goodbye. Wincing in guilt, he backtracked his memory. She'd said something about ordering parts, so she'd be back in a few days and he'd be sure to offer her a coffee or something civilized like that.

Just then the setting sun broke through the pines, streaking past the quaking aspen leaves and casting mottled, moving shadows against the big boulder that marked the eastern edge of the clearing. That was exactly what he'd been looking for, just that tone and timing of light.

Quinn threw off any thoughts of visitors and began sketching furiously, capturing his new vision for the entry of the house. Losing track of the world around him was a high price to pay, but it always got Quinn just what he wanted. At work, anyway. And if he concentrated hard enough, he never had to think about the rest of his life, or lack thereof.

CHAPTER TWO

The man—she didn't know his name and didn't want to—roughly tugged her pants to her knees and pushed her facedown over the table.

"Don't say a word."

She nodded and bit her lip in desperate anticipation. When his calloused, unfamiliar hands touched her hip, she jumped and gasped. The tension was already winding tight within her, a serpent looking for release.

Holding her steady with one hand, the man pushed the head of himself against her opening. No stroking, no preparation. He just guided himself close and shoved hard and deep. It didn't matter. She was already wet.

Marguerite screamed.

LORI SET THE BOOK DOWN with a guilty glance around her. Joe hadn't returned from his towing run yet, but she still felt bad because she was sitting in Love's Garage, surrounded by her father's tools, and totally aroused from reading a dirty book. Sure, it was a Saturday, but this wasn't even borderline professional behavior. She should've at least retreated to her house.

Maybe to the bedroom. She eyed the clock. Three hours more to go. Although she *was* the boss....

The phone rang, cutting off any chance she could slip off to her bedroom for some personal time. "Hello?" She tossed the compilation of erotic stories onto the worktable.

"Lori, it's Ben."

"Hey, Ben." He was calling to tell her he'd been wrong. He must be.

"I know I must have shocked you the other day. Are you doing all right?"

"Sure, I'm fine." Just tense and irritable and restless.

"Good. I'm still waiting on more information. Old cases take a backseat in the state system, of course. But in the meantime, I wondered if you could answer a few questions."

Lori blinked. "Um, sure. But I wasn't here when the acci—when he was hurt."

"I just mean some general thoughts. Did your dad have any enemies? I don't mean Capulet-Montague kind of stuff. Just some guy he never got along with. Maybe a garage owner in Grand Valley he was stealing business from. A customer accusing him of fraud or theft."

"Oh, I don't think so."

"A woman? Was he dating someone, or maybe a few someones?"

She blinked again, struck by how strange the idea was. "Not that I know of."

"Okay. That's fine. It's nothing urgent. I just want

you to keep these questions simmering in the back of your mind. Write down anything you think of. Any reason at all someone could've been after your father. Money and passion are the two most common denominators in these situations."

"Yeah, but…" Lori closed her eyes and rubbed her free hand over her face. "Ben, I'm sure it was just some stupid barroom brawl. Nobody wanted anything from him. He didn't *have* anything."

"You're probably right, but I wouldn't be doing my job if I didn't consider every angle. I don't mean to upset you—"

"No, I'm sorry. I can't say I'm happy about this, but it means a lot that you're looking into it. I'll help any way I can."

"Thanks, Lori. Call me if you think of anything, or if you just need to talk, all right?"

Just after she hung up, Joe roared into the lot with a suddenness that made Lori jump. Dust floated up in his wake while she rubbed her eyes.

"Nothing serious?" she called hoarsely when he descended from the cab.

"Flat tire. Nobody can change a flat tire anymore, you ever notice that?"

Yes, of course she'd noticed, and had said as much the first thousand times they'd had this conversation. Still, the auto clubs paid them thirty dollars a pop to fix a flat, so the decline of manly civilization was just fine with Lori. Joe inclined his head toward the phone.

"Another run?"

"No, just a personal call." She eyed him as he pulled a handkerchief from his pocket and wiped sweat from the nape of his neck. He looked old, suddenly. He'd been older than her father by a few years, but they'd been as close as brothers. And Joe had been like a second father to her.

He'd worked in the garage since before Lori was born. But he'd been more than an employee.

Joe had picked her up from school countless times, applauded her achievements, lectured her about boys and drinking. She wouldn't have been able to care for her father if Joe hadn't been there to pick up the slack in the garage. She hadn't been able to pay him enough for essentially running the garage for those first few years, but Joe had never complained. Not once.

And he'd known her dad better than anyone.

"Joe, can I ask you something?"

He shrugged and dropped into a chair. "You know you can ask me anything. Shoot."

"I've been thinking about my dad lately. I wasn't here those last few months before his accident. What was his life like after I left?"

Joe shrugged. "Same as always, really. Work. Fish. Grab a beer."

"Was he dating anyone?"

She must have surprised him. Joe tucked his chin in. "Dating? Nothing serious that he ever mentioned. There was a waitress over in Grand Valley he stepped out with sometimes, even when you were still here. A woman over in Eagle he saw once or twice. But he

was a loner. After your mom left…" He squinted up
at her. "He wasn't much on relationships after that."

Lori cringed. Her mother had run off when Lori
was five. She'd left both of them behind and never
looked back. She'd died about eight years ago from
liver failure. Hepatitis C. So Lori was officially an
orphan.

"She wrote me once," Joe said, shocking Lori so
much that she gasped.

"What?"

"Your mom. She wrote to me. You were probably
fifteen by then. She wanted to know how you were
doing."

"But…why did she write to *you?*"

Leaning forward, he rested his forearms on his
knees and stared at the floor. "She was too ashamed
to write to your dad, maybe. I wrote back to tell her
how amazing you were. Smart and hardworking. I
never heard nothing after that."

Lori cleared her throat. "You don't think she ever
got in touch with my dad?"

His eyes rose quickly to meet hers. He held her
gaze for a long moment. "He never said anything
about it."

"Yeah." Nodding, she kicked the cement with her
boot. "I guess she never did. Thanks for telling me,
Joe."

"You bet, darlin'. Anything else you want to
know?"

"No. I'm gonna head up to Quinn Jennings's place.
If there aren't any calls in the next thirty minutes,

you can go. Just forward the phone to my cell." She grabbed her book to head for the door, but Joe cleared his throat and stopped her.

"Say, before you go… Have you thought anymore about selling your dad's lot?"

Lori managed not to groan. What was it with that piece of land? Sure, it bordered a good stretch of the river, but it didn't hide access to an old silver mine. Or maybe it did. "Joe, I'm sorry. I'm just not ready. I know it's been a year now, but my dad was so happy when he bought it. You know what I mean."

Joe held up his hands and offered a sad smile, the sympathy in his eyes a familiar comfort. He'd made an offer on the land soon after the accident when he'd realized she was having financial problems, and if she was going to sell to anyone, it would be to Joe. He loved that place and fished there all the time, even though his fishing buddy was gone.

She joined him sometimes, and it was as if her father was there with them, too. Just like the old days. Her two favorite people in the world.

Joe's scarred fingers closed over her elbow. "No pressure, Lori. You just say the word when you're ready to discuss it. Say, whatcha reading there?" He stood, starting to reach for the book, but Lori danced out of his way.

"I'll see you Monday!" she called, grabbing her keys to head for Quinn's cabin.

After rolling down the window and speeding out of the lot, Lori shoved a CD into the player and turned it up way too loud. The wind wreaked havoc on her hair, but for once, Lori didn't care. The loud music and the beautiful day chased away her ghosts, mostly because she wanted them to.

Whatever had happened in her life, whoever she was, she needed to be free of it, just for a moment. Her hair, the one thing she loved about her looks, bounced and writhed in the wind. The music thrummed a sexy beat through her body. And the cool air made her cheeks glow pink.

She was twenty-nine years old. An orphan, sure. A single woman with no prospects. But she was hardly dried up and done. What she needed was a distraction.

Ben had stirred up dusty memories, and if she didn't distract herself, she'd find herself living with ghosts. It wouldn't be a long trip for her. She was living in her dad's house, driving her dad's trucks, doing her dad's work. If she wasn't careful, she'd turn into a fifty-nine-year-old man with a salt-and-pepper beard and hairy arms.

She needed a distraction. She needed to be a *girl*. No, not a girl. A woman. A fling would offer that much at least, and give her something pleasant to think about while Ben screwed with her life.

Or would it? She'd had casual sex before, and fireworks hadn't exactly exploded behind her eyes. Firecrackers, maybe, down a little lower. *Pop!* And that was it. Night of adventure over. What the hell kind of distraction would that be? She needed...*more*.

In all honesty, Lori had never been as aroused in a man's arms as she was reading the erotica that Molly had her hooked on. And despite the rumors around town, she wasn't the least bit interested in women. So what did that mean? Did she need more...kink? Did she want a stranger to treat her with rough force like that last story she'd read?

"God, I don't think so," she muttered to her steering wheel.

Did she want to be tied up, spanked, or passed around a werewolf pack? Because she'd liked all those stories, too. Laughter bubbled up and made her snort. That werewolf fantasy would be a hard one to pull off. She'd have to troll through the forest in high heels, just praying one of the scruffy campers was actually a raving beast.

Her truck roared as it strained up the steep climb to the summit, but Lori barely noticed the impressive view. She was too busy analyzing her sexual needs.

No werewolves then, but what about all the other stuff?

She hadn't been at college long enough to go out with more than one boy, no time for experimentation, and since then she was just...dating. Barely. Her frustrated groan broke in two when she hit a rut in the road. *Dating.* She'd only met a few men she'd even wanted to sleep with and couldn't imagine asking any one of those guys to spank her.

Though Jean-Paul probably knew how to spank a girl. He'd probably done it dozens of times. Maybe she should call him. Maybe—

"Oh, for God's sake," Lori growled. She didn't even *want* to be spanked. She just wanted to have a spectacular orgasm or two. She wanted spark and sizzle and a whole damn conflagration.

Her life was about to speed past thirty, but a real relationship was out of the question. She might not have a plan to escape her life, but she wasn't ready to surrender to it completely. Someday she would leave Tumble Creek, find a way to move on. But for right now she wanted...more. Any excuse not to think about her problems.

Instead of worrying, she wanted to be glowing, moaning, panting. *Wet*. Just like the women in those books.

New shoes definitely wouldn't do that for her, but it would be a start. A signal that she was ready and willing. And maybe, just maybe, the perfect stranger would come along and coax her to slip those shoes off. Or, better yet...order her to keep them on.

Lori gunned the engine and climbed toward the sky.

"HI, QUINN," A voice said from right beside him. Much as he wanted to keep taking notes for his latest idea, Quinn resolutely put the pencil down and turned toward his visitor. When he saw her familiar curly brown hair and green eyes, he smiled.

"Lori!" He pulled her into a hug.

"Oh... Hi!" she squeaked, and Quinn quickly let her go.

"How've you been?"

"Good. You know...the same." She shoved her hands into the pockets of her gray coveralls as a gust of wind blew up from behind her. Her curls bounced, tugged by the breeze, and her cheeks turned pinker as he watched.

"Well, you look great. Want a cup of coffee?"

"Um, no, I don't think so. I'd better just get to work. I got those parts in last night."

"Come on. Have coffee with me. I feel bad about last time."

"What about last time?" she asked, though she walked into the cabin when he waved her on. With her hands in the pockets, Quinn noticed the way the baggy coveralls pulled tight across her ass. He was pretty sure he hadn't seen her in anything but coveralls in the last five years. Maybe ten.

He edged past her to start up the small coffee machine he'd plugged into the generator line. When he spun back toward Lori, she was turning in a slow circle.

"Are you actually living here?"

He glanced toward the bed. "Sometimes."

Her boots clomped against the scarred wood floor. Quinn looked from the steel-toed leather up to the delicate shape of her face and shook his head.

Lori frowned. "Why are you shaking your head at me?"

"Nothing. Yeah, I've been staying up here most of the summer."

She cast another doubtful look around the tiny one-room cabin. "Where do you keep your suits?"

"Back at my place in Aspen. I head there every

morning to shower and dress. The solar water heater isn't particularly effective after a cold night up here."

"I guess not! I can't believe it's so cold up here in the middle of August. It was nice in Tumble Creek." She shuddered, eyeing the coffeemaker.

Quinn laughed and grabbed a mug to pour her the first cup.

She glanced out the window. "You must get a lot of bears up here."

"Bears? I don't know…"

She waved a hand. "They're all around here, Quinn. So…what did you mean about being sorry for last time?"

"When you came by to look at the backhoe I was a bit absorbed in my work."

"A bit," she said with a grin.

"I didn't even realize you were here until you were gone, then I felt like a complete idiot."

Lori waved a dismissive hand. "Don't be ridiculous. I've known you long enough not to be offended. You've always been that way. What did your dad used to call you? Doctor Distraction?"

"Yeah." Quinn grinned.

"But I am glad you emerged from your daze long enough to offer me coffee this time." She raised her cup in thanks and then gulped half of it. "Nice. I'm almost warm enough to go back out in that wind."

"Hold on." Quinn knelt down to rummage through the wooden box he kept next to the counter and dug out a knit cap. He tugged it over her hair. "This will help," he murmured, as he concentrated on tucking a dozen stray curls under the cap.

"Stop!" She tried to duck away. "I don't like hats."

"It's cold."

"The coffee is enough." She finally evaded his hands and yanked the stocking cap off, then stood, straightening out her hair and glaring at him.

"And I've always thought you such a simple woman. Who knew you were quirky *and* irritable?"

Lori rolled her eyes and tossed back the last of the coffee. "I should be done in about forty-five minutes."

"Wait. Don't storm out." He pasted on a mock serious look. "This is turning out even worse than last time. I'm sorry I tried to put a hat on you. I apologize. That was inappropriate and horrible. I don't know what I was thinking."

Amusement immediately replaced the annoyance on her face, and Lori laughed. "I just don't like hats, okay? Drop it."

She'd always had a great smile. In the rare moments on the school bus when both of them hadn't had their heads stuck in books, Quinn would sometimes hear her laugh and turn to see her brilliant, wide smile. Not often, but that only made the smiles seem more important. And now? Now she was just a mystery. Unknowable and completely self-contained.

But she still had that smile.

He realized just how glad he was to see her. "Thanks for coming up to fix my machine, Lori."

"You're welcome, Quinn," she called sweetly as

she stomped toward the door in her big boots. "Give me an hour. Then we can discuss my bonus."

LORI PULLED A few more curls back into sproinginess as she stared at the backhoe's engine. She made very sure that she appeared irritated instead of slightly excited. Those hands she'd wondered about had stroked over her forehead, her cheeks. Elegant as they looked, Quinn's fingers were slightly rough, raspy from the work he'd done here on the mountain.

But it had been a fraternal sort of touch. As it should have been. Quinn was her best friend's brother. He thought of her as a little sister or possibly not at all.

"More likely the latter," she muttered, and forced herself to get to work.

"You say something?"

She jumped and banged an elbow on the angled hood. But Quinn didn't notice. He was already back to staring down at his drafting table. "What are you working on?" Lori couldn't help but ask.

He looked up, blinking as he always did when he surfaced for air.

She repeated the question.

"Oh, plans for the house."

"But you've already started building." She glanced toward the gray lines of concrete she could just make out at the edge of the meadow. "The foundation looks set."

"Yeah, I've completed all the floor plans. Actually, I had everything done, but now I'm stumbling over the design details. I keep changing them." He smiled in a self-deprecating way. "I do this every day for other people, but it's much harder working on a house I plan to live in for decades. A brilliant new idea will come to me, then the next morning it's clearly crap. I think I have a new sympathy for clients and their ever-evolving ideas."

"That's probably a good thing." Lori looked around at the meadow and the trees and the blank expanse of sky suspended above the cliff. "You come here for inspiration then?"

His eyes lit up. "Exactly! The light, the color... shades and hues that change from minute to minute. I need to get the windows just right, the height and shape of them. The texture of the walls against the light. I need to know what the views will be in morning and afternoon and evening." His hands gestured, and Lori greedily watched every arc, every twitch.

"That evening you were here," he continued, "right after you left, the sun burst through the aspen, and I finally realized just the type of window I should place above the front door. The exact grade of stone to use on the fireplace where it rises up to the second floor... Shit, I'm sorry."

Lori shook off the spell he'd cast with his bright eyes and deep voice. "What?"

"Sorry. I know I tend to go way past the boredom mark for most people. Not just computer engineers are nerds, I'm afraid."

"No, I think it's amazing! You look like you're in love."

"Oh." He actually blushed. This tall, successful man standing in front of a log cabin in a flannel shirt. He blushed.

"It's sweet!" Lori assured him.

"Yeah, great. *Sweet*. The ultimate nerd compliment."

She couldn't help but laugh. When he scowled, she laughed harder. "Give it up, Quinn. I'm not going to feel sorry for you. Even if you could convince me you're a nerd, you're still hot and rich and successful. Poor baby."

Shaking her head, she set to work on removing the old starter. Maybe he *was* nerdy in the strictest sense of the word, but she knew plenty of girls in her junior high class who'd thought him tantalizingly mysterious before he'd gone off to college. Bookish and distracted took on a whole different meaning when the boy in question was also gorgeous and kind.

"Hot?" she heard him ask, and looked up to see him leaning against the porch rail watching her.

"Huh?"

"Hot. You said I was hot." He kept his mouth serious, but his hazel eyes danced with laughter.

This time Lori's face heated. She waved her wrench in his general direction. "I was just stroking your ego."

"Well, nice work. It felt good, your stroking."

She growled in frustration. "Go away. I can't work with you staring at me."

"You mentioned a bonus earlier. What did you mean?"

Something playful and husky had entered his voice, confusing her. And the word *stroking* was still echoing through her limbs. "Nothing," she blurted out. "I just hoped you'd let me borrow the backhoe sometime. When you're done with it."

"That's all?"

"Yes. Now could you please leave me alone?"

"But you're in my office." The aspens shook in the face of a gust, as if confirming his words.

"Fine. Look at your trees then. Not me."

"I don't want to be inhospitable." She thought his gaze flicked down her body in a quick caress, which was silly since she was in her standard gray coveralls.

Suddenly, she really hated what she was wearing. It was Saturday. Maybe she should have arrived in a tank top and cutoff shorts with a plan to find many reasons to bend over while working. Of course, that would be before the frostbite set in.

Lori turned her back. "Fine then. Work and talk."

"About what?"

Shrugging, she made sure to sound casual. "Where was the first place you went in Europe? You studied there, didn't you? Tell me about it."

After a long moment of silence, he did. His voice softened after a time, as if he were talking to himself, but Lori absorbed every word and stored it away for later.

CHAPTER THREE

THE BRIGHT RUBY PUSHPINS were reserved for special occasions. Shaped like faceted jewels, they made Lori smile each time she used one. She rolled the pin back and forth between her thumb and finger, then pushed it carefully into the word *Córdoba*.

Quinn's story deserved a ruby pin. He'd described the buildings of Córdoba with passion, eyes sparkling, hands shaping the arches and doorways of the ancient city. He'd spoken of domes and spires and mosaics like an artist speaking of love or sex. And Lori had gotten turned on listening to him, embarrassingly enough. Maybe her fetish was architecture.

Once the pin was perfectly even with all the others, Lori stepped back to take it in. Pins covered most of Europe and spread out from there. Blue and black and yellow and green. Each pin representing a story someone had told her or she'd read in a book. Each color a measure of her desire to visit that place. The ruby pins... Those cities would be her first stops.

Someday.

She'd planned her escape from the first day of sixth grade, when the new teacher had shown pictures of her summer trip: sixty days of backpacking through Europe. Lori had felt her heart swell with lust. That passion had grown, building upon itself with every book she checked out from the library, every documentary she watched on PBS. It had filled her up all the way through high school, leaving no room for interest in boys. All her concentration had gone into saving and studying to get into Boston College.

And she'd done it. She'd gotten into the international business program, and even scored a coveted scholarship to spend a semester at a university in the Netherlands for her sophomore year.

Lori's heart spasmed, throwing sparks of pain against the walls of her chest.

Her dad had been so proud, refusing to even admit to a hint of loneliness during the four months she'd been at college. And then—

"Jesus," Lori cursed. Skulking down memory lane was one of her least favorite activities. She spun away from the map and hit the light switch, plunging her old bedroom into darkness. Before she'd made her way down to the first floor, the doorbell rang, and Lori sprinted the last few steps.

When she opened the door, Molly rushed in and pulled her into a hug. "You really want to go *shopping?*"

Lori pulled away and her gaze fell on the *Aspen Living* magazine she'd left on the couch. A pair of shoes she'd been lusting after for three days graced the back cover, not that she could afford them.

"Yeah, I think I do."

Molly looked from the magazine to Lori's face and nodded solemnly. "All right then. Let's go buy some shoes."

"Okay. And…and a dress."

Already turning toward the door, Molly froze to stare openmouthed at her. "My God. Are you serious? I thought you were all about jeans."

"I was. But I'm turning over a new leaf. I think."

"A new, *sexy* leaf! Considering how good you look in jeans, I think you're about to rock this town. And I just saw the perfect dress for you last week. We are going to have *So. Much. Fun.*"

Lori couldn't help but grin back at her. "Okay."

"I made reservations at Peak for nine, so we've got a full four hours. Let's do this."

She nodded. "Let's do this."

Once they were in Molly's cherry-red SUV and on the road to Aspen, Molly gave her a searching look. "Soo…"

"What?"

Her friend shot her another meaningful glance, but Lori just shrugged blankly.

"So…" Molly said, "is this an 'I'm every woman,' Oprah kind of makeover? Or is it a 'that guy is hot and I want to do him' kind of makeover?"

Lori glanced down at her too-short nails, noticing that she hadn't quite gotten the grease cleaned from one of them. She clenched them into fists. "Both maybe. I don't know why, but I just feel like buying some heels. Looking like a girl. *And* I want to do someone."

"Who?" Molly's eyebrows had flown nearly up to her hairline. "Who is it?"

"I don't know."

"Ooo, did you see him at The Bar? The café? Is he one of the mountain bikers in town for the race? Maybe—"

"Whoa, there, paperback writer. I mean I don't know *who* I want to do. Just someone. Someone tall and strong and cute." *With nice hands,* something in her head added without her even considering it.

"Oh, my God!" her friend cried. Lori had a sudden, strangling fear that Molly was about to yell something about Quinn, but she didn't. "Lori's gonna get her groove on!" she squealed instead, just before she started singing "Super Freak" in a loud, off-key alto.

"All right. Okay. I want to ask you something serious. Ready?"

Molly pulled her mouth into a severe line and narrowed her eyes, though her nostrils still flared with amusement. "I'm ready."

Tiny raindrops pattered against the windshield as they neared the summit, and Lori chose to watch those instead of her friend's face. "Um... Those stories you write? Are they always...? Um..."

"Excellent? Why, yes, they are."

"Shut up." Lori drew a breath. Molly liked to crack jokes, but she was a good person and a great friend, and the only one Lori could even dream of talking to about these things. She set her shoulders and plowed ahead. "I'm asking if they're always stories about things *you* like?"

Molly turned her narrowed eyes toward Lori. "Are you asking if I like S and M?"

"No! I mean… No, I don't care about whether or not Ben ties you up and makes you call him Daddy."

"Nice," Molly snorted.

"I'm just wondering if you can write about things you're *not* into. If you find some things exciting, even if you'd never actually do them."

"Absolutely," Molly answered quickly, making Lori wonder if she and her writer friends had these types of conversations all the time. Some of the tension left her shoulders.

"I've got a friend," Molly went on, "Delilah Hughes. She writes stories about pretty heavy submission and bondage. Stuff I'm totally not into. But her books are beautifully done, charged with emotion and conflict. Very sexy. I love them. And Ben always appreciates it when I read them, if you know what I mean."

Lori rolled her eyes. "I think I might."

"But sometimes it's not really a matter of what you're into. It depends on who you're with. There are—" Molly wiggled her eyebrows meaningfully "—*things* I'd do with Ben that I'd never do with anyone else."

"Deer," Lori called out, thankful for the opportunity to change the subject. She had the answer she wanted.

The car slowed to a crawl as Molly drove by the doe staring from the shoulder of the road. They both watched until it finally burst into flight and disappeared into the trees. Silence reigned while Molly concentrated on the road, but if the doe was part of a herd, the rest had stayed well hidden. Two minutes later, the mist cleared, and sunlight exploded around them.

"Hey, we're out of the clouds!" Molly cheered, and she was right. They'd been thrust into a beautiful, sunny evening, and the air inside the truck warmed by fifteen degrees in the bright rays.

When Lori rolled down her window, the green scent of wet grass poured over her. She breathed deep.

"So what is it?" Molly asked, lowering her voice to a stage whisper. "Spanking?"

A gnat flew down Lori's throat. Or else she was choking on mortification and horror. Coughing, she glared and shook her head.

"Oh, come on. Everyone likes to read about spanking. Or a three-way. Is it two men? Is that what you're thinking about? I've never done that. You should do it."

"No! No, no, no! I don't think I want to try any of those things, I'm just…missing something."

"Okay." Molly relented, and reached out to pat her hand. "I get it. You're restless and horny. Maybe you should go stay in Aspen for a whole weekend. Get a love nest at The Lodge. Pick up a cute guy. I'd come for moral support, but I think the Chief might object."

"Definitely."

"But you'll think about it?"

Lori felt a little shiver of nervousness. "I don't know. Let's get through tonight, see how it feels."

"Deal." Her friend glanced away from the road to grin at her like a proud mama. "My little girl is all grown-up."

"You're embarrassing me, Mother."

Molly let out one of her loud, boundless laughs, the kind that pulled everyone in whether they felt like laughing or not. Lori was no exception.

So she laughed into the wind, a weight rolling from her shoulders to bounce away into the forest. But without the weight, she felt a little hollow once she'd stopped laughing. Lori cleared her throat. "So Ben thinks someone might have killed my dad."

The car jerked, hitting the soft shoulder for a brief moment that raised up clanging pebbles. *"What?"* Molly gasped.

"He stopped by the other day while you were at the store to tell me he was reopening the case."

"What do you mean? He thinks someone came into your house and killed your dad?"

"No, he thinks someone purposefully bashed his skull in ten years ago. He didn't tell you?"

"Oh, Jesus," Molly breathed. The truck slowed considerably. "No, he didn't tell me. You know what a stickler he is about confidentiality. But…why would he think your dad was killed?"

"There's some evidence, but nothing concrete. I honestly don't want to talk about it tonight, but I wanted to tell you. Just in case I have three martinis and start blubbering."

"Oh, but, Lori, you're—"

"No, seriously. No talking about it. I need a night

out in the worst way. So let's have fun. Show me a good time."

"You're sure?"

"I'm sure."

Molly watched her for a long moment, then turned determined eyes back to the road. "All right then. I have my mission."

THE MAÎTRE D' SMILED over his shoulder for the second time since he'd started leading them toward a table. Lori felt Molly's elbow dig into her side and nudged her back, but she couldn't help a little thrill of excitement. The man was flirting with *her*. Lori Love. And she was flirting back.

She smoothed a hand nervously over the flared skirt of the midnight-blue sundress. Without Molly's encouragement, she'd never have even tried on the strapless silk dress, much less paired it with a pair of deep red shoes. But now she felt daring and feminine and sexy. And giddy as hell.

"Ladies," the host said with a charming purr, sweeping his hand toward a table that overlooked the street outside.

"Thank you," Lori said, trying not to giggle like a teenager when he winked at her.

"Paul will be your server tonight, but I'm Marcus. Please let me know if there's anything else *I* can do for you."

"We will, thanks."

By the time she'd settled into the chair he held out, arranging her skirts carefully so they wouldn't get wrinkled, Lori could feel that Molly was about to burst. She looked up to find her grinning over her clasped hands.

"You look so pretty. And you're glowing, Lori!"

"Maybe I put on too much blush."

"Maybe you're in heat!" Her eyes dropped lower. "My God I'm a genius. That dress is perfect for your body."

"Thank you for helping me. I even look like I have boobs."

"How crazy is that?"

Lori kicked her with one brand-new shoe.

"All right, I'll be serious. You look gorgeous, so keep an eye out. There isn't a man here who'd be able to resist you."

"*That's* being serious? I'm ridiculously short, I've got a face like a grumpy pixie, and there's black grease under my nails."

"You look like a *hot* pixie tonight, darling. And everybody knows that pixies are little whores."

"Hey, I think I read that book!" They were both snorting quite unsexily when the waiter came to take their drink order.

When he hurried away, Molly went suddenly wide-eyed. "Oh, my God. Look!"

Lori swung around, and immediately spotted the person who'd caused Molly's shock. He was handsome, tall, and he had exquisite hands, though she couldn't see them from this far away. Quinn was standing next to a table on the other side of the restaurant, a napkin clutched in his fist, and his eyes locked on...Lori.

Her heart flipped as she spun back to stare down at her silverware. When she'd first looked at herself in the mirror at the store, she'd had a brief, mad wish that she'd run into Quinn tonight. And here he was. Maybe she *was* a pixie.

When she noticed Molly smiling up as if her brother were getting closer, her heart fluttered.

Where the hell were those drinks? Flirting with a stranger was one thing, but now she had the acute sense that she looked foolish. A fraud. A sow's ear trying very hard to become a silk purse, or whatever that damn expression was. She pulled nervously at a curl and wondered if she'd already licked all her lipstick off.

"Hey, Quinn!" Molly said, and Lori nearly knocked her bottle of mineral water over.

When he didn't reply, she couldn't stand the suspense and had to look up...straight into his hazel eyes. "Lori?" he breathed. Heat climbed up her chest, burning all the way up to her hairline.

"Hey," she managed to croak. It didn't help that he looked unbelievably elegant. His dark gray suit was set off perfectly by a white shirt and silver-green tie. He'd seemed like plain old Quinn this morning, but she was abruptly reminded that his life was a world away from hers.

"Hellooo?" Molly interrupted. "I'm Molly, your loving sister."

"Hey, Moll." His eyes didn't leave Lori's. "What did you do to Lori?"

"Got her horny with my award-winning writing."

"Gah," Lori choked, and broke free of Quinn's eyes to shoot an outraged glare at Molly. Her friend grinned in response, but her mouth got more serious when she looked up to Quinn, then down to Lori and back up again.

"Why?" she drawled. "What did *you* do to Lori?"

He opened his mouth but didn't say a word, then seemed to shake off whatever shock he'd been laboring under. "You look beautiful, Lori. Really amazing. I'm afraid my new client thinks I've got epilepsy now. I choked on a piece of jicama when you walked in."

"Oh! Thank you."

"That color is amazing. Like blue steel."

"I...just..."

Molly tapped his arm. "Quinn, that blonde is waving at you. I think she's pissed."

"Shit," he muttered. "I'd better go. It's probably not professional to get caught drooling on my mechanic. I'll see you soon, all right?"

"Oh. Yeah. Okay."

Despite his words, he stood staring at her for so long that she got dizzy from holding her breath. Then he grinned and walked back to the fancy world where he belonged.

Lori couldn't help but watch him the whole way, and goose bumps rose on her skin when he turned halfway to his table and winked at her.

"Lori," Molly said in a very steady voice. Suspiciously steady.

Bracing herself, she turned back to face the scrutiny. "Hmm?"

"Lori, are you interested in being spanked by *my brother?*"

Hot and cold rushed over her at the same time; she leaned forward, almost landing her chin in the pomegranate martini she hadn't even seen arrive. "You are the worst friend in the world!" she whispered. "I can't believe you'd ask me that!"

Molly seemed unfazed. She lifted her glass and took a sip, eyes unwavering in their focus. "You were just asking me about dirty things, Lori Love. Remember? And then Quinn walks over here and stares at you like you're a raspberry truffle dipped in honey cream."

"He… A what?"

"I'm sorry. That was too much, huh? Too erotica-y? Too much creamy goodness?"

Lori wrapped her fingers around the stem of her martini glass. "God, you are strange."

"Don't change the subject. Do you want to do dirty things with my brother or not?"

"No!" Her brain seemed to vibrate at the word, like an internal lie-detector test. "Of course not. I just fixed his backhoe. That's it."

"Got his engine running?"

"Stop it."

"Hey!" Molly protested. "I could've said something about being a hoe, but I didn't."

Frustration built up inside her, but when it boiled over, it just disappeared, steam spreading out into the air. The curses she wanted to yell morphed into laughter, and she collapsed against the linen table-cloth. "Can't you ever be serious?" she gasped.

"I'm working on it, I swear. But I have to save it all up for Ben so he won't lose his mind. You only have to tolerate me for short periods. Suck it up. Anyway, I'm supposed to be showing you a good time, remember?"

What could she do but nod? Molly was her best friend, and her life had been one long gray haze before Molly had returned to Tumble Creek last year. It had been so much less gray since. "Okay, I suppose I can tolerate you. By the way... Did Quinn say he was drooling?"

A smile started small on Molly's lips, but it gradually spread into a wide grin. Her eyes sparkled like happy jewels. "That," she answered, "is exactly what he said."

Lori polished off her drink and then stared down into the empty glass. She tried even breathing, but it didn't seem to work. "I-think-I-want-to-do-dirty-things-with-Quinn," she forced out, and then raised her heavy gaze to Molly's. "But I can't."

The sparkle left her friend's eyes and she finally got serious. "Why? I admit, we won't be able to gossip about the details, but I don't have any objection otherwise."

"He's your brother."

Molly placed both her hands flat on the table and

leaned slowly forward. "I only have circumstantial evidence," she whispered, "but I'm almost certain he's not a virgin."

"That's not the point. The point is I'm not looking for a relationship, I just want to use someone for sex."

A throat cleared from somewhere just over her shoulder. When she turned to see the waiter standing there, she wasn't even embarrassed, just incredibly relieved it wasn't Quinn.

"Shall I give you another moment?" He was turning away before Lori finished explaining that they hadn't looked at the menus yet.

"He's very tense," Molly said.

"Well, then he shouldn't walk up on people so quietly."

"No, I meant *Quinn*. Quinn's very tense. I think he could handle being used. Might be good for him. He has trouble sleeping."

"I'm not going to use your brother! And I don't think he's volunteering."

"Oh, he's volunteering," Molly scoffed. "I think he's ready to have his tires rotated, if you know what I mean."

"No, I *don't* know what you mean. Is that supposed to be sexy?"

"Absolutely."

"Okay, I can see we're moving away from serious here." Lori sighed. "So let me put this simply. I'm looking for a little fun. No attachment. And definitely not someone I'll see all the time afterward. Quinn is not an option."

Molly rolled her eyes. "How many times have you seen Quinn in the past decade? Five or six times?"

"Are you determined to pimp your brother out?"

She slumped and waved a dismissive hand. "Fine. Never mind. Whatever you do, don't sleep with Quinn. Anyway, you've got another option. Our waiter is talking to the maître d'—I think he's passing on your secret message."

Lori twisted around to find both men smiling in her direction. Great. She suddenly felt less like a powerful sexual creature and more like prey. She'd exposed her soft underbelly, now one of them would move in for the kill.

Finally picking up her menu, Lori just shook her head. "I think heels and a dress are enough for this weekend. I'll cross the sex bridge next week."

"Oo, the sex bridge," Molly murmured, looking over her own menu. "All right, we'll see how that works out. By the way, Ben said to tell you he might stop by the shop on Monday."

"Why?"

She shrugged. "I don't know. I thought it was something to do with his truck, but now that I know about your dad, I'm not sure. Just make sure you're not standing on the sex bridge when he gets there. He might accidentally get on it, and wouldn't *that* be embarrassing?"

Picturing Ben catching her in a compromising position, Lori burst into laughter. He'd had enough embarrassment via Molly over the past year, and she didn't want to put him through any more, but the thought still struck her as hilarious.

Enough with worrying about men. Tonight she was going to have fun. Let the boys watch from afar. And maybe...maybe even drool a little.

CHAPTER FOUR

THE SUN BEAT DOWN, hotter than it had been all summer, burning Quinn's back. If he were working at his site, he would've already ditched the shirt, but he wasn't working. Instead, he was in Tumble Creek, watching Lori.

He hadn't expected to find her in the garage on a Sunday, but there she was, balanced on the bumper of a half-ton pickup, her small body swallowed by the depths of the engine well. A long, muttered curse bounced off the hood of the truck, something so blatantly obscene that it turned him on. Who'd have thought such a pretty little thing could have such a dirty mouth? Even more shocking, who would've thought those coveralls could so thoroughly hide those curves? Not that she was buxom, but last night his eye had recognized the beauty of each perfect proportion. Though not until *after* he'd recovered from the shock of glancing up and spying some sort of ultrafeminine doppelgänger of Lori Love.

Speaking of spying… Maybe it was creepy of him to stand outside unannounced.

So he said, "Hey, Lori," and then watched her head rise into a quick and nasty crash with the truck's hood. "Damn," he rasped, rushing forward to help. The cursing started again, which would have made him smile if he weren't worried about her skull.

"Are you okay?"

As she clutched the top of her head, Quinn eased his hands around her waist and lowered her to the ground. "Are you bleeding?"

She slapped his hands away and cursed some more. "You scared the hell out of me!"

"Sorry. You want some ice? Let's get some ice."

"I don't…" Her shoulders slumped. "Okay, fine." She led the way through the garage and into the house, fingers gingerly exploring her scalp the whole way. "I think it's all right actually."

But Quinn didn't pay any attention; he was busy inhaling the scent of home-cooked food. "My God, that smells good. I was going to ask if you wanted to go grab dinner, but you've already got plans, I guess."

He glanced over to find her staring at him, hand still pressed to her head. "Dinner?"

"Yeah. You've already got something in the oven?"

"Yes."

When she didn't offer anything more, Quinn felt his stomach sink. "So you're busy?"

She looked from him to the oven, her green eyes wide with…anxiety? Strange. "No, I'm not busy."

Well, she wasn't exactly enthusiastic, but he didn't plan on giving up that easily. He'd been thinking about Lori Love since yesterday afternoon in his cabin. He'd been thinking *seriously* about her since last night.

"It smells delicious, did I mention that?"

She finally lost her shocked expression and smiled, rolling her eyes at his obviousness. He'd never claimed to be slick with women.

"Fine, Quinn Jennings. Since I've already cooked dinner, would you like to stay and help me eat it?"

"That's a fantastic idea! I'd love to. Now let's get some ice."

"My head feels fine. I've got a thick skull. And lots of hair." She glanced at the clock as she balanced a boot on a kitchen chair to loosen the laces. "It'll be ready in about fifteen minutes. Just give me a second to change. There's beer in the fridge."

His shoulders had already begun to turn toward the ancient beige fridge when his eye caught the motion of her hand rising toward her zipper. He changed direction, turning back toward Lori as she moved the zipper down. The coveralls gaped, and Quinn watched, entranced, as a white tank top was exposed.

At that point, he half expected her to step out of her uniform wearing nothing but a thin white tank and a pair of panties. But Lori tugged the coveralls down with no ceremony, revealing a faded pair of jeans. And the tank top wasn't that thin, either. Damn.

Seemingly unaware of his train of thought, Lori toed off her boots, pulled off the coveralls, and tossed them over the chair before heading for the bedroom.

Her walk seemed captured on a slow-motion camera; Quinn imagined her hips swaying in nothing but a pair of skimpy blue panties and reached blindly for the handle of the fridge door. He needed a drink.

He might not be better with women with a beer or two under his belt, but he forgot how bad he was, at any rate.

After popping a bottle open for Lori, he downed half of his in a few quick swallows. What the hell was he doing here, anyway? Looking to ruin a perfectly good friendship? His track record with relationships so far was zero and… Hell, he didn't even know the number, which proved the point. But every time he put down his work lately, he started thinking about her and that smile.

Lori Love was an enigma. Though she and Molly had been friends in school, they hadn't been best friends. Molly had been popular and slightly flighty, while Lori had embodied the stereotype of the scholarly girl. Nose always in a book, extracurricular activities planned with an eye toward college applications, or so Molly had claimed. Lori had studied hard and spent her free time working in Love's Garage. Quinn had no idea what had happened to her after that, except that she'd gone to Boston College on a full scholarship, then come home when her dad was injured.

And now she seemed like a typical female mechanic, if there was such a thing.

Wandering into the living room, Quinn let his architect's eye take in the lines of the fifties construction. Nothing had been changed since the original build as far as he could tell. He wasn't even sure the walls had been painted since then. Certainly the decor hadn't been updated. Nothing here, absolutely nothing, gave him any clue as to who Lori had become.

Ancient bowling trophies crowded the mantel above the moss rock fireplace. A lamp made from a bowling pin sat on an unremarkable oak table. The couch was frat-house chic.

This was her father's house, plain and simple. But her father had died over a year ago. Was it grief that kept her from making the place her own? Quinn raised the dusty blinds on one of the small windows and found a view of the garage yard. The sad sight burned through his stomach. He could see why she kept the windows closed.

A creaking floorboard alerted him to her presence, and when he turned, Quinn forgot about old decor and broken-down cars. Her jeans and tank were gone, replaced with white capris and a flirty little red shirt that showed off her shoulders. She chewed on her lip and tugged a few brown curls into compliance. He let his eyes slide all the way down to her bare feet… and bright red toenails.

"Nice toes," he said stupidly, and watched them curl against the carpet. Clearly he needed to finish the beer. Who the hell told a girl she had nice *toes?*

When she'd had enough of him staring at her feet, Lori spun for the kitchen and opened the oven. "Another few minutes," she muttered. "I'll make the salad." By "make," she apparently meant "get out the bag" because she cut open a plastic bag and dumped the salad into two bowls while Quinn smiled at her back.

Her shoulders were straight and beautifully pale, brushed by shiny, bouncy curls as she moved. He caught her profile as she went back to the fridge for salad dressing and couldn't help but lose himself in the careful line of her throat and chest. Her breasts were small, but they rose in a graceful curve that drew the eye. No wonder she wore that baggy outfit at work. The men in her employ would get nothing done if she showed up like this.

"Do you want to go to The Bar after dinner?" he blurted out.

Her head popped up and she frowned. "Why?"

"Because I didn't bring any wine."

"And you think they'd have good wine at The Bar?"

Well, she had a point. The place was so old and crusty it didn't even have a real name. "To Aspen then," he corrected. "There's a great wine bar on Hopkins Avenue."

"Did you talk to Molly today?" Lori suddenly demanded.

"I—"

She cut him off by slamming the dressing bottle onto the counter. "Damn it, I told her I didn't want to date you!"

Quinn wondered if the air conditioner had just kicked on with a vengeance. All the pleasant warmth of the evening vanished in an instant and left him in the freezing cold. "Really?"

"Yes!" Lori ran her hands over her face, then shook her head before she met his eyes. "I'm so sorry,

Quinn. I'd love to date you, honestly, but that's not what I'm looking for right now."

Now he was confused. That sounded a lot like, "It's not you, it's me," except that they'd never even gone to lunch. "I see," was all he could say.

"I can't believe this," she muttered.

"Look, I just wanted to take you out for a drink, and maybe we could—"

"Whatever she told you, I am *not* going to use you for sex."

The imaginary air conditioner switched off. So did his brain.

"Not that I wouldn't love to!" she went on. "But it's really about random, meaningless fun, not dating. I'm not in a good place for dating right now. I'm sorry you were dragged into this. She just won't drop it."

"Who?" he rasped.

"Molly! What did she tell you to get you over here?"

Quinn clutched the beer bottle tighter, feeling the smooth glass press his skin, grounding himself so that he could make his brain work. "Molly hasn't called me in weeks."

Though she'd been reaching for her own beer, Lori's hand froze just an inch from the bottle. "Excuse me?"

"I'm not quite sure what you're talking about."

Her hand fell away to hover near her side. "That doesn't… No. Why would you be here if Molly hadn't called?"

Maybe she wasn't as smart as he'd always thought.

"Lori, I came over to ask you out. Period. It's not that complicated."

"Oh." The pink started right at the skin just above her shirt and floated inexorably higher, past her collarbones, then up her neck to her jaw. Her cheeks flamed redder than the rest of her skin. "Oh, God. Are you sure?"

"Very sure. But what were you saying about using me for sex?"

Her body tilted slightly to the left, then the right. Alarmed, Quinn was moving toward her, meaning to grab her elbow and help her to a seat, but the oven timer went off and the sound snapped her straight.

She moved stiffly to the oven, grabbed a hot pad, and in a moment she was standing at the counter, staring down at a perfectly roasted chicken and a loaf of hot bread. "Okay," she said to the poultry. "Okay."

"Lori—"

"No, just… Let's have dinner. I'm sorry there's not more. I was just going to have a salad and… Oh, Jesus."

Quinn let silence fall, utterly unsure of how he should proceed. His thoughts were ping-ponging back and forth, running into each other like drunk kids in a mosh pit. When Lori moved, grabbing plates to set the table, he jumped on the opportunity to give them both time and took her beer and the bottle of dressing.

Sex. Lori Love wanted sex.

He grabbed the salads and carried them over while Lori brought the chicken.

No dating. Just sex. Nothing else.

He watched her hips as she hurried back to the fridge and let himself imagine. Sex. With Lori. The images came easy and quick.

Once the food was served and all the busywork ran out, they both lowered themselves slowly into chairs and looked anywhere but at each other as they dug into the salad.

Though he'd never been into meaningless sex, Quinn wasn't above liking the idea of it. And, actually, it would solve one of the more serious problems in his life: he was a terrible boyfriend. Seriously bad. Out of all the women he'd dated, not one had been happy for more than a month.

He forgot things, important things like dates and birthdays. On the phone, he had the attention span of a gnat. Worked late more often than not and liked to read books about engineering when he got home. It was a sad measure of a relationship when a woman grew jealous of *New Physics in Architecture*.

Quinn started on the chicken.

Considering his track record, asking Lori out in the first place had probably been idiotic. But if they kept it meaningless and casual… None of his shortcomings would matter, would they? They'd simply go their separate ways, some very nice memories between them.

A few minutes later, Quinn set down his fork and raised his eyes. Lori kept chewing for a few moments, until she noticed his attention and swallowed hard.

"What?" she asked.

"Did you mean what you said?"

Relief softened the anxiety on her face, but her smile popped into place with too much brightness. "No! No, of course not. I was obviously joking. Duh."

"Mmm-hmm." He stared at her until she squirmed, then stared some more.

Her smile vanished. *"What?"*

"Because if you weren't joking—and I don't think you were—then I'd like to volunteer."

"Volunteer?" she breathed. "For what?"

Quinn took a deep breath and placed his hands flat on the table for balance. "I'd like to have meaningless sex with you, Lori Love."

THE ROOM WAS spinning and hot. A convection oven of mortification spiced with a hint of lust.

Quinn Jennings had just propositioned her in the most inappropriate way. The last thing she'd ever expected.

"We can't do that," she blurted out.

"Why not?"

Because I like you, was her first thought, but that was ridiculous. Did she want to have sex with someone she *didn't* like? If so, how could it possibly be any good? She reached for the next thing. "We know each other."

"Um… Were you planning on hanging out at a rest stop or something?"

She gasped in horror. "No!"

"Bathroom at a club?"

"Quinn!"

"Well, you know my name and where I work.

That's about it, and I'd hope you'd want to know at least that, even if you picked somebody at random."

"I just…" God, it sounded so sordid when he described it. Then again, she'd been wanting sordid, hadn't she? And yet that guy at the restaurant had been cute and polite and interested, and the idea of taking him home had left her cold. "I know a lot more than that about you, Quinn. I know your sister and your best friend. It would be too awkward."

He frowned at that, his straight brows descending into an angry V. "Not as awkward as being hurt—or worse—by some stranger you decided to experiment with. It would be really, really stupid for you to hook up with a complete stranger. Is that really what you're planning?"

"Hey!" she protested, but couldn't think of anything more than that. Just those few words made her flush with embarrassment, because he was right. Risk was fun until it actually got risky. But still… "You sound like your dad when you say things like that."

Anger simmered in his gaze, but he quickly tamped it down, closing his eyes for a moment. When he opened them again, his face flushed with regret. "I'm sorry. You're right. I just don't want to think of you putting yourself in harm's way. Especially when you have a willing victim right here."

"Victim, huh? That's flattering. Thanks, but no thanks." He grabbed her wrist when she pushed back to leave the table. Lori froze, hovering an inch above her chair.

"I didn't mean it that way. Honestly, Lori, I'm the perfect candidate."

"Do this a lot, do you?"

"Of course not. Never, in fact."

She hadn't realized that jealousy had crept inside her skin until it slunk away. Jealousy over what? *Quinn?* When her thighs began to tremble from exhaustion, Lori slowly let her body collapse back into the chair.

He watched her with very serious eyes. "I'm no good at relationships, Lori. I work too much and I forget about all the boyfriend stuff and end up carelessly hurting any woman in my life. I'm inattentive and distracted…" He shrugged, gaze leaching from serious to weary. "I suck at being a boyfriend, but you don't want a boyfriend.

"I like you. I respect you. You know me, but not so well that I won't fit into your sordid plan. Just well enough to be sure I'm not going to drug you and post dirty pictures on the web."

Another point in his favor, though her career as a mechanic didn't hinge on a spotless reputation. Maybe it would be exciting to be caught up in an internet sex scandal. Maybe she'd get more customers. Or maybe she'd die of embarrassment.

Quinn's fingers shifted, and she realized he was still holding her wrist. Her heartbeat jumped as his skin slid against her pulse, heat smoothing against that delicate, beating place usually covered by thick leather work gloves. The nerves in that one square inch gasped to life, then quickly spread the word to their neighbors. Warm prickles tingled up her arm.

She jerked her hand away and shoved to her feet. "Do you want some ice cream?" Not bothering to wait for an answer, Lori rushed to the fridge and yanked open the freezer.

"Plus, I find you very attractive," Quinn added as if that were the least of her concerns. But those few words froze her lungs as she banged the tub of ice cream down.

Shit. He found her attractive? *Very* attractive? It could be true, or it could be an attempt to get some free sex from a woman who was offering. Just as she tried samples of things at the fancy grocery store in Aspen. She didn't particularly want cranberry-flavored waffles, but she'd eat one if it was pushed in front of her.

Just as Quinn would eat her if she lay down naked in front of him.

Her cheeks burned as she scooped vanilla ice cream and thought of Quinn lapping her up. The strength of her yearning shocked her into panic.

"I can't!" she groaned. "I—" A loud knock stuttered through the house.

Gasping with relief, she darted for the door. Her relief didn't die even when she opened the door to find Ben standing there, looking for all the world like bad news in a uniform. But whatever he was there for, he was only saving her from having to reject Quinn. Or not reject Quinn. Either prospect seemed terrifying.

"Lori," he said, hand tipping his Stetson down a

fraction of an inch. Lori frowned. An awfully formal gesture from a man she'd known forever.

When she waved him in, Ben's gaze slipped past her, eyebrows rising for just a moment before he looked serious and official again. "Quinn," he said with not a hint of inflection at finding his best friend in Lori's living room. "How's it going?"

"Great," Quinn answered. "I think."

Lori blushed and felt Ben's eyes noting each shade of pink as it rose up her cheeks. Damn cop eyes. "I apologize if I'm interrupting your evening," he said.

She shook her head. "No! No, we had something to eat. But we're done now. Quinn was just leaving!"

"Huh," he said from behind her. Lori didn't turn around.

Ben's eyebrows rose again. "You sure?"

"Yes!"

Quinn cleared his throat. "Well, all right then. Lori, why don't I give you a call about that bill tomorrow."

"I don't—"

"We'll discuss the details then."

Oh, jeez. He wasn't going to drop it. But at least she'd have time to think before then. And, knowing Quinn, he'd forget to call anyway.

"Thanks for dinner, Lori. It was a very pleasant surprise." He brushed past as she nodded, holding her breath at the touch of his arm against her shoulder. His skin felt so *hot*...

Well, of course it was hot—98.6 degrees, as a matter of fact. Nice and toasty and no different from anyone else. Unless, of course, he was a *werewolf!*

"Lori?"

"What?" she barked, trying to pretend she wasn't staring at the door that had closed behind Quinn a few seconds ago.

"Look, I was going to come by tomorrow, but I was walking past and thought I'd stop by tonight. I'm sorry if I interrupted something." A tiny question hovered in those words, but she pretended not to hear it.

He cleared his throat. "I have notes on your dad's treatment in the emergency room, but do you think you could get me copies of any X-rays or scans that were done?"

"Sure. Why?"

"I want to have the medical examiner take a look at those, too."

She crossed her arms tightly and nodded.

Ben flipped out his notebook and jotted something down. "What about the motive question? Did you think of any possibilities?"

"No. Nothing."

"Nothing? No rivalries? No bad blood?"

"Not that I know of."

"And what about girlfriends?"

The idea of her father dating felt as bizarre now as it had two days ago. But maybe the stranger part of it was just how odd it seemed to her. "I honestly don't know. I asked Joe about it, and he said my dad dated occasionally but there was never anyone serious. I had no idea he even dated. He kept it from me." She laughed a little. "I'm beginning to think it's weird that I can't answer these questions, Ben."

"No," he said immediately. "This is normal when a child—even an adult child—is answering questions about a parent. Believe me, it's usually a bad sign if a kid knows too much. Your dad was your dad, and he kept his private life private. That's just what he was supposed to do."

"Okay." She felt tears welling, and nodded quickly.

"The officers investigating at the time came up with the same information. As far as they could tell, there wasn't a woman in his life. So you weren't left out at all."

"Okay." The tears finally spilled over. She tried to wave him off, but Ben was having none of it.

He cursed and reached out to rest his hands on her shoulders. "I'm sorry. I shouldn't have dropped in and ruined your Sunday like this. I'm heading to Molly's in thirty minutes. Why don't you come with me?"

Lori felt tempted for about five seconds. Then she remembered the lingerie Molly had picked up in Aspen the night before. "Um, no. I think I'll just stay here and let you two have your evening. I've got invoices and…stuff."

He objected a few times, but Lori finally got him out the door and shut it tight behind him.

She needed some ice cream. Or a drink.

Probably both.

CHAPTER FIVE

"I'll take care of you," Rafael whispered. Then she felt the scrape of his impossibly sharp teeth against the tender skin of her neck.

"You can't protect me from everything," Jodi protested, breath catching somewhere between a gasp and a sob. His hands held her still, her naked back pressed against his chest, ass snug against his erection.

"I can." His surety vibrated over her skin, raising goose bumps. Finally, he loosed his grip and slid one hand down her arm to caress her hip. He teased her, stroking circles over her skin until his fingers found her sex and she cried his name like a prayer. And then his long, sharp teeth sank deep into her neck....

LORI SIGHED AND tossed the book toward the end of her bed. She'd been flipping through the pages since she'd awoken at 5:00 a.m. Too early, but she couldn't get back to sleep and even the best of the stories couldn't hold her interest. She'd lived all of Monday as if she were moving through water, every movement taking more energy than it should. It looked as though Tuesday would be more of the same.

Lori found herself wishing she could sink deeper into depression, deep enough that she could lie down and sleep for a good twelve hours. As it was, she seemed to be hovering between anxiety and the blues. Restless and lethargic at the same time. And seriously confused.

Ben must be wrong about her father's injury. She wanted him to be wrong. And all the reports weren't in yet, so Lori could still hope.

Her dad had been a good man, but he'd been rough-and-tumble. Sometimes, especially after her mother had left, he'd hit the town to get good and drunk. And he'd seen nothing wrong with throwing a few punches around if one of his drinking buddies pissed him off. Hell, his injury had happened at the now-defunct biker bar at the edge of town. Fistfights were part of the recreation. So he'd gotten punched and fallen against a stray rock, and whoever he'd been fighting with had taken off to save his own ass. The reconstructed scenario made total sense, and she'd never once doubted it.

Until now.

Damn Ben Lawson and his determination to run an organized police department. His persistent inquiries were working, at least on her. She'd spent hours lying in bed last night, trying to puzzle out this mystery. What had changed in his life? What had shifted?

She'd gone to college, yes. But how could that have inspired a crime? A mysterious drifter hadn't moved into her room. What else? There hadn't been any personnel changes, according to the records. Sometimes her dad had paid the occasional worker off the books, though. She'd have to ask Joe about that.

But there was one other thing that had changed while she was gone. A big change for her father.

He'd bought that land.

He'd purchased it just a month before his attack. Seemingly out of the blue. He hadn't mentioned it to her until after the purchase, and Lori had been too wrapped up in college life to ask any questions.

Aside from this house on a lot chock-full of ecological hazards, that riverfront land was the only thing of value her father had owned.

Yet another developer had called about it on Monday. So at least two developers were interested in that twenty-acre plot. Why?

Lori covered her face in frustration.

If her father really had been assaulted, and *if* it had been premeditated, the land was the only motive she could think of. And that was the extent of her revelation. No who or how or why. She was going to have to spend the day going through his records, and those would probably tell her nothing at all.

"Crap," she muttered, as she pushed herself off the bed. The red numbers of her clock glared 5:30 a.m. at her, as if she'd done something wrong. Dawn would be breaking by now, and if she couldn't sleep, she needed to walk, wandering bears be damned.

She pulled on the sweatpants and T-shirt she'd left next to the bed and padded to the bathroom to brush her teeth and fix her hair. Her curls were the only thing pretty and feminine about her, as far as she was concerned. Her nose was a bit too snub, her eyes and mouth nothing special. But since she'd learned to tame her hair into big loose curls with some very expensive product, she made sure never to leave the house without fixing it. If she let it get frizzy and dry, she'd look as washed-up as she felt.

Once she felt bouncy and minty-fresh, Lori tugged on her running shoes and headed for the door. The purple light of the rising sun only hinted at warmth, but she didn't mind. It fit her strange and icy mood.

Birdsong swelled in the silence of the morning. But once again when her shoes hit the gravel of the parking lot, she couldn't hear anything but that hated sound, so Lori pivoted and hurried directly for Main Street. Her destination was the river, and she could actually reach it through the junkyard, but there was no path along that stretch. Plus she really didn't care to pick her way through ancient tires and rusted struts.

Several large pickup trucks passed her as she walked, kicking up diesel fumes as drivers raised a solemn hand in greeting. The old-timers didn't really wave around here. Too much emotion. The cowboys in the movie *Brokeback Mountain* had reminded her of most of the men of Tumble Creek, minus the secret gay sex, she supposed. Though if it were secret, what the hell would she know about it? Regardless, the men of Tumble Creek and the surrounding ranches were stoic and hardworking and not inclined to superfluous laughter. Or words.

They certainly weren't artistic and funny, not like Quinn.

The thought of Quinn made her mouth pull up into a smile as she passed The Bar. Quinn hadn't called on Monday, despite his threat. If he were any other man, she'd assume he'd gone home, thought over the offer to be her lover and decided a quick disappearing act was in order. But it was Quinn, and she had no doubt he'd been locked in his office, furiously sketching out architectural plans for twelve hours straight and giving not one thought to his scandalous offer.

He would call at some point, when he returned to the real world, and he'd apologize profusely for his forgetfulness, but Lori was thankful for the brief reprieve. She had no idea what to say if he pressed the issue. "No," probably. If she had any sense at all. Quinn was *not* the man to act out her fantasies with. It would just be too...*intimate.*

Wrinkling her nose in embarrassment, Lori turned onto the steep, potholed road that led down to the river. She was so focused on her feet and the loose pebbles that threatened to roll her down the hill, she didn't even notice that she wasn't alone.

"Hey!" a deep voice called, startling her into a stumble that nearly took her down.

"Fuck me," she yelped, arms flailing.

"Anytime, babe," Aaron Thompson shouted like the idiot he was.

"Thanks for rushing up to help," Lori snapped back. "Good way to make use of those muscles."

Completely missing the point, Aaron smiled and flexed his bare biceps. It didn't really matter that it was only fifty-five degrees out and much colder in the water, Aaron was already dressed for maximum exposure in a sleeveless, skintight neoprene wet suit and a lean red life vest. Lori was pretty sure he never wore underwear. He certainly didn't have any panty lines, though she could see the clear bulge of his manly junk. As usual.

"You finally coming for that private white-water lesson I offered?"

"Not in a million years."

"What if I bring along a friend? I did this girl in Aspen last weekend who said she was bi. I told her about you. She seemed, you know—" he wiggled his blond eyebrows "—into it."

"Aaron," she bit out, then made herself count to twenty. Lots of people in Tumble Creek assumed she was a lesbian because she didn't date much and she fixed cars for a living. She'd actively encouraged this belief in Aaron's case, because she'd grown tired of him stopping by after his last river run of the day to show off his tight neoprene package. Especially after the time she'd caught him rearranging his goods to offer his best side just before he'd stepped into the garage.

Lori shuddered at the thought and watched Aaron's pretty blue eyes drop lower to check out her chest. She crossed her arms.

"Aaron, listen. *Please.* I will never sleep with you. And I will never sleep with anyone else in front of you. Nor," she interrupted when he opened his mouth to speak, "will I sleep with someone you know and then tell you about it. Is that clear enough? Just drop it, all right?"

"But…" He looked confused, not believing even a gay woman wouldn't want to sleep with Aaron, god of the hot river guides. A deep crease of thought appeared between his eyebrows. "But I thought we were friends."

"Oh, for God's sake. I don't even know what to say to that."

He shrugged, all traces of thinking gone from his face. "Whatever. Just call me if you ever decide to switch teams."

"I…" There was no reasoning with a man who was such a bizarre combination of nature boy and gigolo. "I'll see you later."

He winked and turned back to the work of unknotting a thick poly rope. Lori's eyes wandered to his ass, and he must have expected just that, because he turned his head and caught her looking.

"Reconsidering?" he offered in a smooth purr.

"No! I just…" With a growl, she spun and stomped off toward the narrow path that had been worn through the grass, Aaron's laughter fading behind her. She didn't want anything to do with that man's ass, but no one could help but stare at the two perfect globes of muscles perched on top of his bulging thighs. How much time did he spend working out anyway? And how long did it take him to pour himself into that suit every morning? Jesus, she'd seen the hollows on the sides of his ass cheeks.

He'd be perfect for a fling. "If only he weren't Aaron," she muttered to herself, then the words hit her brain and she stopped dead in her tracks. A pebble pressed against the ball of her foot so hard that she felt it through the sole of her shoe. But she didn't move.

Aaron was perfect for a fling because he *was* Aaron. He was young, hot and eager. He'd do anything she asked him to. And there was absolutely no danger of it developing into something deeper. Perfect.

And not the least bit tempting.

Not like Quinn.

She pressed her weight harder to her right foot until the pebble felt like a thorn. Her thoughts of Quinn held firm, unaffected by the pain. She wanted him. And she needed the distraction, really needed it. This thing with her dad, it could go on for months. And she had nothing—nothing—to distract her. Except Quinn and his offer.

Lori lifted her foot and kept walking, keeping a close eye out for any sign of bears ahead. If it were springtime, she wouldn't be out at all. In the spring, the bears were not only hungry, they had baby bears to protect. "Eek," she muttered.

The river rushed and roared beside her, always louder than she expected despite that she'd grown up two hundred feet from it. Once it hit Grand Valley it was a wide, smooth ribbon, but here it jumped and dropped and boiled, finding its way through sharp rocks and steep ledges. It was a little like her life, actually. Boring and calm one minute, chaotic as hell the next.

But if her life was going to be chaotic for a while, maybe she should enjoy the ride.

So Quinn wouldn't be a perfect fling. He was too familiar. Too nice. Too smart. But he was right about one thing, he'd be better at a fling than he'd ever be at a relationship. Lori could vividly remember walking into the girls' bathroom at a varsity basketball game to find a beautiful blond cheerleader weeping loudly into her hands.

"He never calls. Ever! And last night my parents were gone for the night, and he didn't even show up. We were going to do it and he didn't even remember!"

"Quinn's just like that," her friend had assured her.

"He hates me!"

"No, no! He's so smart, RaeAnne. He's got so much stuff to think about. College. Basketball."

The cheerleader's sobbing had grown louder, and Lori had hustled out, wide-eyed.

Smiling at the trail, she hauled herself over a fallen pine tree and jumped to the packed earth below. She'd been stunned by that conversation at the time, just the idea that Quinn—sweet, quiet, big-brother Quinn— could make a cheerleader cry. Could make a cheerleader cry about wanting to *do it* with him. What a strange and disturbing idea that had been.

And now here *she* was wanting to do it with him. Not crying over him, at least, but certainly confused.

It felt strangely natural, as if that moment in that high school bathroom had been the first point on a meandering trail that led to an inevitable affair between Quinn Jennings and Lori Love.

But maybe it was a terrible idea, inevitable or not. Maybe it would end with her crying in a bathroom somewhere. Maybe she'd even be wearing a cheerleader's uniform at that point. Just a lonely, kinky mess, wearing a short skirt and no underwear as mascara ran down her cheeks.

Her laughter bounced off the rock wall on the far side of the river, as if to confirm her decision. Sex with Quinn was a good idea, even if it turned out to be a bad one, because her nights would be spent pacing around her house, leaving angry messages for a forgetful lover, instead of tossing and turning and worrying about an investigation she couldn't control.

She didn't want to think about what might have been done to her father, didn't want to imagine that someone had stolen his life and all her plans. So until Ben called to tell her his suspicions were unfounded, Lori would think about Quinn instead.

QUINN GLANCED AT his watch, then back to the road that led in a straight line from his condo to his office. It would be a busy day, but he felt as relaxed as if he'd just checked out early on a Friday afternoon. An hour swimming laps would do that for you, but it was more than just the loose exhaustion in his muscles. He finally had the vision he'd been chasing for Brett Wilson's new home. The two-acre lot halfway up Aspen Mountain was flat and perfect for building…aside from the fact that Brett wanted a view of his favorite ski run from his living room. A ski run that sat on the wrong side of a jagged wall of granite.

"Buy another lot," had been Quinn's first suggestion upon walking the land. The builder had insisted that Brett Wilson would pay a premium if Quinn could make it work.

Quinn would be collecting on that premium now, though it had been the challenge of the project that had driven him to take it on rather than the money. He'd spent days turning possibilities over in his head, but the swimming had finally unlocked the puzzle for him, as it often did. Something about the rhythm and the echoing solitude worked like meditation for him.

He was picturing the cantilevered jut of the suspended living room when his cell rang. The sound tossed a sudden thought into his brain, where it exploded like a white-hot cherry bomb.

It might be Lori.

"Holy *crap*." Quinn scrambled to grab the phone, but the front wheel hit a slight buckle in the shoulder of the road, and when he jerked the car back onto the blacktop, the phone skittered away.

"Shit." He'd forgotten to call her. "Shit, shit, shit."

He pulled into a lot, threw his car into Park and dived across the seat to grab the phone.

"Hello?" he nearly shouted.

"Good morning, Mr. Jennings." The cool voice of his office manager flowed across the ether. Jane. Just Jane.

Collapsing back into his seat, Quinn let his head hit the headrest. "Morning, Jane."

"I hope I'm not disturbing you. I wanted to remind you of your schedule in case you were heading straight to a site this morning."

"No. No, I'm coming in. But remind away." He raised one eyelid to glance at the clock—8:30 a.m. Yes, he'd most definitely missed Monday by a mile.

"Here we go," Jane said, just as she always did before running through his appointments. "You've got a preliminary consult with Jean-Paul D'Ozeville at ten this morning. Lunch with Peter Anton of Anton/Bliss Developers at twelve, a conference call at three about the lecture in Vancouver, and then the benefit dinner with Tessa Smith at seven."

"The what?"

"The fundraiser for the Aspen Music Foundation. You bought tickets weeks ago. I believe Ms. Smith wanted to meet Sting."

Quinn thought he could detect a sardonic hint in her words, which would have surprised him if he hadn't been busy reeling over the shock she'd just delivered.

"Tessa and I broke it off last week."

"Well, she called yesterday to be sure you hadn't forgotten."

"Uh…right." He vaguely remembered Tessa's shouted assertion that she was not going to let him back out of such an important event.

"And," Jane continued, "she went to dinner with you on Friday?"

"Yeah. Apparently I forgot to cancel that, too."

His office manager cleared her throat. "I don't see any more dates on your schedule. As long as you don't accidentally agree to any other shared meals, this should be your last evening with Ms. Smith."

"Good. I'm not— Jane, are you laughing at me?"

"Certainly not, Mr. Jennings. If there's nothing else I can do for you, I'll see you in a few minutes." The line clicked dead, confirming his suspicion that she was, indeed, laughing at him. As he deserved. What kind of man found himself on not one, but *two* accidental dates?

Of course, Tessa was defined by her persistence. Quinn wasn't normally apt to notice when women flirted with him, but women like Tessa didn't wait for a man to notice, they simply assumed their place. So it was that one evening Quinn had looked up and found he was dating a big-breasted blonde who wore frighteningly tall heels. His developer friends had been impressed. Quinn had simply been too apathetic to break it off until Tessa had gotten clingy. Then it had been an easy decision.

Speaking of easy decisions…

Quinn dialed information, got connected to Love's Garage, and then wiped the sweat off his brow while he waited.

"Love's Garage," a very feminine, very *grumpy* voice answered. Not good.

"Lori, it's Quinn. Don't hang up. I am so sorry I didn't call yesterday. I—"

"Forgot?" she asked sharply.

Lying would be wrong. Really wrong. "I wouldn't say *forgot,* exactly…"

"It's no problem, Quinn. It gave me time to think."

Not good at all. He wanted sex with Lori Love. It was slipping from his grasp, making him realize just how *much* he wanted sex with her. Time for brutal honesty. "You're right. I did forget. I've been working on this difficult site, and… Okay, you don't want to hear that. I'm so sorry. I know it's insulting and degrading and…" He tried to think of a few more choice adjectives that had been applied to his forgetfulness in the past.

"It's fine, Quinn. I'm not mad."

He would *not* let this slip away from him on a wave of polite distance. "Of course you're mad," he pressed.

"Nope."

"Then why do you sound so strange?"

"Because I'm on my back under a car?"

"Oh. Seriously?"

"Yes." Her voice dropped. "But it's nice and private under here."

Quinn turned that odd comment over in his head for a moment. Was it possible she really wasn't angry? Or was false relief making him stupid? Still… "And you need privacy because…?"

Her long pause stretched through the distance between them, tightening their connection like a wire about to snap. She'd had time to think, and surely that was a bad thing. Planning and forethought couldn't be the quickest route to a red-hot affair. But maybe…

"Does your offer still stand?" she blurted out in a near whisper.

Quinn's heart turned over so quickly he felt dizzy. "Yes," he answered with a casualness he didn't feel.

"Because I think maybe it's a good idea. If you still do."

Strangely, he thought of her stretched out under that car, her feet and ankles vulnerable, available to him. He could stroke his hand down the instep of her small foot, kiss her painted toes, curl his fingers around her delicate ankle, smooth his palm up the inside of her rising calf. In his fantasy world, she only wore boots and thick denim when he wanted her to. Today, she was barefoot, wearing a little flowered skirt as she labored beneath chrome and steel. Her—

"Quinn?" she breathed into the phone.

"Yes, I still think it's a good idea."

Her relieved sigh made him smile.

"So," he ventured, "should I just stop by tonight to service you?"

A wheeze burst over the phone line, followed quickly by the clang of something heavy and metallic. Quinn grinned at the Mexican Food sign on the building in front of him.

"Oh," Lori squeaked just before she coughed. "Oh, I guess. That would, um… Tonight?"

"I'm teasing you, Lori."

"Oh, thank God. Jesus, Quinn. That was cruel."

"Sorry." Not that he was sorry at all. "I was actually thinking maybe we should go to dinner. Unless you'd prefer I just come over and drop my pants. I've got an hour free before lunch."

"Quinn." Lori's voice had dropped to a tone he suspected she used with her employees.

"All right. Dinner first. Unfortunately, I've got a previous obligation tonight. What do you think? Tomorrow?"

"That soon?"

"Yes." He left it at that. No point letting her mull over her decision any longer. And, frankly, he couldn't wait.

"Okay." The little squeak was back in her voice, making him smile. It thrilled him that she was nervous, that he wasn't just some old friend who'd climb into her bed and make her feel comfortable and safe. He wanted her tense and excited. "What time?" she asked.

Quinn didn't bother trying to think of his schedule. It had never once cemented itself into his head and never would. "Six-thirty."

"Okay, I'll meet you at your office."

"No, why don't I—"

"Listen, Quinn. I'm not interested in sitting here in my living room in a dress and heels for hours, waiting for you to remember our plans. I will meet you at your office."

"Oh. I see. All right."

She hung up with no added pleasantries, leaving Quinn staring at the restaurant sign for a few stunned seconds. "No chance am I forgetting this date," he said to no one at all. "I'll be there with bells on."

He was still wondering what the heck that phrase meant when he pulled up to his office two minutes later. One more date with Tessa, and then he'd be Lori Love's meaningless fling, hopefully for a good long while.

LORI ROLLED OUT from under the car, wiping her hands on a rag. "Joe," she called as she stood and stretched. "Will you be okay on your own for a few minutes? I've got a quick errand to run."

After Joe gave her a thumbs-up, she walked out and headed for the office of her Realtor. As she strolled along the cracked sidewalk, she realized how good this felt, confronting something. She'd been passive for so long, swept along by her life. Now she was taking control of a few small things. Finally. Maybe this would snowball into a real life.

"Fat chance," Lori muttered, but she was smiling when she opened the door of the tiny Main Street office. "Hi, Helen!" she called to the tall blonde at the back of the room.

Helen Stowe looked up from pouring coffee, her big hair bouncing with the movement. "Hey, Lori! What can I do for you this morning?"

"Oh, I just had a couple of questions. How are you doing? I thought you were going to meet me and Molly at The Bar last week."

Helen shrugged as she took a seat at her desk and waved Lori over to the chair that faced it. "You know. I just got busy."

"We're dropping by on Friday. Why don't you come along?"

"Oh." Helen's heavily mascara'd lashes fluttered. "I don't... I would, but... If..."

"Helen." Lori sighed. "Did you break it off with Juan?" Juan was the manager and bartender of The Bar. He was also ten years younger than the newly divorced Helen.

"No," she whispered, the quiet word trembling in the air. "He..." One fat tear escaped her lashes and tracked an ashy line down her cheek.

"Oh, Helen."

"He said he was tired of hiding our relationship!" Helen gasped. "He said I was ashamed of him, but I'm not! It's just..." That one tear was just the first of many, and Lori's stomach sank.

"I'm so sorry, Helen."

"It's my own fault," she said, as she yanked open a desk drawer and pulled out a box of Kleenex. "I never should have started dating him. He just doesn't understand what it's like to be a fortysomething woman dating a younger man." She leaned forward, eyes a bit wild. "Do you know they have a *word* for it now? They call women like me 'cougars'!"

"Yeah, I've heard that."

"It's mortifying!"

"Well, it's kind of trendy, actually."

"Trendy?" Helen screeched. "Do you know what Juan's mama would say if she found out? She's been after him to start making babies for years! If he brought home some dried-up old floozy like me, she'd probably call the priest over to perform an exorcism!"

"Helen," Lori said softly.

Helen blew her nose and hiccupped.

"Do you like Juan?"

Her face crumpled again, and Lori had her answer.

"If you really like him, don't you think you should give it a chance? Give *him* a chance?"

Though her tears continued to flow, Helen shook her head. "My husband left me, Lori. He left me after twenty years of marriage. I can't go through that again, and you can damn well bet your ass that Juan would leave in a few years. Hell, I'm about to enter menopause. He probably doesn't even know what that word *means*."

Lori sighed. "He's a nice guy."

Helen straightened her spine and took a deep breath, setting her impressive cleavage quivering. "Yes, he is. That's why I'm not going to tie him down to an old biddy like me."

Though she didn't usually think of old biddies as buxom women who wore stiletto heels and shirts cut down to there, Lori gave in and nodded. Juan's mother probably wouldn't approve of the heels and cleavage, either. Having grown up in Mexico, she likely had some pretty conservative ideas about women, at least with regards to her youngest son.

"Now, I'm going to go freshen up," Helen announced, "and when I come back, we will discuss your real estate needs."

Wow, that sounded official. Lori looked oblig-

ingly over the photos of available properties until
Helen returned, pink nose powdered and eyelashes
freshly coated in mascara. "Now, what can I do for
you, Lori Love?"

"I'm afraid I'm not looking to buy anything, but I
did have a question about my dad's property."

"Yeah?"

"Chris Tipton's been in touch a few times about
buying the land and some guy I'd never heard of
called on Monday. Has anyone else contacted you?"

"Oh, sure. I'm sorry, you said you weren't interested in talking about it, so I didn't call you."

"It's okay, honestly. I'm not interested, but I am
wondering what all the fuss is about. Who else has
asked about it?"

"Hold on." Helen spun her chair to a tall filing
cabinet and riffled through until she found a thin
file and pulled it out. "Here we go. Someone from a
company called Anton/Bliss Developers called last
month, and there was a call from The Valiant Group
in the spring. Other than that... I see I noted somebody called to ask about the land last week, but didn't
leave any information. The other two left numbers
and asked me to contact them if you ever showed any
interest in selling. Should I call them?"

"No," Lori said quickly. "But will you give me
their names and numbers?"

"You're not going to try to do this on your own,
are you? Because, honestly, these are some big companies, and whether you use my agency or not, I'd
recommend consulting an attorney and—"

"I'm honestly not looking to sell right now. But I'm beginning to wonder if I'm sitting on oil or something. Have you heard anything?"

Helen shrugged. "Not a thing. I'll keep my ears open, but it's a beautiful spot and there's a lot of rich folks around here."

"Yeah." Still…her dad had bought the land for less than seventy thousand dollars. It had been just as beautiful then, and there had been just as many Aspen people around.

Helen offered her a paper with the information.

"Thanks. If I ever do decide to sell, I need to know just how much it's worth to these people."

"Why *don't* you sell it, Lori? Your dad's gone now and, correct me if I'm wrong, but you were never interested in running the garage, were you?"

"I just…" Not wanting to think about her dreams and her fears and her money problems, Lori shook her head. "It's complicated."

"All right." Helen patted her hand, her smile conveying sympathy and maybe a little pity, too. Great. "I'll call you if anything else comes up. Let me know what you find out."

"Deal. And think some more about Juan, will you?"

Helen just glared, but Lori didn't let that get her down as she left and hurried back toward the garage. She had *something* now, a clue. Maybe it had nothing to do with ten years ago, but it was still a mystery that needed to be solved.

A mystery *and* a fling. She almost had a real life for the moment.

CHAPTER SIX

Jamal's blue skin deepened as she watched. Amy felt her breath quicken and clutched the towel tighter to her body. She'd only just become used to the beautiful sapphire-blue tint of his flesh, and now it was darkening, flushing to a tone closer to twilight.

"Are you okay?" she asked.

His gaze swept down her body. She was still wet from the bath and the tiny scrap of towel fell only to the very tops of her thighs. "I'm aroused," he answered in his usual forthright tone.

"Ah, I see. Hard to hide on your planet, I guess." She laughed nervously, then gestured back toward the bathing room of his ship. "I'm done."

"My turn?" His gaze rose, and when it met with hers, she gasped. His pupils had tightened to a narrow feline shape. He reached for the button of his trousers.

She couldn't help but watch, and when he pushed down the tight black fabric, Amy's heart pounded in shock. Yes, he was aroused. He was also very big. And blue. And textured with little ridges that skipped down the entire length of his shaft. *Ribbed,* they called it back on earth. *For added pleasure.*

The towel slipped from Amy's grasp and Jamal began to purr.

LORI SNAPPED THE BOOK shut on her favorite story and fanned herself with it. It might be awkward to start her date with Quinn already melting with arousal. Or maybe not.

She glanced at the cherrywood clock on the mantel of his office fireplace. He was already twenty minutes late, but Lori had assumed he wouldn't be here until close to seven, and so had his secretary. The woman—Jane, she'd said—had waited until Lori arrived before leaving.

"I left a message on his cell phone," she'd explained. "He'll probably be here by seven. If you make plans with Mr. Jennings again, you may want to fudge the time by thirty minutes."

"I already did," Lori had said, and the woman's cool expression had immediately warmed.

"A smart move. There are magazines on the—"

"I brought a book to read."

Jane's eyebrows had risen. "Very smart, indeed. Your reservations are for seven-fifteen. Have an enjoyable evening."

Another tick of the minute hand sounded from the clock before Lori heard the distinctive thud of a car door closing outside. She tucked the book into her purse and stood, smoothing out her skirt as she rose. The dark gray linen dress would probably be hopelessly wrinkled before the night was out, but she loved it and it had been on sale. And it went with the red shoes. Lori simply couldn't afford to buy another pair for this date, and she didn't think Quinn had seen them the first time anyway. She was just tugging the plunging neckline of the dress up when the door flew open.

Her neckline fell right back to its original position as Quinn burst into the room, cell phone to his ear. Her phone started to ring, then cut off when he snapped his phone shut. "Lori!"

"Hey, Quinn."

"I'm sorry, I lost track of time."

"I know." Even if she had been irritated with him, her annoyance would have disappeared in the next moment. Quinn's eyes lost the glint of panic and focused on her chest. Then his gaze dipped lower, sliding over her hips and legs and down to her shoes.

"Wow."

She smiled.

His eyes rose, moving even slower this time, until he finally met her gaze. "My God, Lori."

"What?" she asked coyly, trying not to let the smile turn to a maniacal grin. "Is something wrong?"

"I'm just glad I'm not eating any jicama right now, that's all."

Laughing, Lori didn't notice that he'd moved closer until he took one of her hands in his. Her eyes popped wide-open just as he leaned close to kiss her cheek.

"Oh," she blurted out as too many things hit her at once. His heat, the scent of his shampoo, the bare rasp of his cheek against her skin. And his lips. On her. And then he stepped away before she could jump his bones.

"You look unbelievably beautiful," he said easily, as if that weren't the first time a man had said that to her. "Are you ready to go?"

"Yeah, I've been ready." More than ready. Ready to skip dinner altogether. That book had been good, but Quinn was something better. His gray suit pants fit perfectly, framing slim hips, and the French-blue dress shirt stretched across those wide shoulders.

"Sorry," he said again, reaching for a suit jacket that hung on a coatrack. The shirt grew taut, then looser again before it was hidden beneath the coat. He pulled a tie from his pocket, flipped up his collar, and proceeded to dress in front of her. As if they'd just woken up together. As if they'd just finished having sex.

God, she wanted to do him.

He glanced at his watch. "We'd better get going."

If this were one of her books, she'd put a stop to this dinner business. She'd unzip the back of her dress and strip down to her brand-new underwear and matching bra. Tell him all she wanted to eat was him. Tell him she wanted it hard and fast and *now*.

But she was just Lori Love, girl mechanic, and she didn't have the guts to put what she wanted into words even if it was the whole point of this date. Pitiful.

Maybe she should call the whole thing off. If—

His hand left a two-inch trail of white fire down her upper arm when he touched her. "Shall we?"

Throat frozen with wants and demands and dirty words that she couldn't force out, Lori couldn't speak. She couldn't say what she wanted, but God she *wanted*. Wanted this just for herself and no one else. So she took the hand Quinn offered and silently led him out the door.

He didn't say anything, either, just waved her toward a silver car that was parked at a panicked angle near the entrance. Lori looked over the car and felt her body settle back into her skin. This was something she knew. Her throat opened up.

"Nice car."

He glanced at the Audi A6 as if he'd never seen it before. "I guess. It's got four-wheel drive."

"Ah. Of course." Nothing about the horsepower or the supercharged V6. The car got him where he wanted to go and that was that. Everything in his life functioned as a simple vehicle for his passion and skill.

She wondered suddenly if Quinn had sprung fully formed from the head of Zeus, because he was certainly nothing like his parents. Mr. Jennings had run the town feed store, and Mrs. Jennings was a no-nonsense housewife, the daughter of a rancher. He came from people who drove American trucks with big engines and oversize tires. People who never dreamed bigger than wanting to own a few more acres of land than their parents had. People like her.

Quinn was different…shiny and polished from

the constant flow of letting his own dreams wash over him.

When he settled into the driver's seat and flashed her a smile, Lori's throat froze again, so full of need that she wondered if she'd cry. She wanted sex with him, there was no doubt about that. But maybe more than that, she wanted a little of that glow to rub off on her bare skin, wanted to feel what she'd felt as a younger woman.

Her glow was long gone, now she just wanted a taste of Quinn's.

THE WINE ARRIVED like a gift from a sympathetic god. Or as if Quinn had ordered it when she was pretending to look at the menu and wondering if they would have sex that night. The waiter had clearly come and gone without her ever noticing. Which was just fine, because now she had the unexpected relief of a whole bottle of white wine to give her courage.

This affair had seemed only slightly frightening when Quinn had been his normal nerdy, distracted self, but his distraction had vanished at the most inopportune time. Every time she looked up from the menu his hazel eyes were focused on her, unwavering and not the least bit clouded by distant thought.

"Why are you looking at me?" she finally demanded.

"We're on a date."

She watched greedily as he tipped the bottle and poured golden light into her glass. "So you're always an attentive date?"

Quinn's eyes crinkled at the edges when he smiled. "Probably not, no. But I'm trying to figure you out. It's taking all my powers of concentration."

She shifted. "I'm simple enough."

"Hardly." His eyes dipped to the tiny bit of cleavage she'd been trying to cover earlier. "You're a complicated woman."

"Oh, yeah. I'm deep and mysterious, all right. A real enigma."

"Mmm." His eyes narrowed in study. "I can tell you're trying to be funny—"

"Trying?"

"But you really are a mystery."

She arched an eyebrow, irritated by the scrutiny. "An exotic taste of the underclass, Quinn?"

His faint smile faded. "What's that supposed to mean?"

"Nothing." Nothing except there wasn't anything mysterious about her. Just another girl stuck in her hometown, going nowhere. Maybe she could sell the movie rights.

"Since this is our first date, I'll let that slide. But don't think I'm not paying attention. We'll talk about your issues later."

Lori shook her head. "There are no issues during a meaningless affair. I'm an empty shell."

"Mmm." His smile returned, as did the spark of sexual interest in his eyes. "You look particularly soft and warm for an empty shell."

She resisted the urge to tug her neckline up again.

"Now back to your nonissues," he pressed. "I've

been thinking about you, Lori Love. What's with the heels and dresses?"

"I'm a girl." The wine pushed warmth deep into her muscles, forcing out some of the tension. She was a girl. And she *was* soft and warm.

"Does this have something to do with those books Molly writes?"

The wine receded a little, traitorous and unreliable as far as courage went. Lori swallowed more to keep herself from choking on panic. "You told her about us? What else did she say? She shouldn't have told you anything."

"No, I didn't tell her. She just happened to mention that you were a fan."

"Good."

"Why?"

Lori took her turn to study him, look him over. He was handsome and so sexy in his bookish way. His hands so elegant that she wanted to pick one up and stroke it. Suck a finger deep into her mouth, just to get them both hot and wondering. But she couldn't do that kind of thing if she was always thinking of Quinn as Molly's big brother. He was her sex object now, pure and simple. And he was waiting for an answer.

"It's hotter this way," she forced out, and watched his eyebrows head for his hairline. "A secret affair. Discreet. And naughty."

"Naughty," he repeated, though his mouth hardly moved.

"Yes."

God bless the wine that had loosened her tongue,

because the spark of interest in Quinn's eyes exploded into fireworks of lust. "I have absolutely no interest in telling my sister a damn thing."

"What sister?" Lori countered.

Quinn threw back his head and laughed, while Lori thought about licking her way up that strong, tanned neck.

A passing man interrupted her daydream. "Quinn," he said in surprise, reaching out his hand. "How you doing?" His deep Texas drawl rumbled from a barrel chest.

"Great! Lori, this is Bill Adkinson. He owns one of the big title companies in town."

Lori shook his hand and tried hard to listen politely to the men's conversation, but her mind had gotten stuck on a sudden thought.

Maybe she could use Quinn for *more* than sex. Maybe she could use him to figure out why her land was so interesting to so many people.

"Sorry about that," Quinn said, clueing Lori in to the fact that his friend was walking away.

"Oh, no problem. I thought it was interesting."

He smiled. "Really? Because you looked a little glazed over there."

As she laughed, she decided on her approach. "Hey, do you know Chris Tipton? He was in my class in high school and I hear he's a big developer now."

"Sure, Tipton & Tremaine."

"Do you work with them?"

Quinn shook his head as the salad plates arrived. "Most of my clients are individual home owners. Big developers want too much of a say in the design. I prefer to work from scratch. It's more fun."

Shit. "So you don't work with developers at all?"

"I worked with a few when I was first starting out. It's a good way to get your name out there. But now I only pick up projects with Anton/Bliss. They do some really great work on small, upscale developments."

Anton/Bliss? That was one of the names Helen had given her. Jackpot! "So are you working on anything for them right now?" She took a bite of spinach salad and tried to look casual.

"No, not really," he answered, and the bubble of hope growing in her chest deflated. "I've got my hands full with about a dozen builds going on right now. Summer is busy as hell, of course. And then there's my personal project, which is taking more time than I…" His gaze slid down to her chest. "Um, Lori?"

"Hmm?" Well, what had she expected, some grand revelation that, yes indeed, he was working on a top secret project for Anton/Bliss involving the very land that Lori had inherited from her dad?

Quinn cleared his throat. "You've got salad dressing on your, ah, chest."

Worried she'd ruined her new dress, Lori glanced down, only to find that her linen dress was safe. But a tiny drop of honey dressing clung to the rounded top of her cleavage, slowly sliding its way toward the very low, very wide V of her neckline. Lori caught it with her finger and raised it to her lips, licking away the dressing before it occurred to her that she was in a nice restaurant and not The Bar.

"Oops," she said around her finger. Cringing, she looked up at Quinn, thinking she'd better apologize, but his expression stopped her.

Lids heavy, hazel eyes blazing with heat, he watched her mouth, watched her slide her finger out. His gaze narrowed even more. She licked her lips and his own pressed tight together. When she wiped her hand on her napkin, his eyes fell back to her cleavage.

Lori forgot all about Anton/Bliss and decided her attention would be better spent concentrating on eating. Fast.

Good Lord, Lori Love was a sex object. Who could've known?

Her dress was cut down to a very interesting place, the wide V showing off the barely rounded tops of her breasts, and leading Quinn's brain on an intense analysis of whether or not she was wearing a bra. If she was, it was constructed of a little scrap of nothing, and he very much wanted to know what that nothing looked like.

He'd managed to carry on a conversation all through dinner, answering all her questions about the cities he'd visited in Europe. But then she'd excused herself to use the restroom, and Quinn had been treated to the sight of her walking away, bloodred heels pointing the way to pale, delicate calves. Her thighs would be even paler. And her ass...

"Okay," he breathed. Time to get it together or he'd be nursing a hard-on through dessert.

But, damn, she was cute.

If he were reasonable, he'd just accept this for what it was: a sex gift dropped, almost literally, in his lap. But he wanted to know the why of it. Why him and why now? She hadn't answered the question about Molly's books.

Quinn crossed his ankle over his knee and leaned to the side to peer into the compact red purse she'd left on the floor. Here was a clue that she might temporarily *look* like a character from *Sex and the City*, but she didn't act like one. She'd left her makeup behind. Good. He liked the natural pink of her mouth. Such a relief after the gobs of shiny gloss Tessa had worn. Not even bubble-gum flavored or anything. Just sticky.

Earlier, he'd spotted the spine of a book that didn't quite fit into her purse, and now that Lori was away, he couldn't resist plucking it out to spy.

It really was one of *those* books. Erotica, Molly called it. Quinn winced at the giant, naked pecs of the oiled-up muscleman on the cover and flipped the book over to scan the author names. No Holly Summers, Molly's pen name, thank God.

Eyes widening, Quinn quickly read the description of the first story. "Wow."

A plain librarian hires a coldhearted private investigator to investigate her own past. But the ex-cop refuses her money…and demands more intimate payment for all the long, hard hours he's put in.

Blinking, Quinn scanned the other four story descriptions, managing to be shocked by each one in turn. He'd been happy to hear about Molly's success as a writer, but he'd studiously avoided any and all details about her work. Clearly, that had been a wise idea. But as long as she hadn't written any of these…

He thumbed open the book, and began to read. Halfway through page three, a lightning-fast hand darted in and snatched the book from his fingers.

"What are you doing?" Lori hissed.

"Research."

"Research?"

"You never answered my question about the books."

Glaring a laser beam of anger into his head, Lori shoved the book back into her purse and dropped into her chair. "That was a hint that you were supposed to drop the subject."

"But I didn't. I want to know what all this is about."

"All what?"

"Lori."

She looked down at the table. The tips of her ears turned red. Her hands clutched each other against the tablecloth, knuckles growing whiter by the second. Shit, now Quinn felt like an asshole. "I'm sorry."

Lori just shook her head. Oh, God, what if she was crying? What had he said that would make her cry?

He reached across the table to wrap his hand around hers. "Lori?"

When she looked up, her expression was stubborn, her face pink, but there were no tears in her eyes. "I've never, um…"

Quinn's stomach fell, leaving a vacuum that

sucked at his lungs and heart. *Holy crap.* "Lori? Are you saying…?" He leaned closer. "Are you a virgin?"

"No! Oh, God, no. I turn thirty in two months!"

His stomach snapped back into place, weak from all the travel. "But you said… Okay. Good. I mean, not that I wouldn't be honored…"

"It's not that. It's just that I've never really… There are things I want to experience and I— Shoot, I don't know how to say this. I really don't." She glanced nervously around the restaurant.

Quinn poured her the last glass of wine, then watched while she drank it too fast. The crème brûlée arrived in a ramekin shaped like a fish, and whatever the hell that was supposed to mean escaped him entirely, but then he was busy trying to analyze Lori and her stammered words.

Her lips closed around one of the raspberries that had been scattered over the dessert. A tiny drop of deep red juice stained her mouth for a moment before she licked it away. Boy, did she have great tongue.

"Is it that you've never had an orgasm?" he finally ventured.

Her steady gaze seemed to give him an answer, but then she tilted her head a little, puzzled. "I don't think that's it." She looked around again before dropping her voice to a near whisper. "I mean, I've had orgasms. But on its own, coming is just coming."

It was Quinn's turn to look puzzled, and he felt he was doing a pretty good job of it. "I don't know what you mean."

"Well, hell's bells, Quinn, I don't, either." She

smiled again, finally—he'd been missing that—and shook her head, making her curls brush her neck. "If you help me figure it out, I promise to make it worth your while."

"Deal," he said, before she could take that back. "So tell me about the books."

"No."

"Come on, Lori. We're going to have sex. Isn't that a little more intimate than talking about it?"

"No, it's not!" She pulled her hand from his and crossed her arms. "You're asking me what my fantasies are, and we've never even kissed."

"We've never even kissed, and we know we'll be lovers, but *that* doesn't bother you?"

Lori reached for the wineglass, but when she saw it was empty, pushed her fingers into her hair instead. Then she blinked, pulled her hand carefully away from her curls, and patted them back into submission.

"You'd better tell me, Lori. Or I might read the wrong story and show up at your house with a turkey baster and a giant pink bunny suit."

"A what?" she asked way too loudly, causing heads to swivel in their direction.

Quinn raised his eyebrows and wiggled them until Lori deigned to laugh. It wasn't long before she had to lay her forehead on the table to try to compose herself.

Quinn offered a friendly wave to the people still watching Lori as she snorted into the tablecloth.

"A turkey baster?" she squeaked.

"What, the bunny suit's okay with you?"

"Stop it," Lori gasped. "My mascara is going to run."

Taking advantage of her incapacitation, Quinn leaned down to retrieve the book. "Just give me a hint. A title. A number."

Her deep breath whispered past her lips in a long, long sigh. She inhaled just as slowly, making him wait before she finally gave in. "Number one," she said. "And…number four."

He glanced down. "But number four is about an alien."

"I *know*."

"I'm human."

Lori finally raised her head to glare at him past her smudged makeup. "Oh, for God's sake, Quinn. He's just blue. Otherwise everything else is the same. They never have any tentacles or extra…actually, sometimes… But the guy in this story is normal."

"Okay, one and four." And thank the sweet Lord she hadn't mentioned number two, because that was about a woman and man *and* his best friend. Quinn wasn't going there, not even for Lori.

The bill arrived, and as soon as he'd paid it, Lori straightened up and nodded. "All right. Your place or mine?"

Quinn jerked back in his chair. "Pardon?"

"Where are we going to do this?"

"*Do this?* You've got a nice way of making a boy feel special, you know that?"

Lori closed her eyes, brow wrinkling in stress. "I'm sorry." She waved her hands as if there were cobwebs brushing her face. "I don't know how to do what we're doing. I'm feeling a little freaked out, and I don't mean to be rude, but I just want to get it over with."

Her eyes opened while Quinn was still bouncing off the triangular walls of offense, shock and amusement.

"Quinn, I'm sorry. I know I'm being rude, but I just need to get through this first time, you know? Oh, God." Her green eyes filled with sudden tears. "I'm turning into a monster."

"I do feel sort of like a harem girl being called up for the sultan's latest pleasure."

"Story number five," Lori whispered.

"Exactly. Shall I prepare myself for you, mistress?"

"God!" She surged to her feet, swaying a little on heels she wasn't used to wearing, then spun and headed for the door.

Quinn grabbed her purse—and the book—and followed.

"Lori?" It took him only a moment to spot her. She stood at the corner of the next side street, facing his car, just at the edge of a pale circle of light falling from one of the old-fashioned lampposts. As he watched, she reached down and slid one red heel off, then the other.

Glancing back at the sound of his steps, she raised her shoes in a gesture of defeat. "I'm no good at this."

"It'd be a little strange if you were."

She just shook her head.

Despite his grand plans, Quinn was nearly overwhelmed with the urge to pick her up, kiss her senseless and drag her home to his lair. Lori was usually nothing if not strong and sure, but right now she looked as fragile as cracking glass. And why was that a turn-on? Some ancient, embarrassing male fantasy of saving a beautiful damsel in distress? What century was he living in?

A slight wind rippled the material of her skirt and tugged at the brown spirals of her curly hair.

"Lori, the whole point of this is for you to have a good time. It's supposed to be hot and mindless, right? But tonight you're worrying and thinking way too much."

"I'm sorry."

"Don't be sorry. I don't want you to be someone else. Just yourself."

She threw her arms out in a jerky motion, the shoes almost hitting him in the chest. "I don't want to be myself anymore! Don't you get it? That's what this is about!"

"I get it." The air of fragility burned off in her frustration, but Quinn's need to touch her remained. He tucked the book into his coat pocket and reached for her arm to pull her closer. "But I want to do this with *you,* because of you. If you're looking to find a new side of yourself, I'm fine with that. But I don't want you to play at being someone else."

Her chin jutted out. "What if that someone else is wearing a cheerleading uniform?"

"Well… All right then, we could talk about that."

She laughed, a choked sound of relief that faded away when he pulled her gently forward, not stopping until he could feel the heat of her body a hairbreadth from his.

He brushed his hand over one of her curls, letting it insinuate itself between his fingers. "I've never touched your hair before."

Her eyelids fluttered. "Sure you have. That time you attacked me with a hat."

"Not like this. Not real touching. It's very soft. And I think it likes me."

"It likes everything, including twigs and bushes. I wouldn't feel too flattered if I were you."

When he trailed his thumb down her temple, the sardonic smile fell away and she actually shivered. Her eyes closed. Quinn felt flattered despite her warning.

"Lori." He leaned down and pressed his lips to hers for a brief, gentle kiss.

"Mmm?"

Her face tilted up, inviting him to kiss her again, so he did. How could he not? And though he kept it just as soft as the first, his nerves stirred when her sigh swept over his mouth. His heart beat harder. He'd been about to say something. Something important…

Right. "Lori, we're not going to have sex tonight."

"Hmm?" When she leaned a little closer, her breasts brushed the cotton of his shirt.

That seemed like a sad place to stop, so Quinn closed the last half inch between them and felt her small, strong body press against his for the first time.

Electricity swirled through him like floating threads of pure heat. Imminent sex or not, there was no reason not to touch her.

So he kissed her again, a real kiss this time, a kiss that asked her to open her mouth and let him in. She did.

He'd never thought about what Lori Love might taste like, so he didn't know why he felt surprised. But he was shocked at the rightness of her, sweet and sexual on his tongue, the most feminine thing he'd ever tasted.

Quinn didn't bother resisting the urge to have more of her. Moving slowly forward, he backed her out of the light and up against the side of the car. When he pressed his hips against her and deepened the kiss, Lori gasped. Her hands clutched at his waist, and she tugged him closer, harder. Her tongue slid over his, more urgent and needy as each second passed, until the logical thing to do became obvious.

Quinn dropped her purse and lifted Lori onto the hood of the car. He fit himself between her legs, and pulled her snug against his growing erection.

Oh, Christ, that felt good. Lori seemed to think so, too, if he was reading her little whimper correctly, but he wasn't thinking straight, so maybe it wasn't—

She thrust her hands beneath his jacket, tugged up his shirt and stroked her palms up his back. Yes, definitely good.

Her tongue sliding over his, her breath hitching, her sex pressing the perfect pressure against his dick… It was all sublime. Beautiful. He sucked gen-

tly at her bottom lip, memorizing the texture before
he kissed his way over to the sweet curve of her neck.

Lord, she tasted good. Clean and simple, no scent
except her skin. Her breath was a rushing beneath
his mouth, so loud he could feel it as he sucked and
kissed.

"Oh," she gasped. "I don't—"

She broke into silence when he rocked against her
sex. He wanted her to feel how hard he was, needed
her to know what she did to him. Her muscles jerked
when he nipped beneath her ear.

"Quinn! I don't think… Oh, God, that feels good."

He dragged his mouth all the way down her neck
to press his teeth to her collarbone.

"Oh! We need to go somewhere. Not here. We
need…" Her body stiffened enough that even in his
haze of pleasure, Quinn registered it. "Wait, what did
you say?" she asked.

He shook his head. He'd been too busy relishing
the texture of her skin against his tongue to say a
word. Raising a hand, he cupped the soft mound of
her breast, then licked up her neck to her jawline.

Her fingers dug into his back as her knees opened
farther.

Yes. That was better. He was cradled by her thighs
now, her sex the perfect concavity to hold his hardness.

"Quinn."

"Yes," he answered. Yes, yes, yes. She shivered
and began to arch her neck back, but that shock
of tension raced through her again, and she sat up

straight. He felt the tight hold of her fingers in his hair just before she pulled him back. When he opened his heavy eyes, Lori was staring him down with a surprising lack of warmth.

"Did you say we weren't going to have sex tonight?"

"Yeah."

"Why would you say something like that?"

The world began to lose its smoky haze, and Quinn suddenly registered that he was halfway to having sex with Lori right here. In public. On top of a car.

He smoothed her skirt back down toward her knees. "I'm sorry, what were we talking about?"

Lori crossed her arms and glared, but he got distracted from her anger by the way her arms pushed her breasts up. The lacy edge of a black bra peeked above the linen.

"Quinn Jennings!" She slid off the car and forced him back.

"I'm sorry. What...? Um, right. No sex."

"You're *telling* me we're not having sex?"

"Yes."

"First of all, you're not the one to decide whether or not we have sex. Secondly—"

Quinn shook his head. "Sorry, darlin', but you hired me for this project, and I need to do all the research before we get started."

"I... *You*..." she sputtered. "I did not *hire* you!"

God, she was adorable. "You're too easy to tease, Lori."

Her lips tightened until they nearly disappeared.

"I may be unarmed right now, but I want you to be very aware that I have access to lots—" she poked his chest "—and lots—" another poke "—of heavy machinery."

He grabbed her wrist and pulled her back into his arms. "Don't be mad. I want to have sex with you. Tonight. Now. In that dark alley right there while unsuspecting people walk past. I want to push up your dress and pull down your panties... Are you wearing panties, by the way?"

"Yes!"

"Good, because I want to tug them off and slip my fingers inside you while you try to keep from screaming. And while you—"

"Yes," she insisted. *"Now."*

"No." He tried to keep the sorrow from his voice. "you wanted a—"

"Look, buddy, this is what I hired you for, so let's get to it."

Quinn laughed, though he kept a close eye on her fisted hands as he chuckled. "No, the deal is that you get a torrid affair. Not a one-night quickie."

"So we'll do it again tomorrow." Her jaw inched out in frustration when he only shook his head. "I am not going to beg you."

Quinn grabbed the book from his jacket and tapped the cover. "Depends what I read in here."

She finally hit him then. Her knuckles bit into his shoulder with surprising force. "Ow!"

She muttered, "Sorry," without much enthusiasm.

"Okay, all joking aside... You said yourself that

you want something more than what you've had before. That's a lot to put on one man, especially a man who doesn't get out much. So the least you can do is trust me on this. It'll be better if you wait."

"If *I* wait?"

Stubborn girl. "We're talking about you here. What you want. What you need."

She stared him down as if she was searching for a sign of truth in his eyes. As the seconds passed, her face lost a bit of its frustration. "You really wanted to do it, too? Just now?"

"Hell, yeah."

Her curls bounced with her nod. "Fine. I can wait then. How long?"

"Not fucking long. I'm no martyr."

"Good."

Apparently she wasn't the type to hold a grudge, because Lori sealed the deal with a kiss that curled his toes and drew his fingers up into fists. The taste of her hit him again, as if it were the first time.

Quinn knew right then that he was about to have the best summer of his life.

CHAPTER SEVEN

THIS WAS THE WORST DAY she'd had in months. The worst day since her father died.

Lori tossed a disgusted glance toward the cuckoo clock her dad had hung in the garage. Nearly five o'clock.

She was relieved one of the mechanics had ripped the bird out long before. If it were still there, Lori would have picked up a sledgehammer as soon as it showed its ugly face. Unbelievable how a clock could take its sweet time ticking away the hours.

But she was almost to the end of the day now. In three minutes the broken perch would emerge from the door with a sick squeal of gears. Then Esteban would come by to pick up the keys of the tow truck for the night calls, Joe would pack up his things, and even Lori would be nearly free. Only one customer scheduled to pick up, and he would be here by five-thirty.

Not bothering to stifle her sigh, Lori wiped her arm across her forehead to catch the sweat before she turned back to the lug nuts of the left rear tire and pushed as hard as she could against the wrench.

She hated rotating tires above all else. It was boring work—and for her, heavy—and it didn't satisfy her need to take something broken and make it purr again. Tire rotations were even more tedious than oil changes. At least with the oil, you could see the satisfying change from black to clear brown liquid.

When her hand slipped off the wrench and crashed against the wheel, she wasn't the least bit surprised, not that it hurt any less just because it was expected. "Shit, shit, shit!" If only her last torque gun hadn't burned itself out last week. She was going to have to scrape up the money for a new one. The men were grumbling, especially since she'd broken the news that she wasn't planning to fix the hydraulic car lift that had given out in June.

Wussies.

"Lori," Joe called over her shouting. "Chief Lawson's on the phone."

"*Fuck!* Tell him I'll call him back." Damn it. Ben had left a message on the machine earlier, asking her to get in touch. He'd sounded serious and official so, of course, Lori hadn't called back. She didn't plan on returning his call this time, either. Not today. Tomorrow maybe, when she wasn't tired and furious and hurt.

Quinn had dropped her at her truck last night, given her another of those deep, searing kisses, and let her drive away. Fine. She'd reconciled herself to it. Waiting could be good, she could see that. A good hour of her night had been spent fantasizing about getting Quinn back between her thighs. The moment her alarm clock had blared to life, so had

Lori's sex drive. When would he call? When would he come over?

So, yes, she'd been tense before she'd ever rolled out of bed, but it had been a good tension. A deliciously tight anticipation that squeezed gently at her body. And then she'd made the mistake of retrieving the Aspen paper from her doorstep.

She got the *Tumble Creek Tribune,* so why the hell did she subscribe to the Aspen paper, too? And why the hell had she opened up the society section?

Quinn Jennings, one of Aspen's most eligible bachelors, shows his support for the arts by escorting Ms. Tessa Smith to the Aspen Music fundraiser.

And there he was, pictured in unflinching black and white at that "previous obligation" he'd mentioned on Tuesday. It must have been a glamorous party. Sting was standing right next to him, and on Quinn's other side, hand on his arm, was a woman apparently named Tessa Smith.

She was beautiful. Stunning. Blond and tall and lean. Model-thin except for a pair of giant round breasts squeezed high by the corset-style bodice of her pale dress. Hollywood white teeth. Thick black eyelashes. Long, elegant arms accented by the perfect bangle bracelets.

The same woman Lori had glimpsed at Quinn's table last Saturday.

Oh, God. Lori felt nauseous just thinking about

it. A comparison to last Monday's gossip column in Tumble Creek's paper just made it worse.

> Our little Lori Love is a late bloomer. Word is that she was spotted in Aspen last week buying a very pretty dress with a female friend. What's next? Perhaps some fluffy kittens painted on her purple tow truck?

The contrast was clear. Lori was a tomboy playing dress up for the amusement of her neighbors. Quinn was a high society bachelor who dated models and hung out with Sting. That summed it up nicely.

Lori was no longer puzzled by Quinn's easy suggestion that they not jump into sex. He'd been riding the wild silicone waves of women like Tessa Smith. Now he needed time to acclimate himself to Lori's flat terrain. Regain his land legs.

Men who were interested in women like that were not interested in girls like Lori. And she'd felt so pretty during those forays into Aspen.

She *had* been pretty. Or maybe cute. But definitely not beautiful. Girlish, as opposed to womanly.

Lori looked down at the thick suede work gloves covering her hands, and wondered that she'd ever thought anything different. She was a pity fuck, pure and simple. How utterly humiliating.

"Miss Love?" a gravelly voice asked from the direction of the tiny garage office. She forced her heavy head up to look at Esteban. "I got the keys. I'll be on call until six."

"Got it," she answered.

He turned to gather up the clipboard and paperwork he'd need, while Lori stared at his back. This was the type of man she should have set her eye on. Stocky and silent. Arms covered with tattoos. Hair shorn down to a brutal and practical buzz cut. No aspirations beyond owning a kick-ass muscle car as far as Lori could tell. Or maybe he was saving up to buy a tow truck and plow gear so he could work on his own terms. Regardless, he was one of her kind.

Though, hell, he probably liked giant fake boobs, too. They all did.

When Esteban straightened, he caught her watching and frowned. Lori frowned back.

"Lori?" Joe's voice broke in. "You okay?"

"I'm fine."

"What's going on with the chief? He sounded serious."

"It's nothing."

He watched her carefully. "You've been acting odd. You want to talk? We could grab a beer at The Bar."

"No, thanks." She'd managed not to snap at the men throughout the day, or not more than normal. But she was entering the red zone of bitchiness now and just wanted to be alone. Beer, hell yes. Company, no.

She felt guilty when Joe's brow creased with concern, but she managed to ignore it. He didn't say anything more, just waved goodbye and crunched out onto the gravel. Esteban had vanished. She was alone.

Fitting the wrench back to the lug nut, Lori ignored

the fact that the wheel blurred before her eyes and managed to get through the last five minutes of her task without letting any tears fall. Then she backed the pickup out of the bay, stowed the keys beneath the floor mat, and called the owner to come pick it up.

As soon as she'd locked up the garage, Lori hit the fridge.

"Oh, God no," she groaned when she saw the contents. In her attempt to become a sexpot, she'd brought home a bottle of wine instead of a six-pack. The thought of walking across the street to the market made her even wearier than the thought of drinking wine instead of beer, so Lori grabbed the bottle, pried out the cork, and headed for the tub.

She felt deliciously melodramatic swigging straight from the bottle, and she needed all the delicious she could get tonight. The swigging worked. A half hour later, she was sprawled out on her old bed in the upstairs bedroom and staring blearily at the TV. Her favorite Travel Channel DVD carried her away to the canals of Venice, though she felt inexplicably grumpy as she floated along on the opaque water.

But the red wine tasted Italian enough, and the cool breeze from the open window felt like a river breeze caressing her naked arms. Then again, she probably wouldn't be riding in a gondola wearing a wife-beater and her favorite panties.

Molly had given her a days-of-the-week set for Christmas, and though Lori hadn't been able to find Thursday's pair after her bath, the sparkly cursive "Saturday" still made her smile. If a bit weakly.

She was just floating toward the Grand Canal when a completely unacceptable sound rose up from the first floor. Lori turned up the volume on the TV and crossed her arms, but the knocking returned, followed quickly by the chime of the doorbell.

"Screw you," she muttered. Quinn had probably psyched himself up and returned to take the plunge. Probably decided to just get it over with as quickly as possible. He was too nice. She never should have told him her plans. Of course he'd feel responsible for taking the task on himself, just to keep her from doing something stupid with a stranger. "Bastard."

By the time the doorbell rang a second time, Lori was pissed again, the wine only making her anger more reasonable.

"He wants to see me? Fine." Lori muted the TV, then took her bottle and stomped downstairs.

When she flung open the door and found Ben Lawson standing there, she didn't miss a beat. Here was another man she was pissed at. Lori put her hands on her hips and glared. "What do you want?"

Ben's eyes traveled quickly down her body, then back up, widening as each second passed. A pink tinge colored his cheeks as his gaze finally fixed on a spot high on her forehead. "I left you a couple of messages."

"And?"

"And I wanted to talk to you. Could you put some clothes on?"

"No," she snapped.

"Lori." He sighed. "Is Molly here?"

"No. Why?"

"Because I thought maybe this was another attempt to get me to look at your ass. I'm not sure why you two think that's so funny, but you do."

"She's not here. And I don't want to talk to you. That's why I didn't call you back, genius. And that's why I'm not getting dressed. Go away."

"Lori."

"No. You've clearly got bad news and I am not in the mood."

His gaze dropped from her hairline to her eyes, and the granite of his shoulders softened to something closer to limestone. "Is something wrong?"

"I've had a bad day, that's all. Shouldn't you be out rescuing people from bears or something?"

"Bears?" This time his gaze slid lower, all the way down to the wine she held in her hand. She'd feel more secure in her wildness if she'd managed to drink more than a quarter of the bottle. "I think Molly's a bad influence on you."

"You think? Look." She jiggled the bottle. "I'm a lush now. Though at least I'm not drinking from one of those fancy boxes that Molly likes."

Ben's sigh was familiar. He used it often enough around Molly. "Do you really want me to come back tomorrow? Because you might be better off adding to this bad day while you're still in it."

Damn it, she could hardly argue with that. Ben was right, probably because he had years of experience delivering bad news to people. She felt her resentment rumble back an inch or two, and get mixed up with sympathy for him.

Careful not to spill any of the red wine on her cheap brown-flecked carpet, Lori gestured with the bottle toward the couch. "Fine. Come on in. You're dripping doom all over my stoop anyway."

It turned out to be less than she'd expected, but still jarring to hear it said aloud. Ben hadn't found some forgotten photo of the assailant's name scratched into the dirt before her father had passed out. No, the evidence was all strongly circumstantial.

"The medical examiner confirmed the previous findings of blunt force trauma to the head. She also looked over the CT scans and X-rays." He glanced up from his notes at that point. "In her opinion, those injuries couldn't have been caused by a fall unless he'd fallen headfirst down an incline."

Lori made a soft, involuntary noise and looked away. "But the blow was to the back of the head."

"She said something about the angle of the force."

Staring at the blank TV, Lori nodded, then took a swig from the bottle.

"I'm sorry," Ben said.

In an attempt to keep from crying, Lori made herself speak calmly. "I've been going through his records. He bought some land about a month before the…injury."

He leaned forward. "Land?"

"Yeah. It looks like he bought it directly from the bank. I thought that might mean it had been foreclosed on."

His pen scratched furiously against the paper as he asked questions about the date of purchase and the bank. Lori got up to get the papers she'd found, and Ben stood with her, still writing.

"I'll get to this first thing in the morning," he said when she handed him the papers.

"Thanks." She started for the door, but Ben's hand fell on her shoulder to stop her.

"Are you okay, Lori? What's going on?"

"Besides my father's murder?"

He paused, and his fingers tightened gently on her shoulder. "Yes, besides that."

I'm a failure, Lori offered, but only to herself. *Sexually, financially, socially, educationally, professionally. A failure.* But that was something she'd never said aloud, even to herself, and something she'd never, ever say to another human being.

"Why don't you come over for dinner," Ben offered, his cop voice falling completely away. "Molly's making lasagna. And it's store-bought, so you don't have to be scared."

She laughed at that, but even to her ears it sounded a little shaky. Ben pulled her into a hug, his strong arms radiating warmth and security.

"Lori, please tell me what's going on."

Lori clutched the neck of the wine bottle tighter. "It's girl stuff, Ben. And it's not serious. It's just depressing."

"Early onset menopause?"

"Shut *up.*" She laughed, and shoved him hard with her free hand.

He gave her one of his rare smiles. "My mom's been having weird conversations with Molly recently. I can't help but absorb it."

"It's nothing, honestly. Just boys. Now go."

His smile snapped to a frown. "What boys?"

"Go!"

"All right, but I'll be watching the *Tribune* for clues."

"Great." Shoving at his shoulder, she turned him, then placed her hand flat against his back and started pushing him toward the door. Or more likely he allowed himself to be pushed. Regardless, she got him out of the living room and he turned the knob and opened the door. She pushed him right out onto the stoop and down the two steps to the narrow sidewalk.

The only thing that alerted her to a change was the sudden unyielding hardness of the muscles beneath her fingers. Her pushing ceased to work. "Ben?" she huffed, giving him one last little shove that didn't even shift his shoulders.

Shrugging, she spun on the ball of her bare foot to flounce back inside. That was when she saw Quinn. Standing in the middle of the front lot. Glaring.

"What do you think you're looking at?" she shouted.

Quinn didn't hesitate. "A woman in her underwear. Outside in the open. With a man who's supposed to be my sister's boyfriend."

Air hissed out between Ben's teeth, and Lori shuffled quickly through her memories, trying to remember if the two men had ever exchanged blows before.

They'd been best friends for years, and neither was inclined to violence, but there was a first time for everything. Lori touched Ben's arm, just in case.

"Fuck off, Quinn," he growled, but Lori didn't hear any real heat behind the words. He looked over his shoulder at Lori, then to Quinn, with the same alertness he'd shown the other day when he'd found them together, but he didn't say anything else before getting in his official police vehicle and driving away.

Quinn didn't say anything else, either; he just stared at her, his vicious frown caught somewhere between bafflement and frustrated anger.

Lori did her best to convey only one emotion with her glare. Complete and utter pissiness. She crossed her arms—ignoring the pain when the bottle banged against her elbow—and stared him down.

AN OPAQUE CLOUD of debris had settled over Quinn's mind, pelting his thoughts with grit and tiny bits of shrapnel. It was hard to think clearly through the mess of confusion.

All he could process was that Lori was in her underwear.

Outside.

Outside, yes, but looking just the way he'd fantasized she'd look in her underwear.

Except in his fantasy she hadn't been with his best friend.

And she hadn't been angry. Or drunk enough to drink straight from a wine bottle.

As if she'd read his scrambled thoughts, Lori

arched an impatient eyebrow and raised the bottle to her lips for a hearty gulp. Fury flashed through him, uncalled for and totally real.

"What the hell is going on here?" he barked.

She gestured with the bottle, a long sweep that encompassed the house and the lot. "It's my Thursday-night pajama party, Quinn. Me and all the other girl mechanics get together to have a pillow fight and lure men off the streets in our butch underwear. Is it working?"

Quinn tried to hold his tongue and failed. "Apparently. Ben's already been here, hasn't he?"

Her lips smiled, but there was no humor in her eyes. "Yep. In and out. And all the free coffee you can drink, but you might leave with a few grease stains."

His grand plans for seduction were spiraling into obscurity. The last thing he'd expected to find was her already undressed and entertaining Ben. And what the hell was she so enraged about?

Lori must have gotten tired of glaring at him, because she finally shrugged and headed for the front steps. Quinn followed and caught the door before it could slam in his face. "What is your damn problem? Are you still pissed about Wednesday night?"

"Yeah, because I'm that sensitive about not getting to the glory inside your pants, Quinn."

He followed her in and slammed the door. Hard. But that didn't relieve his baffled anger, it only pushed it up another notch. "What is your problem? I'm the one who just walked in on a very questionable situation. Shouldn't you be explaining yourself? Jesus, you're not even dressed!"

"Did we ever agree to be exclusive?"

"Excuse me?"

"We never made any promises about dating other people. It's just a fling."

His vision flashed a dull red with each pulse of his heart. *"We haven't even slept together yet.* And he's your best friend's boyfriend!"

Lori rolled her eyes. "Look, you're off the hook, all right? I don't want you making any grand sacrifices for me, Quinn. Just get back to your Aspen women."

"I don't… What the hell are you…? What Aspen women?"

"You know, the ones with the fake boobs and the fake eyelashes and fake tans. The ones who look like centerfolds instead of tomboys."

What in God's name was she talking about? Quinn threw up his hands and shrugged, exasperation turning the gesture violent. Lori apparently felt violent, as well, because she stalked over to the table, banged down the bottle and snatched up a newspaper. He only knew it was a newspaper because it landed on his face a half second later.

"That doesn't help clear things up!" he shouted as he crumpled the sheet in his hand.

"There's a picture of you in there with Dream-Whore Barbie. That *obligation* I believe you mentioned. Not exactly a horrible burden, huh?"

Anger still swirled through his chest, but beneath it

Quinn felt the floor of his stomach drop a few inches. Dream-Whore Barbie? That could only be—

He snapped the paper straight and looked right into the wide, white smile of Tessa Smith. Shit.

"No wonder you didn't want to do me the other night. You were probably still worn out from the night before. She looks like she does Pilates."

She did do Pilates, damn it. Quinn shook his head. "No. No, Lori. That wasn't a real date."

"No? You mean you're not sleeping with her?"

He watched her eyebrow arch up, a challenge he couldn't counter. Shit. "Not anymore," he offered pitifully.

"Not," she bit out, *"anymore?"*

Though frustration began to fuel his anger again, Quinn was suddenly struck with the realization that Lori was hurt. He'd hurt her feelings. Most of his rage fell away and slid like spilled ice across the floor. What a seduction this was.

Time for a hurried explanation. "We used to date. I broke it off two weeks ago—"

"She was at that restaurant with you a week ago."

"Uh, yes. A misunderstanding. And when I broke it off, she insisted that I still take her to that music fundraiser and I wasn't seeing you yet, and… I only took her to the fundraiser and then home. Not even a kiss."

Her hard expression didn't soften. "But you did date her. And sleep with her."

"Uh." Was there a good answer? No, there was not. He left it at "uh."

"You liked her." She came close enough to tap the paper so hard that it fell from his fingers and floated away. "You liked that. And *that* is not *this*." Her hand swept a scornful path over the front of her body.

"No, it's definitely not."

When her face darkened to the color of blood, Quinn realized what he'd said.

"I don't want that kind of woman," he blurted.

Lori stalked back to her bottle of wine and slammed back a shot of red. When she looked at him again, her face was calmer, but her eyes might have been a bit too shiny. "Stop being so nice, Quinn. Just stop. You dated her, so you liked her. I'm not a delicate flower. I appreciate what you were doing for me, but... I want a fling, not a handout. So, thanks, but I'm not a grenade you need to throw yourself on."

"A grenade...?" Quinn shook his head, wondering again how this had all gone so wrong. He'd stayed up half the night reading. First the stories she'd suggested, then the rest of them, because what the hell. And he'd been looking forward to coming over and starting their little adventure. More than looking forward to it. He hadn't been able to sleep, which wasn't unusual. But he also hadn't been able to concentrate on work, and that was a first. He'd wanted to rush the clock forward so he could come over here and give her what she wanted.

And now? Now it was off the rails, and if he hoped for any chance at all, he had to tell her the truth. The embarrassing truth.

So he did. "Tessa is not my type. I wasn't really interested in her at all, but she was…persistent."

Lori narrowed her eyes in clear doubt.

"She wanted to go out with me, I guess. Because one day I looked up and I was dating her."

"That's ridiculous."

"Yes, it is. But at some point, I was distracted during a conversation and I said yes when she suggested dinner. Then I was on a date, and I couldn't not be nice, and a few hours later we were in bed together."

"Just like that?"

"Damn it, I know it sounds absurd, but this is my life, Lori. Absurdity. If you don't pay attention to the world around you, you find yourself involved with…"

"Dream-Whore Barbie."

"That's not very nice."

"No, it's not. I'm not nice all the time, and it throws people off because I look like an elf."

"A sexy elf," Quinn said automatically, apparently surprising her, because Lori lost her frown and actually laughed.

"You sound like your sister."

Her smile started a slow burn of relief that melted some of the ice from his muscles. "It honestly was an obligation. And she's honestly not my type, Lori."

"Ha!" She didn't believe him, but at least she seemed to consider it a benevolent lie.

"So, truce?"

"Ah, screw it," she muttered, reaching for the bottle. "Fine. Here's to a truce." She tipped it back and then offered him the wine.

Not wanting to be rude, and still a little dizzy from the whole strange encounter, Quinn took a drink, too. A long drink. More like chugging, actually. "Nice vintage," he rasped, as he finally set it down. "Now I don't suppose you'd care to explain the whole underwear-in-the-parking-lot aspect of this?"

She shrugged. "I just got out of the bath, and Ben happened to stop by at an unlucky moment."

Unlucky. Right. Now that he finally had the time to focus completely on the picture she presented, Quinn was even more shaken. Her panties covered everything, but seemed somehow sexier for it. And her tank top... Well, it wasn't made out of thick twill. The white cotton looked painted onto her small breasts. Her nipples pressed hard against the friction, and he could just make out the faint shadow of the darker skin of her areolas.

Speaking of shadows... Quinn let his gaze drift lower. No shadow, but his attention was drawn by the blue sparkle of something decorative winking from the front of her panties. He wasn't close enough to make it out, but maybe he could get closer.

"I did my homework," he murmured, and watched her jump a little at his words.

Her eyes flew to meet his. "Homework?"

"Yes." There had been a clear common thread in the two stories she'd liked. Both heroes had been aggressive. Not rough, per se, but not the least bit tentative in getting what they wanted. On the drive over, Quinn had felt slightly nervous about that. Not that he considered himself passive, but he was always

considerate in bed. Maybe even polite. But these stories weren't about gentle encounters, they were about
hard lust.

Quinn wasn't nervous anymore.

They'd been staring at each other for a good thirty
seconds, neither making a move. Lori's eyes got
wider. Quinn's got narrower. His anger had morphed
into something much better.

When he took a step forward, her hands twisted
together.

"Quinn?"

"Hmm?" Not willing to stop and let her think—
what did thinking have to do with fantasies?—Quinn
closed the last two feet between them and pulled her
into his arms.

"What...?" she gasped before he caught the sound
against his lips. Ah, yes. Just the taste he'd spent the
whole day trying to recall with perfect clarity. Lori
sprinkled with wine.

She was stiff in his arms, but while the old Quinn
would've immediately set her back and let her go, he
was a new Quinn. A man determined to give her what
she needed, even if she had no idea what that was. A
man shaped for her wicked pleasure.

He smiled against her mouth and swept his tongue
in to brush against hers. The tiny sound she made
seemed very positive. Her arms crept around his
waist. Quinn backed her up and set her on the table,
fit himself between her parting thighs, and picked up
where they'd left off on the hood of his car.

THIS WASN'T RIGHT. She was so mad at him. So mad that he didn't truly want her.

But now his mouth was working magic, his tongue making promises about what the rest of his body would do, and his hands...

"Mmm." She sighed at the feel of his fingers sliding along the hem at the back of her tank top. Those long, elegant fingers, exploring her back. Now slipping up her spine. Now splayed across her shoulder blade, her bare skin.

He pulled her closer to him, a rough little jerk that pressed her sex hard against him. Oh, God, he was hard already, which made her feel better about the damp state of her underwear. His dick pressing against her made her aware of her own heat, her own slickness. Lori pressed back and felt him shudder.

His mouth broke away, breath harsh as his lips trailed down her jaw. She drew in a desperate gasp, overwhelmed already by the feel of his teeth on her neck and his hand sliding around, pulling her shirt up as he moved.

She was about to be nearly naked, exposed to his eyes and hands and mouth, and Lori was just tipsy enough to be thrilled instead of self-conscious. Some evil part of her brain whispered that she should be worried about the comparison to tight silicone, but she beat that voice down and stomped on it with imaginary work boots. Those steel-toed monsters were good for something.

Quinn's hand finally found her breast, fingers

curving under the slight weight, thumb dragging over her nipple.

"Ah," Lori cried out, unable to hold back the startled sound. Embarrassing to be so affected by such a minor caress, but it felt so damn good. Because of the wine or the adrenaline or because it was Quinn... She didn't know and didn't care. This was it. Just what she'd been looking for.

Quinn tore his mouth from her neck with a curse and his hands fumbled roughly with her shirt before he managed to yank it up over her head. Before she could clear the hair from her face, he was on his knees in front of her, eyes blazing.

He growled, "Lean back."

"Wh-what?"

"Lean back on your hands."

Uncertain but fully willing to take a chance, she put her hands flat on the table behind her and arched her back.

Quinn smiled a pirate's smile. "That's it."

When she glanced down to see what he meant, Lori thought that her breasts looked smaller in this pose, pulled high and taut. Before she could protest, his hand came into her line of sight, fingers trailing a butterfly touch over the curve of one breast.

"Beautiful," he murmured. "Unbelievable. I've been imagining you for days." His thumb brushed her peaked nipple again, and the skin crinkled tighter around it. Lori held her breath, watching.

One long, elegant finger traced the edge of her areola. "Like late dawn. A cool white sky warmed by pure blush pink." It would've sounded sweet if his thumb and finger hadn't closed over her nipple just then, squeezing pressure into a nerve that ran straight to her sex.

Lori closed her eyes and tried to breathe and feel and memorize it all as it happened. His fingers soothed, then squeezed again. She was gasping for air when wet pressure closed around her, and then his teeth, scraping fire.

"Oh," she yelped, spine arching even farther. His hand closed over her other breast while his mouth worked, and Lori descended into pure pleasure. She'd never particularly enjoyed it when a man paid attention to her breasts. In fact, at times she'd found it vaguely physically disturbing, an irritant. But now she was so turned on, she wanted more, harder, something close to pain.

Lori gave up her pose and reached for Quinn's hair to pull him greedily closer. He bit her—as reward or punishment, she wasn't sure, but she enjoyed it all the same.

"More," she groaned, and felt his hand tighten over the other breast. Then his mouth sucked harder while his teeth closed down and Lori wondered if she was bruising his skull.

When he tried to pull away, she didn't hesitate to twist her fingers into his hair, hard.

Quinn's gaze flashed up to meet hers, his eyes sizzling with furious passion. Lori met it with her own. She wanted to hurt him, make him cringe even as he moaned with pleasure, so she squeezed her fists as hard as she could, trying to force him back to his task.

He growled, but didn't obey. Instead of bending his head, he surged up and lifted her from the table. "Bedroom?"

"Can't we do it here?"

"Bedroom. Now."

She pointed and he moved, apparently unimpeded by the way she wrapped her legs around his waist. He was still fully dressed in a suit and tie, and the fabric rubbed against her naked skin, pointing out her vulnerability. Lori didn't mind at all. As a matter of fact she felt good and dirty. She leaned up and bit Quinn's neck, happy that it made him stumble a little.

He lurched into the small hallway where her bedroom door stood wide-open and waiting, and Quinn headed straight for the bed. She dug her heels into him to urge him on.

It worked. He kept going until his knees hit the bed, then he let them both fall to the mattress, bracing his own weight on his hands. Lori didn't want his weight at a safe distance. She wanted it on her, in her, pressing her down, down, down.

But when she reached for him, he slipped away. Before she could catch her breath to shout a protest, she noticed that he was struggling out of his suit coat.

He caught her eye. "Take off those panties, Lori Love."

She blinked and blinked again, caught between surprise and a tiny whisper of self-consciousness.

"Now," Quinn clarified, and what could she do

but obey? As his hands rose to tug off his tie, Lori reached for her underwear. She wanted to close her eyes but didn't. Somehow his surety made this so much easier. So, eyes wide and locked with his, Lori got up on her knees and slid her panties off.

For a long moment, his gaze didn't waver. His eyes burned into hers. And then he looked down.

His hands continued their work on the tie as he stared at her nude body. He pulled the end free of the knot in a long, whispering motion that seemed almost threatening. Lori shivered, and he met her gaze once again.

His shirt parted as he popped the buttons open. "You are going to take back what you said tonight. About this being a grand sacrifice on my part. A handout. You *will* take that back."

"I… Mmm…" Did he want an answer now? Because she was slightly distracted by the skin being revealed. The muscles of his chest worked as his hands moved. They bunched and relaxed, and when the hell had Quinn grown muscles? Amazingly, when he tugged the shirt from his pants, a six-pack marched down in faint lines beneath his skin. And then his shoulders shrugged free of the pale blue cotton, and—

"Oh, my God," Lori gasped. Those *shoulders*. Wide and tight and…*wide*.

"Something wrong?" he asked, glancing back toward the hall.

"You lift weights?" she asked.

"No. Why?"

"You did not look like that on the basketball court in high school."

"Like what?" He shook his head. "I swim."

"To *where?*"

The male ego kicked in, if a bit belatedly, and Quinn's laughter sounded very pleased. "I swim sometimes when I can't sleep."

"Mmm. Molly says you have insomnia."

"I do."

"I can see that."

That chuckle again, like the sound of sexual promise. "You're making me blush."

She meant to say something funny, something about giving him a real reason to blush, but Quinn reached for the button on his slacks and the words turned to mush in her mouth. When he stopped with the button and failed to reach for the zipper, the mush turned to concrete. Lori watched like a tiger eyeing its prey. *Come on. Come on. One step closer and I'll have you.*

Quinn made a humming sound. "I like you looking at me like that."

"Great," she croaked. "Let's look some more."

"You look hungry."

"Uh-huh."

He stalked toward her, pants still firmly in place. "But I want you starving."

"What? No. Come on. You've been reading too many books." She wanted him naked and hard and pushing into her right this moment. He put one knee on the bed. "Take your pants off, damn it!"

"Shut up," he answered just before his mouth caught hers.

A punishing kiss. How many times had she read that stupid phrase in books? It had always seemed ridiculous to her, but if there was such a thing as a punishing kiss, this was it. Hard and demanding and hot. Quinn's tongue licked roughly against hers, and his muscled arms forced her down to her back. This kiss didn't ask for anything, it demanded that she yield. *A punishing kiss.* And Lori was suddenly a dirty girl who needed that control and correction. *Oh, God, yes. Yes, I am dirty. Finally.*

Quinn didn't stop kissing her, but he did start exploring her body, trailing his fingers down her side, then back up to tease her breasts. Shivering, she reached for him, thrilled to finally get her hands on his nakedness. God, his skin felt like silk stretched over the strength of his arms. She slid her palms everywhere—up, down, around to his back. He was hard and smooth until she got to his chest, where crisp hair trailed down to the waistband of his pants.

His fingers teased and teased, venturing as low as her navel before dancing away again. By the time he lifted his head, she was gasping, her heart sucking too much oxygen from her blood. When he licked at one nipple and then the other, Lori pressed her mouth to one big shoulder and bit down to try to stifle her need.

Quinn grunted, but neither the direction of his hands nor the pressure of his mouth changed. She was wet and tight and empty, and she needed him to touch her sex *now*. His fingers teased over her hip bone. *Now, now. Please.* She let her knees fall open. *Please.*

His fingers—those elegant, artistic fingers— slipped into her dark curls, setting her nerves on fire. Her jaw trembled as she panted into his shoulder. "Quinn," she begged. And then finally, finally he touched her, the tips of his fingers sliding along the wet line of her sex, up and down.

Lori gasped hard, but she still heard his sigh. As if the feel of her relieved something deep inside him. "Damn, you're wet," he whispered as he dragged one finger over her clit.

Her hips jerked, rising up, desperate to get more of his attention. Her body's plea worked. Quinn circled her clit once more——Oh, God—and then he slid one long finger deep inside her. She thought that felt good, but then he withdrew and pushed two fingers into her body, stretching her tight.

Lori broke. "Oh, God, Quinn. Oh, that feels good."

He fucked her with his hand, and Lori gave up her hold on his shoulders and grabbed for his wrist.

"Yes. Yes. Ah, *Quinn*." He'd curved his hand in some miraculous way so that every movement rubbed her clit at the same time as he thrust deep inside her. She dug her nails into his arm, making him hiss. He repaid her by closing his mouth over one nipple and sucking hard.

"Quinn," she cried as all the nerves in her body began to shimmer. A vague sensation of floating lifted her away from the world for a long moment, and then her body pulled Lori back down into her

skin just as she shattered into a million glittery bits. Her own scream floated to her ears as her hips jerked against his hold.

When she finally went limp against the bed, his touch left her and the mattress shifted. Lori wanted to open her eyes to see what he was up to, she really did, but she was too busy wondering how she could have lived without that for three decades. That…that *climax*. So much more than just an orgasm. That impossible melding of strength and utter weakness warring for control of her body.

The sound of a zipper lowering floated through the haze. Lethargy vanished like a bubble popping, and Lori's eyes flew open.

"Well, hello there," Quinn said.

"Hello." She sighed, stretching hard, muscles sighing with pleasure.

"My God," he growled. "You're gorgeous."

"Mmm. I think you're just horny."

"That, too." He sat on the bed to tug off his shoes and socks, and Lori couldn't resist shifting close to press a kiss to his back.

He growled again.

She liked that, so she licked a little way up his spine, then back down. This time he hissed. Lori liked that even more. When she wrapped her arms around his waist, the skin of his back pressed against her cheek, and she nuzzled him, breathing him in, the warm scent of skin and hint of fresh sweat. He was sweating for her. For *her*.

Spreading her fingers wide, Lori smoothed her

hands down the front of his thighs, then dragged them back up, letting her nails scrape against the fabric of his pants. The deep breath he took echoed through his body and into her ear, then it froze; he was waiting.

Smiling against his back, Lori pushed her hands slowly toward the open zipper. She held her breath, too, anticipating this first touch. The metal scrape of the zipper, then the soft, hot fabric of his boxers, and beneath that… His thick, solid length filled her hand. *Oh, yeah.* Lori stroked.

Air rushed into his lungs, then just as quickly out. She curled her fingers as far as she could past the barrier of his underwear. He felt big. Excitingly big. *Yes, yes, yes. Please let him be big.*

She normally didn't care about such things, but this was her fantasy. Fantasy did not accommodate normal or average or reasonable. She wanted everything.

Eyes shut tight, Lori sneaked her hand beneath the thin fabric and finally touched him skin to skin. Another hiss from Quinn. Lori answered with a pleased sigh.

Hot. God, he was hot. And so damn *hard.*

Lori scooted up to her knees and pressed her breasts against Quinn's back. They both moaned, though Quinn's moan could have been the result of her firm grip on his cock. Didn't matter. It was all good. Really, really good.

To reward him for having such a lovely erection, Lori slid her hand all the way up, then slowly back down. She caressed him, pumped him, teased him.

She rubbed her thumb over the head, dragged her nails down his shaft, teased her fingertips over his balls.

Something crinkled loudly. *Crinkled?*

"Uh, Quinn? What was that?"

He held up a condom, the wrapper creased from being clutched tightly in his hand. "Condom," he gasped.

She grinned. "What are you doing to that poor thing?"

"Hanging on. Very tightly."

"Mmm." She stroked him some more, rubbing her breasts against his back with each motion. She didn't stop until she could feel him shaking. Then she let go and scooted back on the mattress.

Quinn stood with a speed that shocked her. His pants seemed to disappear, revealing only a brief glimpse of taut buttocks before he spun around to follow her across the bed. "If you were trying to drive me crazy, you've succeeded."

Lori giggled, surprising herself. She never giggled. But she'd also never driven a man crazy before.

His fingers curved around her ankle and tightened, sending a shock up her leg. Then he grabbed her other ankle, and the shock went farther than her leg. Her sex seemed to forget that it had been nearly numb with satisfaction just minutes before. It wasn't numb anymore.

Quinn tugged her closer, then he rose up on his knees and it was Lori's turn to forget to breathe.

Oh, yeah, he was big. Not gargantuan or freakish. Just… "You're gorgeous," she whispered.

He gave a quick shake of his head, eyes roaming over her body.

"Yes, you are. Perfect." Lori sat up to trail her hand over him again, just for the joy of seeing her fingers on the dusky flesh of his erection. His cock jerked at her touch.

He growled her name and leaned in, forcing her to lie back again. When he followed her down, his weight was like the sun against her naked body, hot and soothing and happy.

Lori wrapped her arms around him, bent her knees so her thighs framed his hips. She kissed him with all the joy and relief that coursed through her blood, and Quinn kissed back with hot desperation. Then his fingers wound into her hair and tugged her head back.

Wow.

When his teeth closed on her neck in a less than gentle bite, Lori yelped, but her cry turned to a groan when his fist tightened in her curls.

Oh, wow. This was almost…*rough.* Goose bumps pushed against her skin, setting it tingling.

"I'm going to fuck you now, Lori."

"Okay. Yes, absolutely."

The head of his cock brushed her wet flesh, and Quinn let it slide against her before grunting, "Shit," and pulling away.

"No, no, no," she muttered, but Quinn was a good guy, and he ignored her. The plastic crinkled again as he ripped open the protection. He was right, of course, but that one touch of his naked flesh made her greedy and unwise. That made her smile, too. She'd never, ever been so horny she'd turned stupid.

It occurred to her that maybe she should be doing something more than lying there awaiting his services. But she didn't want to do anything else. Despite that she was on the fast road back to crazed horniness, her limbs were still liquid. So Lori lay there and watched him work, watched him hold his impressive erection in his hand as he rolled the condom on, watched him turn his attention back to her with a predatory glare.

"Now?" she breathed, trying not to sound too eager even as she begged for it.

Quinn wasn't fooled. A smile spread slowly across his face. His eyes glittered. "Now? Hmm, I'm not sure…"

"Quinn Jennings—" she lifted one leg and pushed her toes none too gently against his stomach "—you get down here right now and do me, damn it."

His gaze traveled from her foot to her knee to her thigh, and then to a very specific spot between her legs. "All right," he said simply. And then he was on top of her, kissing her, sliding one hand between their bodies to be sure she was ready. Completely unnecessary, of course. She was more ready than she'd ever been.

His kisses got rougher, as rough as his fingers plunging into her, and she arched up to him, trying to hint, trying to urge him on. When his fingers left her, she whimpered in anticipation, nearly frantic by the time he guided his wide, blunt head to her opening.

Every neuron in her brain focused on that glorious pressure, the stretching of her sex. She couldn't be distracted with kissing anymore, so she turned her face aside and struggled to breathe as Quinn filled her up.

And fill her up he did. She thought he must be as deep as he could go when he drew back and thrust even deeper. Lori gasped as his hips pressed snug to hers.

"Lori," he whispered. "Fuck."

"Oh, God." Her breathing was too loud and too fast, and she felt so…different. Overwhelmed. Full of Quinn and pleasure. "God, you're so big," she gasped. "So big and good."

His laugh was more of bark really, crowded with tension. "Men pay women to say things like that."

"Hell, I'll pay *you*. A lot." Her voice cracked on the last word, because he was drawing back, pulling out, and when he thrust into her it was just as rough as his fingers had been.

He'd been right about one thing: this was no gentle sympathy screw. He fucked her hard with long, steady strokes, each one seeming to sink deeper than the last. Lori clutched at his shoulders, pulling him closer, luxuriating in the feel of his muscles rolling beneath her hands.

Her mouth formed the word *Yes,* over and over again, a whisper or a shout, she wasn't sure.

"God, you're tight."

"Yes," she answered.

"Christ."

"Yes."

Quinn thrust harder. "Is this what you wanted?"

"Yes!"

His body shifted up, slipping free of her hands. He reached for one wrist and pressed it to the bed, then the other, and she was trapped against the mattress.

Jaw trembling with shock, Lori opened her eyes to find Quinn staring down at her. His hips pumped faster, harder. *"This* is what you wanted," he growled, not a question this time.

And it was what she wanted. Oh, it was. His strong arms held her down while he used her with no love or tenderness, just lust. Lust that made him so rough that his hips slapped against her with every thrust.

Lori curled her hands to fists and pulled her knees higher. Everything was tightening around her, winding up like a coil. She didn't want this to end, she wanted to hover here forever.

Minutes passed, or seconds, or no time at all. Quinn's hold on her arms grew tighter. A rasp took hold of his breath.

"Not yet," Lori muttered. "Not yet. More."

"I…"

"More. Please, just a little more."

A drop of sweat rolled down his hairline. "Okay. Yeah. Sure." He clenched his teeth together. "More. No problem."

"Oh, God, thank you." She pressed her heels to his thighs to pull him tighter.

He obliged, but his arms began to shake.

"Yes. Don't stop. Don't."

"Damn it, Lori, you're killing me here."

Suddenly, it was all too wonderful. Not only was she having the best sex of her life, but she was pushing Quinn to the edge. She began to laugh. Out loud.

"Wait a minute," he muttered.

Lori laughed harder.

"Wait, are you *laughing* at me?"

"I'm sorry!" It wasn't funny at all, it was just perfect. Delightful. Delicious.

"Well, this makes it easier for me to hold out, anyway."

"I'm sorry!" she cried, laughing so hard now that she couldn't see him past the tears. When she blinked them away, Quinn's smile was the first thing she made out. He leaned down to kiss her nose.

"You really know how to hurt a guy."

"You want a little more talk about how big you are, cowboy?"

He kissed her lips this time. "You're getting sassy, Ms. Love."

When he slipped all the way out of her body, Lori lost most of her sass. "Hey!"

"On your knees, Lori."

"Pardon?"

He was done messing around, apparently, because he very calmly picked her up and flipped her to her stomach. Before she'd recovered, he shocked her even more. Quinn Jennings slapped her ass hard enough to make it sting.

Lori yelped and tried to figure out if she liked it. Was he going to spank her? Oh, my God, did she *want* him to? What if she hated it? It could ruin everything.

But when his hands touched her again, they curved over her hips and pulled her up. "Put your hands on the headboard." His voice had lost any amusement. The words seemed to rumble through the room and trace over her skin.

Lori put her hands on the headboard.

The electric slide of his hand down the small of her back made her shiver. "Good girl."

A jolt of lust swept through her belly, to her absolute mortification. *You do not have daddy issues,* she told her body in her best feminist voice. Her body responded by arching back in a blatant effort to please him. *Hussy,* the stern voice hissed, but hussy was no insult to her greedy body.

Quinn's hands stroked down her arched back and over her ass. She braced herself for a more intimate touch, but when he stroked his fingertips into her wetness, she still gasped.

And then he was pushing back into her body, and how could she have forgotten that feeling in the space of a few moments?

The polished edge of the wood bit into her palms as she squeezed tight, but the fierceness she was ready for didn't come. He was slower, gentler. Lori squirmed.

"Something wrong, Lori?"

"Mmm," she complained, pushing back to meet his thrust.

He leaned over her, braced his hands on either side of hers. His tongue drew fire over her neck, and all the while he was stretching and stroking inside her.

Strangely, a soft beeping sound drifted to her ears. "Quinn?"

"Hmm?" He kept moving, moving, too slow and so beautiful.

"I think your phone's ringing."

He murmured, "I don't think so."

"I think it is."

"Doesn't matter." One hand disappeared from the headboard and curved over her breast, then snaked down her stomach and lower still. The ringing continued, but when he touched her clit, Lori let her thoughts go.

"Ah!" she cried, as Quinn surged deep and rolled small circles over the perfect spot. "Oh, God. Oh, Quinn."

There was no way she could come again so fast and she should tell him not to bother, but Lori's tongue refused to form the words. He was taking her harder again. Harder. Harder.

Lori straightened her arms and pushed back, taking more of him. "Oh, God," she groaned, concentration pinging back and forth between his lovely fingers and his lovely cock. And before she knew it, the impossible happened. She came again. Screaming.

When her screams died to whimpers, Quinn gave up all pretense of finesse. He grabbed her hips in a brutal grip and fucked her hard. As his hips spasmed

against her and Quinn groaned, muscles stiffening,
Lori let her forehead fall to the pillow.

She'd done it.

She'd had dirty, meaningless, mindless sex. And
she'd done it really, really *well*.

CHAPTER EIGHT

HER SWEAT-SLICK BODY was pressed against his side
when he came back to life. She lay facedown on her
pillow. Quinn was flat on his back, panting. His body
felt strange. Wrung out with physical exhaustion, yet
buoyed by the remnants of brilliant pleasure. He let
his heavy gaze wander, amazed that after all that joy,
it wasn't even fully dark yet.

His eyes caught on something disturbing. Quinn
blinked and shook his head. "What the hell is *that?*"

Her body jerked against his. "I… Huh?"

"My God," he murmured, staring at the bathroom
just across the hall.

"What's wrong?"

Quinn sat up, swinging his feet to the floor. "I
think there's gold flocking in there!"

"Huh?"

Totally energized now, he stood and moved toward
the half-closed door. No way. "Are those *gold flecks*
in the pink countertops? Mother of…"

"Quinn!" she growled from the bed. "What are
you talking about?"

He stared for a long, stunned moment at the horrible glory of her pink-and-gold bathroom before he

stumbled back to the bed. Pink tile, white cabinets, and the wallpaper decorated with pink flowers with fuzzy gold leaves. "I'm sorry. I need a minute. I can't believe that gold flocking was staring at my ass the whole time we were having sex."

In response, Lori mumbled something that sounded irritated, but the effect was muffled by her pillow. He collapsed into bed with a groan, and his hand found a very comfortable spot on the curve of her ass. She looked sweet and tousled in the faint late light slanting through the blinds. Really sweet. And really tousled. "What'd you say?"

She raised her face a half inch from the pillow. "I said my dad remodeled it for my mom in 1979."

"Wow. Do you mind if I come back and take a few pictures?"

"What, do you and your architect friends get together and exchange horror stories?"

Quinn couldn't help the flush that gave him away, but he tried his best to mediate it. "This is a legitimate design era. There's nothing to be embarrassed about. It's part of our history."

"I'm not embarrassed! Jeez, you're a freak."

Even past the tangled curls that hung over her face, Quinn could see her skin turn pink, reminding him of just how he'd repaid her sassiness last time. Damn, that had been hot as hell, taking her from behind. He stroked her ass in fond memory.

"You owe me an apology," he prompted.

Surprisingly, she smiled and brushed the hair from

her eyes as she turned slightly toward him. "You're right. I apologize. Your heart was definitely in it."

His heart twisted to hear itself spoken of. A disturbing response. Hmm.

"In fact, I think you're a genius, Quinn. And I think I'm a genius for picking you."

"Revisionist history. You didn't pick me. I inserted myself into your sordid plan."

Lori grinned. "Right again. You are a genius at inserting yourself, Quinn Jennings."

"Ha!" He closed his eyes and let his head sink into the pillow. "I think I'll put that on my business cards. Along with 'big' and 'good' and 'gorgeous.'"

"Hey, what's with the photographic memory?" He could hear the blush in her words.

"Wouldn't that be audio-graphic?"

"Whatever it is, you usually remember very little of any conversation, as far as I can tell. Kind of inconvenient that you remember what I say in the throes of passion."

Chuckling, Quinn patted blindly around until he found her hand, then curled his fingers into hers. "I remember everything when I'm concentrating. A lecture on Syrian arches, a discussion about architectural ostentation in the sixteenth-century, or..." He rubbed his thumb over her knuckles. "Sex with you. All very worthy of intense concentration."

"Wow. Me and sixteenth-century architectural ostentation? I'm kind of flattered." The word broke on a yawn.

"Go to sleep," Quinn whispered, turning toward

her to kiss her hair. She smelled sleepy, warmth spiced with sex. He didn't bother moving away. Breathing her in made him feel he was exposed to some sort of drugged smoke. Opium maybe.

Still, he wasn't tired. He normally didn't go to bed until one. But he was as relaxed as a man who'd just had the best sex of his life, so he didn't bother getting up to find his clothes. Hell, he didn't have the least urge to leave.

Sex with Lori had been unbelievably erotic. A strange combination of feeling free to do exactly what he wanted and knowing he was engaged in seriously dirty behavior with a nice girl he'd known all his life. The knowledge that in the thousands of times he'd said hi or passed her in a hall or waved from his car...that whole time she'd had small nipples blushing pale pink. And tight dark curls that hid her wet and eager pussy. He hadn't known that she would clench her fingers each and every time he brushed her clit, or that she'd mewl like a kitten when she got close to her peak.

And he definitely hadn't known that ordering her to her knees would cause power to explode through his body, as if someone had just shocked his muscles with pure electricity.

Wow.

Her hand squeezed his. "Don't forget your phone," she mumbled.

"What?" Crap, was she asking him to leave? He didn't want to leave.

"Your phone. It rang."

"When?" Glancing over to her face, he found she'd opened one eye.

"It rang while we were having sex. You really didn't notice? I thought you were kidding."

"I was concentrating, remember?" Now that she mentioned it, he could hear the occasional beep of the message reminder. "You know I can't hear anything when I'm working."

"Working?" she sputtered.

Quinn frowned. "You know what I mean."

When she laughed, his body registered warm pleasure. The husky sound swept over him and the bed shook just a little, physically pulling him into her amusement. His heart responded by beating louder. Not that his pulse sped up, it just grew more…forceful. Odd.

Quinn puzzled over that for a few minutes before he realized Lori was asleep. She made an occasional soft huffing sound that wasn't a snore, but he'd characterize it as snoring later just to goad her. Later, like when they went on another date before he brought her home to—

A loud growl from his stomach distracted him from further planning, so he slipped from her bed and pulled on his boxers to head for the kitchen. Surely Lori Love kept bologna around. Or peanut butter.

The phone beeped again, so he grabbed it on the way out and glanced down. His dad's name was on the caller ID, which meant his mother had called. His dad never talked on the phone. Ever. The man considered emergency calls to be the only acceptably masculine use of a home phone. Sighing, Quinn called up the message and leaned against the kitchen island.

"Quinn, it's your mother. I hope everything's good. We haven't heard from you in weeks, and it's awfully lonely out here lately. Your father and I wish you'd think about coming to visit over Labor Day, but I know you've been busy with your work, and we're so proud of you. Call us!"

A perfectly benign, loving message by anyone's standards. And yet it raised Quinn's hackles. She wouldn't be so damn lonely if she weren't still ignoring Molly. Ever since they'd found out about Molly's career, his mother had been playing the wounded party, put upon by the stigma of an immoral daughter, and further put upon by Quinn's defense of his sister.

He deleted the message and stared at the phone. Yes, his parents were proud of him. They'd always been proud. Unfortunately their approval was like a pie: the more pieces they gave to Quinn, the fewer they had left for Molly. And they had always—always—been spectacularly generous with Quinn.

His habit of getting lost in work had started way back in elementary school, when report cards meant it was time for their dad to say something cruelly dismissive about Molly. *Better be glad you're a girl, Molly, or you'd have to worry about filling some pretty big shoes. Or Look, Molly managed to get a check plus in art!*

God, he'd hated that. As a child, his parents had managed to turn their approval into something he wanted to retreat from, and so he had. He'd read and studied and spent days in his room, building models and projects. He'd learned to tune out and lose himself in work.

Maybe he should call his mom back to thank her for that. After all, if he were less involved with work and more involved in a successful relationship, he'd never have been able to help Lori with her sex adventure. This short-term relationship seemed poised to make up for all the long-term ones he'd missed out on.

"Damn straight," he muttered, heading toward the fridge for a Coke.

It turned out she had not only cold Coke, but also an unopened pack of Hebrew National hot dogs just waiting to be eaten. "Amazing woman." Quinn sighed when he tracked down the buns. He scarfed down two hot dogs and a Coke, then threw together one more dog and wandered into the living room, wondering if he should leave even if he really wanted to stay the night.

The sight of her living room chased away his idle thoughts.

What the hell was a vibrant woman like Lori doing in this house? Did she keep the trophies and the old furniture and the bad paintings as a way to honor her father? Or did she simply not care enough to change it?

Regardless of whether she was wearing a dress or jeans, Lori was bright and funny and young. She needed light around her, and color.

Sighing, Quinn shook his head and turned back toward the kitchen, but a quiver of blue light from the second floor caught his eye. He froze and watched the wall at the top of the stairwell. Another flicker of aqua blue. It looked like the light of a television. He jogged up the steps.

There were three doors here, but only one was open. It looked like a teenager's bedroom, and Quinn immediately guessed that it must have been Lori's. The room she was in now had belonged to her father at some point, and this room with the dark pink bedspread and poster-covered walls had been hers. He flipped on the light.

Though his mind was insisting on images of boy bands and Madonna, his eyes were sending him different signals about the posters. Strange. They seemed to be *travel* posters.

"Huh." Some of them were retro thirties ads, but most were just the typical pictures you saw in travel agencies. Rome. Paris. Turkey. Greece. Ireland. Amsterdam. Bavaria. London. The Alps. There were a few more exotic locales like St. Petersburg and Cairo and Madagascar.

Stunned, he spun in a slow circle, as if the motion would somehow create sense from it. A packed bookcase was wedged into the far corner, so Quinn edged between the TV and the bed and scanned the titles. Travel guides and travelogues, every one. Hundreds of them, and more stacked on the floor.

Did Lori travel? She must. And yet a vague conversation floated up from the foggy pool of Quinn's memory banks. Molly had mentioned something once about Lori giving up her dreams to care for her father. Something about Europe and international business.

"Shit," he breathed, heart sinking to press itself against his stomach. He stroked a finger along the spine of one book and then another. *The Single Girl's Guide to France. England on Fifty Dollars a Day.* Hundreds of them.

This room. This was Lori Love's place in this house. And maybe it wasn't as heartbreaking as it seemed. Maybe it was just a simple hobby.

But when he turned to leave, the view of the far wall stopped him in his tracks. On this wall she'd hung a giant map of the world, at least five feet wide. Bright colors were concentrated within the boundaries of Europe before spreading out like tendrils into Asia and Africa and the rest of the map. When he stepped closer, he could see that the jumbles of color were made up of thumbtacks. Hundreds of them. Different shapes and sizes so that it looked as if someone had thrown sticky confetti against the paper in celebration.

But this wasn't a celebration. There were no thumbtacks pushed into Colorado. There wasn't a single thumbtack in the whole of the United States. This wasn't a map of places she'd been. This was a map of where Lori dreamed of going.

He stopped three feet away and refused to look closer. This was private. Not meant for him or anyone else to see.

Turning back toward the television, Quinn made himself stop thinking about the map. He glanced only briefly at the muted pictures of Venice on the screen before he switched off the DVD player and the screen. Then he descended the stairs and turned off the rest of the lights in the house. As he lay back down on Lori's bed, he tried very hard not to indulge in that fantasy of saving the damsel in distress.

This was a short-term fling, and he wasn't a prince sent to save a beautiful princess.

Still, the idea burned like phosphorous in his tight chest.

CHAPTER NINE

A SHOUTED, "OH, shit!" woke Lori from a deep sleep. She bolted upright in her bed, assaulted by too many strange images flying at her, like a scene from that movie *The Birds*. Daylight. The blankets sailing past her face, a naked man jumping from the bed. A naked *Quinn* yanking on underwear to cover his tight ass.

Lori shoved wild curls from her eyes and glanced down at her own naked body. "Oh, my." She pulled up the blanket.

"I'm sorry." Quinn zipped his pants and reached for his cell phone to stuff it into a pocket. "I overslept and I've got a meeting at eight-thirty."

Still trying to process that they'd really slept together, Lori turned toward the clock—7:00 a.m.

"I've got to get home and shower and change."

She nodded.

"I'll call you." Quinn stopped buttoning his wrinkled shirt for a moment to look up at her. "I mean I'll really call you later today. Not 'Thanks for the good time, maybe I'll call you sometime.'"

"I get that. I'm sure I'll see you around."

He hurriedly tucked in his shirt and flashed her a smile, rocking her sleepy little world. "Oh, you'll see me." Then, like a sexy whirlwind, he grabbed his coat, crossed the room to give her a quick peck on the mouth and stole the book from her bedside table before heading for the door. "Homework!" he called, waving the book. "Have a good day, Lori Love."

And just like that, the Quinn tornado was gone, leaving Lori alone with her shock and awe.

"Ho-ly smokes." She'd really done it. And the doin' it had been So. Damn. Good. She lifted the blanket to look down at her body. Same body she saw in the mirror every single day, and yet now it was imprinted with dirty memories of Quinn, like invisible tattoos. She hoped they weren't those press-on tattoos that would wash off in the shower.

She settled back under the covers just so she could lie there and grin at the ceiling. It might have been awkward if he'd stayed. It might have been weird. But now she could just wallow in her self-satisfaction.

Funny, how horny a girl could get while wallowing. And she didn't quite have to be up yet, so Lori thought about Quinn ordering her around in bed and touched herself. It didn't take long. A quick replay of him holding her wrists down and Lori was biting her lip and shaking against her own hand. God, the man was magic even when he wasn't here.

Worried she'd fall asleep again, Lori forced herself up and floated to the bathroom. Of course, the bathroom made her think of Quinn, too, and she smiled at the pink tiles while she waited for the water to heat. Maybe he'd do her in here. Or maybe he'd be distracted by the wallpaper. Okay, no bathroom sex.

Still smiling, she caught sight of herself in the mirror and let out a horrified scream. Sure, her curls were usually messy in the morning, but this was a new level of chaos. The last image Quinn had from their night together was a crazed, naked bushwoman waving goodbye. Yikes.

She jumped in the shower and tamed the curls with hot water. Hopefully he'd been in too much of a hurry to notice.

By the time she'd dressed and had breakfast, Lori's feet were firmly on the ground, but she still felt strong and invincible as she stepped down to the garage and hit the button to open the bay doors. As the metal doors rumbled up, Lori put her shoulders back. She wasn't going to run from her problems today. Today, she'd take control.

Like clockwork, Joe strolled in at exactly 8:00 a.m.

"Can I talk to you for a second?" she asked.

"Sure. What's up?"

"What is it about my dad's land that's so great?"

Joe frowned and leaned against the counter, his graying eyebrows meeting in a V behind smudged glasses. "Well, it's perfect for fishing, the way the river widens out there and slows down a bit. It's quiet. There's only that one house that borders the land. There's a great flat area for building. Why? Are you worried I won't offer you a fair price?"

"No, but…why do you think I wouldn't want to keep it for myself? Build a cabin. Settle in."

"Lori," Joe scolded, crossing his arms. "You can't do that."

"Why?"

"You've got to get out of here, girl. Go back to college."

"There are bills and—"

Joe cut his hand through the air. "You know your dad didn't want this for you. Yes, you've got bills and this place here isn't worth much with all the cleanup that needs to be done out back. That river land is all you've got. Sell it now and pay off the bills and move on, Lori. For your father."

Anger overrode the tears that were burning in her throat. Everything Joe said was true. She knew that. But the truth of them didn't make the math work.

"Unless that land is worth a hell of a lot more than you can afford, then I *can't* get out, damn it. Do you know how much his hospital stays and rehabilitation cost? Do you know what ten years' worth of day nursing adds up to? The hospital bed? The medical supplies? The prescriptions? The ambulance trips when he got infections? The physical therapy? Medicare doesn't cover the best care, Joe, it only covers the bare minimum. I couldn't give my dad the minimum, and I have to pay for the rest myself."

Joe rubbed a hand over his face, the calluses rasping over his stubbled chin. She thought she saw the glint of tears in his eyes. "I know. I'm so sorry. But if you sell out now, it'll be a start. You don't belong here, Lori."

Fear shivered through her. Fear and hurt and anger. Where the hell did everyone think she belonged then? Not here, but where? Shit, all her happy confidence was gone. Poking at old wounds would do that to you, even after the best sex of your life. But she took a deep breath and waded back into dark water.

"I want to sell to you, honestly. But I can't sell this land until I know what it's really worth."

He shook his head. "What do you mean? Haven't you had it appraised? I'll give you fair value for it."

"I know you will. But there's something else going on."

Joe's eyes grew round behind his glasses. "Does this have something to do with the chief calling here yesterday?"

"No, it's just—"

"Lori, if there's something going on, you need to tell me about it. Your dad's not around to protect you, and you're like a daughter to me."

She bit back her guilt. "There's nothing you need to worry about. I'm just confused because I've gotten calls from a few developers who want to talk about that land, too."

He pushed away from the counter and stood straight. "Are you kidding me?"

"No, but I'm not interested in selling you out for an extra ten thousand dollars, Joe. We might not be related, but you're all the family I have left. I just need to find out why these Aspen developers are so interested in the land. It's got to mean something."

"It means their land has gotten too expensive over there and they're looking to fleece us of ours."

"Maybe. You're sure you haven't heard anything about it?"

"Not a word. But… Listen, Lori. If selling to one of those developers will get you closer to college, you do it, you hear me? Don't worry about me. You deserve more than this and I'll do anything I can to help."

"Joe…" She didn't know what to say. "Thank you. I'll let you know what I find out."

"I want what's best for you, whatever that is."

"I know." She was about to ask him more about the land when her cell phone buzzed against her hip. "Yikes!" she yelped and hurried to tug it from her pocket. Things were a little sensitive in that area.

She gave Joe a wave and walked outside to answer it. "Hello?"

"Good morning, Lori Love," Quinn's voice purred.

Her tension vanished, and a goofy smile stretched so far across her face that her cheeks ached. "Good morning."

"I made it to my meeting with a few minutes to spare, so I thought I'd call to see if you'd meet me for dinner tonight."

"Hmm." Lori twirled a curl around her fingers and smiled down at the sidewalk. "Didn't I just see you *last* night, Mr. Jennings?"

"What can I say? It's a torrid affair. Night after night of…*seeing* each other."

Lori laughed, but her laughter turned into a sigh. "I'm sorry, Quinn, I can't. I already told Molly I'd meet her at The Bar tonight."

"Cancel. My sister will understand."

"No, she won't. I can't tell her why, and she'll be suspicious."

"Mmm. Let her be suspicious. I want to take you someplace special. It's okay. I'm her brother. I absolve you of any responsibility to her."

Grinning, she shook her head. "I don't think you can do that."

"Not true," he countered. "My parents live out of state now. I'm the head of the Colorado branch of the family. She's totally under my control."

"Quinn." She laughed, then quieted down when she heard another voice in the background.

"Oops, I've got to get in there." His voice lowered to a whisper. "Meet me tonight? I have to see you again. Please. I can't wait."

Okay, he was just playing into her fantasies now. A red-hot affair. A man desperate to have her. And Lori didn't mind one bit. "All right," she whispered back. "But not too late. I'm on call at ten."

"Six-thirty at my office?"

A shiver raced through her. "Yes," she answered quickly and hung up.

It was irresponsible to call off her evening with Molly, but irresponsibility felt really good all of a sudden. Naughty and wild. But the call to Molly would have to wait. First, she had to get in touch with some developers who were clearly trying to take advantage of a nice girl. Too bad she wasn't a nice girl anymore.

"SHOOT, SHOOT, SHOOT," Lori cursed as she roared down the highway. She was late. She hated being late.

But she hadn't realized until about five o'clock that she had absolutely nothing to wear, so she'd had to race through her shower and run out the door to shop.

Still, the sprint to her favorite store had paid off. There'd been three dresses on the clearance rack in her size, and she'd ended up with a cute little black jersey number that clung in all the right places. Luckily it went with the strappy black heels she'd found at the cheap shoe store next door. Perfect. If only she wasn't ten minutes late. And grumpy.

The phone calls this morning had revealed nothing but the developers' hope that she'd sell. These people were professionals. They'd used phrases like *investment criteria* and *best use,* and claimed that sheer beauty made the land valuable. But not *that* valuable, mind you.

Scowling, she pulled her purple truck into the parking lot of Quinn's office building and screeched to a halt. Quinn's car wasn't there, of course. Lori breathed a sigh of relief and hurried in.

"Oh, hi, Jane."

Quinn's assistant looked up from her computer. "Ms. Love! How are you?"

"Oh, call me Lori, please. I'm fine. I take it Quinn's not here yet?"

"No, but he called just two minutes ago to see if you'd arrived yet. He's right around the corner. Very impressive."

"Huh?"

"I haven't seen him this close to being on time in years."

"Oh, well. Thank you." Lori felt flattered by this strange compliment.

"Please have a seat. Can I get you something to drink? Water or coffee?"

Lori shook her head and sat down to catch her breath, but she watched Jane as she turned back to her work. Despite her reserved air, Jane wasn't as old as Lori had first suspected. In fact, they were probably about the same age.

The woman wore her hair pulled back in a tight knot and her clothes revealed little about her figure, but if one looked a bit closer…Jane was genuinely attractive. In fact, if this were one of Lori's books, Jane would fit in perfectly. The meek secretary just waiting for the right man to notice her and give her a night she'd never forget. Hmm.

"I'm sorry," Jane said, glancing up. "Did you say something?"

Shit, had she hummed *out loud*? "Nothing," Lori chirped, and vowed to keep her musings to herself.

While Lori was lost in thought, pondering the likelihood that Jane was actually the secret mistress of a Greek tycoon, the door whooshed open. "Hi, Jane." Quinn looked quickly around, and when his gaze found Lori in the corner, his eyes lit up. She was sure of it. Her heart beat harder in celebration.

"Lori." He gave her a wicked smile. "I'm so glad you were able to clear your schedule. Someday maybe you'll let me pick you up at your house, so we can have a date that's less like a doctor's appointment."

"We'll see," she answered as she rose. Quinn was playing it cool, but his eyes devoured her as she stood.

"Jane, do you need anything else from me?" His gaze didn't leave Lori's body.

"No, Mr. Jennings, you're all clear until the morning, but don't forget that you have an appointment at 9:00 a.m. As for tonight, the reservation is for seven, but I'll call ahead and let them know you'll be early. You two have a lovely evening."

"Thank you," they said in unison, and Quinn reached for her hand and led her out of the building.

"You look beautiful. Again," he murmured as the door closed behind them.

Before Lori could respond, he caught her around the waist and turned her for a kiss. His mouth stayed gentle and sweet, but the taste of him fanned memories of the previous night to fiery life. Lori was panting a little when he finally let her go. Strange to think that just a few days ago she'd thought of Quinn as rather harmless. Maybe even a bit nerdy.

He took her hand. "We can walk if you'd like. It's not far. Though I never wear heels, so I may not be the best judge."

"I'd like to walk. Where are we going?"

As they began their stroll, Quinn winked down at her. "It's a surprise."

"Does it have anything to do with turkey basters?"

"No. No turkey basters. Or bunnies. Then again, there might be rabbit on the menu, but I have nothing to do with that." He kept stealing glances at her, and Lori flushed, embarrassed by the attention.

"You almost made me late today," Quinn said.

"Should I pretend to be sorry?"

He chuckled. "No, you should not. I definitely wouldn't want you to regret it. I haven't slept that well in years."

"Nice. Are you telling me I rocked your world?"

"No, I'm telling you you're a lot of hard work, woman. I almost got a cramp."

Lori laughed too hard and nearly tripped over a crack in the sidewalk, but Quinn's big strong arm kept her steady. She held tight to his fingers, and glanced over his tall body. No suit jacket today, just a pale pink shirt, the sleeves rolled up to show his tanned forearms.

"What are you thinking about, Lori Love?"

The way he said her name made something deep inside her melt. *Loreluv.* All run together like one soft, precious word. An endearment instead of a name. Lori shook off her shivers and lied. "I was thinking that Jane is very pretty."

"Jane?"

"Yeah, don't you think so?"

"Jane?" he repeated. "I guess."

"Um… Haven't you known her a long time?"

"Sure. She keeps my world running. I couldn't live without her."

"You couldn't live without her and you've never noticed that she's *pretty?*"

"No. She's like a sister to me. And, frankly, I'm fairly sure she thinks of me as a hopeless little brother. So, no I've never noticed whether or not she's hot."

She smiled at the slight horror in his tone. He really did think of Jane as a sister. "Well, she is hot. She's so reserved and professional, I didn't notice it before. The woman is a force to be reckoned with."

"Yeah, she could probably execute a bloodless coup of a midsize country without ever leaving the office. She's priceless. We're here," he added, and gestured toward a nondescript door. Above the pale wooden door, a small canopy displayed the word *Andalucia.*

"What is this place?"

Quinn swept open the door and guided her in with a hand on the small of her back. Spice swirled around her. "A little taste of Córdoba," he whispered against her hair.

"What?" The alcove swallowed them up in darkness.

"I can't take you to Córdoba, but this is pretty close. The owner is from Málaga, another part of Andalucia. The food's amazing."

"Oh." Lori's heart squeezed too hard, hurting itself. Just then, a burgundy curtain at the other end of the alcove flipped open and let in the light.

"Mr. Jennings!" exclaimed a slender man with a thick accent. "It's been too long!"

"Stefan!" Quinn answered, then launched into a stream of gorgeous Spanish. *Gorgeous.* He even slurred his *S*'s in that sexy Spanish way. The man just got hotter all the time.

Stefan laughed at whatever Quinn had said and gestured toward Lori.

"Lori Love," offered Quinn, "meet Stefan Arroyo."

A flurry of Spanish words followed as Stefan ushered them into a large room aglow with evening light. The first thing Lori noticed were the trees. There seemed to be hundreds of potted trees scattered among the small, dark tables. Orange trees and... well, other trees that didn't have little oranges hanging from them. The illusion of a garden was furthered by the ceiling of skylights that had been opened to the breeze.

"Wow," she breathed as they followed Stefan through the nearly deserted room. He led them straight across to a row of French doors, then out onto a large brick patio. Tables ringed a wooden square set into the bricks, and the chairs here were full of customers. Classical guitar music flowed over her on the warm evening air.

"It's so beautiful!"

"*Gracias,* Señorita Love. Though not nearly as beautiful as you are, *mi cara.*"

Quinn's hand settled on her arm. "Very true, but I'll thank you not to dwell on it, Stefan."

Stefan laughed as he seated them at a small corner table, not leaving until he'd placed a napkin onto Lori's lap with an elaborate flourish and a wink.

"This place is amazing," Lori breathed.

"Will you trust me to order for us?"

"Sure." She didn't think tacos and enchiladas were part of the menu in Spain, and her knowledge didn't extend any further.

"Any allergies? Anything you can't stand?"

"Um…just mushrooms. And raw fish."

"All right. No Spanish sushi." He leaned back and smiled at her. "I'm so glad you decided to ditch my sister."

"Shut up. You're going to make me feel bad."

"Poor Lori." He reached for her hand and drew it to his lips to press a kiss to her fingertips. She stopped breathing for a moment, but when he sucked the tip of her middle finger into his mouth, she couldn't help her loud gasp. The gasp turned to a yelp when a waiter chose that moment to walk up to the table. Lori jerked her hand back and nearly knocked over her empty wineglass, while Quinn just smiled serenely.

After the waiter informed them of the specials, Quinn launched into that musical Spanish again. She could pick up only a few words from her semesters of high school Spanish. *Vino. Paella.* And…*baño?* No, that meant bathroom. Lori gave up and just enjoyed the show.

Maybe…maybe if she asked very nicely, he'd speak Spanish to her while they had sex. She could pretend he was a Spanish corsair who'd kidnapped her and forced her to be his personal slave. Alone on his ship with no hope of rescue. The things he'd make her do. Things no innocent lady should know about.

When she realized that silence had fallen around her, Lori looked up to find both Quinn and the waiter staring at her. Her eyes flew wide. "What?" She hadn't spoken out loud again, had she?

"Still or sparkling?" Quinn asked, eyes dancing with amusement.

"Huh?"

"Water," he said carefully, as if he were repeating himself.

"Oh. Regular water. I mean, still. Thank you. Sorry. I was just…"

As soon as the waiter turned away, Quinn chuckled. "You're blushing. What *were* you thinking about, Lori Love?"

She shook her head so hard her hair brushed her neck.

"I didn't get a chance to do my homework today. Is there something I should know about?"

"No! I wasn't…um…"

"Oh, I think you were."

The waiter returned then, rescuing her by presenting a small bottle of wine to Quinn. The two men went through all the fancy wine steps that were required at any Aspen restaurant, and then Quinn presented her with a glass half-filled with deep golden liquid.

"*Vino de Málaga.* It's a bit sweet. I hope you don't mind." When she shook her head, he raised his own glass and tilted it toward hers. "To Spain," he said, "and fantasy."

"Hear, hear," Lori agreed. When the sweet, cold wine touched her tongue, she couldn't help but moan her approval. It was flowery and bright. Too bad she couldn't get tipsy tonight.

Quinn's eyes narrowed. "Remind me to stock up on Málaga wine tomorrow. I like that sound."

"Falling back on props?" Her amusement turned

to a shock of desire when he dragged his gaze down her body.

"Props, hmm? That's something to consider. Thanks for the hint."

"I thought it was more of an insult."

He arched an eyebrow. "Don't make me get out the transcripts of last night. Your insults fall on deaf ears. Although…there was the laughing to consider."

"Hey, at least I didn't *point* and laugh."

"Jesus." He chuckled. "You're cruel. And you're starting to chip away at my confidence."

"I wouldn't want you to get complacent. Complacency is the enemy of hot monkey love."

"Hmm. Ben Franklin?"

Thank God she didn't have wine in her mouth at that moment or it would've gone airborne.

Quinn took her hand again, though he didn't try to suck one of her fingers into his mouth, so Lori relaxed.

"You said you're on call tonight. What does that mean?"

"The tow truck. I'll take any emergency calls until 6:00 a.m."

He frowned. "So someone calls in the middle of the night and, what? You just drive out into the dark to help?"

"Yes. Oftentimes I give them a 'tow,' hence the name of the aforementioned truck."

Deep lines of trouble appeared between his brows. "Does someone come with you?"

She tried not to roll her eyes, she really did. "No,

Quinn. No one comes with me. I go out and tow the car. Sometimes I charge a battery or help someone out of a ditch."

The waiter returned and set down a series of small plates, but Quinn never once broke contact with her eyes. His frown had turned into a glare.

"Lori, that's ridiculous," he said. "You could get hurt. A woman out there alone in the dead of night? What if the guy is drunk? What if he's violent?"

Of course there had been men who'd stepped over the line. Men who'd theorized that a woman on the side of the road at 3:00 a.m. was probably open to all kinds of invitations. She couldn't deny it, which made her mad.

"It's part of my job," she snapped.

"You're, like, five feet tall."

"I am five-two! And don't be an ass!"

"Excuse me?"

"It's my job, Quinn. I've been doing it for ten years now, and you weren't the least bit worried about it for the past decade, so don't be an ass and act concerned now."

He leaned forward and lowered his voice. "I had no idea you'd been out risking your hide in the middle of the night. You could be raped or killed out there, damn it."

"Well, so could my other drivers."

His cheeks turned red and he clenched his jaw tight. "That is the…*most*…unbelievably stu—"

"Stop," Lori realized he was still holding her hand—squeezing it now—and pulled free.

"Lori—"

"No. You don't have the right to lecture me about my life."

When Quinn sat back, eyes blazing frustration, Lori was struck with a sharp pang of distress at the distance. They were only going to see each other for a few weeks. She didn't want to argue, not when they could be doing something much more relaxing.

He took a deep breath and shook his head. "If you go out tonight and something happens, how am I supposed to live with that?"

She needed this back on track. "Listen. Thank you for being concerned. But I'm not your responsibility. This is my job. I'm only on call once a week" —usually— "and I'm careful and smart. If someone is drunk, I have no compunction about calling Ben or one of his officers. I even keep a Taser in the truck. All right?"

"I don't like it," he bit out.

"Fair enough."

Frustration lay tight across his face, but he didn't say anything more. He just tapped a finger against the table in a frantic rhythm.

Lori looked purposefully down to the plates. "Tell me what we're eating."

He kept his jaw stubborn for a few moments more, and then glanced down in resignation.

"Come on," she urged. "Truce."

He glanced up and his mouth softened. "Another truce?"

"Yeah, what is it with you? You're very argumentative."

"Not with anyone else," he muttered, but the tension was melting away.

"Must be all the sizzling passion between us, hmm?"

This time he smiled, and his grin stretched wide and wicked. "That might be it. Here." Quinn offered her a taste of one of the little appetizers. He explained each plate, and she coaxed stories of Spain from him until the paella arrived. Then she was too busy devouring the delicious stew to talk. The sweet wine was the perfect antidote to the spice, and she soon found herself finishing her second glass with a mournful sigh.

"Did you like it?" Quinn asked.

"The wine?"

He glanced around with a slightly embarrassed air. "The trip to Spain."

"I loved it," she answered with complete honesty. It really did feel like a foreign country. The waiters argued softly about something in Spanish. The simple, sensual music stroked down her body as dusk fell, tingeing the air midnight-blue. Tiny white lights were wound through the potted trees and flowering vines, and each time a breeze touched them, they sparkled like stars. "It's perfect."

Quinn stood, surprising her. "Come on."

"But you haven't paid, have you?" She glanced around instead of taking the hand he held out, but Quinn just reached down to tug her up. That was when Lori noticed the two couples swaying on the wooden floor. "Oh, no!"

"Oh, yes. What would a romantic trip to Europe be without dancing?"

"Don't be ridiculous. I don't dance!" But she was on her feet and being pulled toward the middle of the patio.

"It's nothing but swaying. Actually, all you have to do is hold on. I'll move you."

Well, that sounded sort of sexy. Lori stopped dragging her feet and followed.

His fingers wrapped more thoroughly around hers as he brought her around to face him. "That's better," he murmured, settling one big hand on her waist as he pulled her flush with his long body. "Much better."

The music was louder here, slow and lovely as sex, and Quinn began to move with the promising rhythm. Lori did as he'd suggested and just held on, and it turned out he was right. Dancing was kind of nice. He was a good dancer—or a good swayer anyway—and Lori relaxed enough to rest her cheek against his chest.

He smelled good, the natural scent of his skin like pure sex to her now. She closed her eyes and breathed him in, thinking of him naked and stretched above her. The touch of his lips against her forehead sent a shiver of lust down her spine. His fingers spread wider, splaying over her hip.

"Tonight," he whispered near her ear. "Again."

Yes. Yes, *again*. Just like the night before. Only…

Lori clenched her eyes shut. She couldn't possibly ask him.

"Please," he murmured, and Lori's body smoldered.

This was supposed to be her fantasy. If she couldn't ask for what she wanted with Quinn, right here, right now, she'd miss her chance to live a dream. Lori held her breath, gathered up her courage and whispered into his shirt.

Quinn shook his head. "What?"

Lori swallowed and raised her face toward his while Quinn kept swaying, his hips pressed to hers. "Would you, um, speak Spanish? You know, to me?"

Despite being distracted by the rush of blood in her ears, Lori noticed the way his muscles stiffened beneath her hands. *Oh, God.* Then he smiled. "Speak Spanish, hmm?"

She pressed her face back to his shirt and didn't answer.

"Yes, I'll speak Spanish to you, *mi querida.* Do you want to call me Quinto? Or would you prefer not to know my name?"

"Shut up," she said as clearly as she could with her face buried in cotton.

"But if I shut up, how will I speak the dirty Spanish words to you, *mi pequeña gatita?*"

She could either run away or she could laugh, so Lori laughed. Running away wouldn't get her any hot corsair action. And this wasn't her real life. If it were, she wouldn't be slow dancing with a handsome man in a Spanish café.

So once she'd gathered up her courage—again—
Lori lifted her head from his chest, leaned into his
neck and licked him. Quinn growled just like a pirate.

"Estás cortejando peligro, mujer."

Oh, yeah. Whatever he'd said, it sounded wonderful. She bit gently at the tendon in his neck, rubbing
her tongue against his skin, reveling in the faint rasp
of his stubble.

"Eres una bruja. Bastante." He broke the embrace
and pulled her off the dance floor. *"Vámanos."*

The bill was waiting, thank God. Apparently it had
been clear to the waiter that the dessert they wanted
wasn't on the menu. Quinn slapped a stack of bills on
the table, and they were already turning toward escape when a female voice stopped Lori in her tracks.

"Quinn Jennings, is that you?"

Quinn's face froze in a look of such shocked frustration it would have been comical if Lori's heart
wasn't sinking. She could see the woman approaching over Quinn's shoulder, and she was gorgeous.
Of course.

He turned and saw the woman, too. Lori caught
the edge of a smile as he spotted her.

"Yasmine," he said.

Yasmine? Unbelievable. Almost as unbelievable as
how impossibly attractive she was. Mahogany skin,
straight black hair accented with streaks of dark
brown that picked up the color of her eyes even in
the dim light. And she was thin. And tall. Taller than
Quinn in her stiletto-heeled boots.

Her little scrap of a shirt fluttered around her

as she drew closer to Quinn and kissed him on the cheek. The dark jeans looked painted on; the woman couldn't have worn underwear with them if she'd tried. Lori fought the urge to growl and bare her teeth.

"Quinn, I haven't seen you in ages!"

"It's been a long time," he responded, while Lori glared at his back.

"Too long. We should go out for a drink sometime," the woman purred.

He laughed. "I think your new husband might object to that." Finally, he turned and reached for Lori's hand. "Yasmine, this is Lori Love. Lori, this is Yasmine Harrington."

"A pleasure," Yasmine cooed, her eyes flicking down Lori's body in a quick trip.

"Nice to meet you," Lori made herself say.

The woman's skin actually threw off a silky sheen when she raised her hand to touch Quinn's elbow. "I can see I'm interrupting a business dinner, so I'll leave you two alone."

"No—" Quinn started, but Yasmine was already waving her fingers and calling "Ciao!" before he could say more. Really, what was the point anyway? The clarification would be worse than the mistake. *Strangely enough, she's actually my date.*

"Sorry about that," he muttered.

Lori's jaw was beginning to ache, so apparently she'd been clenching her teeth. She unlocked her jaw. "No problem. Look, I was about to forget my purse anyway." She snatched it off the floor and folded her arms. "Ready to go? I've got to get home."

"Home? Why? What's wrong?"

"Nothing."

"Nothing? A minute ago we were about to tear each other's clothes off, and now you're fuming."

"Can we just leave?"

He looked down to her crossed arms. "No, we cannot. Why are you so pissed?"

After glancing around to be sure no one was watching, Lori stepped closer to their table for privacy. "What do you think is wrong? You used to date that woman, right?"

He eyed her warily. "Yes. A couple of years ago."

"Damn it," she hissed. "You told me that Barbie dolls weren't your type!"

"Yasmine does not have fake boobs," he protested.

"That's not what I meant—"

Quinn cut her off. "She's an attorney, for God's sake."

"Oh, great! She's tall and model-y and gorgeous and she's intelligent? Even better."

He threw up his hands. "So? Would you feel better if I'd only dated trolls before? What the hell would that say about *you?*"

"Forget it. If you want to date a girl from the wrong side of the tracks for a little excitement, that's your business. Let's go."

"The wrong side of the..." His jaw muscles clenched and fury leaped to cold life in his eyes. They seemed to change from hazel to pure pale green as she watched. "Yeah, it's hard to go slumming in

Aspen. I had to hit up Tumble Creek to find a girl like you."

"Screw you," she snapped back.

Quinn leaned forward, voice lowered to a dangerous calm. "Don't even try to make this into something weird, Lori. We grew up in the same place, so get over your complex. Unless, of course, this is part of your fantasy. The asshole rich boy and the noble girl from the poor family."

"Fuck off," she growled.

Quinn's fingers wrapped hard around her elbow. "Let's go." He pulled her in a different direction than they'd been heading.

"Where are we going?"

"There's a back way out."

Apparently he was too furious to make small talk with Stefan. Lori was grateful, because there was a good chance she'd burst into frustrated tears at any moment. She was being ridiculous. This was a fling. It didn't matter who else he was attracted to.

Except it did. She felt small and boyish and uncouth. She felt as if she was walking through the middle of a European café wearing coveralls.

They seemed to be approaching a vine-covered wall, and Lori slowed in confusion, but then Quinn reached into the greenery and twisted, and the wall revealed itself as a gate that swung open onto a dark alley.

This ritzy Aspen block might look quaint and pretty from the front, but back here the buildings rose up in two stories of unpainted cinder blocks.

Lori was still glancing around when the gate swung closed with an ominous click.

"I thought we were past this." His voice floated to her like the rumble of a storm and his shadow drew nearer. Lori backed up a step. He followed.

"I want you," he said, the words threatening. "Do you get that?"

Lori nodded. Her eyes were adjusting, and she could see him now as he reached out to curve his hand behind her neck. His fingers felt hot and strong, and not the least bit elegant.

"I want you. *Now.*"

Her heart stopped beating for a moment. She felt the echo of it fade to complete silence before it finally restarted with a hard thump. "Okay," she breathed.

Finally, he kissed her—*a punishing kiss,* her brain volunteered, and it certainly was. Quinn was furious. And when he pulled her hard against his body, she knew he wasn't just furious but also incredibly ready. And just like that, she was ready, too. Wet and hot for him. Quinn backed her up to the wall of the building next door, and Lori went willingly.

When he pushed her against the hot cement brick, Lori began to shake. When he tugged the neckline of her dress down and exposed one naked breast, she groaned. Her bra hadn't gone with this dress, and when his hand closed roughly over her, Lori was so glad.

This was insane. She could still hear the music of the restaurant, could clearly hear people laughing, silverware clinking. She tried not to moan too loudly when he pinched her nipple and sucked her tongue into his mouth, but when he pushed his hard cock against her, she couldn't help her groan. She broke free of his kiss to get air into her straining lungs.

"Es esto lo que deseas?" he rasped. *"Deseas la prueba de mi lujuria?* Do you need me to *show* you how much I want you?"

"Yes," she sobbed. Yes, she wanted him to *prove* how much he wanted her. Leave her with no room for doubt, because her body was so damn full of him.

He cursed against her neck, and Lori heard him tear open a condom wrapper. The sound of his zipper lowering seemed to scrape over all the nerves in her body. Her sex tightened as if she were close to coming.

Quinn pulled up a handful of her dress, then grabbed one side of her panties and yanked them down. Kicking a foot free just in time for Quinn to lift her, she curled her arms around his neck and her legs around his hips. Before she was ready, he shoved his cock deep into her.

"Oh, God," she gasped.

"Yes," he grunted, buried to the hilt inside her. "You're so hot."

His hips shifted away for a brief moment, then thrust hard and fast against her, filling her once again. She cried out, unable to hold it back, but that didn't stop Quinn. He thrust again and again, deeper every time.

"Tómalo," he ordered, *"Tómalo todo."*

"Yes," Lori moaned, not caring in the least what he'd said, just needing to please him. "Yes, please."

Tightening her hold on his neck, she arched her back to take him deeper. He was so hard, so big, that even as wet as she was, the friction rubbed rough against her nerves.

Quinn licked a path up her neck and bit just below her ear. *"Eres mía."*

"Yes."

"Siempre que deseo."

"Yes!"

He pressed her shoulders more firmly against the wall, giving himself the leverage to fuck her harder.

"Oh, God," she groaned. "Oh, Quinn."

He kissed her neck again, sucked her flesh between his teeth while Lori pressed her head hard to the wall.

"Ven para mí, querida. Come for me now."

"No," she muttered. "Not yet." Relaxing her thighs, she let gravity push her more firmly against his thrusts. The new angle pressed his sliding cock against her clit, and Lori couldn't stop her scream.

"Bueno," Quinn murmured even as he raised his hand to her face and covered her mouth with his palm. He took her like that, pressed against the wall, cries smothered by his strong hand, while Lori tried to tell herself that being ravished in a dark alley was not an admirable fantasy. Her sex told her to shut the hell up.

Quinn quickened his thrusts. "Come for me, baby. Come."

Defiant, she shook her head, but when he began to

growl in Spanish—words that sounded suspiciously foul and offensive and threatening—Lori felt her soul slipping down, down, down into pure sensation. Oh, God, she was going to come, and she wanted this to go on forever, didn't want to let go of his muscled body and big cock. But her nerves had all tightened to the snapping point and she couldn't back away.

Just as he muttered, "Ah, fuck, I...can't..." Lori's sex clenched him hard, and she screamed into his skin as the night exploded into pleasure. His body shook and shuddered. His fingers dug into her cheek.

Lori closed her eyes and let it all wash over her. The sound of people talking just a few yards away. The feel of rough cement against her back. Her neckline pulled taut beneath her breast. Quinn's fingers pressed too hard to her jaw. And him...still tight inside her body.

This was sordid. Dirty. Wrong. Jeez, this was illegal.

But every heartbeat pulsed happiness into the tired muscles of her body. Every breath shimmered inside her lungs. Her body *sparkled*. If she opened her eyes, she was sure she'd see light glowing beneath her skin.

His hand slid down to her shoulder, and Quinn's panted breath hitched against her neck. "Lori? Are you okay?"

"God, yes." Her voice was too raspy, so she cleared her throat and tried again. "Are you kidding me?"

"Uh, maybe that wasn't quite the fantasy you had in mind."

"Jesus, maybe it was."

She thought she detected relief in his soft huff of laughter. "You're okay?" He pulled away, his body sliding out of hers.

Lori unhooked her ankles and slowly lowered her feet to the ground, but she held tight to his arms until her legs stopped shaking. Her skirt fell conveniently back into place. "That was…"

Quinn rested his forehead against hers. "Please say something good."

"Hmm. Well, how was it for *you?*"

"It was…Lord, it was…good."

"Just good?"

He cursed under his breath. "Am I allowed to say it was amazing? I feel too guilty. I shouldn't have done that. But it was spectacular." He nodded. "And wrong."

Lori laughed and pulled him down for a quick, hot kiss. "It *was* spectacular and wrong. I'm glad we agree."

"Perfect. Now if you'll excuse me, I'm still at risk of being arrested."

While she chuckled, Quinn turned away. She heard him zip his pants and watched as he looked around for a garbage can. It took a moment before she realized she had her own cleaning up to do. The panties that were hooked around one ankle had twisted under her heel, and while she had been feeling pretty adventurous, she wasn't daring enough to put them back on and find out what kind of disease a dirty girl could catch from an alley floor.

Lori kicked off the black lace and crumpled it up

to stuff into her purse. She popped her breast back inside her dress where it belonged and tried not to picture what she'd looked like a few seconds before.

When she pushed away from the wall, she weaved a bit but finally found a bit of strength left in her knees. The strength must have migrated from somewhere around the region of her heart, because it felt suddenly lonely. A tinge of embarrassment made itself known. Her cheeks flamed.

My God, had she really just done it in an alley a few feet from the innocent patrons of Andalucia? What if someone had heard them? Maybe someone *had*.

Lori grabbed her purse from the ground and dusted it off. "Let's get out of here."

He approached out of the dark. "Did you spot a surveillance camera or something?"

Her gasp echoed against the masonry blocks. She glanced frantically around.

"Well, don't look up, for God's sake. Haven't you ever watched *America's Most Wanted*? Now they've got a full face shot."

"What?"

"Lori, I'm teasing you."

She fought the urge to stomp her foot in frustration but didn't quite succeed. *"Can we just go?"*

She grabbed his hand and jogged as best she could in heels, pulling Quinn out onto the street. Here it was still the deep blue of late dusk. The streetlamps blinked on as she stole a furtive glance around. No crowd had gathered, and there didn't seem to be blue and red lights flashing closer in the distance.

Quinn murmured, "Look at that. Scot-free."

"Hey," she snapped, relief adding fuel to her frustration. "You're the one with the professional reputation to protect. I'd think you'd be more nervous."

The smile he turned on her oozed self-satisfaction. "Don't be silly. I'm Aspen's most eligible nerd. When *I* do it in an alley, sleazy is just plain sexy."

"You…" she stammered. "You're…"

Quinn leaned down and kissed her, cutting off her outrage pretty effectively. His tongue swept all the embarrassment away and made her strain toward him.

"Feel better?" he breathed against her lips.

"Almost." She put her own tongue to work to shut him up. Jeez, they'd had sex just minutes ago, but she was ready to do it again. Now. In the alley. In his car. In her truck.

Her truck.

Lori broke away and glanced at her watch. Nine-thirty. "Crap. I've got to head back over the pass."

Though he sent her a dark look, Quinn didn't argue. Instead, he walked her through the dark, the same path they'd taken earlier in the evening, but so much more intimate now. His long fingers curled loosely around hers, fingertips brushing a secret caress against her thumb.

"I'm sorry," she murmured. "I had no reason to get mad."

He glanced at her, his profile a darker shadow against the sky. "No, there was no reason. I was there with you because I wanted to be. If I wanted that woman so much, I would've kept dating her."

She nodded.

"You know, Lori, we're from the same place."

"Not anymore."

"Damn it, if something like that had happened to me, if my parents had needed me, I would've been in the same spot. We're from the *same place*. Your dad ran the garage, and mine ran the feed store. We both worked hard and we both had a plan. And then something terrible happened to you. That's the only difference between us."

"I suppose." Lori sighed. "But it's a big difference."

"Is not," he countered, making her smile.

"Regardless, it's not a reason to act like an insecure shrew. I apologize."

"You know," Quinn drawled, "if yelling at me makes you want to get your freak on, I might be able to tolerate it."

"Yelling at you does not make me horny. And I didn't yell."

"Mmm. But you did get very mad. And your cheeks got all pink. And your chest started heaving."

"I think me being mad makes *you* horny."

"I think you're right. Wanna fight again?"

Lori chuckled past the wave of desire that washed over her. "If I had the time, yes. Definitely. I might even knock you around a little bit."

"Tomorrow?"

They were already at the entrance of Quinn's parking lot and, God, she didn't want this to end. And if it had to end tonight, she wanted to pick it up tomorrow.

Damn it.

Lori groaned, "I can't," as she stopped next to her lavender half-ton pickup. "I put Molly off until tomorrow, but I can't do it again. I'm meeting her at The Bar."

"What time?" Quinn asked immediately.

"You can't come!"

"I'm not going to come crash your girl party. What kind of loser do you think I am?"

"A horny one?"

"Ha! No, I was thinking I'd be a horny stalker instead, and come see you after your date with my sister."

"Yeah? You'd make a booty call in the middle of the night?"

"Yes, I definitely would."

She leaned against her truck and smiled up at him. "Mr. Jennings, where in the world is your dignity?"

Quinn frowned and made a show of patting his pockets. "Damn, I must have left it in that alley back there. I saw some dignity on the ground near the Dumpster, but I thought it was yours."

"Asshole." She tried to kick his shin as she laughed, but he'd stepped too close to give her any room. Still, it was easy to forgive him when he feathered a kiss over her temple.

"I'm going to Vancouver in a couple of days. Come with me?"

Her smile froze as a band of shock wrapped itself

around her lungs and slowly tightened. "Vancouver?" she wheezed.

"It's a beautiful city. Have you ever been?"

She shook her head, hoping the movement wouldn't set it spinning.

"I'm speaking at a conference on Monday, but I can free up the whole evening to show you around."

Pictures of Vancouver flashed through her head at blinding speed. It was a beautiful place. Not as exotic as most of her dreams, but she'd love to go.

"I can't," she whispered, shaking her head again. "I can't."

His shoulders sagged. "Are you sure?"

No. Her eyes prickled, so she glanced up at the sky to stop any tears before they started. "I've got the garage. I can't get away without planning."

"Damn. We've never done it in Canada. I thought I'd try to pick up a little French along the way."

Lori forced a wide smile. "You pick up the French. I'll buy the Moosehead. We'll meet back here on Tuesday."

"Deal."

She ducked her head under his chin and pressed her cheek to his chest. His heartbeat vibrated through her, thumping loud enough to chase away her sadness. "But keep your phone turned on in the meantime. I just might need you to drop everything and come running in the middle of the day."

"Anything you say."

CHAPTER TEN

THE BLACK SHADOWS of lodgepole pines flew by Lori's open window. She was driving too fast, risking a run-in with a deer or, God forbid, a moose, so she forced her foot to ease off the accelerator but reached for the volume knob on the stereo at the same time and twisted it up.

The wind eased a bit, but the bass of angry old-school Liz Phair kept her frustration fed as she sped down the pass.

Vancouver. She wanted to go, wanted to stroll onto a big plane and drink champagne with her lover as they blasted across the sky toward another country. Canada wasn't exactly Timbuktu, but it wasn't Tumble Creek, either. She wanted to fly away for just a few hours.

But she couldn't.

She'd realized a distasteful truth about herself the year before. Lori Love would date for travel.

An imaginary movie clip played through her mind. There she was, standing at an intersection in short shorts and crop top, waving a handmade sign that said just that: Will date for travel! The dot of the exclamation point was a little happy face. Hearts danced across the poster board. Her ass jiggled when she bounced.

Yes, she would date for travel. In fact, she'd done it already.

When she'd first met Jean-Paul, she hadn't realized who he was. As far as she'd known, he'd been simply a handsome, older European man with a keen knowledge of cars. He'd also been driving the most beautifully restored Aston Martin DB6 she'd ever seen.

Jean-Paul had pulled into her garage by happenstance, troubled by a slow leak in his front tire. After they'd spent a half hour chatting, he'd asked her out, and Lori had been so surprised she'd said yes, regardless that she'd been only mildly curious about him.

Mysteriously, that mild curiosity had developed into a month-long relationship. Though she'd demurred every time he'd invited her out on the town, she'd spent the night at his place half a dozen times. She'd slept with him more often than that, retreating to his bedroom after a dinner prepared by his private chef. Jean-Paul had been smart and interesting, and more than decent in the sack. And he'd also asked her to accompany him on a trip to Greece within a week of their meeting.

It hadn't been a conscious decision on her part. She hadn't said to herself, "I will sleep with Jean-Paul D'Ozeville because he's going to take me to Greece." She'd never have had sex with the man if she'd realized she was only interested in him for his private jet and well-used passport.

But then Jean-Paul had broken the news that

Greece would have to wait, something had come up and he couldn't go until the fall. And Lori had been angry. Not disappointed, but *angry*. She'd made an excuse to get out of his bed at one in the morning and go home. Not her finest moment.

It had taken her a few days of avoiding his calls to realize why she didn't want to see him. She wasn't mad anymore. She was just…no longer interested. Not interested unless the man was going to fly her away to Greece within the next month.

Lori sighed at the memory, her stomach knotting itself with anxiety as she passed the road that led to her father's land and drove into the outskirts of Tumble Creek. She knew the exact source of each light that shone through the dark, even the ones set far off the road. Knew each house and workshop, even if she wasn't familiar with every person inside. This was her home, it always had been, and it would be her home until she cleared her own path out of it.

The relationship with Jean-Paul had taught her that, at least. She had to do it herself. It was too easy to mistake desperation or greed for more genuine feelings. Too easy to use sex as a resource. She'd cheapened herself and lied to both of them in the process.

What she had with Quinn was real, at least. It was real lust and she'd already disclosed her sexual greed. They were equals in this game, and she wasn't going to let herself fall into the role of the cheap mistress again.

But regardless of her big ideals, it had still been hard to say no to Vancouver.

She'd have to try out a poor man next time she decided to use a man for sex, because her scruples were just a bit too mushy in this area. And she never, ever wanted to wake up to the realization that she'd slept with another man for the cost of jet fuel.

As she pulled into her lot, Lori was so absorbed in those depressing thoughts that she had nearly turned all the way into her parking space before her brain registered something amiss.

The shadows on the two bay doors of the garage looked…odd. Distorted. And her headlights picked up flashes of reflected light on the ground as she swung around.

Shaking her head, Lori jumped out of her truck and slammed the door. The floodlight between the two bays was out, so that might be the explanation for the strange streaks of darkness twisting across the doors. Lori was walking closer when her heels crunched against something sharper than gravel. She froze and looked down at shards of broken glass that winked moonlight at her.

The eerie feeling of something out of place was replaced by alarm. Lori took a step back and spun in a slow circle. No dark figure loomed nearby. Everything else looked normal, so Lori raced back to the truck for a flashlight.

The bright beam revealed a swath of glass shards trailing across the gravel that led to the bay doors.

She swept the light higher and gasped so loudly that her own voice echoed back at her.

What she'd thought were twisted shadows were, in fact, deep dents in the metal doors. It looked as if someone had taken a sledgehammer to them. The floodlight hung from the wall by its wires, the thick glass bulbs shattered just like the windows of the garage doors.

The flashlight slipped in her hand, nearly falling to the ground. She was holding it too tight, sweat making the grip slippery, so Lori switched it to the other hand and reached into her truck for her phone. The light beam shook.

Of course, the wind chose that moment to pick up. Something slid across the ground a dozen feet away. Likely just a plastic bag or dead leaves, but the adrenaline rushing in her veins insisted it was something dangerous. Lori pressed her back against the open truck door and swung the flashlight wildly around the lot. The sweeping beam caught shadows and then dropped them, creating movement where there was none. Her panicked breathing grew so loud she was sure someone could walk straight up to her and she'd hear nothing but her own fear.

"Calm down." Her words trembled, so she repeated the admonition. "Calm down." Her brain ceased spasming long enough to insist that she get back in her truck, so Lori did just that. As soon as she'd shut and locked the door she felt better. And she felt downright safe once she'd restarted the engine and switched on the high beams.

"Okay," she whispered. "You're okay. No one's here." Not that she was taking any chances. Lori dialed 911 and held her breath until a male voice answered.

"This is Lori Love of Love's Garage. Someone broke into the garage. Or maybe just vandalized it. I don't know."

"Are you still at the site?"

"Yes." She recognized the voice of Ben's newest officer, the one assigned to dispatch until he racked up some seniority. She wished it were someone a little older and more experienced.

"Okay, are you somewhere safe?"

"I think so." A faint crackle of voices came over the line.

"I'm dispatching officers right now. Tell me where you are, so they don't mistake you for the trespasser."

She nodded. "I'm in my truck in the lot."

"Can you see the suspect?"

"No. I don't think anyone's here. I don't know. Should I check? I didn't think—"

"No, stay in your vehicle. The officers should be there any moment."

Before he'd finished speaking, the faint whine of a siren filtered through her closed window. Within seconds, blue flashes of light were bouncing off the side wall of the building across the street. These guys were good. Or the town was just small. Hopefully both.

The first officer on the scene ignored her entirely. He parked his SUV, unholstered his weapon and started prowling around. When the second vehicle screeched to a halt, Ben jumped out and headed straight for her truck. Lori fought the urge to rush out and throw herself into his arms. Undignified and probably uncalled-for. She rolled down her window instead.

"What happened?" Ben demanded.

She explained as quickly as she could, and then everything was moving at a comfortingly fast pace. Ben ushered her out of her truck and into his, speaking what seemed to be gibberish into a little radio at his shoulder. He switched on a spotlight, and then locked her inside. After a quick conference with his officer, the two men split up and disappeared from Lori's view.

Secure in Ben's truck, Lori began to feel a little silly about her fear. Her heartbeat slowed and, as her blood pressure decreased, all the creepiness dissipated from the scene before her, helped along by the unflinching brightness of the spotlight. The garage had been vandalized, that was all. The house looked secure. No doors or windows stood open, as far as she could see. No dead animals nailed to the wall. No stalkers creeping along in the shadows. Just two dented garage doors.

Well, *one* dented door and one completely smashed, crooked door.

"Crap." That was going to cost a pretty penny. When she got her hands on the asshole who'd done this... Apparently there was a thin line between fear and anger, because Lori felt suddenly furious. She wanted to strangle someone, beat the living daylights out of them. Power rushed into her muscles, signaling the fight part of her instincts. But flight returned with a fury when the door jumped beneath her elbow. Lori screeched.

"Sorry," Ben said as he swung it open. "Just me."

Once she'd detached her nails from his leather upholstery, Lori jumped down from the truck and rubbed her sweating hands against her skirt. When she remembered she wasn't wearing panties, she frantically smoothed it back down. Jesus, had she flashed Ben getting into his truck?

"We didn't find anyone," he said, seemingly unfazed by any dirty bits he might have seen. "You said you saw nothing except the damage, right?"

"Right."

"Okay, let's survey it together, and then I want to walk your house with you. We'll take some pictures of the vandalism and fill out reports, so I'll be here for a while." He flipped out a notebook and his eyes flicked down to her heels. "Were you returning from someplace close?"

She tensed. "No. Aspen."

This time his gaze flicked up to meet hers before he looked back to the paper. "Did you notice any pedestrians on your street, any vehicles you might have passed?"

"No."

"Were you alone?"

The all-business tone of his voice finally got to her stretched nerves. "Could you drop the cold cop attitude? It's kind of annoying."

He scowled and snapped the notebook closed. "Fine. You look like you were on a date. Were you?"

"Why? What does that have to do with this?"

His shrug was decidedly un-cop-like. So was the brief flash of smile. "Nothing. I just want to know what the hell's going on with you. Lori Love in a dress? The world's gone mad."

"Whatever."

"And here's the truly strange part… Molly hasn't mentioned a thing about you dating anyone."

"Hmm. Can we get back to the crime scene? When are the techs going to arrive?"

"The techs?" He sputtered, choking on laughter. "It's just me and old Frank there, sorry. You mentioned boy problems the other day. Care to tell me about that?"

"Good God, are you going to do your job, or do you just want to gossip?"

"That's not gossip. I'm trying to figure out why someone would want to drive a truck into your garage."

She blinked. "A truck?"

"Yeah, but not your tow truck. The headlights have been smashed, but there seems to be no other damage."

"The headlights?" she groaned.

Ben walked her over to the far side of the lot where the tow truck was parked. Sure enough, both headlights had been smashed, as well as the spotlight on the driver's side door.

"All deliberate damage, obviously. Do you know who would want to do this to you?"

"No. I don't suppose you have any idea how much that door will cost to replace, do you?"

"Lori, I'm serious. Have you broken it off with someone recently? Turned someone down?"

"Er…just Aaron."

He wrote that down.

"Seriously, Ben, I don't think he cares that much."

"You never know." He glanced up. "And Quinn? Are you still dating him?"

Lori choked on her tongue. Ben just waited patiently until her coughing stopped. "Huh?" she rasped.

Rubbing his eyes, he sighed. "Come on. Even if I weren't a trained investigator, I would've figured that one out. Molly doesn't know?"

"I don't know what you're talking about!"

"Fine, I'll call Quinn with any questions."

Lori smacked him in the arm before it occurred to her that she could be arrested, then she smacked him again because she was pretty sure he wouldn't press charges. "Don't call him!"

"I won't call him unless I have to." He let the threat sink in for a moment. "All right, let's walk the property and then we'll go inside and you'll tell me exactly what you've been up to for the past week. It's possible this was an aborted theft, but my instincts say it was personal, so I don't want you editing yourself, understand?"

Lori thought of the alley behind Andalucia and lied her ass off. "You got it, Chief."

But it turned out that Ben didn't need that information anyway. When he left an hour later, he was convinced that if the vandalism had, in fact, been personal, it had something to do with the phone calls Lori had made earlier in the day. Lori wasn't so sure. Why would a developer do something so petty?

Ben's expression told her he didn't think it was petty at all. "No more phone calls about the land. If someone is trying to intimidate you, it could be the same person who assaulted your father. And why didn't you tell me about these developers in the first place?"

"I just thought of it today."

"Well, call *me* next time, not your Realtor."

"It seemed like a long shot. It still does. I don't see why you think this was anything more than a couple of drunk teenagers looking for trouble."

Ben scowled. "If you've been watching enough cop shows to think we have a tech department, then you should know that cops don't believe in coincidences. I reopened the investigation into your dad's assault. You made a few inquiring phone calls, and suddenly your shop looks like the front end of my first car. No more phone calls, understand?"

Well, she'd been done anyway. "Fine."

"Now what else are you hiding?"

"Nothing." She shook her head. "Did you find any more information about the sale?"

Ben nodded. "Your dad bought it at auction. It

was foreclosed on just as you suspected. The previous owner was Hector Dillon. Did you know him?"

"Hector?" Lori frowned. "Actually, I think I did. Didn't he own the gravel pit? I think my dad bought sand from him for the plows."

"Yeah, he owned the gravel pit and had a pretty good-sized ranch he and his brother had inherited from his dad."

"The land my dad bought?"

"Yeah," Ben said. "That was part of it. The bank broke it up into a few parcels."

Could that have made Hector mad enough to come after her dad, just because he'd bought a parcel? "You're using the past tense. Is Hector dead?"

"I don't think so. But he moved to New Mexico about five years ago. I haven't tracked him down yet."

"You really think he had something to do with my dad's injury?"

Ben took off his hat and ran a hand over his hair. "I don't know. It's another long shot, but it bears looking at."

"Okay."

"As for tonight—" his voice lowered "—will you please let me drop you at Molly's?"

"No." She didn't like being fawned over or taken care of, didn't like to feel more vulnerable than she really was.

Ben didn't approve of her answer, but he left after eyeing her locks with suspicion.

Lori collapsed onto the couch with a sigh. Crapola, this was going to cost her a bundle. One door could be banged out and made serviceable, but the other was a lost cause. Five of the wheels had popped off and the framework was twisted beyond repair. So they'd be using one bay until insurance came through, and even then... Her deductible was somewhere in the twenty-five-hundred-dollar range.

"Shit."

And the truck lights...those would be out of pocket, too, and she couldn't afford to wait. As it was, she'd have to refer all of tonight's calls to Grand Valley. She'd sold the old hook and chain truck a few years ago to pay off some bills and that meant no backup, so tonight's towing fees were gone.

She was seriously beginning to regret the new dress she'd bought. Shit, it was probably snagged in the back from being rubbed against cement.

Gazing longingly at the fridge, picturing the cold beers inside, Lori tugged the throw off the back of the couch and wrapped it around her.

A full day of work, an evening of dirty sex, and a night of being victimized had all teamed up to exhaust her. She'd figure out what the hell was going on in the morning. Right now she just wanted to curl up and sleep, right here on the couch.

The phone rang.

Lori cursed and curled up tighter.

It trilled again and she realized it was her cell phone ringing from her purse, well within reach. Grudgingly, she reached out and scrounged for the beeping menace. "Yeah?"

"Hey, Lori Love," Quinn's voice purred.

She closed her eyes and wished she were pressed up against him, breathing his skin. "Hey."

"How's it going? Are you in your truck?"

"Yes." Weariness made it easier to lie than explain the truth. She'd feel bad about it some other time.

"I'm calling to check up on you. I hope you don't mind the obnoxious behavior."

"Are you kidding? I've never had a stalker before."

"Great! You're really racking up the new experiences. But seriously, I'm not just calling to track your movements with the GPS locator I secretly installed on your phone—"

"Nice."

"I'm calling to finagle another date before I go out of town."

She smiled and pulled the blanket higher, cocooning herself in warmth. "By *finagle*, do you mean offer to do me again? Because I'll take it."

"Yes, you will," he growled, thrusting her body into immediate arousal. God, he was turning into a wicked, dirty boy and she loved it.

She wondered if she was about to have phone sex with him during her pretend shift in the truck, but Quinn cleared his throat to a more reasonable tone. "But I actually meant something less exciting, unfortunately. I've got a business thing on Sunday, a cocktail party that—"

"Oh, God, no," she groaned.

"Come on, it can't all be trips to Europe and public sex."

"Sure it can. This is a sordid affair, remember?"

"Please? An hour, that's all. Maybe two."

"Sorry. Nope. I wouldn't have anything to talk to those people about, and I have nothing to wear."

"Wear that blue dress. I didn't get to touch you in it."

Lord, he knew how to make her smile. He must have sensed her weakness because he pressed his case.

"I want you with me, and I have to go. This developer is one of my big clients and we're right in the middle of—"

Lori sat up. "Wait. Who?"

"One of my clients—"

"You said a developer. Which one?"

"Er…Anton/Bliss. Why?"

Anton/Bliss. "Okay," she said with an abruptness that startled him into silence. A few seconds passed. "Okay, I'll go with you."

"Ah, so it's name dropping that impresses you. Well, if you're really good I'll introduce you to James Dubbin, the head of Aspen's planning commission. Pretty impressive friends, huh?"

"You're a dork."

"Maybe, but I'm a dork with a hot date for Sunday. So assuming you don't spot me stalking you before then, I'll see you on Sunday night. I'll even pick you up to make it official. Seven-thirty?"

After agreeing, Lori hung up and jumped from the couch, her exhaustion vanished under the flood of adrenaline. She raced to the computer and sat down to do some serious research on Quinn's friends.

"LOOK, MRS. BRIMLEY, I promise your wheel is not about to fall off. You just need new brake pads." Lori rubbed her forehead and glanced at the clock. Molly had probably arrived at The Bar by now. Mrs. Brimley continued to squawk.

"Ma'am, surely you've had bad brakes before? It's a totally normal sound, just bring it by in the morning and— Yes, I am a girl, but I've been working on cars since I could walk. The only time wheels ever 'fall off' is during a serious accident, *and*—" she cut off the old biddy's high-pitched squeal "—I really don't think that bumping the curb at the grocery store qualifies."

The squawking turned to grumbling. God, Lori had hated this woman when she'd run the old movie theater and she was quickly remembering why. Lori glanced at the clock again. "Okay, fine. If you really want me to come tow you in the morning, I will. But it'll be thirty bucks and your insurance will not cover it, I swear. Call me on Monday after seven-thirty, all right? We'll do it your way."

Slamming down the phone, Lori grabbed her keys and darted for the door, glad she'd forgone heels for tonight. Her flip-flops would make faster time on the sidewalk, and they had little fabric roses on them that matched the red polish on her toenails. She actually felt cute tonight, regardless that she'd reverted back to jeans. The jeans were tight, her scarlet tank dipped low, and she knew for a fact there was an extra sway in her hips. All in all, she felt far too cheerful for a woman with her problems.

After carefully picking her way across the rocky lot, she hopped triumphantly onto the sidewalk and started the short two-block trek to The Bar—otherwise known as T-Bar, since the *h* in the sign had long ago burned out. The place was run-down and decorated in the same style as Lori's house, but it was the only game in town, and she and Molly had cavorted there often since Molly's return to town the year before.

Up to that point, Lori had only dropped by occasionally, since she hadn't had a good friend to hang out with. All the women in town had either left after high school and stayed gone, or they'd married young and started families. Strangely enough, the good housewives of Tumble Creek had a marked disinterest in hitting the town with the community's lesbian mechanic.

Just as she stepped off the curb to cross the street, a vibration rumbled through Lori's lower pelvic area, bringing her to an abrupt halt. "Yikes!" she gasped, pressing a hand to her belly. Maybe she should find a better place to keep her cell phone. Or maybe not.

Assuming it was Molly, Lori flipped open the phone and sprinted across the street. "Hello?"

"Lori, where *were* you last night?" For a moment, she couldn't place the frantic female voice, and the vandalism popped immediately into her head. Was this the person who'd trashed her garage? But then she heard the caller draw a deep breath. "I went to The Bar, but you guys didn't show!"

"Helen?"

"You said you and Molly would be there!"

"Oh, jeez." She smacked her forehead and stopped in the street. "Helen, I'm so sorry." An approaching pickup honked, the male occupants whistling as they eased past. Only one guy didn't whistle. He was James Webster, nephew of Miles, the town reporter. She'd fired James a few months before because he'd called her a bitch when she wouldn't advance his pay. His eyes watched her as the truck rolled past, but he didn't quite glare.

"How could you leave me alone there?" Helen cried.

"I'm sorry," Lori muttered. "I had to cancel, and I totally spaced on calling you. Did you and Juan have an argument?"

"Well, no…"

"Regardless, I didn't mean to leave you just sitting there looking lonely."

"Yeah…" Her outrage had faded to a suspicious reticence.

Lori stopped dead in her tracks. "Helen? *Did* you sit there looking lonely?"

"For a little while."

"And then?" Raising her eyebrows, she waited for Helen to end the long silence. She waited in vain. "Helen, did you and Juan get back together?"

"No! No, we did not. But I drank that first beer a little fast. I was nervous, and Juan kept glaring at me. And then…I don't know what happened. I started drinking screwdrivers and you know how those get to me. And then I was crying and Juan was so nice, and I...I woke up in his bed this morning!"

"I see."

"And then I woke up again in the afternoon, and he was gone, and I think he thinks we're back together!"

Lori walked the last few yards to the establishment in question, then leaned up against the wall, trying not to think of the last wall she'd leaned against. "*Are* you back together?"

"We can't be!" Helen shouted. "I'm too old for him!"

"Mmm-hmm. Funny, it sounds like you were just the right age a few hours ago."

"Shut up."

She couldn't stop the laugh that escaped her mouth. "Look, Helen, I'm sorry that I forced you to make sweet, sweet love to Juan last night. *And* this morning."

"Oh, cripes."

"But I told you before, I think you should give it a chance. You two have obviously got some serious chemistry."

"We're from two different worlds."

That struck close to home, so Lori just shrugged. "I am sorry. I'm walking into The Bar right now if you want to meet us here tonight."

"Are you insane?"

"Should I tell Juan you said hi?"

Helen screeched. Then she huffed, "I hate you," and hung up. Poor girl. She had it bad. If only she could relax and embrace the hot sex as Lori was doing.

After checking to be sure the phone was still on that lovely vibrate setting, Lori stuffed it into her pocket and tugged open the heavy oak door. The thick odor of beer drifted over her, happily lacking the stale cigarette stench of years past. Stepping into the dim room, she idly wondered if there were any states where you could smoke in bars these days. Her thoughts were interrupted by a loud inhalation.

"Lori," Molly barked from a few feet away.

Lori squinted toward the bar, waiting for her eyes to adjust. Just as she picked out Molly's blond hair, her friend sprang to her feet and pointed.

"Lori Love, who are you having sex with? And don't you lie to me!"

The whole bar froze—of course it did—and all eyes turned toward her. As she looked around in horror, one of the gentleman had the courtesy to tip his cowboy hat, but the rest of them were too busy smirking or ogling her body. "Molly, are you crazy?" she hissed, rushing toward the stools.

"Me?" Molly countered. "Ben hinted you'd been on a date last night and I didn't believe it. But look at you!"

Panicked, Lori looked down to be sure a boob wasn't hanging out again. "What?"

"You're practically...*dewy!*"

"Dewy?"

"You're all aglow. You think I can't see that? No wonder you canceled yesterday. You probably still had rug burns on your knees. Oh!" She gasped, pointing toward Lori's legs. "That's why you're wearing jeans!"

"You're insane, you know that?"

Molly threw her hands in the air. "Who is he?" she demanded just as the jukebox faded to a new song. The bar watched, collective brow rising higher.

"He?" someone whispered from the vicinity of the pool table.

Great. Just great. Lori collapsed onto a stool and glared at her best friend. "Either keep your voice down or I will go home, pack up my things and leave this town without telling you anything, ever. Got it?"

Molly blinked and then glanced toward their observers. "Oh, sorry. My bad." She raised her voice again. "Nothing to see here, people! I was just kidding around." Then she plopped back into her seat, leaned close and waited.

Clearly, her best friend was a lunatic.

Lori tried to rub the embarrassment from her face. "I need a drink."

Molly gestured frantically for Juan to hurry, then tapped her shoe against the footrest of the bar. *Ping, ping, ping.* Juan grinned and waved before he started mixing Lori's favorite: a green apple martini with three maraschino cherries crowding the bottom. Molly crossed her arms and chewed her lip.

"You've got the patience of a two-year-old," Lori observed, leaning nonchalantly against the bar just to annoy her friend.

"Whatever."

"What did Ben tell you?"

"Not enough."

Lori smiled. "Do you remember last year when you wouldn't tell me anything about your job except that it was secret? You even asked for my advice about breaking it to Ben and you *still* wouldn't give me a hint."

Molly's eyes stayed on Juan as he carried the brimming glass over and gingerly set it down on the bar. "I don't know what you're talking about," she muttered.

"I'm talking about secrets. Naughty, sexy secrets."

Molly's gaze swung back to Lori and locked on. "Drink your drink already, woman. I need details."

Grinning, Lori idly picked up her martini glass and sipped at it.

Molly's eye twitched. "I should've known something was up when I saw Miles's latest column."

"What did it say?"

"Oh, it was just another dig about you being seen in dress. Miles wants to know why you've taken a sudden interest in fashion."

Lori cocked her head. "I wondered why Miles showed up on my caller ID. Must be a slow news month."

Molly growled.

"Okay." Lori finally relented. "I can't give you any details, but I can tell you I've been seeing someone."

"'Seeing' someone? As in having someone over for tea or as in making the beast with two backs?"

"Your imagery is less than pretty, but I have, in fact, been getting down and very, very dirty."

"I knew it! My God, you look like your joints have been lubricated. Whoever he is, he's good. So who is he?"

Lori took another apple-tinted sip. "I'm not at liberty to say."

"Oh, yes you are."

"Am not."

Molly glared. "Don't be childish. Just tell me who's puttin' it to you." Her glare narrowed as Lori happily sipped from her drink. Then her friend's face sprang from suspicion to utter shock in the space of a millisecond. "Ohmigod. Oh, my *God*, it's Quinn, isn't it?"

Crap. "What? No. Don't be ridiculous."

"It is!" She jabbed a finger at Lori's chest bone. "It's Quinn. You're doing my brother!"

Well, at least she was screeching in a sort of whispery shout that probably didn't reach farther than the first few tables. "Shut up already! You're going to get Quinn's name in the *Tribune*. And it's not him," she added halfheartedly.

"You're the worst liar in the world. And I can't even believe you're dating my brother and you didn't tell me. Worst liar *and* worst friend."

Lori sighed and finished off her drink. "I couldn't tell you. It's weird."

"Weird because he's my brother or weird because he likes to dress in latex or something?"

She rolled her eyes. "Because he's your brother."

"Hmm." She pursed her lips. "Yes, I knew this could be a problem. Damn it. Okay, so no details, just tell me what led up to this shameful, disgusting state of affairs."

Juan whistled his way over with the next round of drinks, dark brown eyes twinkling.

"What's he so cheerful about?" Molly whispered when he moved away.

"Helen gave him some of the good stuff."

"I thought they'd broken up."

Lori cringed. "So did Helen, so don't say anything to Juan to get his hopes up, just in case it doesn't work out."

"Yikes. Awk-ward! But enough about them…back to you."

Lori smiled. "All right. Quinn came by to ask me out. I thought you'd talked to him and I told him in no uncertain terms that I wasn't going to use him for sex. Needless to say, he was intrigued with my outburst."

"I guess!"

"So, you know…it developed from there."

Molly's face scrunched up. "I can't get details. Damn it, I wish you were sleeping with someone besides my brother."

"Sorry. There's nothing to be done about it."

"Fine. So what happened at your shop last night?"

Groaning, Lori swirled the liquid in her glass before taking a generous gulp. "Somebody trashed it. Busted out lights and rammed into the bay doors. One of them will have to be replaced."

"How much will that cost?"

"Too much. The guy's coming out tomorrow to

take a look, but I checked online. Whatever it will be, I can't afford it."

Molly cursed under her breath. "Well, what the heck? Who would do that to you?"

Apparently Ben had said nothing about what he suspected, so she kept her mouth shut and shrugged. "Whoever it is, I doubt we'll find them, and I doubt even more they'd be the type of people who can afford to pay damages, so I'm screwed."

She was staring down at the scarred wood of the bar, thinking she should tell Ben about James Webster, when she realized that Molly was uncharacteristically silent. When she looked up, her friend studied her face and then glanced down to the drink in Lori's hand. "What?" Lori pressed.

"Nothing. I'm just trying to decide if you're tipsy enough to broach the subject."

She straightened and frowned. "What subject?"

"The subject of you moving. Why don't you sell, Lori?"

Her mood plummeted. "Not you, too."

"Oh, I'm not the only one who thinks you need to move on? I wonder why. Maybe it's because you're stuck."

Lori set her jaw. "I like Tumble Creek. It's a great place. *You* came back here."

"It is a great place. I know you love it. So do I. But you had dreams once upon a time. Goals that had nothing to do with Tumble Creek. You were going to Europe, weren't you? You planned to travel the world.

I remember, because in high school it sounded kind of scary to me."

"Plans change," Lori muttered. "Life goes on."

Molly crossed her arms and eyed her intently. "Oh, really? Is your life going on? Because it looks like you're standing in place. Sell the damn garage, sell your dad's land and get the hell out of Dodge."

"I can't get rid of the garage."

"Why not?"

She didn't want to talk about this, damn it. Talking didn't do any good, it only made the truth more inescapable. But Molly didn't look as though she would budge on the issue. Fine. "It's not that simple, all right? The damn garage isn't worth that much, and once I need to sell it, it's worth even less. The old dump out back is probably a fucking Superfund site, because I'm pretty sure there was no oil recycling program when my grandfather opened this place. They certainly didn't bother sending the old tires away. Anyone who bought it would want it cleaned up first, because the grandfather clause ends once it's sold. Shit, it would probably cost me money to get out of here!"

Molly blinked. "Oh. I didn't know."

"And I can sell my dad's land, but with all the damn bills, it won't bring in enough to make much of a difference, so what's the point of getting rid of something that made him so happy?"

Lori felt a warm hand close around hers and realized she'd closed her eyes.

"I'm sorry," Molly whispered.

Shaking her head, she swallowed hard. "Hey, I've got a house and a job and a tow truck, right? That's more than some people ever have. In fact, some people leave everything they know to come to this country and have a life like mine. There's no reason to feel sorry for myself."

Molly's hand squeezed hers.

"And I'm good at what I do, so fuck it."

"Yeah," Molly echoed. "Fuck it."

Lori raised her drink to that, and set it back on the counter empty.

"Let's get one more round," Molly suggested. "And talk about something else, huh?"

She had to nod, because she was afraid she'd start crying if she opened her mouth. She was stuck and going nowhere. Her life was complete shit, and she was *still* afraid to throw it away and start all over. She wasn't eighteen anymore. She just couldn't do it.

Molly squeezed again. "I didn't mean to make you into one of those sad, drunk women who sits at the bar and weeps into her drink until she passes out."

"Thanks."

"Hey, maybe Quinn could get you a discount on a new door. He knows lots of suppliers and contractors."

"I haven't told him."

"What? Why not?"

Lori sighed and rolled her eyes. "I don't want to argue about it. That man's got a nasty temper."

"Uh…what?"

"Your brother. He's just like your dad when he gets mad. Blustery and—"

"You're kidding, right? My brother is one of the most laid-back guys around. *Some* might even say removed."

"Well, not with me. We get in an argument every time we see each other. It's ridiculous." And hot.

Juan approached, wiping his hands on a towel, biceps flexing. He'd lost weight since he'd begun dating Helen and was starting to look more like the star football player he'd been in high school. But his smile still looked like a happy five-year-old's. "Another drink, ladies?"

"Just one," Lori said, then added, "I mean one for each of us, of course. Let's not be ridiculous."

"Got it."

Lori glanced over at Molly, and her smile froze. Molly's mouth was hanging open, her eyes glued to Lori's face. "What?"

Molly shook her head and then blurted, "Quinn is totally falling in love with you!"

"What?"

She leaned forward and rested both hands on Lori's knees. "Quinn doesn't argue with anybody. He's too caught up in his own thoughts to get involved in the problems of mere mortals. But he argues with you *all the time?* He's falling for you, Lori."

"No! Are you insane? He's not my boyfriend. We're not even dating."

Molly blew a disgusted sigh past her lips. "Use your brain. You read romance novels all the time.

What are the most obvious signs of true love? Drama! Arguments! Tension!"

"Those are also the most obvious signs of domestic abuse. Those books are fiction, which you should know since you write them." Lori tried her best to beat down the shocked panic bubbling up in her chest. "We have chemistry, all right? It's the sexual tension making us fight. Quinn is *not* in love with me."

"Not yet."

"Not ever. He's not my boyfriend. We're not dating. It's sex. Just sex. I'm using your brother for his body and that is *it*. He absolutely understands that."

Molly squinted. "This is so weird. I feel like Bambi just morphed into a raging nymphomaniac."

"Well, Bambi was a boy, so I'm not sure what you're trying to say—"

"Bambi was a boy?"

"I think so. Didn't he grow up to be king of the forest or something?"

"Huh." Molly shrugged.

"Anyway..." The fluttery pain had finally left her chest, thank God. "I've only been seeing him for a few days. There is nothing deep going on. So let's drop it."

Molly dropped it and only gave Lori a few pointed looks through the next hour.

The idea turned out to be sticky, however, and kept clinging to Lori's mind despite its utter ridiculousness. She had to forcibly pry it off, but finally succeeded at about one in the morning when she drifted off to sleep.

CHAPTER ELEVEN

This was wrong. So very, very wrong. And she was enjoying every second of it.

The tight cords bit into her wrists each time she pulled or shifted against the rope that held them to the headboard. Her ankles were tied also, though not together. No, they were spread wide, tethered to opposite bedposts, leaving her sex exposed and open. Caroline dug her heels into the sheets and lifted her hips, struggling… and offering her lover an even better view. His dark eyes gleamed from within the black mask that covered most of his face.

She'd never seen his face, had no idea who he was, and his anonymity only made this wickedness sweeter. Nervousness drove her blood harder against her throbbing clit, and Caroline moaned.

QUINN NEARLY MOANED, too, thinking of the story he'd read three times the night before. He glanced over to Lori's legs framed against the dark leather of the passenger seat. Did she really want those legs spread apart and tied down? Did she really want him to have complete control over her body?

The book he'd stolen from her bedroom had been fairly well used, clearly read more than once. But that story…that story had fallen open naturally, the spine broken into submission.

He shifted in his seat, drawing Lori's eye. She smiled. "So tell me what you were working on today."

Quinn cringed. "Did I mention how sorry I was about being late?"

"Yes, and I believe I mentioned that I knew you'd be late, so it's no big deal. Heck, I wasn't even going to call for another ten minutes, so you beat expectations."

"Sorry. I was actually ready too early, so I sat down to look over some plans and… Well."

"It's not a problem." She laughed. "Quinn, you were like that in *junior high,* for God's sake. I'm not taking it personally."

"I don't want you to think you weren't on my mind or—"

She put a hand on his thigh and effectively shut him up. He stopped worrying about his tardiness and started wondering if her hand was going to slide a little higher. He had a one-track mind after all, and architecture had been run off the rails the moment Lori Love had opened her door and smiled at him. Sex with Lori was currently the only engine building up steam.

Her blue dress was even more lovely than he remembered, probably because he knew he'd be unzipping it later, letting it fall, exposing her smooth, snowy skin. Was she naked under there? Or was she wearing a pair of demure white panties like she'd been wearing the first time they'd had sex? If she was, Quinn thought maybe he'd tie her up before removing them, leave her looking innocent and sweet as he stretched her out on the bed.

Oh, crap, he had to stop thinking like that. His dick had jumped past pleasantly interested to throbbing. The little circles she was drawing against his thigh weren't helping, either. Her hand slid higher.

"Lori—"

"My, my," she purred as her touch slipped sizzling heat against his erection. "What do we have here?"

"Don't encourage me," he ground out.

She laughed, the husky sound like shot silk against his skin. "Oh, but it's fun. What are you thinking about over there?" She traced his cock, sending bright shocks through his gut.

Quinn pulled into an empty space on the street, thinking bitterly of the underground parking garage on the other side of town. If he were parked there, he'd happily show her exactly what he was thinking of, with only a small chance of being arrested.

Throwing the car into Park, Quinn turned to face the woman torturing him. "I was thinking that after the party, I'd take you back to my place. I have a whole drawer full of ties, and I understand they're quite effective at keeping wicked girls like you under control."

She blinked and yanked her hand back to press it flat to her chest. "What?"

"I thought I'd use one to tie your wrists and maybe one to cover your eyes. As for the others…"

Her face paled, all the blood migrating to two high spots on her cheeks.

"I guess you'll find out." He smiled at the utter shock on her face. "Now, are you ready to make small talk?"

He'd thought of simply taking her back to his condo and surprising her with a little bondage, but he was greedy. If he was cursed with thinking about it all night, he wanted her thinking about it, too. He wanted her aroused while they sipped champagne and smiled politely at the other guests. Wanted her anxious and eager. Nervous. A little scared. *Wet.*

She was staring out the windshield now, eyes distant. When Quinn stroked a finger down her arm, she jumped.

"Ready?"

Lori licked her lips. Her eyes slid toward him and then away.

A surge of confidence rolled through him, jolting the nerves in the deepest parts of his body. He hadn't been sure, hadn't wanted to step over the line, but now he knew. Lori did want this. Wanted it so much she was terrified to admit it, was horrified to have it out in the open. So Quinn wouldn't push her or force her to say it aloud. He'd simply make it happen.

Hoping his arousal had faded enough to save the public any embarrassment, Quinn stepped out of the car and walked around to open Lori's door. When she took his hand, Quinn led her across the street and into the party without saying another word.

OH, GOD. OH, GOD, oh, God.

Lori tried to steady her breathing.

She hadn't paid any attention to which book Quinn had swiped from her bedroom. If she'd thought about it, she might have seen this coming, but sex and unpaid bills had absorbed her thoughts for the past few days.

But now he knew. Knew she wanted to be tied up, maybe even spanked.

"Oh, God," she muttered.

Quinn glanced in her direction but said nothing.

Her brain spun with the compulsion to protest. Stop this thing in its tracks. Deny, deny, deny. But, horrified as she was, she didn't want to deny it. He probably wouldn't believe her anyway—hell, she'd dripped strawberry ice cream on some of those pages—and then she'd be embarrassed *and* unfulfilled. Better to be embarrassed and tied up.

Her face burned at the image as Quinn opened a door and ushered her in. The space was all dark wood and polished steel, packed with faces she didn't recognize. Several of them looked toward her, and then casually away. She was no one here, and for once that was a relief. Even if these people *could* read her thoughts on her face, she'd never see them again.

But Quinn…Quinn knew her too well, and when his hand settled on her back, Lori inhaled sharply.

"Shall I get you a drink?"

"Yes! Please. Definitely."

His lips brushed her cheek in a brief caress before he strolled over to the bar, and Lori stood there like an idiot with her fingers pressed to the spot.

She had to get it together. For God's sake, the person who'd trashed her place might be somewhere in this crowd, and all she could think about was her wrists being tied, Quinn's long fingers pulling the silk tight, his face a mask of impenetrable ice.

When he reappeared at her side, Lori blushed again.

"Champagne?"

"Thank you." She raised the glass immediately to her lips and gulped, wishing she could press the icy cold flute to her burning forehead.

"There's Peter Anton." Quinn gestured with his drink while his other hand curved around her elbow. "I'll introduce you."

Lori froze. "No!" His questioning look stirred her brain to further confusion. "I mean, um…" Shoot. "I need to, uh, step into the ladies' room. You go talk to Mr. Anton and I'll find you in a minute. Okay?"

His sharp gaze stayed focused on her for a long moment before he nodded. "All right. You're sure you don't want me to wait?"

"Nope, I can handle the bathroom on my own. And if I can't, I've got my cell phone."

"Good to hear."

Lori spun toward the little alcove to her left and headed toward the pay phone, a sure sign that the bathroom was near. She wasn't even sure people used pay phones anymore, except as a means to locate the restroom. She glanced back to see that Quinn had already turned away, then popped into the alcove, counted to twenty and stuck her head back out.

There he was, shaking hands with a slight blond man wearing wire-rim glasses. He looked like the pictures she'd found of Peter Anton online, only he was smaller than she'd expected. Delicate as the gentleman was, his watch looked as if it weighed a good three pounds. Definitely the rich Mr. Anton.

Now Lori had the element of surprise. Not that she expected him to spill some deep, dark secret to a strange woman, but her spying would be completely ineffective if he knew the crazy-haired woman in red heels was Lori Love.

Ducking back behind the wall, she finished off the champagne in a few big swallows and hurried into the bathroom to buy a little time. She wanted Quinn to speak with Anton and move on. Then her plan would be ready for execution: share a couple of drinks with Quinn. Start a conversation between him and some other engineering nerd about a fascinating topic. Something like "the structural inadequacies of today's failing bridges." Then slip away for a little reconnaissance while Quinn talked the night away. The perfect plan, as long as she could strike while the nerd iron was hot. Quinn wouldn't be nearly as absorbed by some rich trophy wife's thoughts on bridge deficiencies; Lori had to find the perfect foil.

After tucking more than a few stray curls back

into place and dabbing a little nude lipstick on, Lori slipped back into the party. She spotted Quinn right away by searching out the broadest shoulders in the room. Peter Anton was nowhere to be seen.

Raising her chin, she marched out.

"Hey," he whispered when she wrapped her arm around one big bicep. "Everything go okay in there?"

"Well, it was a close call, but I only got one foot wet."

"Excellent work."

When he lifted his head, Lori was forced out of the private little world he'd created and back into this group of strangers.

"Let me introduce you." A flurry of names and titles floated around her, none of which she'd remember in a few seconds, but Lori dutifully smiled and shook every hand. "And of course, you know Jane," Quinn added.

"Jane!" Lori felt stupidly relieved when she spotted Quinn's assistant at the edge of the group. "I didn't know you were here."

Jane inclined her head and the light gleamed off her simple chignon. "Ms. Love, it's a pleasure to see you again. May I refresh your drink?"

Quinn made a shooing motion. "Would you please go have fun? You're not on duty tonight."

"Hmm." Jane raised an eyebrow. "Then I don't need to remind you that your Monday flight was changed to 11:00 a.m. before I leave?"

"Uh…" Quinn squinted. "Only as a gesture of friendship."

"Of course, Mr. Jennings." Jane smiled at Lori before she weaved her way into the crowd.

Lori shook her head, watching as Jane disappeared. "Is she always so formal?"

"Pretty much. She's sweet once you get to know her, though. I think she's just more comfortable keeping her distance."

"Was she educated at a Swiss boarding school or something?"

"I have no idea. But she *is* very smart. Just a few minutes ago she told me she liked you."

"Really?" Lori didn't like the warm and fuzzy feeling she got from Quinn's revelation. This man was nothing but a friend she was using for sex. Despite what Molly thought, it was going nowhere, so the opinion of Quinn's friends should mean nothing to her.

She told herself the same thing several times over the next half hour as she made small talk with the rich people he hung out with every day. She nodded when she didn't understand the political talk. Laughed at inside jokes that went over her head. Pretended pleasure at every new introduction even as her brain reeled.

But finally—finally!—Quinn introduced her to a likely candidate. Edward's scruffy Afro and smudged glasses marked him as an outsider in this crowd, as did his rumpled jeans and plaid shirt. "Edward just joined Mountain Alliance as their soil engineer. How are you liking it over there?"

Edward mumbled something back, then brought up a problem with some new site with a high water table. So began a conversation about excavation techniques that eventually turned into a friendly argument about the benefits of blasting versus... Well, Lori didn't care. She just said a quick prayer of thanks and slipped away unnoticed.

She needed a better prop than her empty champagne glass, so the bar was her first stop. As soon as she had a water glass in hand, Lori slunk along the edges of the party, keeping her ears open and her eye out for Peter Anton. She didn't quite know what spying on him would accomplish. There'd probably be no talk of that pesky female garage owner. And even if there was a minuscule chance that he'd been responsible for her father's skull fracture ten years before, the man was unlikely to have blood under his fingernails or a mark of guilt on his forehead.

She heard Quinn's name before she spotted her prey. When she turned toward the sound of "Quinn Jennings," she found herself not three feet away from Peter Anton.

"Yeah," he said. "He says we're on his schedule, but he does want us to firm it up within a few months."

The other guy—Bliss, maybe?—nodded. "Well, if we don't have it by then, we won't have it at all. He understands that this is all preliminary and not to be divulged? I don't want this floating any farther than it already has."

Anton's mouth opened, but before he could answer, his gaze landed on Lori. His eyes traveled down her body before he studied her face. Heart seizing,

Lori smiled and moved on, pretending she hadn't been standing in the middle of the crowd, staring. She circled around, glancing over her shoulder in a flirtatious way just in case he caught her checking. He did. In fact, he offered a rather predatory smile as he leaned closer to his companion and resumed their talk. She hadn't meant to make herself quite so noticeable.

"Shit," Lori mumbled and edged over to a large window on Peter Anton's other side. Sure the view was a blank, black square of night, but the people behind her couldn't know that. Lori stared into the darkness and sipped her water, eardrums vibrating as she strained to pick up anything.

A long moment passed of nothing but the hum of dozens of people speaking. A woman laughed as if she'd had way too much to drink. Then, finally, she heard Peter Anton again. "We've already discussed this. He's not going to be a problem."

Quinn? Were they still talking about Quinn? And why would he be involved in anything *secret* that might be a *problem?* Surely this had nothing to do with her land. That would be too much of a coincidence. Or no coincidence at all…

The other man spoke. "I don't like so damn many people knowing about this."

"You're the one who can't stop talking about it," Anton growled.

Their voices lowered. Lori strained to hear.

"What are you doing?"

Lori jumped at the voice coming from just over

her shoulder. Water dribbled down her fingers as she
spun to find Quinn's assistant frowning in concern.

"Hi, Jane!" she squeaked.

"Hi. Is everything okay?"

"Oh, yeah! Great. Super."

"Why are you staring at a blacked-out window?"

"I... Oh." She squinted, noticing for the first time
that not even one distant light was visible in the darkness. "Is it blacked out? I thought there was just no
moon tonight."

Jane's eyebrows lowered. "Are you sure you're
okay?"

She pushed her mortification aside. "Yeah, of
course. Just lost in thought."

"Did you argue with Mr. Jennings? Please don't
take it personally if it seems like he's ignoring you. I
saw him talking with Edward Rubian and—"

"No, no. Quinn's fine. It's just the party. Small
talk is stressful for me." As she got over the shock
of being caught spying, it occurred to Lori that Jane
might hold some secrets herself. And Lori was clearly
a failure at this spying thing. It was probably a good
idea to just try gossip. "So, what's Quinn's relationship with Anton/Bliss?"

"His relationship? He's one of their favorite archi-
tects. I'm sure they'd love to have him in-house, but
he's not interested."

"Is he working on something for them right now?"

"Of course. He usually is."

She could hear caution creeping into Jane's voice,
but Lori took a deep breath and asked one more

question. "Does it have anything to do with Tumble Creek?"

Jane frowned. "Tumble Creek? Why would you think that?"

"Oh, I thought I heard...rumors."

"About Tumble Creek? I haven't heard a thing, unless... Wait. Highway nineteen runs through there, right?"

"That's the pass."

"Hmm. I could swear I heard someone referring to highway nineteen recently."

The tiny bit of anticipation that had tightened her shoulders faded to nothing. "Quinn's house is off nineteen. That's probably what you're remembering."

"Maybe. Yes, I suppose that must be it." But she frowned down at the floor.

The awkward moment drew out for too long, so Lori lurched into a new topic. "Anyway, how did you come to work for Quinn?"

Jane glanced up as if she'd been lost in thought, but then shook her head and seemed to let go of her worry. "I worked in the office where he apprenticed after his degree. Mr. McInnis was so impressed with Quinn he asked him to stay on after his apprenticeship. He'd never done that before. Two years later McInnis retired and encouraged Quinn to open his own practice. He urged me to go with Quinn. I did."

Lori blinked in shock. "That's the first time I've heard you call him Quinn!"

"Oh! I'm sorry. I thought of him as Quinn back then, but he's Mr. Jennings now."

My God, this was weird, wasn't it? Jane looked uncomfortable, too, and suddenly Lori had no doubt of the woman's age. Her eyes behind the glasses were wide and uncertain. Her skin flushed and smooth as silk. Definitely pretty and definitely young.

Jane bit her lip and glanced around, then leaned close. "I work among men, Ms. Love. Not that I think Mr. Jennings would ever be inappropriate, but the men coming through the office… Engineers and surveyors and developers and planners and, oh, God, the *contractors*." She gave a little shudder. "Professionalism is key. Even with the women, because they assume that just because I'm young and working for a handsome, successful man, I'm taking more than dictation from him in the back room." She rolled her eyes and went on. "I'm not well educated. I'm not one of the boys. Propriety is all I have."

Something that felt a lot like deep affection welled up in Lori's chest and bubbled into her throat, forcing her to whisper. "I understand."

"Do you?"

"Jane, are you kidding? Do you know what I do?"

Shrugging, she shook her head, though her chignon didn't shift even a millimeter.

"I'm a *mechanic*. I spent my whole childhood in my dad's shop. And now I've spent my whole adult life in the shop, too, damn it all to hell. So, yes, I know exactly what you mean. I curse like a sailor and never give an inch. I get greasier than I need to, just so they won't call me prissy. Hell, I let the whole town think I'm a lesbian! So, yes, I get it. We're two halves of the same coin, Jane. Lucky for you, you're the shiny side."

The woman drew back in surprise, eyes skittering down Lori's dress. "But you're so pretty and feminine—"

"This isn't me."

"Of course it is."

"No, Jane, this isn't me. I'm playing dress up, and it's fun, but it's not real."

Jane's mouth opened as if she were about to deliver a lecture, and Lori braced herself. Despite the woman's youth, she looked fully capable of delivering some seriously stern shit. But then Jane's brown eyes shifted and her frown popped into a smile.

"Mr. Jennings is looking for you. Finally."

Lori relaxed. "The man does love to talk engineering, doesn't he? But if he's done, I'd better go."

The careful touch on her arm stopped her. "Listen. If I remember what I heard, I'll let you know. As long as it's nothing proprietary to Jennings Architecture, you understand."

Lori didn't bother resisting the urge to give Jane a quick hug. "Thank you. Call me if you ever need a new set of spark plugs. Or a pretend lesbian date. I'm good for either."

CHAPTER TWELVE

QUINN MADE HIS WAY toward Lori through the crowd. He meant to ask her why she and Jane had been looking out a blacked-out window as they spoke, but her cuteness totally distracted him as he watched her smile at his assistant.

She might be a tomboy, but he was finding that there was something spectacularly arousing about a woman who hid her sexiness behind T-shirts and tennis shoes...or steel-toed boots. The dress and heels were like visual foreplay. A secret message.

But unlike some of the other women in the room, she looked real. Not posed. Or even poised, frankly. Dressed up as she was, she wasn't wearing any jewelry, not even earrings. But she looked fresh and warm and approachable.

He wasn't the only one who noticed. Peter Anton stood a few yards away and his eyes were locked on Lori's body.

Seeming completely unaware, Lori turned away from Jane and aimed a smile in Quinn's direction. His heart shuddered.

"Hey, Quinn," she said.

"Hey, Lori Love." Her smile inched wider as it

usually did when he said her full name. "Did you introduce yourself to Peter?"

The grin slipped. "Why?" She glanced in the man's direction.

"Because he's having trouble keeping his eyes off your ass. I thought you two had become friends."

Her spine relaxed a little and the grin returned. "Nope. It must be the gravitational pull of my mojo."

Quinn leaned closer until the scent of her shampoo filled his world. "I think maybe he's got a good eye for the naughty ones." Her lashes fluttered to her cheek. When she took a deep breath, he couldn't help but notice the strain it put on her dress. "I've got a couple more people to talk to, and then we can go."

She nodded, still looking down. A flush rose up her chest, reminding him of the delicate pink of her nipples. His heart shuddered again in reaction, so full of anticipation that it hurt. How strange this was. So new and so comfortable and so nerve-racking all at the same time. The feelings tangled around each other, coiling and stretching through him, expanding the feel of his body, if not the actual dimensions.

The pleasantries he needed to exchange became suddenly less important. He glanced around...

"You go on," Lori urged him. "I'm fine."

He searched the faces around him, evaluating each person's status in the world of Aspen development. He should probably say hello to old Mr. Whitson. Then again, the ancient dandy caught Quinn's eye, raised his brows in Lori's direction and winked. He clearly had his priorities straight. Pretty women first, business later. A lesson Quinn would do well to learn.

"Or—" he turned his eyes back to Lori "—we could go now."

Her dark curls bounced when she shook her head. "Oh, no. Really. This is business. We'll leave when you're done."

Opening his mouth to disagree, he paused when he saw the way her eyes darted over the crowd. Maybe she needed a little more time to ease into the next few hours. She certainly looked nervous. "All right."

"You go. I'm terrified of small talk, so I'll join you after another drink. Is that okay?"

"That's okay. But steer clear of Peter Anton. He's looking particularly handsy and I'd hate to have to punch him out."

"Deal."

Quinn was halfway across the room and still smiling when he heard someone call Lori's name. A very male, very loud someone. Abandoning his path toward Mr. Whitson, Quinn spun on his heel. Just out of curiosity.

"Lori Love!" the deeply accented baritone repeated.

He watched Lori's face go comically blank before she looked toward the bar. Quinn looked, too.

A slim man with wavy black hair sauntered across the room, dark eyes locked on Lori. He was clearly pleased to see her, if the wide and self-satisfied smile was any indication. But how the hell could a French playboy like Jean-Paul D'Ozeville even have met a girl from Tumble Creek?

Locked in the riddle, he watched Jean-Paul wink at Lori—*wink?*—and then open his arms wide. What the *hell?*

Quinn's feet were moving even before the man's arms closed around Lori.

"Jean-Paul!" Lori said, surprised but not shocked. She was starting to smile when her eyes caught Quinn approaching. Then the shock appeared. "Oh," she breathed, but Jean-Paul's smooth voice overrode hers.

"You never call me anymore, *petite.*"

Quinn's feet froze.

"Ah…" Her gaze stayed locked with Quinn's. "Well…"

"You should have come to Greece," Jean-Paul chided. "The sea was magnificent, but not nearly as beautiful as you are tonight."

"Thank you," she stammered. "But…"

The man finally realized Lori wasn't looking at him and eased her away to glance over his shoulder. "Oh, Quinn! How are you, my friend?" One of his hands stayed around Lori, and he actually turned her toward Quinn as if they were a couple.

What the…? The ambient conversation buzzed around Quinn's ears like a swarm of flies. He wanted to swat it away.

Lucky for his nerves, Lori sidled over until Jean-Paul's hand slid away. "Um, you two know each other?" she asked.

"Of course," Jean-Paul answered cheerily. "Quinn

is building a house for me! He is the best architect in town, and you know I will have only the best."

"Yeah." She stepped farther away from Jean-Paul, closer to Quinn, and his possessiveness eased a little. But not his tension. He took her hand and looked at his client.

"Ah, you are here together?" Jean-Paul chuckled. "Well, Quinn, I did not mean to make your face so cloudy." He winked at Lori again, the bastard. "There is no reason to build me an ugly house. Ms. Love and I were friends for only a few short weeks before she flitted on to her next conquest. You are a lucky man."

"Oh, come on," Lori muttered under her breath.

Quinn looked from her to Jean-Paul in growing confusion. Confusion, because this made no sense. No sense at all. Lori didn't date guys like this. She'd made that clear. Hadn't she?

His tongue dried out before he realized his mouth was hanging open.

Jean-Paul looked inordinately cheerful and as indulgent as a favorite uncle. "I will leave you to your evening then. No use wasting that dress on an old friend, eh, Lori? Quinn, I will see you next week when you return from your trip. Good evening, *mes amis*."

After he bowed over Lori's hand like a damned French count, Jean-Paul returned the way he'd come and left Quinn gaping at his retreating back. "What was *that?*"

"Um, anyway…" she mumbled.

Not quite satisfied with that response, Quinn

dropped her hand and looked down to see her crossing her arms. "I must be confused. Because that strange episode gave me the impression that you used to date Jean-Paul D'Ozeville."

"Mmm-hmm."

"Pardon me?"

Lori cleared her throat and looked around as if she wanted to see who was watching before she answered. "Yeah."

"Let me get this right. You, Lori Love, used to date Jean-Paul D'Ozeville, French playboy extraordinaire?"

Lori's chin inched up. "He's not French. He's from Monaco."

He couldn't keep his jaw from dropping again. Had she really just put a fine point on the guy's nationality? *"What?"*

"He's from Monaco. Though, of course, he lived in France for a while when he was on the Formula One circuit, so…" She cleared her throat. "Anyway."

He stared at her until she tapped her ruby-slippered foot.

"What?" she demanded.

"Jesus Christ, Lori, that man is old enough to be your father!"

The grumpy set of her jaw inched into anger. "He's fifty."

"Yes! He's fifty! Do the math."

"Hey, don't be rude."

They stood in the middle of the party glaring at each other for at least thirty seconds before Quinn jerked his head toward the front. "Are you ready to go?"

She took off for the door before he'd even finished the question, and Quinn followed, trying his best not to meet anyone's eyes so he wouldn't have to smile pleasantly. Pleasant wasn't even close to what he felt.

THE JIG WAS UP. There was no point in hanging around the party anymore. After Jean-Paul had yelled out her full name a couple of times just for the hell of it, Lori had made a point of looking around for Peter Anton. He'd been standing only a dozen feet away, staring at her with a less-friendly smile than the one he'd given her before.

Not only had she lost her chance to spy on Anton, but now she was worried that Quinn's plans for the rest of the evening had changed. He didn't seem in the mood. Or maybe he did. He certainly looked as if he might be up for paddling her ass. When he reached the sidewalk, he headed straight for the car. Lori briefly considered not following, but in the end she crossed the street and slid into the passenger's seat.

"What are you so pissed about?" she demanded as soon as he closed his door.

"What the hell do you think?" he shot back. He started the car with a roar and pulled out without looking at her.

"Well, you're behaving a lot like I did the last time we ran into someone *you'd* slept with. So I guess I'd have to go with jealousy."

"I'm not jealous," he muttered. The car sped up.

"No? Wait, I've got it. You're morally outraged that I had sex outside of marriage! No, no, that can't be it…"

Quinn braked hard and turned the corner onto a residential street. It was probably a bad sign that he'd thrown the car into manual. Each time he shifted gears he clenched his jaw. "I'm morally outraged that you slept with *that* guy."

"Does he kick puppies or something?"

He finally glanced her way, eyes glittering with anger. "I can't believe the shit you gave me about dating 'sophisticated' women, when you were dating a European playboy who's nearly twice your age." Despite his anger, Lori noticed that Quinn slowed the car to a crawl when they passed a driveway full of skateboarding kids.

"I was shocked, all right?" he said into the silence. "I didn't think you normally went out with Aspen guys."

Lori's mouth fell open. "Oh, my God. Are you upset because you thought you were the first successful guy I'd ever dated?"

"No," Quinn scoffed.

"Then what?"

"It's just…" His eyebrows fell even lower. "He's just… Jesus, he's such a typical rich guy."

Her snort of laughter probably didn't do much for his ego, but she couldn't help it. "By rich, you mean he has an expensive car and he's building a gorgeous house and he travels the world? Boy, that sounds familiar."

"Yeah, you left out the personal jet and the three homes and the younger women and the whole stable of sports cars!"

"Okay, so he's a little richer than you. Is *that* the problem?"

Quinn swung the car into the steep driveway of a pretty group of condos designed to look like individual cottages. He very calmly set the brake and killed the ignition before turning toward her. Then he just glared for a long moment, mouth a flat, tight line of simmering anger.

After drawing in a long, steady breath, he sighed and relaxed a fraction of an inch. "Okay," he muttered. "It's possible I was a little jealous. It was strange to stand next to some other guy, knowing you'd had sex with him. I was…shocked."

Relief bubbled up in her blood. She knew that look already. He'd lost his temper but he was past it now. He wasn't going to be an ass…and this date wasn't over.

Lori raised one eyebrow. "I *might* be able to understand your reaction. I had a similar response to your absurdly tall ex-girlfriend, if I remember correctly."

"Right. So we're both crazy. Perfect."

"Perfect," Lori agreed, grinning just a little. "But you might be a little crazier. I can't believe you were jealous of a man old enough to be my father."

His eyes narrowed. "Very funny. But you did sleep with him, didn't you?"

"Mmm." She cleared her throat, loudly.

"Exactly," Quinn muttered. When he reached

for her hand, shocks sizzled through her palm. "I'm sorry. Will you accept my apology even though I'm still a little pissed?"

"I guess I'd better. I assume this is your place?"

He finally smiled. "Dare I invite you in?"

"I'm not sure. Did you buy any of that Málaga wine?"

His smile turned wicked. "I did."

"Then let's go, Mr. Jennings."

Quinn was out and coming around to open her door before she could blink. She took his hand and followed him into his home. It was beautiful, of course. Woodsy and bright and amazing. Lori looked over the hand-hewn railings of the stairway and the stained-wood doors and windows, all of it polished to a sheen. The walls were painted a pale sage that set off the warm brown leather furniture perfectly.

"Wow," she breathed. "What a great place."

"Thanks. I credit my housekeeper. She keeps the rustic look fashionable. I've noticed that when rustic gets dusty it heads straight into 'old barnyard.'"

"What happens when you add flocked wallpaper to dusty old barnyard?"

"Ahhh…very retro shabby chic?"

"Shabby. Yeah, that sounds about right."

Quinn disappeared into the kitchen, so Lori wandered over to a black-and-white photo she recognized as one of Ben's. He was good enough to work professionally, in Lori's opinion, and this picture was no exception. Black towers of pine trees silhouetted against perfect white clouds. She could almost see the limbs swaying.

"I've tried to convince him to sell them," Quinn said from behind her. He sneaked an arm around her to offer a glass of wine. "Hell, if he'd just stick an exorbitant price on a few of them, half my clients would decorate their houses with Ben's pictures and he'd be set."

"Molly says he likes to keep that part of his life private."

"Well, considering that his sex life is tangled up with my sister's career, I suppose he's got to keep something out of the public eye." He touched her elbow. "Come outside and see the view."

The deck was small, just enough room for a café table and two chairs, but the view made her sigh. The mountains rose up through a veil of pale green aspen leaves. The highest of the peaks still glowed pink with snow in the setting sun on a few of the northern faces. "It's so peaceful."

Lori took her first sip of wine and closed her eyes to savor the cool sweetness as she inhaled the greenness of the trees. She felt the heat of Quinn's body draw closer, and suddenly his lips brushed her shoulder. Eyes still closed, Lori just breathed.

"I hope I didn't ruin the evening," he said, the words shivering over her skin.

She shook her head and took a longer sip of wine. When he dragged his chin over her shoulder, the barest hint of stubble scratched her chin. *Roughness,* she thought, and that one word recalled the plans Quinn had revealed for the night.

Her lungs ached when she took too deep a breath. Rough. He wanted to be rough with her.

"You're so beautiful," Quinn murmured, mouth still on her skin. His hands settled on her upper arms...as if he was holding her, trapping her against the wooden railing. "So pretty."

She didn't want to break the spell, the sudden danger that shimmered on the air, so Lori didn't even bother to voice her protestation that she wasn't pretty. Let him have his fantasy, too. She wanted to be delicate and helpless, and he wanted her to be feminine and beautiful. Perfect.

And then he pressed his body into her, already hard with lust. The railing pushed into her belly, his hands tightened around her arms, and the fantasy blossomed, swallowing up real life. She was powerless in the face of his strength, and his mouth on her skin made her beautiful.

Lori rested her glass on the rail and arched her head to one side. His lips and teeth and tongue strayed from her shoulder to her neck, sucking and biting along the way. She didn't press into his erection, she just stayed still and let him do as he wanted. Finally, he pressed his hips more firmly to her backside, sucked harder at her neck, and she had to part her lips to breathe.

She barely noticed when his hold slid lower, but she definitely noticed when he pulled her arms behind her back and wrapped one hand around both of her wrists. Oh, God. The hot jolt that shot through her stirred up so much tamped-down need that Lori's brain went dim for a moment. She had a vague thought that she might have moaned but couldn't be sure. Her mind was too busy rejoicing that someone had finally done the thing that she'd been too embarrassed to ever ask for.

His other hand brushed between her shoulder blades a moment before the distinctive sound of a lowering zipper pierced the silence. Her bodice loosened just a bit, and then he stopped.

The reflection of the sun had deepened to umber. The trees shaded the balcony from view and deepened the patio to an even-darker shadow than the rest of the world. Would he strip her here? Fuck her against the rail? Lori's eyes rolled, trying to determine whether anyone could see them. Quinn didn't seem to care. He spread his fingers wide over her chest and slid his hand beneath her dress.

"You were very rude tonight," he whispered as he cupped his hand gently over her breast.

Lori bit her lip and shook her head.

"Yes, you were. Flaunting your old lover in front of me."

He was really going to play this game, invest in the fantasy and not just go through the motions. Lori squeezed her thighs tight together at the sheer pleasure of it. "I'm sorry," she breathed.

"I don't think you are." He rolled one nipple lightly between his thumb and forefinger.

"I am."

He teased her for a long moment, still soft and slow. "I don't find your apology…*sincere*." He whispered the word and squeezed her nipple hard at the same time.

Gasping, Lori arched suddenly away from him, and the hand on her wrists tightened. He hadn't really hurt her, it had just been the shock of the sudden, inescapable pressure that made her shy away. But Quinn couldn't know that. He stroked her nipple gently with the pad of his thumb.

"You need a safe word," he said.

"A what?"

"A safe word. Because then—" he bit her earlobe, increasing the pressure until she gasped "—then you can tell me no as often as you want, and I won't stop."

Oh, good God, she couldn't take this. Her clit was too tight already, primed to seize up at any moment. The thought of moaning *No, Quinn, please don't. Please…*

The intensity of her reaction to the idea scared her.

I can't, she started to say, but strangely enough, the words that came out were, "*Sunset.* My safe word is *sunset.*"

His fingers twitched against her breast, but his voice was smooth as satin. "Excellent. Now back to your apology."

This was embarrassing. She couldn't do it. She wouldn't. Her blush already burned so hot that it hurt.

Quinn pinched her nipple again, hard, and Lori gave up.

"I'm sorry!" she cried.

He nodded, his cheek rubbing her hair. "Maybe. But I'm not sure I believe you. Do you think you can convince me?"

"Yes." Oh, yes, she was sure she could.

Slipping his hand out of her dress, Quinn stepped back, though he kept control of her wrists. The silk tightened around her straining ribs as he pulled the zipper up and nudged her toward a door set at a right angle to the one they'd come through. When he reached past her and opened the door, a wide bed filled her vision. *His* bed.

Her hesitation was genuine, though it was only caused by surprise. Quinn pushed her forward. He slammed the door shut with his foot and plunged them into night.

Good. She could do this in the dark, pretend his wasn't a face she'd see for years to come. She could get on her knees for him, beg him not to hurt her, do anything he asked…

One little click and light flooded the room. Lori cringed from it, heart jumping in shock, but the light faded to a warm, soft glow before Quinn dropped his hand from the switch. Not dark, but nearly dreamlike.

But that bright light had shocked her from her desire, pushed her head above the water for a brief, unhappy moment. "Quinn, I don't… Shit. Are you sure you want to do this? I don't want you to do this if—"

"Hush." It wasn't an order. Not at all. It was a caress, a friendly touch of a word. A reassurance. "I've been looking forward to this all day, Lori, so hush."

She swallowed her mortification. "All right."

While she'd been worrying, Quinn had apparently grabbed a tie, because he turned her around, pulled her wrists together in front of her and began wrapping them tight. The silk was too fine to hurt her skin, but there was no mistaking that he meant her not to escape. He wound the ends around several times to provide a cushion, then tied one knot before repeating the process. She couldn't move. She tried to wrench her arms apart and achieved nothing but horniness in the process. Quinn watched her struggle and smiled.

"Turn around," he ordered.

Lori turned—a stuttering, nervous movement. She caught her heel on the carpet and nearly fell before his hands curved over her shoulders to steady her. She started to say, "Thank you," but the second syllable stuck on her tongue when Quinn swept another tie over her head and covered her eyes.

Her world went black, but she was alone in this darkness. Quinn could see everything. Blood rushed to her skin, opening her nerves up to the sensation of air pushing around her each time he moved.

"Is this okay?" he whispered.

Was it? She felt so damn vulnerable. But she'd chosen this game, hadn't she? In the bare space of a second, as the rasp of the silk pulling into a knot slithered against her hair, Lori made her decision. If she was going to do this, she'd do it right, damn it.

So she gave the correct answer. "No."

His hands, falling away from the knot he'd tied, froze in their descent. He paused for a moment, then she felt the rush of his movement as he jerked his hands back up to undo what he'd done.

"I've already apologized," Lori said. "Please don't do this."

This time his hands fell away entirely. She felt him move back, away from her, and her shoulders were cold without him there. She couldn't hear anything, not even his breath. Certainly not her own, because she wasn't breathing.

Finally, he let out one long, soft sigh. A tug on her dress, a brush of warmth, and her zipper slid down.

She remembered to breathe then, and the expansion of her ribs pushed the dress open. It slipped off. And Lori was wearing nothing but her panties and heels and two silk ties.

THANK GOD LORI couldn't see his face, because Quinn didn't think there was anything resembling icy control in his expression. Probably he looked more like a teenage boy presented with his first naked woman, because that was what it felt like.

Somehow, her tied hands and covered eyes made her more exposed, more naked than any woman he'd ever been with. And, hell, she was still wearing panties. Pale blue satin and modestly cut, they turned him on more than a garter belt and G-string could have. She didn't look as though she'd dressed for sex. She looked as though she'd been caught unawares.

Quinn turned her and helped her sit on the bed so he could take off her shoes, as well. Her lips were parted as he knelt down and slipped the heels off, her nipples hard and deep pink. The tie gleamed black against her pale skin, darkness against light.

He slipped his hands between her knees, parting them so he could kneel between her thighs. "You're mine tonight, Lori." Surprisingly, the words felt sincere on his lips. He *had* been jealous. He still was. To know that she'd let that rich old bastard between her legs? Quinn wanted to push her so far that even the memories of other men would cease to exist. The strength of his feelings didn't bear examination. Not now.

"You're mine," he repeated, slowly exploring the curves of the tops of her thighs.

"Yes."

He'd never been interested in domination before and wasn't even sure he was interested now. What excited him was Lori. Her response. The thought that he could do this for her, turn her on in a way no one else had…that was what made his dick throb. That and the idea that his doing whatever he wanted was part of her fantasy. Definitely a game he could get into.

Putting his faith in the belief that Lori would stop him if he went too far, Quinn slid one hand past her hip and up her back. He wound his fingers into her curls, tightened his fist and pulled her head back. The movement arched her breasts forward, and Quinn took quick advantage.

Her nipple was a hard pebble against his tongue and it only got harder as he sucked. He set his teeth gently to her flesh, scraping. Lori's soft cry filled the room and swelled louder when he applied more pressure. After licking the pain away, he moved to her other breast to do the same.

"Oh, God," she gasped. "Oh, God." They'd barely started, and she sounded out of breath and nearly out of control. Each time he bit, her gasps got more strained. "Please," she begged. "Please don't."

Quinn's dick swelled to unbearable tightness. Surely he'd never been so hard. "Please don't what?"

Lori pressed her lips together.

"You want me to stop?"

Her lips turned pale under the pressure. She didn't answer.

Quinn swirled his tongue lazily around one peaked nipple, then sucked hard and fast to make her gasp. "No? Tell me how much you like it," he ordered.

"No."

"Your job, Ms. Love, is to show me how sorry you are." He dragged his tongue up the curve of her breast and kept going all the way to her throat. "You're not doing a very good job." He nipped her neck.

"I'm sorry!" she cried.

"Show me." Holding her still, he finally put his lips to hers and kissed her deep and hard. Lori kissed him back as if she wanted to devour him. When he broke away, she tried to follow, but he pulled her head back. "Convince me," he growled.

She nodded against his hold. Quinn let her go and stood. He shouldn't like this so much. His hands definitely shouldn't be shaking with desperate, angry need when he reached for his belt. But when the belt buckle opened with a clink… Lori licked her lips.

She *licked her lips* as if she could already taste him there, and Quinn gave up even the idea of restraint. Once again, her fantasy had become his.

When he lowered his zipper, Lori's breath hitched and quickened.

He wasn't going to last. Hell, he could probably will himself to an orgasm right this second. And there'd be no chance to indulge all of Lori's needs if he spent the next hour obsessed with trying not to come. A strategic, temporary surrender seemed in order.

Smiling, Quinn wrapped his right hand around the base of his dick and slipped his left hand behind Lori's neck. "Convince me you're sorry," he growled, and Lori took him eagerly into her mouth.

NEARLY VIBRATING WITH stark arousal, Lori lay panting on the bed, still tied and blindfolded, still fully immersed in the game. The taste of Quinn's come lingered on her tongue. He'd zipped up his pants just a moment before and left the room. What did it mean?

Ears straining, she tried to hear something over her rushing blood.

He'd used her. Thrust himself into her mouth until he exploded. And Lori had loved every second of it. She was squirming, aching, throbbing, and each thrust of his hips had pushed her closer to climax. She'd swallowed every drop of his come, then licked at him until he'd finally shuddered and jerked away.

Where was he? Was he coming back? She had a vague notion that isolation and abandonment played a part in bondage, but this aspect of S and M was no fun to her. She didn't want to be a slave, she just wanted to be dominated for one night. Okay, maybe two. Once a week, tops.

She was enjoying it just as much as she'd feared she would.

"Here." His voice startled her into a little jump. "Sit up."

Lori sat up, and Quinn pressed something cool and smooth into her hands. The wineglass. She raised it to her lips and gulped the wine. Not to wash the taste of him from her mouth, but just for the pure liquid courage. The cold wine quickly pushed more heat into her veins. Quinn took the glass away.

"Are you done?" she blurted without meaning to.

"Done?"

She swallowed, mouth dry despite the whole glass of wine she'd just downed. "Are you done fucking me?"

The clink of Quinn's glass touching the table seemed loud enough to echo. "I haven't started fucking you yet."

"I know, but—"

"And it's insulting that you haven't noticed. Stand up."

When she stood, knees trembling, Quinn immediately pushed her panties down. Any worry that he'd lost interest in this game vanished when Quinn slid the edge of his hand roughly along her sex. Though the movement was rough, the sensation wasn't. She was wet enough to turn anything into a smooth glide. A hum vibrated up her throat.

"I guess you haven't gotten what you wanted yet."

She shook her head, goading him as if he really were some volatile sadist, but Quinn just chuckled.

"Lie down," he said, and she did. When he reached for her wrists and tugged her hands over her head, Lori tried hard not to smile. But she failed. She'd been waiting a long time for this, and as his fingers tied another knot and secured her to the headboard, she couldn't help a grin that was half delight and half nervousness.

Quinn kissed her, a friendly peck on her smiling lips. "Stop it," he whispered. "You're ruining the mood."

"Sorry."

Her giddiness faded when he stood, the bed dipping and then springing up at the loss of his weight. She was stretched out on the bed, totally naked, blind, hands tied above her head. A quick tug confirmed that she couldn't move.

Was Quinn watching her? Was he undressing now? Did he have more ties? Would he spread her legs and pin her down? She didn't even know if he was in the room.

The vulnerability of her position washed over her, and any urge to smile was swept away on that wave. Instead of grinning, she squirmed.

"Spread your legs." His voice came from the foot of the bed. She squeezed her thighs tight together. "Open your legs, Lori. I want to see you."

The clink of his belt confirmed one of her questions. He *was* undressing, and though her lust had faded to a simmer, it sprang back to a full boil at that one tiny sound.

"No," she whispered in answer. A faint shushing sound to her left warned her just a moment before his hand closed over her thigh. Lori wrenched away, rolling to her side, and when she did, adrenaline exploded into her bloodstream. Nerves she'd thought already raw shrieked up to a higher level of awareness.

He reached for her more roughly, fingers digging into her hip, pressing sparks of pleasure through her whole body. Suddenly his hot, naked chest was pressed to her back and his heavy thigh pressed her own legs tight together.

"Where do you think you're going, sweetheart? You're tied to my bed."

Yes, she was. Oh, God, she was tied to his bed, hands stretched above her head, and his strong arm curled around her waist to pull her flush against his body. He was hard again already, full and long and pressed to her ass. His hand cupped her lower belly, fingers just brushing the dark hair between her legs.

"I can do anything I want." His words tickled her ear. "Anything. And you can't stop me. So open your legs."

Lori bucked against him, trying to get away and not moving an inch. He thrust his hand between her clenched thighs and found the wetness he'd inspired. When he rubbed her clit, Lori cried out.

"Jesus, you're wet. You can act like you don't want this, but you do. Admit it, Lori. Beg for it."

"No! Don't." Her own words crashed through her body, making her shake. "*Please.* Please don't."

His stroking grew rougher. She was so close.... And then he let her go.

"You want me to stop?" His hand slipped up her stomach, away from her sex, and Lori cried out in sorrow. He cupped her breast and plucked at her nipple as he ground his erection against her ass. She arched into him, silently begging.

"You want to be fucked," he growled, voice rough as an animal's in her ear.

Jesus, she wanted him so much, she was losing track of the story. Her body rebelled. It wanted him and it wouldn't let her mouth form the word *no.* But she wouldn't say yes. She wouldn't.

Quinn rolled away and left her alone, air cooling her burning back.

Please, she mouthed into the sheets. The faint rip of plastic tearing caught her attention, and Lori rolled to her back to try to track him. A condom wrapper? Was he going to take her now? She tugged on her hands just to feel the dig of the restraints.

God, this was so good.

He jerked open her knees before she could resist, and then he was between them as she bucked and arched, pressing her shoulders back as she lifted her hips away from his.

She was trying to fight him but he was too strong. Quinn gripped her ass in his hands, keeping her high off the bed, and rose to his knees to meet her. Suddenly, his cock was sliding into her in a shocking invasion. He buried himself to the hilt in one brutal shove, eased by the wetness he'd caused. Lori screamed.

He jerked slightly at the sound, freezing as if waiting for her to shout out the safe word.

As if. Lori squirmed and whimpered until he lowered her to the mattress and braced himself over her body.

"God, you're gorgeous," Quinn said. "I could do this forever."

Was that a threat? Or was it something deeper? Something that had nothing to do with this game? She didn't want to think about forever, all she wanted was his body filling her too tightly, the smell of his skin hot against hers, the weight of his hips pushing her down.

He thrust, pushing a deep cry from her mouth that he answered with a growl. "Tell me you like it."

"No," she whimpered. "I won't."

Quinn pressed his mouth to hers, rubbing his tongue against hers with brutal pressure as he thrust again. He wound one hand into her hair and tugged her head back. His mouth dragged over her jaw, teeth scraping her skin. Lori let the shock of these small pains sink into her flesh like sunlight.

Sweat slicked their skin, setting Quinn gliding against her thighs when he sank himself deep again. "Tell me," he demanded.

She pulled against the ties, gritted her teeth against

the tight pressure squeezing her in so many places. Her wrists, her scalp, her shoulders pulled taut. And, of course, the tightness of her sex, filled with his width every time he pushed brutally into her.

He could be anyone. He could be a man she'd met in a hotel bar and taken up to her room. He could be a faceless stranger, using her now, doing anything he wanted.

And yet this was so much better. With Quinn.

He kissed her neck tenderly then, pressed his lips gently just below her ear. "Tell me," he whispered, as tender as any lover, though his fist tightened, pulling her head farther back.

"Fuck me," she finally whispered. "Please. I want you to fuck me."

Quinn reared back and hooked his arms behind her knees to draw her legs wider. Then he gave her what she wanted, taking her rough and fast. Slamming his hips into hers so hard that she began to inch up on the bed. Lori arched up into him, taking him as deep as he could go.

"Say it," he grunted.

She could barely hear him now. Her mind was turning in, anticipating the orgasm that was slowly washing up her body, a tide coming in, a wave hovering before it broke.

"You want this, damn it. Beg for it."

So she did. She begged him to fuck her harder. And her desperate, vulgar words pushed the wave higher until she finally went under, screaming, jerking against the ties. Her voice cracked and faded to nothing before the last spasms had even gripped her. Quinn thrust again and again until he finally jerked into her with a guttural shout.

Time passed. Long minutes while the sweat cooled on her face. Quinn's breath rushed over her shoulder, the sound of a man who'd poured his heart and soul into her. For the first time since the night had begun, she wished her wrists were free so she could curl her arms around his neck and pull him impossibly close. She wanted her eyes open and surveying his face to see the thoughts there.

She must have shifted, because he lifted his shoulders a few inches, the movements sluggish.

"Here," he murmured. "Here." The blindfold slid up, but Lori kept her eyes closed, trying to adjust to the small amount of light that leaked through her eyelids. He sat up and worked at the knot until it loosened enough to let her free. She jerked her arms free and wrapped them around Quinn's chest, pressing her face into his shoulder.

He whispered her name and rolled her to her side so he could get his arms around her, as well. "Lori," he said again. *"Jesus."*

"Yeah," she agreed, wanting to apologize, needing to reassure herself that he'd liked it as much as she had. But if she asked, what if he said no? She'd have to grab her clothes and fly out the door, and God, she just couldn't move right now.

He kissed her head. "I didn't hurt you." It should have been a question, but perhaps he was thinking the same thing she was. Perhaps he was thinking he couldn't ask his question, because the answer might kill him.

Lori took a deep breath and pushed away from him. She raised her head and met his worried eyes. "Quinn Jennings," she said, her voice shaking only a tiny bit, "that was the best thing I've ever done."

His eyes went wide. Lori noticed a bit resentfully that his lashes were much longer than hers. "Ever?" he repeated.

"Ever. It far surpasses that time I talked myself into riding the tallest roller coaster on the East Coast."

His eyes went wider still. "*That* was your best thing before?"

"I'm afraid of heights. So yeah. I was pretty proud."

"And now you're proud that we just screwed like crazy people?"

"Yes," she answered before her cowardice got the better of her.

They stared at each other, silent for five or six breaths, while Lori's stomach sank lower and lower. Until, finally…Quinn smiled. "Yeah, I'm kind of proud of myself, too. I was a fucking sex *ninja*."

She'd thought the orgasm great, but the laughter was even better. They both had to wipe tears from their eyes before they settled into each other again, and the giggles hit Lori every few seconds for a good fifteen minutes before she finally fell asleep.

That night she dreamed of masked ninjas prowl-

ing through her room, watching her sleep. Strangely
enough, despite their frightening masks and glinting
eyes, they all seemed quite friendly.

CHAPTER THIRTEEN

LORI WOKE UP ALONE in a big, strange bed. A first for her. *Another* first.

Grinning into the dark, she sat up and looked around for a clock. Only five in the morning, but that was hardly a surprise. They'd fallen asleep pretty early, after all.

The curiously sore muscles of her stomach complained when she collapsed into the pillows. She was clearly in for a deliciously achy day. She'd been ridden hard and put up very, very wet.

"Hell, yeah," Lori groaned, glad that Quinn wasn't next to her. She was embarrassed, just as she'd expected to be. But she only needed a minute. One minute of embarrassment and then she'd get over it, whether she was ready or not.

But for a full sixty seconds she simply lay in Quinn's bed, taking deep breaths as heat rushed over her skin in waves. The bondage part hadn't been particularly embarrassing. It was the "I'm sorry, please don't hurt me" part that made her blush. It also made her wet as hell, and she spent the rest of her minute of mortification wondering how many times Quinn would be up for that in the next few weeks.

Sweet, nerdy Quinn…who'd have thought he'd play the role of demanding captor so damn well? "It's always the quiet ones," Molly had once said about Ben. Obviously Molly Jennings was a woman who knew what she was talking about.

Just in case Quinn had only wandered away for a few moments, Lori stretched hard and relaxed back into the bed. She could pretend to be asleep if he came back in…unconsciously roll onto her stomach and pull the sheets out of place. He wouldn't be able to resist the glimpse of her naked ass, but he wouldn't want to wake her, either. So he'd ease back into bed and run a careful hand up her thigh. Slide his fingers gently between her legs, just for a quick touch, but then he'd find her already soaking wet, ready for him. Lori would whimper a little, shift her knee higher.

Was she asleep or awake? Quinn wouldn't know, but he'd be so damned hard, he'd have to have her. He'd ease off his shorts and kneel between her parted legs, stroke his dick down her ass until he found the slick niche of her sex….

Lori moaned and rubbed her fingers over her throbbing clit. Shocks radiated up her belly, urging her to finish the job, but there was no good reason to get herself off when Quinn couldn't be more than a hundred feet away. Much better to surprise him with a little morning quickie.

The floor radiated warmth when Lori set her bare feet down. She found her panties quickly, but resisted the idea of zipping into the tight bodice of her crumpled dress. Instead, she grabbed Quinn's dress shirt and fastened only two of the middle buttons. *Sexy*. After a quick detour to his bathroom, Lori set out to find her prey.

The kitchen and living room were empty and the patio door still shut tight. Lori headed upstairs and walked straight into what must be Quinn's office. The large loft took up most of the second level. It looked out over the two-story living room below, and the outer walls were set with a half-dozen windows. Quinn sat in front of one of these windows, a big lamp blazing light onto a huge drafting table. He was hunched over, wielding a very complicated-looking ruler and a black pencil. He didn't look up.

"Hey, Quinn," she said, surprised at the throaty whisper that emerged from her mouth.

Quinn didn't seem surprised. In fact, he didn't seem to notice anything at all. "Hey," he muttered.

Well. Sexy, indeed. She thought of dropping the shirt altogether, but even sheer nudity wouldn't work if he didn't look up from his work. Better to keep the shirt on and her pride intact. Plus, the blinds were open.

Glancing around to see what view the neighbors might have, Lori's eyes fell on the big, paper-strewn desk a few feet to Quinn's right. She cut her eyes back to him, then to the desk again.

Hmm. If he was too busy for sex, maybe she could get some work done, too.

Feeling like a James Bond villainess—spying right under the hero's nose!—Lori sidled over, her peripheral vision locked on Quinn. His eyes didn't so much as shift in her direction.

At first, she only stood there, looking over the files and letters tangled up in haphazard piles. Nothing said "Tumble Creek," which would have been helpful, and none of the papers had been stamped with a big red "Top Secret," either.

After looking over her shoulder to confirm Quinn's continued absorption in his work, Lori dared to use one finger to shift a few files around, glancing at the labels on each. Paper rubbing against paper made a much louder sound than she'd ever noticed before. It scraped and dragged and crackled.

Good Lord. Her hairline prickled with sweat, but Quinn worked on, undisturbed. Encouraged by his complete lack of attention, Lori turned back to the desk and began picking files up.

When she lifted the third one, the file beneath it stopped her heart for a startling moment. *Anton/ Bliss,* the tab read, *Project 29-10.* Lori pulled it out and spread the file open.

Inside was a sketch of a gorgeous house fronted with a huge, two-story porch. The supports of the porch were polished pine logs, thick enough to be whole tree trunks. The house sat amidst mature aspens and lush grass. At the very bottom of the paper, a ribbon of water edged onto the idyllic scene.

Her father's *river?* Maybe. But she couldn't possibly be so lucky.

She flipped the sketch over to see the pictures beneath, but aside from one set of floor plans, the other papers were only notes. Numbers and abbreviations that she couldn't decipher. Finally, the last page was an email from Anton/Bliss discussing a proposal for a *riverfront* collection of homes.

"What are you looking at?" Quinn's voice fell on her like a ton of bricks.

Lori gulped so hard that she choked on the air.

"Hey," he said, his voice drawing closer. "Are you okay?"

She dropped the file and spun around. "I'm fine!"

His raised eyebrows slowly lowered. So did his eyes. "Good. You certainly look great."

"Um. Thank you."

"You look...*tousled.*"

Well, she wasn't worried about being embarrassed anymore, but she did raise a self-conscious hand to her hair. Quinn shifted closer and sneaked his arms around her waist. His kiss was a welcome relief. A deep, knee-weakening welcome relief. By the time he ended it, Lori was sitting on the files she'd been pillaging before.

Quinn eased back a bit, his thumb idly stroking the small of her back. "How long have you been up here?"

Oh, jeez. "Ah. You know. Just a minute."

"Huh. I bet it was longer than that."

Frozen, she tried to think of an excuse for what she'd been doing.

But Quinn surprised her. "I'm sorry. I didn't mean to ignore you."

"I... Uh..."

"I'm just kind of an ass sometimes."

He didn't suspect a thing. Lori shook her head and grinned in mad relief. "You can't ignore someone if you don't even know they're there."

"Damn." He winced and let her go. "You're right. It's really bad. I'm so sorry. Will you forgive me if I make you breakfast?"

"Quinn, you were working. It's no big deal. What are you doing, anyway?"

He shot a frustrated look at the drafting table. "I'm working on the house. What else?"

"*Your* house? Can I see it?"

"Really? I wouldn't advise letting me talk about it. An hour from now you'll be begging me to stop."

Electricity arched between them at his words. Their eyes locked. And then Quinn grinned.

"Come on. I've got you at my mercy again. I might even tie you to my office chair and make you beg me for more detailed descriptions."

Lori rolled her eyes and headed for the drafting table, trying to pretend she wasn't blushing.

"Wait!" He jumped in front of her and held up a hand. "Let me get it ready. Just a sec." After opening a few storage tubes and laying out the huge pieces of paper within, Quinn nodded and motioned her forward.

She tried not to smile at the nervous way he crossed his arms, but she couldn't help it. Still, the smile fell away when she rounded the table and got a look at the full-color drawing before her.

His home was gorgeous. Of course it was. But it wasn't what she'd expected. She'd thought he must be building a lodge-style home, framed with polished pine logs and hewn timbers. But this structure looked less like a mountain lodge and more like a mining office.

The wood plank walls glinted silver with age, as if the house had already survived a hundred years of winter. The steep roof was corrugated metal, the foundation and chimneys jagged rock. In the middle of the tall, narrow wing of the main part of the house, three huge square windows were stacked up to the roofline, creating what looked to be a full thirty feet of glass.

"Wow," Lori breathed.

His head turned toward her, then back to the table. "This is reclaimed wood," he said, touching the thin vertical planks of the walls. "The roof is steel, and photovoltaic sheets will be laminated to the south-facing rooflines. Flexible solar panels," he explained, before she could ask.

"It'll use radiant heat, of course. You wouldn't believe the advances made in solar power these days. There's a great new system that runs heated glycol through deep sand beds, and that will be bolstered by a geothermal system."

"Mmm-hmm."

Quinn peeled back the top sheet, and Lori sucked in a deep breath at the sight of the other side of the house. *"Wow."*

A rear wing jutted out from the back of the house like an off-kilter T. The farthest edge seemed to disappear into a cliff wall or at least lean against it for support. This side of the house consisted almost entirely of windows.

"It's amazing, Quinn."

"Do you like it?"

"Don't be stupid. Of course I like it. It's beautiful."

"Would you like a tour?"

She blinked, then turned toward Quinn to find him waiting with a little boy's smile, tentative and excited at the same time. "A tour?"

The smile bloomed into full-out delight. "Yeah. Come on." He grabbed her hand and tugged her toward the desk chair.

"Wait! I'm happy to listen. You don't have to tie me up."

"I won't. Not yet." He sat her in the chair, spun her toward the computer and tapped a few keys.

"What is this?"

"A drafting program." The computer whirred for a few moments before Quinn's home popped to life on the screen. It looked even more impressive from the angle of someone standing on the front drive. Quinn showed her how to direct the view, and soon Lori was walking toward the front door.

"Wow," she said again as she moved inside the house and spun the view around. "Wow." She barely had time to take in the antique wood struts of the two-story ceiling before Quinn pointed toward the kitchen, urging her on. The kitchen was dark, distressed wood and copper accents, lit by tall windows set above the cabinetry. She wanted to linger there, pretend she was resting her weight against the countertop while Quinn made her breakfast. But he waved her forward.

"Is this a tour or a race?" she complained, but Quinn pointed to the large room beyond the kitchen. She glided forward obediently. And then she saw what he wanted her to see.

The living room. Or maybe the office if the desk and tall bookshelves were any indication. She didn't really care, because all she could see was the glass wall that looked out over the view beyond. Hundreds of square feet of mountains and trees and sky. It was gorgeous on the computer. It would be breathtaking in real life.

After staring at the computer-generated view for a few minutes, Lori noticed something odd. The long glass didn't stop at the far wall, because there was no wall. There was only rock. The house really did disappear into the mountain, or rather, the mountain was part of the house.

"How did you *do* that?" she whispered.

"It's dry rock," he said. "Meaning it's not wet. When I found this land, I knew immediately what I wanted to do with this house, but I had to wait until the next spring to be sure it was feasible. I couldn't have snowmelt dripping into my house three months of the year."

"Does the glass go into the rock?"

"No, it's just hand-shaped to fit the contours perfectly. And caulked, of course. The beam above it does go deep into the rock for support."

"Amazing. It feels like you're outside."

"Yeah." She could hear the grin in his voice. "Here." He pointed toward the kitchen door, but Lori pushed his hand away.

"You're worse than a first grader. Let me relax and look around!"

"Okay. Sorry." He tried to look abashed, but failed. "I'll let you look." Backing away, he jerked his thumb toward the drafting table. "I'll be over here. Take your time."

"Thanks."

"Let me know if you have any questions."

"Got it." She clicked the mouse and retraced her previous steps so she could start at the beginning again.

"Don't forget to go out the back door."

"All right already! Jeez." But she was smiling as she complained, enjoying his pride and pleasure. Quinn was like a boy with his first crush. How amazing it must feel to be so skilled. To create a work of art and know your own worth as you did it.

Her eyes blurred with tears as she stared at the dream Quinn had created for himself. Summer fling or not, he'd been her friend first, and she was proud of what he'd done.

A half an hour later, she pushed the chair back from the desk and sighed. "It's amazing."

"Thank you," Quinn said so quickly that she doubted he'd been working at all.

"I've never seen anything like it. Not that I've seen a lot of custom-built, multimillion-dollar estates." She heard him set down a pencil.

"I'm not that rich, you know."

Arching an eyebrow, Lori spun the chair around to give him her best look of sardonic doubt. "Uh-huh."

"Seriously."

"Is this about that argument we had yesterday?"

"Not really. I just don't want you to think I'm one of those guys. All of my money is tied up in this land. The building is taking so long because I'm trading for labor."

"You're what?"

"I'm bartering. Designing houses for the contractors and foremen in exchange for a steep discount. The suppliers are a bit more complicated, but I'm working on them. And some of the work I'll do myself, of course."

"Still…you're not exactly struggling."

He shrugged, leaning a little farther into his stool. "I was lucky. I interned with an amazing architect. He took me under his wing, and when he retired, he urged a lot of influential people to give me a chance. I wouldn't be even half as established now if it hadn't been for Walter McInnis."

Lori darted a glance at the mess of files on the desk and wondered if she should risk it. But she had nothing else to go on, so there was little choice. "McInnis hooked you up with people like Peter Anton?"

"Exactly. Those kinds of developments were my bread and butter the first couple of years. Now I can be a bit more choosy."

"But I see you're working on something for them now." She inclined her head toward the desk, and

Quinn frowned. Her heart rate kicked up to panic mode when he said nothing. "Ah, I saw a drawing of a house."

"Oh, right. That's just a proposal. Some hush-hush deal that hasn't gone through yet. They wanted to get it on my radar because they're planning a big campaign as soon as it's official, I guess."

Lori felt her eyelids flutter. A riverfront deal that hadn't gone through yet? This could be her land. But it made no sense. It was Tumble Creek. Who the hell would buy a multimillion-dollar home they could access for only a few months a year? Sure, they could get up there during the winter, but all their rich friends would be on the other side of the mountain, so what was the point?

"Did you like the house or something?"

Lori stopped biting her lip and tried to look like someone who wasn't thinking of stealing her lover's top secret paperwork. "Sure. It was nice. I'm just trying to think of what river it could be. The Roaring Fork is surrounded by federal land in most places."

He shrugged. "Must be one of its tributaries. God knows these developers wouldn't hesitate to call a stream a river if it meant more sales."

"You don't know where it is?"

"It's not official, so I couldn't very well go and walk it anyway. And neither could they. They only gave me some general ideas to work with." His mouth twitched down a little. "Why? What's up?"

"Nothing," she said too loudly.

"I hope this doesn't have anything to do with Peter

looking at your ass last night. Because I like your ass, too, if that's what you want to hear."

She grinned on a rush of relief. "That's all I needed. Thanks."

His smile didn't match hers. He didn't look relieved at all. "Lori…" he said, a sort of a question in his voice that faded away before he could ask it.

Crap. He must suspect she was up to something. She tried very hard not to look at the file. What kind of a girl planned on stealing something from a man she was sleeping with, anyway?

He met her eyes briefly before his gaze drifted to the ground.

Maybe *he* had something to hide. Maybe he was sleeping with her just so he could get access to the exact dimensions of her property! Bastard!

"Lori," he started again. "I've been thinking."

"Oh?"

"Last night was…"

She blinked, trying to keep her eyes in her head despite the abrupt subject change. She'd been worrying about the wrong thing. "Yeah?" she croaked. Last night was *what?* Amazing? Scary? The kind of freak show he never thought he'd get himself involved in?

A change of subject had seemed ideal, yet now Lori thought longingly of the top secret real estate minefield she'd been tiptoeing through.

"Last night was fun. More than fun."

"Um… Thanks."

His eyes rose to meet hers. "It's all been more than fun."

"Thank you. Again." Premonition made her skin tighten with anxiety. "And I agree. This has been great. You've been great. Definitely."

He narrowed his eyes at her as if he were trying to figure something out. Her face flushed and the heat seeped inside her, leaching deep into her body.

She said, "Anyway," about to break for the door and make her escape, but Quinn interrupted her flight.

"I think we should give this a chance."

The words fell into the room like a rock. A heavy rock that might break something if it kept rolling toward Lori. She took a step back and shook her head. "What?"

"We should give this a chance. Us, I mean."

"Um…"

"It doesn't have to be a summer fling. It could be more. A lot more."

The rock rolled solidly onto her chest and sat there, defying the laws of gravity. Molly had been right. Quinn's temper had been a very bad sign.

She said, "No," just because that's all she could get out.

"Come on. We're great together. We've known each other since you could walk. The sex is amazing." His smile screamed nervousness. "And we're friends."

"This is…" She swallowed against something solid lodged in her throat. "I don't know what you're talking about. This can't be anything more."

"Why?"

"Um…because I won't see you for at least six months while the pass is closed?"

Quinn shrugged as if that was nothing. "Plenty of people have long-distance relationships."

"Yeah, in college. And those usually work out so well."

"Lori, we're not in college. We're adults. There's no reason we couldn't make it work. We could make an effort to see each other every few weeks, at least."

She stood up too fast and had to put a hand on the desk to steady herself. "No, that's *not* what this is. I made that clear to you. You volunteered to have a purely sexual relationship with me. I can't handle anything more. My life is a complete mess."

"So? This doesn't have to be a messy part of it."

"'So?' That's it? That's your response?"

"Yeah, that's it. I'm not asking you to marry me, Lori. I just want to keep seeing you."

Okay. Okay, maybe her panic was a bit of an over-reaction. Quinn was right. He wasn't asking to marry her. He hadn't even mentioned love. So why was her heart throwing a tantrum in her chest, screaming for her to run, run, run?

"Let's not argue, all right?" Quinn said softly, any sign of a smile long gone from his face. "I didn't mean this to be some grand declaration. Just think about it. That's all. No big deal."

What kind of a person was she that she just wanted to shout "No!" and stomp from the room? He was being reasonable, though he *had* gone back on the whole premise for this relationship. In the end she only nodded and tried to ignore the rabid butterflies dive-bombing her stomach.

Quinn wasn't in love with her. He hadn't said that at all. The man just wanted to draw out his encounter with a kink-obsessed, no-strings-attached lover. What guy *wouldn't* want that?

When Quinn mentioned breakfast again, Lori jumped on the chance to leave this horrible subject behind.

Everything was going to be just fine. The meaningless, mind-blowing sex would continue, and no one would get hurt.

No harm, no foul.

Lori pulled into her deserted lot with a sigh of relief. It was only seven in the morning, and she was stuffed full of pancakes, physically exhausted and still reeling from the emotional roller coaster of being Quinn Jennings's lover. Regardless of those tense minutes in his office, they'd managed to get in a few more orgasms before they'd made it to the kitchen. A much better way to change the subject, and she'd been sure to convey her gratefulness to Quinn.

But all in all, she was glad she'd escaped without more deep talk. She couldn't handle sincerity right now. She just couldn't. And she'd cut off any chance of that on her way out of his house by sprinting upstairs to steal the Anton/Bliss file. She couldn't possibly have deep feelings for a man if she was willing to steal from him, right? And Quinn would never love her if he found out about it. Not only was the file a good clue, it was also an insurance policy against an unwelcome complication.

The stolen item in her hand reminded her of just how screwed up her life was, so Lori gave more than a passing look to the yard of the garage as she headed for her front door. Everything looked fine. No further destruction had befallen the property during her night away.

She unlocked the door and pushed it open, trying to ignore the sadness of the room that greeted her. It was almost noon, but her house was dark and silent. No family or friends inside. No cheerful kitchen or bright garden awaiting her attention. Just her sad, brown couch sitting on her sad, brown carpet. Hell, even her walls were looking slightly muddy.

A redecoration was long overdue. First, she'd waited because it was her father's home. Regardless of whether he'd be conscious of it or not, it would have been wrong to change his home around him, even if she'd had the time or money to do so.

And now that he was gone, why hadn't she changed anything?

Lori set down her purse with a sigh. She still didn't have any money, but that wasn't truly the reason. She could paint, at least. Put away the bowling trophies and buy a damn slipcover for that horrendous couch. But she didn't. Because sprucing this place up was a clear admission that she meant to stay. Making her father's house into her own would be a declaration: this is my place in this world. This town, this house, this work is mine.

And though she was afraid to leave—even though she *couldn't* leave—neither could she take the steps that would mean staying.

Like redecorating. Settling down. Falling in love.

Her life was in permanent limbo.

"God, I am a grade A loser," Lori muttered, kicking off her heels. But she was a loser who'd had her world rocked the night before, and that was something.

Her cell was almost out of power, so Lori headed straight for the kitchen to plug it in, wrinkling her nose a bit at the heavy tinge of oil in the air. Another strike against her home design skills. Motor oil probably wasn't nearly as popular a scent as vanilla or lavender. Still, if she bought some nice candles, there was the danger the whole place would blow. Even if the petroleum fumes didn't catch fire, the ancient layers of dust might.

When she drew a deep breath, meaning to heave a loud, pitiful sigh, fumes stung her nose. "What the…" That was definitely *not* normal. Even she wouldn't live in a house that smelled like a working refinery. Lori dropped her phone on the counter and yanked open the door to the garage office.

Thick air cascaded over her, making her cough, but the source wasn't the office. Everything looked in place and normal. She rushed for the next door, her mind perfectly blank. The blankness stayed when she opened the door. Nothing registered. She took one step down and stopped.

Swirls of gold and black twisted across the floor

of the garage, deepening to dark brown sludge near the drain. She stared for a long time before she realized that the swirls were actually liquid. Oil. One of her oil barrels had sprung a leak.

"Oh, no," she moaned. Despair traveled up her chest and spun through her head as she looked over the damage. The horror slowed down the workings of her brain, so it took her a moment to process what her eyes told her. In fact, she was staring at an overturned barrel for quite a long time before her mind signaled alarm.

It wasn't a leak at all. Her gaze skipped from left to right, feeding her more information. Not just one overturned barrel, but three. Both of the most popular weights of motor oil, plus the barrel that stored the used oil for recycling. All of them had been unplugged and dumped. Her gaze kept moving, touching on various things. The clogged drain, the cover of the work pit, the workings of the air-pressure system, now two inches deep in oil. How was she supposed to clean this up? How was she supposed to fix this?

She took another step down, then stopped herself. The phone. Her boots. When she turned, her legs protested the weight, trembling beneath her, but she could hardly feel it. And it didn't matter. Shaky or not, they worked, and soon enough, she'd pulled on her unlaced boots and grabbed the phone.

"I need to report an act of vandalism," she said to the dispatcher. She gave the details she thought necessary, then hung up. Her jaw hurt, her throat burned, and further talking was simply out of the question.

She needed to get fresh air in here, and there seemed to be a relatively dry path around the far edge of the room. As her phone rang in her hand, Lori stepped down and picked her way toward the cabinets on the far wall. She was almost there, just passing the damaged air-pressure system, when she got careless. She put her foot down too casually, didn't balance it just right, and began to slide. Suddenly, her legs were in front of her.

Lori reached out, trying to catch herself as she went down, but instead she punched the bolted edge of the air tank. Her hand exploded in pain and she kept falling. A deep, fleshy thunk filled her head just before the world went cool and black and liquid around her.

"LORI? LORI! DAMN IT, FRANK, be careful. I don't need you hurt, too. Lori, can you hear me?"

Lori ignored Ben's voice and concentrated on trying not to throw up. Her head was rolling. Then again, her body was moving pretty uncertainly, too. She felt whoever was carrying her slide in slow motion, then catch himself before falling. Though she thought about being worried, she couldn't summon the will.

Eventually, the world steadied around her. Heat soaked into her back and she felt concrete against her skin. Her front sidewalk, all warm and cozy in the afternoon sun, just like it had been after she'd run through the sprinkler as a little girl. She was sighing with pleasure when a hand gripped hers and set bone scraping against bone.

"Ah!" she screamed. "Fuck!" The words hurt her head, and Lori was suddenly furious. "Let go!"

"Lori," Ben's voice murmured, warm with relief. "Thank God. What happened?"

"My hand," she groaned, and the fingers let her go.

"I'm sorry. I didn't realize. The ambulance should be here any minute."

"Don't need an ambulance."

"Quiet."

An extraordinarily annoying mosquito began to buzz in her ear. She tried to brush at it before it got louder and turned into a siren. Too many people surrounded her. Something cold slid under the neckline of her dress. A metallic snick rang in her ears.

"What the hell?" she cursed, struggling to sit up.

"Lori," Ben Lawsons's voice cut in. "They need to get the dress off you or the oil could hurt your skin."

She looked down at herself, at the strange sight of her new dress paired with steel-toed boots, like a candid peek into her recent life. But now her beautiful blue dress was soaked with grease and cut at the neckline and even the boots looked ruined.

"Fine. Just get me a blanket, would you?"

The paramedics handed her a blanket and Ben moved away to talk on the phone. Her blood pressure was measured, her neck braced, her hand splinted. More lights flashed as she lay staring at the overhang of her house. These lights weren't like the others. They were orange.

"Who's that?" she asked no one, not expecting a reply, but Ben answered from somewhere behind her.

"It's the county. They're calling up the EPA to monitor the spill."

"Oh, son of a bitch. This is just great."

"Can you tell me what happened before they cart you off to the hospital?"

She gave him the short version. Heck, there wasn't much to tell.

"Were you at Quinn's all night?"

Her neck didn't budge when she tried to nod. "Yeah."

And then Molly was there, crying and holding Lori's unbroken hand, and it was such a relief to watch someone cry for her that Lori felt better even though her head was pounding. "Hey, Moll," she murmured. "Say something funny."

Molly shook her head, but relented in the same moment. "Don't go toward the light," she sobbed.

Even Lori herself couldn't believe it when she managed a laugh. "Deal. I'll tell my dad to go take a flying leap if I see him beckoning."

With a loud, wet sniff, Molly nodded. "Okay. Good." She flipped open her phone, but kept a hold on Lori with her free hand. "I'll call Quinn."

"No! Why?"

"He should be here."

"He should not. He's not my boyfriend. And anyway, he's on his way out of town today."

Molly just looked at her, phone still menacingly open.

"Do. Not. Call. Quinn." Lori ground out.

"He'll be furious if I don't."

Lori played her best card. "You're making my head hurt with this shit!" She didn't have to call tears to her eyes; they were already there, waiting.

"Oh, God," Molly gasped. "Don't cry. I'm sorry. I won't call him." She closed the phone and put it away.

Good.

Lori wanted him here. Wanted to lean on him and let him take care of her. But after that conversation this morning, leaning on Quinn wasn't an option. That kind of thing led to crying and cuddling and quiet moments and deep talks. That kind of thing led to love. And if she'd thought her life was screwed up this morning... Well, this afternoon it was completely in the ditch, engulfed in flames. There was no room for company.

CHAPTER FOURTEEN

THE FLIGHT ATTENDANT'S mouth was moving. "Have a nice day," she might be saying. Or "Thank you for flying with us." Whatever it was, Quinn couldn't hear it past the rush of hot blood pounding against his ears. He could only respond to her by politely aiming his glare in another direction.

After Vancouver, the Colorado air felt thin against his skin as he descended the narrow steps to the tarmac. Too thin to cool him down. When he'd called Ben and accidentally stumbled onto the news of Lori's accident, his only emotion had been fear. Once Ben had assured him that Lori was out of danger and everything was fine, his stark fear had been replaced with worry for Lori and hurt that she hadn't called him.

But throughout the afternoon as he'd tried in vain to arrange an earlier flight home, as he'd left message after message for Lori, as he'd slowly worked his way across the continent from Vancouver to Denver and Denver to Aspen, anger had built inside him. It seemed that getting closer to Tumble Creek was like drawing closer to a red-hot grill. From a distance it looked like nothing...no flames, little smoke. But a closer view revealed waves of shimmering air over the glowing coals. Closer still and you stumbled onto the sudden danger of a blast of superheated air singeing all the hair off your body. Quinn wouldn't have been surprised to look into a mirror and find that his eyebrows had vanished in the heat of his own fury.

Thanks to the small proportions of the Aspen airport, Quinn was in his car and headed closer to the source of his anger within a few minutes. Twenty more minutes—most of which he couldn't recall later—and Quinn's tires were throwing up gravel in the lot of Love's Garage. The sun glinted like flames off of the windshields of the parked vehicles as he slammed out of his car and headed for Lori's house.

He wasn't the only one angry with her, apparently. As he approached, he could hear the sound of shouting from within.

"But what the hell were you thinking, trying to walk through that mess?" a man's voice boomed, the words carrying easily through an open window in the living room.

Lori's reply was too soft to hear.

"You could have killed yourself."

Whatever she said, it was dismissive.

"Damn it, just sell that land and get out already. I don't even care if it's me anymore, just get the best price you can and get out of here."

Frowning even harder now, Quinn banged on the door. The voices froze. When the door opened, it was Lori's mechanic, Joe, holding the knob. "Hey," he said. After a glance back at the couch, Joe shook his head and brushed past Quinn. "I'll see ya tomorrow."

Quinn just stood there in the open door, staring over the back of the couch at the top of Lori's head. She must know it was him. He'd left enough messages letting her know he was on the way.

More than twenty-four hours had passed since her accident. More than twenty-four hours and she hadn't called. Hell, he'd still been in town when she'd been hurt.

Quinn closed the door softly, his hand shaking. "Are you all right?" he asked first.

Her head nodded.

"They kept you overnight at the hospital?"

"Just for observation," Lori muttered.

Circling the couch, he finally got a look at her. Eyes swollen and skin pale, she cradled her hand, encased in a bright white cast, against her chest. Some of his anger wanted to crumble like sand. Quinn tried to shore it up.

"What the hell is going on, Lori?" When she shrugged, his anger stopped crumbling and solidified to concrete. "I missed you today," he growled. "I missed you and you wouldn't answer my calls, and I wanted to feel some connection, so I called Ben just to fish for news about you. I wasn't expecting to hear that you were in the hospital."

She stared at her lap.

"I wanted to feel a *connection*. How fucking stupid was that?"

"I'm sorry," she whispered, "but it's not your business."

Despite her brutal words, he was overwhelmed with the sudden urge to touch her. Still furious, he laid a gentle hand against the side of her face to assure himself that she was fine. "Lori. I can't believe someone hurt you."

"It was my fault. An accident."

"But somebody *did* this. More than once, according to Ben. Why?"

"I don't know."

He gritted his teeth. "You don't know? Or you don't care to tell me?"

Her face finally tilted up and her dull eyes met his. She very pointedly said nothing.

Quinn latched on to what he'd overheard. "Does this have something to do with your property?"

The skin around her eyes tightened almost imperceptibly. "Why don't you ask some of your developer friends about that?"

That seemed such an inexplicable shift of topic, Quinn felt momentarily dizzy. "Why would my developer friends be interested in Love's Garage? Not that it's not...special."

"Never mind. There's no way to tell who's done this. It's just vandalism, just kids, probably. I was stupid enough to get myself injured. Nobody hurt me."

"This isn't just vandalism—"

"It is. Ask Ben. Hell, it could be some kid I turned in for drunk driving after an accident. Who knows?"

Muscles burning, Quinn began to pace the short

length of her living room. The sight of the ugly moss
rock hearth made him madder still. "You're in danger. Regardless of how you feel about me and my
inconvenient interest in your life, I'm staying here."

"No, you're not."

"I'm not going to leave you alone."

"Yes, you are."

Quinn spun around and glared at Lori. "What the
hell is wrong with you? We've been friends for years.
You need help. Let me help you. Don't tell me a damn
thing if that's the way you want it, but let me stay."

She reached out slowly for the chenille throw and
wrapped it around her body, the cast making the
movements awkward. Nearly a full minute passed
while she tucked it beneath her legs and fiddled with
the edges. She didn't look at him when she spoke.

"My garage is ruined. It's going to cost thousands
of dollars to get it back in working order. My septic
tank is full of oil. Some of the oil leaked out into the
gravel, so I have to pay the EPA to monitor my soil
and test my well for the next couple of years.

"The insurance company finds the whole thing
'suspicious,' so God only knows how long they'll take
to pay whatever they're willing to pay. And I've got
to find some way to get everything up and running,
or I can't pay my workers. I'll lose the trucks. I'll…"

He took a step toward her, but she shook her head.

"I just want to be alone, okay? I can't *do* this right
now, Quinn. I can't do anything right now, so please
go away and leave me alone."

His anger tumbled into alarm. She was serious.

She'd rather be alone and in danger than with him. "Please let me stay. Or at least go sleep at Molly's. Just don't stay here by yourself, damn it. *Please*."

Her good hand emerged from the cocoon of the blanket and rubbed at her eyes. She seemed to consider his perfectly reasonable request for a long while.

"Fine," she muttered, and the beast clawing through his chest paused to listen. "You can sleep on the couch." Without a glance in his direction, Lori lurched to her feet and swiped a prescription bottle off the coffee table. "I'm going to bed. My hand hurts."

She shuffled away.

"Hey," he called, "have you eaten anything today?"

Her only answer was the slamming of the bedroom door. Pitifully, this did nothing to ruin his relief. He could stay. He could watch over a woman who didn't want him around and find out what the hell was going on.

After grabbing Lori's keys off the table, Quinn headed for the front door. He'd take a quick look around the grounds, grab his overnight bag from the car, and then he'd call Ben and threaten a law enforcement officer with physical injury in an attempt to get more information.

But instead of hunting down the creep who'd been harassing Lori, Quinn stepped onto the sidewalk and ran straight into his turncoat sister.

Molly grabbed his arm. "How is she doing?"

"She's fine. She doesn't want to see anyone."

"You're not leaving her alone, are you?"

"No, I'm not leaving her alone! And you'd damn

well better start apologizing or there's a good possibility I'll never speak to you again."

Molly crossed her arms. "She asked me not to call you. What was I supposed to do?"

His throat burned with remembered panic. "Call me."

"I wanted to, Quinn. I swear I wanted to. But she said you were on your way out of town and… Well, you're not really her boyfriend, are you?"

"Yeah, thanks. I've heard that a little too often in the past few days. I'm just an emotionless sex worker. I get the message."

"I'm sorry!" She reached for his arm again, but Quinn shook her off.

"If you want to make it up to me, send your boyfriend over here. I want to know what the hell is really going on."

Molly, regret seemingly forgotten, rolled her eyes. "He's not going to reveal any 'official police business,' not even to you."

"We'll see."

"Ooo, tough guy," she muttered, then quickstepped backward when she caught his glare. "Fine, I'll send Ben over. Tell Lori I'll come by later."

Quinn nodded, but he was already heading toward the back. The police couldn't be here all the time, and Lori Love needed his protection, whether she wanted it or not.

A FULL TEN HOURS after she'd fallen asleep, Lori woke up, still groggy. Her heart had traveled to her broken hand while she was unconscious, and it beat there, larger and stronger than it had been when it lived in her chest.

Reaching blindly for the bottle of pills she'd set on her bedside table, Lori fumbled until her fingers closed around it. "Thank God," she breathed, gripping it so tightly that it bent inward. She was still chasing the pill down with water when the phone rang. Not her cell phone. That had been ruined in the oil. She grabbed the cordless phone from its base with an infuriated growl.

"Yeah?"

"Lori Love?" a woman's voice asked in a very professional tone. A lawyer who'd heard rumors of a workplace accident, perhaps?

"Yeah."

"Lori, are you all right? Mr. Jennings said you'd been injured in an accident."

"Oh, hey, Jane. I'm okay. I broke my hand, but I'm fine." She lay back down on the bed to wait for the painkiller to kick in. She'd timed it at seventeen minutes the night before. Amazing that only two bones had fractured; it felt more like twenty.

Jane was saying something, but Lori had zoned out. "I'm sorry, Jane, what did you say?"

"I said maybe I should call you back tomorrow."

"No, I'm good. I haven't had any coffee, but I should be okay."

"All right, well, I wanted to tell you that I remembered what I'd overheard. About highway nineteen?"

Lori's eyes blinked open. "Seriously?"

"It's not much, but… Have you ever met Harry Bliss?"

"He actually goes by *Harry* Bliss?"

Jane snorted. "Yeah. Anyway, maybe because of his name, he's a bit of a blowhard. He talks too loud and likes to look important. He's always on his cell phone. A couple of months ago, he was in the office waiting for Mr. Jennings to show up for a meeting and he got a phone call. If Mr. Bliss doesn't want people to eavesdrop, he shouldn't leave the volume turned up to walkie-talkie levels."

Lori nodded, as if that would encourage Jane.

It seemed to work. Jane took a deep breath and her voice lowered considerably. "The man on the other end said 'the committee is open to the reclassification of highway nineteen.' Do you know what that means?"

"Reclassification?" Lori frowned. "No."

"Well, Mr. Bliss said if it happened, it would probably happen in December, and they'd have to move before then or too many people would know. He specifically said, 'Every Tom, Dick and Harry will have their finger in the pie.'"

"The pie?" This didn't give her any more info at all. "Did they say anything more about this reclassification?"

"No, that was it. I'm sorry. I was hoping it would mean something to you."

Lori threw her good arm over her eyes. "I don't think it does. But it's a good starting point. Thank you so much."

"You're welcome. I hope it helps with…whatever it is you're doing."

Despite her pain, Lori managed a smile. "I promise to fill you in as soon as I figure it all out. Deal?"

"Deal."

She hung up and took a deep breath against the pain.

Okay. Things were urgent now. She couldn't screw around any longer.

Lori had never thought of her debt as a mountain, the way they showed it in those debt-relief commercials. Mountains were majestic and gorgeous. Deadly, yes, but chilling in their beauty. No, her debt was a mine shaft sinking her deeper and deeper beneath the rocky spine of the world. Every day that passed, the interest dripped, wearing away the stone like water. Every week brought new explosions that dropped her another hundred feet. And the gravity was so heavy down here, pressing her into something small and hard. She just couldn't handle it anymore.

Despite that the pain meds hadn't quite kicked in, Lori forced herself from bed. She ran a bath because she couldn't get her cast wet, but she didn't spend any time soaking. Instead she simply washed up, pulled on her capri pants and a tank top and headed out.

The sight of Quinn asleep on her couch stopped her dead in her tracks. Somehow she'd lost track of that confrontation during the night, and she'd lost her will to fight him, as well. Perhaps because he looked vulnerable and sweet with his feet hanging off the end of the sofa and his arm stretched wide toward the coffee table. He just looked like Quinn, and not some threat to her heart.

He must have been up half the night if he was still sleeping so hard, so Lori tiptoed past to grab her keys and get out. She might not know anything about a re-classification of the highway, but she now had just enough information to find out. And not a moment too soon. Whether or not Ben solved the mystery of what had happened to her dad, she had to sell that land. There was no longer any choice. Any sentimentality she'd had left had drowned in that pool of oil in her garage.

The drive to Aspen struck her as particularly beautiful today. Maybe because the painkillers had kicked in, maybe because she'd spent too many hours in bed. Regardless, she felt strangely peaceful as she pulled up to the three-story office building and let herself in. There was no security guard or receptionist, just a board listing the names of the occupants. Lori found the one she wanted and headed for the second floor.

When she opened the door to Chris Tipton's office, her peace burned away in the furnace blast of shock. Un-fucking-believable.

"Yes?" the skinny blonde asked in a dismissive tone.

Tessa, Lori thought. *Tessa Smith,* otherwise known as Dream-Whore Barbie. The woman raised perfectly waxed eyebrows as Lori continued to stare.

"Uh, sorry," Lori stammered, then shook it off. Tessa Smith and her very round breasts had nothing to do with her today. "I need to see Chris Tipton, please."

"*Christopher* Tipton isn't available at the moment, but I'd be happy to deliver a message."

Christopher, she scoffed inside her head, but only offered a polite smile. "Is Christopher in? I'm certain he'd be interested in talking with me if he is."

Her eyebrows rose even higher, her shiny mouth turned down. "Mr. Tipton is in a meeting."

"Just pull him out and tell him Lori Love wants to talk, all right? It's important." If she'd been hoping to see a flash of jealous horror on the woman's face, she'd hoped in vain. Of course Tessa Smith had never heard of Lori. Mechanics didn't often make it to the society page, and Tessa didn't look like the type to read the *Tumble Creek Tribune.*

Tessa didn't even seem particularly put out by the request. "Well, give me a minute then. I'll see what he says." When she stood, she towered over Lori. The heels she was wearing pushed her nearly to six feet. Were they all that tall?

Whatever jealousy Lori might have been feeling turned into something more like pain. This was Aspen, where even receptionists looked like models. Where women still wore mink coats and men owned private jets. Quinn fit in here. He was an artist commissioned by royalty. But this was no place for her, even if she could get up the courage to fall for Quinn.

Tessa Smith reappeared from the hallway she'd stepped into, a welcoming smile pasted on her face.

"Mr. Tipton will be out in just a moment. Please have a seat."

But before Lori even had a chance to look around for a chair, Chris came striding around the corner. "Lori Love!" he called.

"Chris," she answered, just to let him know that he might be wearing an expensive suit and calling himself "Christopher," but she remembered that he used to French-kiss his own fist in sixth grade. When he pulled her into a hug, she remembered the time he'd kissed *her* in seventh grade. He hadn't worn such nice cologne back then.

"Come on into my office. Tessa, would you bring in some mineral water for Ms. Love?"

"I'm fine, thanks," she protested.

He was handsome in a used-car-salesman kind of way. Too smooth for her taste, but when he put his hand on her lower back and walked her toward his office, she didn't protest. If he wanted her charmed, she'd act charmed.

"What happened to your arm, Lori?"

"It's my hand, actually." She watched him from the corner of her eye. "There was an accident at my shop."

"Yikes. That sounds ominous."

"This is the worst of it."

He looked guileless as he led her into his office, but used-car salesmen usually did. "So," he said as he took a seat behind his shiny desk. "I'm hoping you're here to talk about your land. Not that I wouldn't welcome a visit otherwise."

"Right. Well, lucky for you, I *am* here to talk about the land."

"Wow. I can't thank you enough for coming to me with this."

"No problem, but you might not be thanking me in a minute."

His smile didn't budge. "Why not?"

"Because I know about the talk of reclassifying highway nineteen."

This time, the smile definitely dropped a notch. "The what?"

Lori crossed her legs and wished she'd thought to wear a dress and heels so she could play the part of high-powered landowner more convincingly. "Come on, Chris. If you want to play games with me, I'll go to Anton/Bliss. They seem pretty serious about getting that lot. Maybe they'll be willing to treat me with respect."

The smile headed down two more notches and became a straight line. "I take this seriously. What do you want?"

"I want a legitimate offer, not the crap I've been handed before." She brushed a piece of imaginary lint off her pant leg. "We both know this reclassification could change everything."

"Jesus. How did you find out about it?"

"How did I find out that you've been trying to cheat me?"

Chris leaned back in his chair, looking a bit deflated as he reached into a desk drawer for a bottle of water. "Look, I wasn't trying to cheat you."

"Yeah, right."

"Give me a break, Lori. There's no guarantee the state will agree to improvements. Winter maintenance alone could approach a million a year. Buying your land is still a huge gamble at this point. It could all fall through."

Winter maintenance? Whoa! "They're going to keep the pass open all year," she breathed, not quite believing it. If they opened the pass, that would change everything, and not just for her.

He stared at her for a long moment, a bit of the color leaving his face. "Goddamn it. I can't believe I just did that. You didn't know, did you? You totally played me."

"I knew something, just not everything. And it's my damn land anyway, so pardon me for screwing you over."

He had the decency to smile at her, even if it did border on a smirk. "Hell, I wasn't going to get the land anyway. Anton/Bliss has a heck of a lot more capital and clout than my firm does. My best hope was that you'd sell to me because I've known you for years."

"Huh. Well, I don't really play by the hearts and unicorns rules of business, so you wouldn't have had much luck there."

His wide smile was back. "It was bound to get out anyway. Too many people know about the rumors already. Offers are being made to other landowners. You got hit first because yours was the best undeveloped lot. Riverfront, totally level, right-of-way access that runs through public land, large enough to be broken up into two dozen lots, if need be."

She nodded, trying to absorb it all.

"Fly-fishing cottages are the new thing for the wealthy. Skiing in the winter. Fishing in the summer. All of it within commuting distance of an airport and five-star restaurants. Of course, these rich guys always overestimate the amount of free time they have. The caretakers spend more time in the house than they do."

Well, the mystery was solved then, but not the right mystery. She couldn't imagine this had anything to do with what had happened to her dad a decade before. "How long has this talk been going around?"

He shrugged. "I heard about it a few months ago, because Peter Anton and I were dating the same woman." Chris winked at her. "She liked me better."

"Congratulations. And since we're being honest here…"

He took a drink and raised his eyebrows for her to continue.

"Do you have any idea who's been trying to intimidate me into selling?"

With a wet cough, he set the water down. "*Intimidate* you? How?"

Lori raised her broken hand.

"Good God, are you kidding me? Somebody did that to you?"

Shrugging in response, she let him believe the worst in the hopes that he would reveal something. But Chris shook his head hard.

"No way. I don't know anyone who'd be involved in that sort of thing. I mean, some of these guys are hard-asses, but there are always other deals to be made. Your land isn't worth that kind of trouble."

"Yeah," she muttered. "I guess not. Thanks, Chris."

"You should talk to the cops," he called as she walked out.

And he was absolutely right. Time to turn this over to Ben completely. The more she found out, the less she could see how any of this had to do with her father's attack. First, there was only a *chance* that the vandalism had anything to do with the pass. And even if it did, the idea that the same proposal had been floated ten years before and inspired someone to hurt her father was even more far-fetched.

The truth was that her father's attack had probably been random. Dark night, cheap bar...not much of a mystery. And her vandal? Hell, it could be any one of the half-dozen people who had outstanding bills with the garage. It could be bored teenagers. It could be that shitty mechanic, James Webster.

For a few days there it had seemed almost a relief that she would be able to lay all her troubles at the feet of some nefarious stranger. Her father's years of suffering, his death, her stagnant, stunted life, even her financial problems. But life was complicated. People were rarely felled by one grand blow of fate, rather they bled out slowly from hundreds of small, careless cuts. Just as she was bleeding now. It was slow and painless enough that you could ignore it for just the amount of time it took to become fatal.

"Bastards," she muttered to no one. She switched off the radio and drove back to Tumble Creek in silence.

"SHE'S HERE," BEN said, relieving the burning worry that had taken over Quinn's body.

"Where?" Quinn barked into the phone.

"She just pulled up to the police station. She's coming in now and looks fine."

"I'll be right there." He snapped his phone shut and walked out the door.

Quinn had spent a full hour going mad. After the night spent talking with Ben, finally getting the truth about what was going on, he'd tossed and turned all night. The little surprise he'd found on the kitchen table hadn't helped his stress. The Anton/Bliss file from his home. And now that he knew about the riverfront land, he understood her strange interest in his business associates. Maybe even her interest in him altogether. After all, this affair hadn't started until after Ben had begun the investigation.

It seemed there was a very good chance that Lori had been using him for more than just sex. For some reason, though it had felt fine to be used for his body, the idea of being used for information hurt like hell.

So he'd had a long night and had been running on very little sleep when he'd awoken to find Lori missing. Well…not "missing" according to Ben and his idiotically strict standards. Ben had maintained that

Lori had simply gotten into her truck and gone somewhere, but Quinn hadn't liked that at all.

What if she was investigating dangerous people?
What if she was disoriented from the blow to her head
and driving aimlessly on back roads? What if she'd
taken too many painkillers and driven into the river?

Quinn had wanted Ben to at least have his men on
the lookout for her as he refused to mount a full-on
search. They'd argued about it, but it hardly mattered
now. Quinn was jogging across Main Street, headed
right past the back of Lori's purple truck.

She was safe. She was alive.

He was going to kill her.

Ben was speaking when Quinn pushed through
the door. "You should not have done that," he told
Lori in a stern voice.

Quinn reached her just as she was shrugging.
"What did you do?" he demanded as he wrapped his
arms around her. "Are you okay?"

"I'm fine!" she protested.

"What happened? Where did you go?"

Lori let him hug her but didn't exactly respond.
"Calm down. Everything's fine. I just went to see
Chris Tipton."

The developer's name brought Quinn's brain back
to reality. "I see." He dropped his arms and stepped
back. "Did you steal any of his files while you were
there?"

Lori's head snapped back as if he'd hit her. Her
mouth worked as if she would speak, but she didn't
say a word. The response triggered a wave of guilt

that tugged at his heart, but Quinn ignored it. "You should have at least hidden it," he muttered.

"I'm sorry. I really am."

"Why didn't you just *tell* me?"

She shrugged and looked at the floor. "I thought maybe you already knew."

Quinn drew in a deep, deep breath, pretty sure he was about to start yelling, but Ben stepped between them, hands up.

"You two can hash this out later. Lori, I need to know what happened with Chris." He jerked his head toward his office and Lori headed for it. She walked away without one glance back.

Quinn hadn't even noticed the other people milling around the station, but there they were, eyeing him as if he were a stranger. And he was now. A stranger in his own hometown, and apparently a stranger to the woman he was sleeping with.

Odd that this casual, meaningless affair was driving a dull stake through his chest. Determined to escape the creeping feeling that his heart was suffering catastrophic damage, Quinn headed for Ben's office.

"It's the pass," Lori was saying as he walked in and closed the door behind him.

Ben glanced up at him, then back to Lori. When she didn't protest Quinn's presence, Ben relaxed back into his chair. "What about the pass?"

"There's talk that it might be maintained through the winter. The state is looking at the numbers."

"What?" Ben's chair screeched when he sat forward. Shock turned his face to stone. "Year-round?"

Quinn leaned hard against the closed door, the logic of it hitting him like a gust of wind.

Ben rubbed his face. "You're kidding me. Right?"

"No. It's nothing definite yet, but there's enough of a chance of it going forward that people are interested in my land."

Shock melting back to anger, Quinn clenched his fists. "So someone is trying to pressure you into selling before anyone finds out that your land is valuable."

"Maybe. I don't know. I talked to Chris Tipton, and I honestly don't think he's involved. He didn't think anyone else would stoop that low, either." She looked over her shoulder. "They're your friends. Do you think Peter Anton or Harry Bliss or one of the other developers would trash my garage?"

Would they? He shrugged. "I don't know, but I'm perfectly willing to beat the truth out of them. At the very least, they tried to fuck you over."

Lori smiled, and the sight of it set off an echo of pleasure inside his chest. He hadn't seen her smile in days. "Thank you," she said. "But I'm ready to give this all over to Ben—"

"Oh, thanks," Ben chimed in sarcastically.

"I can't deal with this anymore. It's too much. I've got to sell that land, and I've got to do it quickly. If you can figure this out, Ben, I'll be free to cash in without worrying I'm selling to a criminal."

He nodded, then quizzed Lori on which developers she'd been looking into, taking the time to chew her out for not keeping him in the loop.

"You checked out James Webster?" Lori asked without enthusiasm.

"Yeah," Ben answered in the same flat tone. "He's got an alibi. I'm still tracking it down, but it's pretty solid."

While Ben was busy writing in his notebook and Quinn was trying to rub the tension from his neck, Lori let her head fall back and stared at the ceiling. "The land deal is obviously not a decade-old issue," she said.

Ben sighed and set down the pen. "No, I don't think so. I'll check it out, just in case, but it seems unlikely. I did track down Hector Dillon, by the way."

The name meant nothing to Quinn, but Lori perked up. "And?"

"He'd moved on to Arizona. He had a record there. But he died two years ago."

"Oh. But you think he could have had something to do with my dad?"

"It's possible. I don't know."

Lori slumped back into the seat. "Ben, I honestly don't think my dad's attack had anything to do with the land. I think it was random."

Did Quinn have the right to kneel down next to her and take her hand? She clearly didn't want him involved in her life in any meaningful way, but he couldn't just let her sit there alone, talking about her dad's skull being bashed in. He pulled the second chair close to her and took her hand in his as he sat. She didn't pull away. In fact, her fingers curled into his as she closed her eyes.

"I don't know," Ben muttered. "It just doesn't feel random to me. Something's off."

Lori shrugged, the gesture weary. "It was the middle of the night at a biker bar. What better place to find trouble?"

Ben said, "Yeah," but the frustration in that word came through loud and clear. He wasn't buying it and there was nothing he could do. Quinn understood, because he felt the exact same way. He'd do anything to help her, but what the hell could he offer? Aside from beating some business associates to a pulp.

"I could wear a wire," he blurted. "I could wear a wire and ask Peter Anton what he knows." His offer raised Ben's eyebrows, but more importantly, it drew another smile from Lori.

"That's sweet," she said, as if he'd offered her a bouquet of flowers.

"Well," Ben murmured dryly, "if it comes to that, I'll keep your offer in mind."

There wasn't much left to discuss. Five minutes later, Lori and Quinn were walking out of the station, awkwardness like another person wedged between them. He got in her truck without asking permission, and they drove the short distance to Lori's house in silence. His shoulders were burning with tension by the time he stepped through her front door, but he bit his tongue and let her go about her business.

Lori checked her messages and went to the bathroom. Then she got a glass of water and took a pain pill before pulling a paper-wrapped package from the freezer and putting it in the fridge to thaw. Quinn just watched, leaning against the back of the couch.

Finally, she rolled her shoulders and turned to face him. "Okay," she said and took a deep breath.

"You thought I might be involved in all this?"

Lori shook her head. A curl fell over her forehead, resting there for only a moment before she pushed it back. "No. I didn't think so, not really. It seemed like a possibility, once I realized you worked with Anton/ Bliss, but I know you're not that kind of person."

"And you?"

"Me?" she finally breathed. "Am I that kind of person?"

His throat tightened as he waited for her answer. Had his body just been a perk? An added little bonus in her quest to solve a mystery? If so, he'd been even more meaningless to her than he'd thought.

"It occurred to me that maybe you'd know something," she said, "but…after we were already dating. Not before. If that…if that makes a difference."

It did. God, it did, but he was too relieved to make his mouth work.

"I'm sorry, Quinn." Lori blinked rapidly. "I felt like I couldn't tell you. But I knew what I was doing was wrong. When I used you to get close to Peter Anton and when I stole that file. I was just desperate…"

"If you'd trusted me and told me about it, I could have found out about the pass long ago."

"Yeah," she murmured. "But those people are part

of your work, Quinn. And your work means everything to you. What we had was just…it was just sex."

What we had, she'd said. Hell, he'd gotten used to the "just sex" part of it, but now it was past tense? Boy, he was inching down the ladder of pride, wasn't he? At first he'd cringed at being dismissed as a sexual machine, and now he was praying she'd use him for a few more days.

"Ben agrees that you shouldn't be alone at least until he's interviewed each of the developers. I'd like to stay. Here. Or you can come to my place."

It wasn't a good sign when Lori looked at the floor. It was an even worse sign when she shook her head. "I think I'll stay with Molly. Everything's too confusing right now."

She was right, of course. It was confusing. He was still pissed at her, and hurt, and now was not the time to talk about the future. And neither of them were in the mood for sexual fantasy. His work here was done, and Lori didn't need him anymore. So why did he feel desperate to stay?

But he hadn't sunk to begging yet. That was something. "All right. I'll help you get your stuff together."

It didn't take long. The garage was already closed up. Lori only packed one bag. It seemed that mere seconds had passed and suddenly Quinn was standing next to the open window of her truck, saying farewell.

"Call me if you need information about anyone," he offered.

Lori nodded.

"Or if you want to talk. About the land or about your dad."

"Okay."

"Be careful. Stay with Molly."

"I will."

He stood there a moment longer, fantasizing once again of rescuing Lori Love. She'd turned out to be a damsel in distress after all, but not the innocent, helpless kind. No, she was a damsel of a different sort. The brave kind who fought and lied and stole and did really dirty things with the knight in shining armor. Just before she sent him on his way with a pat on the back. And that was that.

Quinn stepped back and gave Lori Love a little wave. Her lavender truck pulled out of his life in a cloud of dust.

He'd let her go. But only for a little while.

CHAPTER FIFTEEN

AFTER FIFTEEN MINUTES of washing, Molly had finally reached the bottom of the stack of dishes in her sink. Lori dried the last plate, set it on the rack and wiped sweat from her forehead. "You really need a dishwasher," she complained to Molly.

"I told you, I use paper plates. But apparently you're too fancy for that."

"Yeah," Lori snorted. "That's me. Anyway, it's hard to cook a roast on a paper plate."

"Lori, look at me," Molly ordered. "*Stop cooking.* I've found that's the easiest way to avoid dirtying pots *and* pans. Not to mention utensils. And real silverware." She grabbed a plastic spoon, pulled a carton of ice cream from the freezer, and dug in. "Mmm. It's even more delicious eaten on a spoon you don't have to wash." She licked the spoon clean and dug right back in.

"Remind me not to try the chocolate."

Molly growled, baring her teeth. "It's all mine. Stay away from my precious!"

Laughing, Lori turned back to wiping down the counter. She didn't cook this often at home, but the past three days had been hard for her. She didn't like staying at someone else's house, taking up their space and privacy. She felt Molly deserved some home-cooked meals in exchange, at the very least.

Harry Bliss was out of town and not returning Ben's calls, and Ben insisted she not return home until Bliss showed up. Though she loved spending time with Molly, Lori desperately wanted to be in her space, in her own home. Truthfully, she wanted to lie in bed for a few days and just think. And cry. And eat her very own carton of ice cream.

"I'm going out," she said as she passed Molly and went to slip on her tennis shoes.

"You'd better tell me where, or Ben will have no choice but to spank me. That man is a *hard* taskmaster."

Lori snorted. "Good Lord, you're not even subtle anymore. I don't think you can call it a double entendre if the first entendre's not even there."

"Sorry. This new book I'm reading is super naughty. I'm distracted."

She rolled her eyes and headed out the back door, but Molly cleared her throat.

Lori stopped. "All right." She sighed. "I'm going out to my dad's land. It's all I've been thinking about for weeks, and I haven't set foot on it all summer."

"Okay, but…" Molly's voice sharpened with caution. "Just don't go near it if you see any rich developers hiding in the bushes with nets. They're not hunting deer. They're after you, little girl."

"Yeah, yeah." She let the door close behind her as she muttered, "I'm more worried about bears." Rich developers, after all, didn't like to get mud on their Italian loafers.

As she pulled out of Molly's driveway, Lori rolled down her window and took a deep breath of air. It was cool and a bit humid, strange weather in the mountains. The air was usually bone-dry here, the sun like a brutal heat lamp on summer afternoons. But today clouds strolled languidly across the face of the sun, dulling its power, and the air was cool with moisture. It felt like the spring mornings when she used to go fishing with her dad.

Over the past twenty-four hours, Lori had come to the slow realization that she'd never really mourned her father. He'd died gradually and she'd shifted her expectations over that time. Then one day, finally, he'd been gone, as natural as if he'd faded away in the sun.

Right after his injury there had been shock and sorrow. That had been followed by hope and fear and adjustment and resignation and lots and lots of hard work. There'd been grief, too, both before and after he died, but only when she had time for it. And only when she'd let herself feel it.

She wanted to find a way to be with him now, and grieve his loss.

Despite the rutted dirt road, the ride along the river was soothing. She wouldn't think about what it might look like lined with huge houses that would stand empty for months at a time. She'd only think of her dad standing hip-deep in that cold river, stained

fishing cap pulled low on his brow, hands flicking
the delicate fly in and out of the water.

She could almost see him, so at first she wasn't
surprised to see an ancient pickup pulled off to the
side of the lane, its tires nearly hidden by deep grass.
For a moment, as she slowed and pulled her truck in
behind it, she thought that she would get out and really see him there. Not a visiting ghost, but real life
after a bad dream.

But when she switched off the ignition, she came
back to herself. It *was* his old truck, but he hadn't
driven it here. She'd given Joe that truck five years
before and he'd been driving it longer than that.

Lori stared at the open tailgate in surprise. When
she'd had to shut down the garage, Joe had told her
he was going camping. No surprise. Joe camped a lot.
But she had no idea he'd been camping here.

She slid out of her truck and walked on down the
road until it narrowed to nothing more than a trail.
The narrow path through the grass rose up a hill before curving out toward the river. Thunder rumbled as
she edged carefully along the cliff. The water jumped
and swirled below her. About a hundred feet on, the
land opened up again and the trail dipped back down
to the meadow that stretched out from the riverbank.
When Lori spotted the small tent near the water, she
felt her throat close up. She was glad Joe had been
spending time here, since she hadn't.

A narrow spiral of smoke drifted up from the side
of the tent. As she drew nearer, she saw Joe, hunched
over the fire, a whole fish roasting on a stick.

He glanced up at her approach, eyebrows not even rising in surprise.

"Lori," he said. "What are you doing out here?"

"I didn't know you camped here, Joe."

He shrugged. "It's a beautiful place. Your dad sure knew this river. I hope you don't mind."

"Of course not. I'm glad someone's getting pleasure out of it."

Joe pulled another stump close to the fire and motioned her to it. A wave of contentment crept over her as she took a seat and lapsed into silence. Sitting with him here was almost like sitting with her dad. This was what it would have been like had he still been alive.

Joe shifted in his seat. "No more trouble, I hope."

"No," she answered. "None."

"How's your hand?"

"It's good." Actually, she hadn't thought about it once today, aside from the inconvenience of trying to help wash dishes, so it was obviously healing.

"Chief Lawson find anything?"

Lori stretched out her legs with a sigh. "Nothing. But I think I know what it's all been about. The land."

He turned slowly to face her. "The land? Why would you say that?"

"Someone wants me to sell. Quickly."

His lips parted, jaw hanging open for a moment before he shook his head and closed it.

"I can't be sure," she assured him. "I heard a rumor. Ben's trying to chase it down now."

Joe sighed and looked up at the sky, then he swept

a long, lingering glance around them. He looked at the campsite, the meadow, the wide sprawl of river. Then he nodded. "I'm sorry, Lori. I'm sorry for everything."

"Thanks, Joe."

He pulled the charred fish out of the flames and set it carefully on a rock. "It's not right the way you've been living here, and I couldn't seem to convince you to go. I thought you needed a little nudge out of the nest, you know?"

She paused in midnod, frozen solid as ice. Unease prickled up her arms like an army of fire ants. "What...what do you mean, Joe?"

"I could hardly bear watching you take care of him for all those years, but I kept telling myself you'd be fine. Eventually, you'd be fine. After he died, I thought you'd go back to school, but you didn't even want to talk about it. You should never have gotten caught up in all of this. I had to do something."

"Joe," she breathed. Her head buzzed with adrenaline. "Joe, are you saying... Were you the one vandalizing my garage?"

His white hair whipped across his forehead in the wind, then pressed back close to his scalp, the pink showing through. "It was just small stuff. The hydraulic lift. The torque guns. The doors. And then... I never thought you'd get hurt in the oil spill. I liked to have died when I heard that, Lori. I just thought if things got a little more dire, if your bills were too much, you'd have to sell the land to me. Then you could pay off that debt and move on. I even thought maybe you'd leave the garage in my care. I could keep running it, and you wouldn't have to worry about a thing." He gave her a pained smile. "You've got to fly away, little bird."

Little bird. He hadn't called her that since she was twelve. Tears burned her eyes. This made no sense. Joe loved her. How could he have done these things? "I don't understand," she murmured. "You wanted me to sell the land to you? Give you the garage? That's what you wanted?"

"No. It wasn't about the land anymore. I've been saving up for thirty years. I've saved a lot since your dad... Well. I've got nearly a hundred and twenty thousand now. I wanted you to have it."

"In exchange for the land?" she demanded. Her muscles were aching now, her hands trembling. Not Joe, her mind insisted. Not Joe.

"I was going to give the land back to you! I don't want it, not anymore. I was going to leave it to you in my will, and then you could sell it again, you see? I'd pay you for it now, while you need the money, and then you could have it back, Lori. I didn't want it for myself, I swear."

It actually made perfect sense. And yet it didn't. "Why didn't you just tell me your plan? Why do it behind my back?" *And terrify me in the process,* she left unsaid.

Joe threw one hand up in exasperation. "You wouldn't have agreed to that in a million years. You're too proud, always have been. Nothing like your mother. That woman would take help from a person before he'd even offered."

He was staring into the fire now. Joe picked up a stick and poked thoughtfully at the edge of a charred log. "That time she wrote to me? She wanted money. She'd been gone so many years and it didn't bother her at all, reappearing like a ghost."

Her neck had tensed into a burning knot. Her broken hand remembered that it was supposed to hurt and started throbbing. "I thought she wanted to check up on me."

Joe didn't seem to hear her. "I wouldn't send the money. I couldn't do it. Despite everything, I never thought she'd leave you. It's hard to see the truth sometimes, and I just didn't want to see she was that bad of a mother."

"Joe." Lori stood. She wanted to leave. Run until she was so exhausted that her brain would cease to think. She could forgive Joe for wrecking her garage. She could. He'd had good intentions, despite being totally misguided. But there was something else in his voice now. Some deeper sorrow. An older memory.

"Joe," she choked out. "You're scaring me."

"I'm sorry," he whispered, the words scratchy with unshed tears. "I'm so sorry. She didn't want to take you with us, and I couldn't leave without you. So I stayed and she moved on, and good riddance to bad rubbish. I couldn't have loved her after that anyway. What kind of woman could leave a little child behind?"

Lori clutched her broken arm to her chest. "Joe…"

Oh, *no.* Oh, no. "Joe, did you… Were you with my mom before I was born?" The truth suddenly seemed obvious, but Joe's brow furrowed with confusion. Looking up at her, he shook his head.

"No. That's not it. I'm not your daddy, even if I wish I was. But I did love her. I'm ashamed to admit it, but I did. After they were married and you were born—" Joe's shoulders slumped "—it seemed like she'd gotten what she wanted out of your dad. She was bored and pretty, and I was young and stupid. I'm so sorry."

This is a motive, her brain was spelling out to her in slow and careful tones. *A classic love triangle.* Except that her mother had run off thirteen years before her dad had hit the asphalt of that parking lot.

Her foot slid back. She inched away. "I'm going to go now, Joe."

He stood. "No."

"Joe," she pleaded. "I don't want to hear this."

"It's been killing me for a long time now, Lori. This is my chance to tell you the truth."

"No," she begged him.

"She wrote to me. She'd been gone more than ten years, and here she just up and waltzes back in from out of the blue, looking for money. I wouldn't give it to her. I wrote back and told her how amazing you'd turned out to be and how much she'd missed out on by being stupid and selfish. I guess that didn't sit too well. She called me and told me she was going to tell your dad everything."

Her tears were blinding her. Lori tried to wipe them from her eyes, but they kept coming back.

Joe hung his head. "I waited for the explosion. I knew if he found out, he'd ride me out of town on a rail. I'd have lost my best friend and I'd never have seen you again. I was scared to death, Lori, but nothing happened. She never called or wrote again. I thought it was over."

Lori took a step back and stumbled over a clump of grass. With the cast on her wrist, she couldn't catch herself in time, and landed hard on her butt. Joe rushed over and pulled her up and right into his arms.

"I'm sorry, Lori," he whispered, and she began to sob. She cried for what he was saying and what it meant. She cried because she was scared of him, and yet she buried her face in his chest and sobbed while he held her.

"He was going to sell me the garage," he explained. "We'd had a plan from the time your mama walked out. I was going to work for him, put in my time and then buy him out. He could retire then, buy his land and spend his days fishing. At some point we stopped talking about it, but I guess I just didn't notice."

Joe's hands rubbed over her back in a soothing rhythm. "One day I heard he bought a piece of land off the bank. He kept putting me off when I asked him about it. Wouldn't say a word when I tried to talk about buying the garage. I'd put twenty years into that place, and I wasn't going to work as a damned mechanic until the day I died. He'd promised me,

Lori. And all of a sudden he wouldn't answer one damned question."

Lori breathed in the scent of wood smoke on his clothes, tainted by the metallic stench of fresh fish. How many times had she smelled this exact combination on her father's shirt? "Did you kill him?" she asked on a whisper. "Did you do it?"

His deep breath roared in her ear. "I'd been drinking. I drove past and saw his truck, and I was so pissed at him. I waited for him to come out. He'd been drinking, too. It didn't take much to get us screaming at each other. I accused him of screwing me over and going back on a promise. I told him he was a goddamned liar and a greedy one at that. He just looked me up and down like I was trash. 'Joe,' he said, 'I didn't want to have this discussion, but you won't let it go. I'm not selling you the garage, because I'll be damned if I'll let you buy the roof you were fucking my wife under.'"

She pulled away. She had to.

Joe let her go. "She'd told him after all. I wasn't mad. It wasn't like that. I was scared. He was like a brother to me, and the thing with your mom seemed like a whole other lifetime. But I saw in his eyes that he'd finally decided he couldn't live with it. You and your dad were my only family and I was full of terror and I panicked. I don't even know why, Lori, I swear. I just saw that rock and I wanted to stop him from walking away."

She must have been backing up, because Joe

reached toward her and she scrambled back faster. "Don't touch me."

"Ah, God, Lori. I'm so sorry. My little bird. It's been killing me, all these years."

"Don't," she sobbed. In between the hard beats of her heart, Lori suddenly registered a new sound. The distant grind of tires rolling on gravel.

Joe stopped. His eyes rose over Lori's shoulder. She kept backing away, and then she turned and ran. She didn't want to hear any more.

QUINN WASN'T SURE what the hell he was doing. At first, he thought he'd just drop by and find out how Lori was doing. A man could drop by his sister's house any time he wanted. It wasn't weird.

But she hadn't been there. And Molly had given him directions to Lori's land as if it were natural that he would come find her here. When the dirt road had disintegrated to ripples and ruts, he'd snapped out of his mental auto drive.

What was he doing, following her to this private spot? He wanted to see her, yes, but he didn't have any right to intrude. She didn't want his help, didn't even want his company.

Quinn pressed his foot to the brake, reconsidering. He had no right to interfere. He should go back to his place and console himself with the little bits of information he could glean from the *Tumble Creek Tribune*. The week before, Miles had finally linked Quinn's name with Lori's. Sadly, the sight of their names together had made Quinn's heart spasm.

Staring aimlessly out the windshield, Quinn caught a glint of the sun against metal ahead. He squinted. Her truck was there, pulled over in the high grass.

Stopped in the middle of the dirt road, Quinn stared at her purple truck.

He should go. He should.

Turning the wheel hard, Quinn started to swing the car around. Midturn, he braked so hard that his head snapped forward.

There was another truck there, parked just in front of Lori's. Well, hell.

He popped open the door without even thinking, and started toward her truck. One raindrop hit him, then two. Then ten. The raindrops became music on the river, barely audible over the water rushing along the rocks on the banks. Just as he reached a bend in the road, he heard another sound, high-pitched like the call of a hawk.

Glancing up toward the clouds, he saw nothing but the rain falling toward him and hunched back down to avoid it.

"Quinn!" the hawk cried, shocking him to a complete stop.

He raised a hand to his brow to shield himself from the rain, and his eye finally caught sight of movement ahead of him. Dark curls whipped in the gusts of wind. *Lori.*

She was running toward him—*running!*—and he started to smile just before he registered her waving hands and panicked eyes.

Fear exploded through his veins, and Quinn sprinted forward.

He could hear the strain of her lungs even from twenty feet away.

Finally, she was right in front of him. "Lori!" he yelled, as she held her good arm straight out to push him back. His hands were on her. She wasn't bleeding.

"It was Joe," she panted. "It was Joe."

Quinn shook his head. "What was Joe?"

Stumbling, she pulled him toward her truck, clearly exhausted from running through the knee-deep grass. Quinn glanced back, but he followed her to the road. "What's wrong? Why were you running?"

"I just have to get out of here. And I think… I think I have to go to the police."

Alarm flared back to life under his skin. He put an arm around her shoulder and ushered her toward his running car. "Are you okay?"

Shaking her head, she yanked the door open and nearly fell inside. Tears flowed down her face.

He slammed the door and jogged to the other side. As soon as he was in the driver's seat, he grabbed Lori's hand. "What happened?"

"Joe… He was the one who attacked my father."

He pulled his phone from his pocket. "He's here?"

"He's camping on my dad's land. He just…*confessed*. Everything. He and my dad got into an argument and… Jesus, I just freaked out and ran, and…"

"There's no reception," Quinn said with a frus-

trated curse. "Let's go. We'll tell Ben. It'll be okay."
He reached for the gearshift just as Lori gasped.
When he followed her gaze to the top of the trail
ahead, Quinn saw a man standing in the distance,
his features blurred by the falling rain.

"Is it Joe?" Just in case something awful was
about to happen, Quinn eased the car into Drive.
But the figure only stood there, watching. Then the
man raised a hand and gave a little wave, as if he
was seeing them off before he turned to head back
up the trail.

"Lori?" Quinn murmured.

She nodded. "Go. I think you can get service near
the highway."

Not liking the flat tone of her voice, Quinn took
her cold hand again and squeezed it tightly.

"He did it," she whispered. Rain dripped off her
nose. "He killed my dad. He said he didn't mean to."

Quinn's body jerked in shock, but he tried to speak
calmly for Lori's sake. "I'm sure he didn't."

She was shivering hard, despite the heated seats.
"But…he was his *best friend*."

Those were the last words Lori spoke for a long
time. She huddled silently in Quinn's front seat as
he cranked up the heat and drove as quickly as he
could back toward civilization. They were nearly to
the highway before his cell phone showed signs of
life. Lori didn't even look up as he called Ben and
explained what had happened.

Ten minutes later, Ben arrived along with what
seemed to be the entire Tumble Creek police force.

The trucks raced past them, heading toward the campsite. Quinn just waited silently, cradling Lori's hand in his own. Her shivering finally stopped. The rain faded to a mist and then ended altogether.

They waited.

By the time Ben pulled up next to them in his truck, the sun had emerged to glare off every wet surface.

Quinn got out and opened Lori's door, frowning at her stiff movements. "Did you arrest him?" He didn't understand the careful look Ben shot him, but he put his arm around Lori's shoulders just in case.

"He wasn't at the campsite," Ben said. "You say you last saw him on the trail?"

She nodded.

"One of the men noticed some marks at the edge of the trail, just at the top of the ridge. It's awfully slick there right now."

Lori shook her head. "What do you mean?"

"There are shoe prints in the mud, and some slide marks just above the water. Joe's things are still at the campsite."

"He probably ran," she insisted.

Ben nodded but gave Quinn that same look again.

Quinn understood it now. "Why don't I take you home, Lori? You can get changed. Ben will let us know what they find."

"I don't want to go," she insisted.

"You're cold. Let's at least go get changed. Then we can come back and wait."

"No."

What could he do? Tired of trying to silently communicate with Ben, Quinn convinced Lori to at least sit in the car. Then he made his way back to Ben.

"What is it you're trying to tell me?"

Ben glanced toward Quinn's car. "People don't normally just make a confession like that and then go on their way."

"You implied he might have slipped."

"Yeah, that's what I implied. But I'm not sure why he would've been that close to the edge in the first place."

"Oh. Shit."

"Yeah. I'd better get back. I'll let you know as soon as—"

Ben's radio squawked, interrupting him, and he walked away to listen to the garbled message. When he turned back, his face was grim. Lori must have seen it. She got out of the car and stared at him.

"I'm sorry," Ben said. "They found him in the river just past the campsite."

Lori's whole body stiffened. "What?"

"I'm sorry," Ben repeated.

"He's…dead?"

"Yes."

"But…he was just right there. He waved goodbye. He…" Her face drained of all its color and Quinn reached for her. "Oh," she murmured. "Maybe…"

Ben's gaze strayed to the ground for a brief moment, before he looked back to Lori. "It was an accident. And the river's only a few feet deep there. It was over quickly."

"But, do you think…?"

Quinn didn't let her finish the question. He pulled her into a hug and held her tight to his chest. "Let me take you home."

Her hand clutched at his shirt. "We can't just leave him here. Not like that. I can't believe he…"

"All right. Okay. Ben, how long will it be?"

"Hopefully no more than an hour, but it could be longer."

"We'll wait in the car."

Ben's head dropped. He put his hands on his hips and stared at the ground for a moment before he shook off whatever emotion had gripped him. "I'll try to speed it up. I need to ask you both some questions, but it can wait till tomorrow. Keep her warm."

"I will."

She fell back into her silence in the car. Quinn could only watch helplessly and wait.

Two hours later, it was over. Lori was bundled into his bed in a sweatshirt and socks, warm and dry and still silent. He'd rescued her, finally, and found that it didn't feel nearly as good as he'd imagined.

CHAPTER SIXTEEN

A FLUTTERY YELLOW butterfly hovered just an inch above the tanned skin of Lori's knee. It moved slightly closer, then away, then closer still. She'd heard they were attracted to the salt on people's skin, but she was pretty sure she hadn't started sweating yet. It was only 11:00 a.m.

Mesmerized, she watched as it drew ever closer. For some reason it seemed important that it land. That exaggerated importance was likely a result of her recent descent into complete, trancelike inaction. For the past seven days, she'd done nothing but sit in a lounge chair on the front sidewalk of her house.

On each day, Quinn had stopped by to bring her lunch. Sometimes he came for dinner, too. Sometimes he stayed the night.

She was leaning on him, and it felt nice, and that scared her to death. But she seemed incapable of doing anything but showering, making coffee and sitting on this sun-faded chair until Quinn delivered something for her to eat.

The butterfly finally landed. It folded its marigold wings, and Lori released a silent breath. Good.

A few minutes later, a car pulled into the lot, gravel

pinging against its underside, but the butterfly didn't move. She kept her gaze tightly focused on its tiny antennae.

"Hey," Quinn's voice said. "How are you doing this morning?"

"Good."

The wings twitched when he stepped closer, then fanned open. "Did you make a new friend?" he asked.

Lori smiled. "I think I did. Though it might be more interested in my lavender lotion than my winning personality."

"Mmm." Quinn stared with her for a while, then cleared his throat. "You want to come for a ride with me?"

"Sure," she answered before she realized that a ride would entail not only chasing off the butterfly, but also getting up from her lounge chair. Crap. "Well…"

"Come on." Quinn reached for her hand and the butterfly fluttered up, zigzagging away from her leg.

Lori sighed. There was no point staying now anyway. She shoved herself to her feet and let Quinn pull her toward his car. Once she was in the passenger seat with wind rushing through her curls, Lori found herself waking up a little.

"It's a beautiful day," Quinn ventured.

Lori looked around. It was a beautiful day. "Yeah," she agreed. "This is nice, actually. Thank you."

One deep breath seemed to open up some closed door inside her. A second breath chased out the damp, stale air that had filled her up.

She'd been grieving, she realized. Finally. For her father and for Joe, too. Maybe even for the woman she'd wanted her mother to be.

When she glanced over at Quinn, he smiled and took her hand. She smiled back. "Where are we going?"

"Up to my place. I thought maybe you'd like to vary the angle on your tan a little bit."

She arched an eyebrow at him. "Oh, yeah? Do I still get lunch?"

"Yes, there's lunch, too. I'm quite clear on what my duties are."

"Good."

His thumb trailed over the inside of her wrist, reminding Lori of the very first time he'd held her hand. A lifetime ago. Now the summer was almost over. Quinn would go back to Aspen. And Lori... Well, Lori didn't know what she was going to do.

But Quinn seemed confident in his plans. He drove them through the tunnel of trees that was his driveway, then parked right next to the old cabin.

"Are you going to tear this down?" she asked.

"No way. I love this place."

"I'm not sure it goes with your house."

He shrugged and got out to open her door. "It's my house," he said as she took his hand and stood. "If I say it goes, it goes."

"I guess you're right."

They didn't head toward the cabin, though. Quinn tugged her toward the white lines of the foundation. She thought he was offering another tour, but they skirted the cement walls and circled to what would be the back of the house. When she looked up, she found herself facing the view she'd seen on Quinn's computer. And in real life, it was just as breathtaking as she'd imagined it would be. As she watched, an eagle circled by before gliding out of the range of her sight.

"It's so amazing."

Quinn's only response was to tuck one of her curls behind her ear. He let her look for a moment, then pulled her farther on. The rock dropped two feet lower here, so Quinn jumped down and lowered Lori by her waist. A few steps farther and the rock dropped again. This time Lori jumped on her own. Her muscles stretched with life. It felt good to move.

"Careful here," he cautioned, gesturing toward the very edge of the rock. Beyond it, Lori could see nothing but blue sky and treetops. She followed Quinn to the right and down one more drop before she spied the quilt spread out on the rock.

A picnic. In the wilderness. Lori glanced around. "Aren't there bears up here?"

Quinn froze and spun slowly toward her. "What is it with you and bears?"

"They're dangerous," she insisted.

"No more dangerous than mountain lions or rutting elk. And I swear I've never seen a bear on my lot. So, is it a phobia?"

"No! They are *deadly* animals!"

He sighed. "Just spill it already."

"Oh, fine." She blew a curl out of her eyes. "It's no

big deal. When I was a little girl, my dad and I went camping in Yellowstone. The rangers were always giving lectures about bears. Stay away from them. Don't get out of your vehicles to look. Keep your food in bearproof containers and don't store food in your tent. Frankly, it was scary. On our third day there, we drove the northern part of the park and finally saw some grizzlies. And everyone—everyone—was getting out of their cars to take pictures. I was sure the bears would start eating them at any moment. I got really upset. Terrified. There may have been a few nightmares involved.

"Then a few weeks after we got home, I went to take the trash out, and there it was. A bear, digging through our garbage. I thought it was the end of me. I don't know how long I stood there, shaking, but the bear finally stood up, looked at me, and left. The end."

Quinn crossed his arms and tried to look serious. "Shut up."

"I'm sorry." He coughed to hide a laugh. "It's not funny. But I think we're safe here. I don't think bears like cliffs."

She could tell he was making that up, but Lori tried her best not to worry. Beyond him, the picnic awaited, and she could see real china and wineglasses, along with a sweating bottle of wine sticking out of a tub of ice. Quinn had put a lot of effort into this.

Lori walked determinedly over to the blanket and sat down. Quinn joined her, and once her anxiety receded, she realized she could hear running water. For a brief moment, she thought of the river before she shoved those thoughts away and slammed a mental door. This wasn't the river. It was just a tiny waterfall trickling down the rock face to her right.

"It's beautiful here." She sighed.

"This is my favorite spot. I'm going to put in some rough steps, but otherwise I won't change it at all."

"Good. It's wonderful the way it is."

Silence reigned over their meal as Quinn served up fruit and sandwiches and cucumber salad, all of it still in containers from the fancy Aspen market. They faced the view as they ate, each comfortable with their own thoughts.

Once she'd polished off her frosted brownie, Lori groaned and lay back on the quilt. "Thank you for bringing me here. It feels good to get out."

"I thought maybe we could talk," he said, and Lori's muscles tensed despite the hot sun and perfect breeze.

Talking. That was never good. Never. She stayed as still as a deer frozen at the sound of a snapping twig.

"I've been thinking…" he started. Another bad sign. "You know I don't want to end this, Lori. I've already made that clear."

"Mmm."

"I want you to come live with me."

"What?" She'd worried he was about to make a grand declaration of love that she'd have to wiggle away from. But *this?* This was crazy. "I can't come live with you!"

"Sure you can."

"I live in Tumble Creek."

"Come on, Lori. There's nothing left for you in Tumble Creek. You don't belong there."

Lori's jaw fell open. He'd said it so casually, as if it weren't her whole life he'd just tossed aside. "It's my home," she forced past her tight throat.

"It's where you live, sure."

"It's my life.'"

When he sighed, he sounded exactly as if he were dealing with a recalcitrant child. "You don't *have* a life."

Wow. Lori squeezed her eyes shut. When she opened them and looked up, she saw a tiny puff of cloud drifting across the never-ending sky. "Did you really just say that?"

"Somebody needs to say it. You're dying there, Lori. You already said you were going to sell your dad's land. It's the perfect time for you to move on. And I thought… Well, I thought I'd love it if you came to live with me."

The cloud slowly tore in two. "You thought I could just move in with you, no problem."

He paused for just a moment. "Yeah."

"You thought I could sell my dad's land, close the garage, pack up and move in with you."

Despite his obtuseness, Quinn finally seemed to pick up on the tone of her voice. "Um…" he muttered, "yeah."

"And would you take care of me? Pay for everything? Fly me around the world to keep you company on trips? I wouldn't have to worry about bills or work or responsibilities?"

This time his answer was more a hum than a word.

"Thanks," she snapped. "But no thanks." When she scrambled to her feet, Quinn jumped up to follow her.

"Lori, I'm not suggesting you hang around and eat bonbons while I go out and bring home the bacon. You need to get back to school."

"I can handle my life on my own, thanks!"

"Oh, really?" he countered. "Because you haven't done a damn thing in ten years!"

She stopped so quickly that Quinn plowed into her back and nearly knocked her over. "*Fuck. You. I was kind of busy for most of the past decade, ass-hole. I couldn't exactly go hang out with the kids on the quad.*"

When she started to turn away, Quinn grabbed her arm. "Don't give me that," he growled. "I like you too much to put up with your self-pity. You could have taken summer classes at Western State. You could have signed up for an online course. Hell, you could have done more than that in the past year. You could hit the road and *see* something instead of sitting in your old room watching travel videos."

Her gasp echoed off the rock walls that surrounded them. "You…" Oh, God. Had he looked in her old bedroom? Humiliation washed over her skin in a wave of fire.

"Shit," he cursed, rubbing a hand over his face.

"I'm sorry. I know I'm saying this all wrong. But, Lori, you're wasting your life."

She swallowed the tears that wanted to rise. "There's nothing wrong with being a mechanic, you arrogant shit."

"No, there's nothing wrong with being a mechanic if that's what you love doing. And there's nothing wrong with Tumble Creek, either. But you never *wanted* to stay here and work in the shop. You've never even pretended you wanted to. You had dreams when you left here ten years ago, and you've got dreams now."

She jerked her arm from his grip. "I'm not an eighteen-year-old kid anymore."

"No, you're not eighteen. But if you want to go to college, you can work at some crappy job in between classes just like any other freshman. Hell, you don't even have to worry about an apartment if you want to live with me. So what's so different about it? What are you afraid of?"

"What's so *different?* Are you serious?"

"Yes, I am serious."

"What's so different is that when I left here to go to college, I had a family and a home. I had a father. I *belonged* somewhere. No matter where I went, no matter what I did, I could always come home. But if I sell everything and leave Tumble Creek with noth-ing…I won't belong anywhere, Quinn. If I'm not Lori Love the girl mechanic, I'm *no one.*"

"That's not true. That's not who you are."

"Well then, *who am I?*"

"Lori…" He threw up his hands in frustration. "You can be anybody you want."

"Like your live-in mistress."

"Oh, come on! I want to be with you. And you won't even consider a long-distance relationship."

"Quinn…Jesus." A tear finally leaked from her eye and she swiped it off her cheek. "You're asking me to give up everything—*everything*—to be your girlfriend."

"No, it's not like that."

"No? All right then. Why don't you sell *your* business and come live with *me?*"

"Don't be ri—" He cut off his own words and paused for a moment, hand still held high as if he'd finish his sweeping gesture.

"Yeah, it'd be ridiculous. So please don't ask me to give up my little life to come live in yours."

His hand fell. He dropped his chin and stared at the ground. She watched him for a long moment. She looked at his broad shoulders and the way the sleeves of his green T-shirt stretched tight against his biceps. She traced the muscles down to his forearm and thought of the way those crisp hairs felt under her fingers. This moment was a memory, even as she lived it. It was a memory she needed to gather up and take home with her. His dark gold hair ruffled in the breeze when he looked up. His eyes were swirls of brown and green.

She'd never have another lover like him. She knew that. Even if she traveled the whole world.

Quinn rolled his shoulders and shook his head.

"I don't want you to give up anything for me. Not for me."

"Good."

"I just want... I want something *better* for you. That's all."

Lori took a deep breath and let it out as slowly as she could. The urge to scream and cry faded away. She met his gaze. "Regardless of whether my life is perfect or not, it's not for you to decide that it's worthless. Nobody has that right."

"I didn't—"

"Now, will you take me home? I just want to go home."

"Lori..." The word was a plea, but what the hell did he want from her?

She shook her head and walked past him. When she got to his car, she heard the locks pop open and got in. He joined her, and the silence between them was no longer comfortable, but it lasted the whole way back.

When he pulled to a stop in front of her door, Quinn reached to turn off the ignition, but Lori stopped him with a hand on his arm. "Don't. This is over, Quinn. It's already September. The summer is done. You knew it was never supposed to be anything more than that."

He looked at her hand for a long time, her fingers curled over his flesh. He stared at her skin on his. Then he shifted his narrowed gaze to her face. "You're being a coward, Lori. And you know it."

She didn't disagree. She couldn't. So she just got out, calmly closed the door, and walked into her father's house alone.

CHAPTER SEVENTEEN

"You can't love me," she groaned, bowed under the pain of the idea. When he'd found her she'd been broken and used. A trollop thrown out like rubbish in the alley. And now she might be cleaned up and beautiful, but no amount of soap could make her pure.

Sebastian might want her, but he couldn't possibly love her. She wouldn't let him.

"I do love you," he whispered. "And you will be my wife."

Anna shook her head and pulled him back down into the tousled sheets. She kissed him to hide her sorrow, opened her body to his. He let her have her way for now, and that was all she needed. In the morning she'd be gone, and Sebastian would give up these foolish notions of love.

LORI CLOSED THE BOOK with a sigh. Reading just wasn't the same anymore. None of the heroes were as interesting as Quinn, and the sex wasn't nearly as hot as what she'd had this summer.

The third week of October and snow was already

falling. The pass was closed. The idea stirred up a dull ache in her chest.

She'd been doing well though. Really well. She'd come to terms with what Quinn had said to her, probably because most of it had been true.

Lori *was* scared. She'd been scared for years, ever since her father's injury. Little bits of her courage were scattered across the country. Some of it in Boston where she'd received the phone call. Some of it floating high in the sky in the trail of the plane that had flown her home. But most of it had fallen away in Grand Valley in the hospital where she'd spent weeks by her dad's side.

When she'd left Tumble Creek, left her father, something bad had happened. That logic had been seared into her head, along with the mantra *If only I'd stayed.* So even after his death, the idea that she might just trot away and try again had given her a cold chill. But with no money to make her way in the world, she hadn't had to face that terror. Lori didn't have that luxury any longer.

Joe had created a living trust in her name. Her first instinct had been to turn her back on the money and pretend it wasn't there. But when she'd realized the amount in the trust was almost the exact amount of her father's outstanding medical bills… Well, it had only been right that Joe's money go toward those expenses. She hoped it would bring his ghost some peace.

Lori had found some peace for herself, surprisingly enough. Just knowing what had happened to her dad had relieved a hollow burning she hadn't even known was there. Even a painful truth was better than no truth at all.

She'd been able to pack the trophies away and take down those horrid paintings her dad had loved. She'd thrown out the burnt orange curtains and raised the blinds. And then she hadn't been able to stop. Pale yellow paint, a midnight-blue cover for the couch, a pretty crystal lamp she'd found at the outlet mall.

Her bedroom was even brighter with its stark white comforter and brown-and-pink pillows. The bathroom had been a problem. Retiling had seemed a bigger project than she could handle, but she had dared to pry out the countertop and replace it with faux granite and a brushed nickel faucet. To offset the pink tile, she'd papered the wall in pinstripes of pink and brown.

Thoughts of Quinn had kept her company in that bathroom, of course. There'd been no avoiding him. How many times had she thought of calling him to laugh at the sparkly gold countertop or the even more horrid wallpaper she'd found beneath the flocking? How many times had she picked up the phone?

She missed him. She missed him every day. As brief as their affair had been, it had been imprinted on her soul. He hadn't just been a fling. There was a small possibility she'd actually believed that at the time, but now there was no escaping the truth. She was in love with Quinn Jennings, or damn near close to it.

But one truth did not cancel out another. Her life was still a sticky mess, and falling in love wouldn't make it any better. She had to figure her life out for herself.

And she was. The land was up for sale, overseen by the savviest real estate lawyer she could find. An equity line had given her enough cash to give a small severance package to her last full-time employees when she closed the garage for good. The oil cleanup was slow, but nearly completed. The last thing on her plate was a plowing contract to fulfill for the town this winter, but after that... Well, after that her life would change somehow, whether she was ready or not.

As for today...she had absolutely nothing to do unless the ground suddenly froze and let snow pile up on the road. Lori stared out the window, hating the fat white flakes. Somehow it had been easy not to reach out to him when she knew she had the option. But now the idea scratched from the inside of her skull.

Lori stretched out on her fake-suede couch cover and stared hard at the ceiling. She was busy getting her life together. If she was still around next May, then maybe she'd drive over the pass and knock on Quinn's door. Maybe she'd ask him to dinner. Maybe she'd be ready.

But what if a buxom blonde answered the door?

"Jeez Louise." May was seven months away, and what were the chances that Quinn wouldn't stumble into some other woman's bed in that time, even accidentally? Just the thought made her stomach hurt.

She had to press a hand to her belly to keep it from turning, but she *wouldn't* call him. There was no point. Her life was in flux and would be for a while.

And though he'd been an arrogant ass, she hadn't exactly been Mary Sunshine. Hell, he'd probably said
good riddance and moved on already.

*He could be giving some girl a cyber-tour of his
house at this very moment.*

"Oh, God," Lori groaned, and grabbed one of her
soft yellow pillows to press it to her face.

Even if he's dating, she told herself, *he doesn't
mean it.* She'd gotten flowers on her birthday two
weeks before. No card, no signature. Just a huge bouquet of dozens of Gerbera daisies. They could only
have come from Quinn. She'd cried, but she hadn't
called him. And she wouldn't call him now.

She wouldn't.

Desperate for distraction, she inched the pillow
off her face and grabbed the latest *Tribune.* The gossip headline only made her feel worse. *Local Realtor confirms she's dating former football star Juan
Jimenez. "We have a lot in common," Helen Stowe
claims.* Helen had finally done it. She'd risked everything for Juan. She was holding her head high and
marching bravely into love.

Lori dropped the paper and pressed the pillow
back to her face. The cotton muffled the world pretty
effectively, but she was sure she could hear those
damned snowflakes sliding down the glass of her
front window, mocking her.

"Hey, idiot," his sister said cheerfully over the phone.

Quinn scowled at the sketch on his desk. "What
do you want?"

"I just thought I'd call to see how you're doing. I worry about you."

He snorted. "Since when?"

Molly didn't answer.

"Look." He sighed. "I'm fine. Never better."

"Quinn, the last time I saw you, you looked like an umbrella."

"O-kay… You're not making any sense at all. Is Ben keeping your prescriptions filled?"

"An um-ber-el-la," she said slowly, emphasizing more syllables than were actually in the word, as if that would give it more meaning.

Quinn grunted.

"You're skinny as a rail but your shoulders are freakishly wide. An umbrella."

"Jeez. Thanks." He glanced over at his left shoulder. Okay, he'd had to have a few suits taken in at the waist. But surely he didn't look freakish. He was just having more trouble than normal sleeping. "Anyway, thanks for calling."

"Quinn!" she yelled before he could set the phone down. He raised it warily back to his ear. "She's doing really well. Why don't you call her?"

"No," he answered, and hung up before she could say more. Molly had been outraged at his stupidity. *You actually told her she didn't have a life?* She'd called him a clod and an idiot and worse than that.

At some point it had begun to sink in that he'd acted like a dick. He'd lived through so many failed relationships that when he felt as if he'd found the right one, it had been so *clear* to him. So obvious.

And somehow he'd failed to see that it might not be so clear to Lori.

Pure stupidity.

The girl had been through hell and back in the past year. The loss of her father, the destruction of her business, the ultimate betrayal of a man who'd been like an uncle. Quinn had had no business pressuring her like that. He'd been an idiot and ruined everything, and there was no way he was going to crawl back and pressure her again.

Well, not right now anyway. Maybe in a few months. Maybe next year. Definitely when he read about her dating somebody in the online edition of the *Tumble Creek Tribune*. Luckily that hadn't happened yet.

Time. He owed her that at least. But he *would* try again.

In the past, the longer any one relationship went on, the more and more time he devoted to work. That hadn't been happenstance. *He* was the one ending things, escaping from a connection once it got too deep. Fading away until the other person gave up.

But with Lori… He didn't want to lose himself in architecture. It wasn't that he couldn't work. It wasn't that he was slumped over his desk, fading away. He could work just fine, thank you. But the moment he set down his pencil, he thought of her. When he finished a project, she was the one he wanted to show it to.

When he'd dated in the past, he would look up from hours of concentration and think, "Oh, shit,

I'm late and she's going to be pissed." But now he expected to look up and see Lori standing there smiling and tapping her foot.

She understood him.

Too bad he hadn't taken the time to understand her.

"Time," he murmured. That was all she needed.

After a glance out at the lazy snowflakes, Quinn began to pack up. Time for a swim and then more work.

"Good night, Mr. Jennings," Jane said as he passed her desk.

"Any meetings tomorrow?"

"Nothing tomorrow," she replied.

Hand on the door, Quinn stopped and looked back at Jane. "Do you think I look like an umbrella?"

Her eyes went wide and she shook her head, but Quinn saw the way her gaze darted to his shoulders. Sighing, he slumped against the closed door. "I screwed things up, Jane. Badly. I just want to give her some time."

Jane's face softened, losing all its stiff professionalism. Lori had been right. Jane *was* pretty. "Okay, but don't take too long. I like her. And she's the only woman who chases the thoughts from your eyes."

"Yeah," he said, and walked out into the snowy day. But just as he reached his car, the snow stopped. While he stood there, one hand on the roof, the sun came out. Quinn looked toward the mountain pass that led to Tumble Creek. It sparkled.

Lori had closed the garage permanently. He'd seen

that in the *Tribune* a couple of weeks before. And Molly said she was doing really, really well.

It had been five weeks. Maybe she'd had enough time.

Quinn thought back to those books she liked. There weren't any damsels in distress in those stories, but there weren't any wussy heroes, either. Lori didn't need saving anymore, but maybe it wouldn't hurt to ride up on a stallion and ask if she wanted a ride.

"A stallion," he muttered in disgust. He'd clearly read one too many of those books in the name of research.

But then Quinn thought of something. Something big. And yellow. Something powerful enough to get over a snowy mountain pass and nimble enough to maneuver around the snow gates. And most importantly, something Lori wanted to ride.

He'd promised her a bonus for her work and then never delivered. He couldn't live with that all winter, could he? She was counting on him.

Confident that he had the perfect excuse to see Lori Love, Quinn opened the door of his car, threw in his portfolio, and rode off into the sunset.

LORI PACKED ANOTHER VHS tape into the big box and tried not to wince. It hurt to get rid of her travel tapes, but it was the next thing on her list, and she was sticking to it. If there was one sure sign someone was stuck in the past, it was a collection of VHS tapes. Lori wiped her dusty hand on her sweatpants and grabbed another tape.

Greece. Cringing, she tossed it in the box.

The posters were long gone, rolled up in tubes and stuffed in the closet. She'd have pictures of her own soon. She didn't need posters. She'd go through the books next and get rid of any that were more than five years old.

The last VHS tape fit neatly in the box. Lori stood up and looked around. "Damn, I'm kind of awesome."

Dust motes danced crazily under the force of her words, so she moved her awesome ass to the window and heaved it open. The snow had stopped and it was close to fifty degrees. Beautiful. As she looked out at the wet, happy dandelions that were already encroaching on the unused lot, something rumbled in the distance.

Lori frowned and leaned closer to the glass. A deep sputtering sound echoed down the street, then faded away. Shrugging, she was just starting to turn back to her work when something yellow flashed between the hardware store and the gas station. She paused and watched the top of her fence line out of curiosity. From this side of the house, she couldn't see the front of her lot, just the very corner of the wooden fence that surrounded it.

Something tall and metal and yellow slid past. Gravel crunched as if it were turning in. Then the awful sputtering stopped.

"Huh," she breathed. Maybe someone wanted to slip her a hundred dollars to tune up a bulldozer or something. She was watching the side lot closely when Quinn walked into her vision.

Lori jumped back and frowned at the windowsill. For a couple of weeks there, she'd thought she'd seen him everywhere. At the grocery store, at the diner, even passing by in a car full of teenagers. But those had been brief glimpses of men with light brown hair and wide shoulders. She'd never hallucinated him entirely before.

Holding her breath, Lori leaned forward to look again, and the doorbell suddenly chimed. Her forehead hit the window with a sharp crack. "Oh, my *God!*"

It couldn't be him, could it? She was wearing red sweatpants, for God's sake. And he couldn't be here anyway. The pass was closed.

She'd finally lost it. The stress of the past year had been too much.

The stoop wasn't visible from here, but she pressed her face hard to the glass, regardless, straining to see. It was just the bulldozer driver. Or it was just the UPS guy, and the sun had hit him in some weird way that added five inches of height and a few more of shoulder. Or...

Lori gasped.

Maybe it was the driver of an old, beat-up backhoe.

A man stepped backward, head tilted up. "Lori, is that you?"

"Ah!" She stumbled back from Quinn's voice. Not only was she wearing red sweatpants, but she'd had her cheek squished against the window like a two-year-old making faces. How was she supposed to present a vision of burgeoning success *now?*

No, no, no. It wasn't supposed to happen this way. She'd planned to casually drop by his place next summer. She would just happen to be wearing tight jeans and expensive heels. She'd mention her trip to Europe as if it were nothing. She'd be wearing the right day-of-the-week underwear for once.

Oh, God, it was Friday and she was wearing Thursday. A perfect storm.

"Lori?" he called.

She dropped the pants. And the underwear. "Just a second!" Naked from the waist down, she raced out the door and down the steps. The window was open, so she ran faster, hoping he'd keep staring at the second story. She nearly fell when she got to the bottom step, but held back a scream by sheer force of will. She would *not* be found sprawled at the bottom of the stairs wearing only tube socks and a tank top.

She spotted her jeans on the floor as soon as she hit her bedroom and tugged them on in record time. "One second!" she screamed as she sprinted for the bathroom to pat her hair into something bearable. She swiped the sweat off her forehead, took a deep breath and went to answer the door.

Quinn looked very troubled when she tugged the door open so hard it slammed into the far wall. His smile looked a little sick. "Um, hi."

"Hi!" she said too brightly.

He glanced past her. "Is this a bad time?"

"No, not at all!"

"Are you all right?"

"Sure, I'm great!"

His eyes traveled down to her chest and back up. "You're, um, kind of breathing hard. Do you… Am I interrupting something?" He looked behind her again, his jaw tightening.

"No, I just ran down the stairs and…" Wait a minute, did he think she'd been having sex? Lori smiled. "Whoever he is, he'll wait. What can I do for you?"

Quinn's eyes snapped back to her face. *"What?"*

She laughed, wheezing a little since she was already panting. "I'm just cleaning, you dork."

"Oh," he said. Then "Oh!" again as a wide smile spread over his face. "Okay, good. I just wanted to… Uh, I hope you don't mind me stopping by."

"Not at all," she chirped. "What's up?"

"I told you I'd bring you the backhoe, so…"

"Really?"

He swept his hand out and Lori darted out onto the sidewalk so that she could see past the corner of the house. "Oh, my God! You're going to let me use it?"

"I am. It's your bonus, remember? I'm done working for the season, so I thought I'd…" He paused to clear his throat. "You know. Just drop it by."

"But how did you get over the pass?"

"It's got a lot of traction. It wasn't that bad."

She shook her head, eyeing the snow stuck deep in the backhoe's tracks. "But isn't the pass *closed?*"

"Um…yeah." He pushed the hair off his forehead and Lori's heart flipped at the gesture. "I kind of drove around the gate. The snow isn't that deep yet. And, all right, it was terrifying."

She laughed, but her nerves were jangling. What

was so important that he'd broken through the pass during a storm? Not just the backhoe, surely. Was he here to declare himself over her?

"You can keep it until spring. I'm definitely not trying to go around the gate again. I think I almost slid off the mountain at one point, but it was hard to tell with my eyes closed."

As she grinned and nodded like an idiot, Quinn crossed his arms and glanced nervously toward the lot. "So anyway, I guess I'll just…"

Was he leaving? He couldn't go now! "I'm sorry. I'm being rude. Come in. Please?"

He followed her into the house without a word.

"Do you want some coffee?"

"No, I'm fine. Hey, look at this place!"

Her mouth went suddenly dry as he spun around. Her decorating skills were amateurish. She knew that. But Quinn kept smiling as he turned.

"It's a bit feminine for my taste," he said. "But it suits you." When he finally looked at her, his eyes were warm light. "I thought of yellow for you actually."

"You did?"

"Yeah. I had a fantasy I might break in and fix this place up for you. But even I knew that would be a bit heavy-handed. See? I'm learning."

Her fluttering heart paused, frozen with hope, then it beat harder than ever. "Come see the bathroom."

Quinn laughed out loud at the sight of it. "It looks great."

"I saved the countertop for you. It's in the garage."

"Seriously?" His laugh turned to pure delight. "That's perfect." Crossing his arms, he leaned against the doorjamb and met her gaze. "So you anticipated maybe seeing me again someday?"

Her heart shook. "Someday, yes. Just not on the day they closed the pass."

"I couldn't wait." His voice was lower now, soft and deep.

"Is something going on?"

"No," he said. "I just couldn't wait anymore, Lori. I'm sorry. I know a backhoe isn't a grand romantic gesture. Or maybe it is. I didn't really mean it to be. I just…"

She was sure her heart was responding to that, but she couldn't feel anything beyond the pull of his hazel eyes. She shook her head.

"I'm sorry," Quinn said again, "for what I said to you. I wanted to say that in person."

"Thank you."

"You're an amazing person. And you'll do amazing things when you're ready, and I know that has nothing to do with my schedule or my ideas or my life."

Something bubbled up inside her. "I'm taking classes," she blurted out, then wanted to cover her eyes in embarrassment. But she didn't. "I enrolled at the University of Colorado. I'm taking online classes." Her eyes filled with tears, though she wasn't sure why. And when Quinn's arms came around her, she didn't care.

"In international business?" he asked, his breath warming her hair.

Lori sniffled. "No. Accounting."

He pulled back and bent down to meet her eyes. "Accounting? Really?"

"I loved doing the books for the shop. So I thought I'd try it out and see if I liked the courses. I do."

"That's great." He looked so proud that she folded herself back into his arms and held on. He didn't feel as if he wanted to tell her good riddance. Not at all. In fact, his arms tightened around her and he sighed against her temple.

"Have you had dinner?" she ventured.

Quinn shook his head.

"I've got hot dogs."

"Perfect," he answered. And it was. They sat at her table and ate hot dogs, smiling in between bites.

"I really am sorry," Quinn said after he finished his second dog.

Lori set down her beer and folded her hands together. "You were cruel—"

"I know. It was—"

"But you were right. Not about me becoming your kept woman, but about everything else." She smiled to break the tension, but Quinn still looked miserable. "It's okay, Quinn. Honestly. I was so mad I had all the energy I needed to start getting my shit together. Your evil pep talk worked."

"Well…good. You look great. And the house looks like it belongs to you now. And the accounting classes… I'm happy for you, Lori."

"Thank you." She finished her hot dog and was wiping off her hands when Quinn cleared his throat.

"Thanks for dinner. I'm staying at Ben's tonight. Maybe you'd consider going out to Grand Valley for lunch with me tomorrow?"

"Oh. Don't you have to work?"

He tipped his beer in her direction. "I think Jane will be thrilled if I call in sick. In fact, I think she'd insist."

"Do you have to go now?"

Quinn leaned back in his chair and looked at the ceiling. "I didn't come by to try to insert myself back into your life."

"But you're so good at inserting, remember?"

His sudden laugh was so loud it startled her into a jump. "How could I forget? I had new business cards printed. Poor Jane was scandalized."

"Liar."

Quinn sighed and aimed a tired smile in her direction.

"Stay," Lori whispered. "At least stay for another beer. We'll talk. If you get too drunk you can walk to Ben's." Or *you can just sleep here,* she left unsaid. She wondered if he'd notice if she replaced his half-empty bottle with a full one.

She still didn't think she was ready for a permanent relationship with Quinn, but she couldn't bear the idea of him leaving now. She just wanted to get close to him, smell his skin, maybe lick his throat just a little bit. Her body felt drawn to him, her skin pulling to get closer. But he still hadn't answered her invitation. If he left, she'd have to embarrass herself by sneaking through one of Ben's windows in the middle the night. And Ben had a gun.

"I'm going to Europe in June!" she blurted out in desperation, feeling stupid even as she did it. Bragging about something not worth bragging out. But Quinn's jaw dropped.

"Are you kidding me?"

"I'm not. I'm going to get a little more money out of the land than I'd expected. I'm selling it on speculation and I'll let the developer take the risk. They'll either be very sorry or very rich. And I'm taking a six-week trip to Europe. Finally."

"Lori… *Wow.* Six weeks?"

"So will you stay and tell me about your favorite buildings in Paris? It's my first stop."

Quinn didn't even answer. He just grabbed his beer, took her hand and led her to the couch. She asked a few questions and then he was off, describing cathedrals and libraries and ornate palaces. She didn't take notes. Hell, she didn't even listen. She just watched his face shift from seriousness to reverence to awe. His hands shaped and turned, gesturing toward structures she couldn't see.

Lori melted into the couch. He was a work of art. A man made beautiful by his passion. She could watch him for hours. She could have sex with him *right now.* When he finally came to a stop, Lori breathed out a deep sigh.

"You're amazing. If you ever looked at a woman like that, she'd be in deep trouble."

His brow lowered and his eyes finally came back into focus. "Pardon me?"

"Nothing."

He glared at her. "I hope you're not serious."

"Oh, come on, Quinn. You're like a different person when you talk about architecture."

"You think I like buildings more than I like you?"

Lori cringed and didn't answer, trying to be diplomatic. But apparently Quinn didn't appreciate the diplomacy. He set down his empty bottle with a thunk and stood, holding out his hand. "Come on."

"What?" She took his hand and found herself towed toward the bathroom. *"What?"*

"Look," he said, facing her toward the mirror. He stood behind her, hands on her shoulders.

She looked…and realized she'd forgotten to put on a bra under her tank top. Not a terrible mistake, considering.

"Look here," he whispered. He wound one of her curls around his finger. "You're beautiful, Lori."

She cringed a little.

Quinn shook his head. "You're amazing. A work of art and engineering."

"I'm pretty sure I'm not."

"Look." He wound her curl a little tighter. "Your hair is arabesque tracery…"

She started to shake her head.

"Falling down to hide the fragile volute of your ear." His lips touched her ear and paused there for a moment, mouth brushing her skin in a butterfly touch.

Lori shivered.

"And here…" His hand slid down her throat to rest against her chest. "Your collarbone, a formeret, sweeping out to your shoulder. I've traced it in my mind…" Lowering his mouth, he pressed his lips there, following the shape of the bone with a trail of kisses.

Lori's heart thundered and her chest tightened until she couldn't breathe. Quinn's words wound around her, the consonants brushing her skin. Was this really happening?

"The lancet arch under your arm—" he brushed his fingers down her bicep "—and the perfect rounded vault of your breast."

She watched his fingers spread over her breast and curve beneath the slight weight as her knees went weak and helpless. He paused there, looking at their reflection in the mirror.

As they both stared, Quinn raised his hands and slid both thin straps off of her shoulders. Her top fell, exposing her breasts. Lori gasped and heard the gorgeous sound of Quinn sighing behind her. He slid past her and dropped to his knees.

"Here." He breathed the words against her breast. "Your nipples are delicate rosettes, straining to be noticed. I *notice*." Before his words had finished shivering through her, he put his hot mouth to one nipple and drew it gently into his mouth. He sucked at her until she moaned, then dragged his wet mouth lower. "Your ribs…" He nuzzled each individual line of her ribs. "Your ribs are molded struts forming the frame of your body."

"Quinn…" she gasped, but he moved lower still.

His tongue dipped into her belly button. "Your navel is a circled niche hidden in the curve of your belly."

When he reached for the button of her jeans, Lori let her head fall back against the cool wood of the doorjamb.

She felt him tug and heard the zipper and was afraid to open her eyes and find that she was dreaming. She'd thought of Quinn's body every single night, even when she was furious with him. But she'd never imagined the beautiful words coming from his mouth.

Her jeans slid down her legs. Lori stepped out of them and heard them hit the far wall. "The quadripartite," he breathed, his voice so rough she could barely hear him, "where your thighs arch up to meet at your sex. And your sex…" Both his hands touched her, his fingers slipping into her curls while his thumbs slid lower, parting her.

Lori whimpered.

"Your sex is a gothic portal molded of delicate palmettes. Something too beautiful to have been created by man. Like nothing made of stone. I know. I've tried to build you in my mind. I've lain there at night sculpting your shape behind my eyes." His wide thumbs traced the lines of her sex, tightening her belly into coils.

"And finally…" He spread her gently and dipped his head to touch his tongue to her. "Finally, the hidden keystone of your whole body."

When he licked her, she moaned. She couldn't hold

it back and didn't want to. His words were flying through her, swirling around inside her chest, her head. And his tongue was pressing at just the right spot. Sobbing, she came within seconds, her body rushing to meet the pleasure he offered.

Before she'd stopped shaking, Quinn lifted her up and carried her to her new bed. He made love to her slowly. There was no roughness or dirty talk. There were no ropes and harsh words. It was just Quinn and his body on hers. Lori held him tight to her, even the thrust of his sex not close enough for what she wanted. She wrapped herself around him and took him in and cried as he reached his climax.

Quinn brushed her hair from her eyes and kissed her tears away. "I like you more than buildings, Lori Love," he whispered, causing more tears to fall. "A lot more. I won't tell you how much. Not now."

"I missed you," she choked out.

"I missed you, too. And I've been thinking…"

She froze beneath him. "Oh, no."

"Seriously." He rolled to his side, but kept her body tight against his. "Ben's going to move in with Molly."

Lori pulled her chin in to look at him. "She hasn't said anything to me."

"She was trying to be delicate, I think. You're sitting here with a broken heart and— Oof!" He pressed a hand to his damaged ribs. "Anyway, Ben's going to rent out his house. I thought maybe I'd lease it for a year."

"What?" She shook her head. "That makes no sense. You can't leave your office."

"No, I can't. And I wouldn't want to. But it's winter now. I can't go out and visit sites, so my time is occupied with planning and drawing and meeting with clients. There's no reason I can't work from here for a week or two every month. And in the summer, it will be no problem. I thought maybe, if I behaved myself, you'd consider giving me another chance. Just dating. That's all."

His face swam in front of her. Not from tears, but just her reeling mind. "Just dating?"

"You need time. I know that. I don't want to pressure you, but I don't want to give you up, either. I like you *more* than buildings, Lori. And I think that deserves a chance, if you do, too."

"You'd come here for me?"

"I would. You were right. I asked you to sacrifice everything and that was shitty."

"Mmm."

"But my ego can't take more than one more rejection, so just make it quick if you never want to see me again. But you'd better sound like you mean it, because I can still feel the imprint of your fingernails on my ass."

"Shut up!" she gasped, relieved at the chance to laugh. While she was still laughing, Quinn kissed her and didn't stop for a long, long time. When he finally let her go, she'd melted into the covers.

Quinn took a deep breath. "Will you let me move temporarily into your town and take you out to dinner a few nights a month so you don't forget me this winter, Lori Love?"

"Aren't you going to get down on one knee while you ask that?"

"I didn't want to scare you." He punctuated his joke with a yawn. "Plus I'm really tired."

"Yes," she answered, "I will." Smiling, she stroked his hair for a few minutes, thrilled that she could touch him again. "And, Quinn…? Do you think you might… Um… Will you meet me in Córdoba?"

She held her breath, waiting for an answer that didn't come. Awkward. "Quinn?"

He didn't answer, so Lori scooted down a little on the bed to see his face. Her studly erotica hero was dead asleep.

Lori snuggled close, pulled the comforter over both of them, and fell fast asleep. She dreamed of dancing with a handsome stranger in a café in Spain, and strangely enough, the stranger had elegant hands and a keen interest in the local buildings. And he called himself Quinto.

* * * * *

Summer love can last a lifetime....

**A dazzling new story from
New York Times bestselling author**

SUSAN MALLERY

Small-town librarian Annabelle Weiss has always seen herself as more of a sweetheart than a siren, so she can't understand why Shane keeps pushing her away. Shane has formed the totally wrong impression of her but only he can help her with a special event for the next Fool's Gold festival. And maybe while he's at it, she can convince him to teach her a few things about kissing on hot summer nights, too—some lessons, a girl shouldn't learn from reading a book!

Summer Nights

Available now!

www.Harlequin.com

PHSSM687

**He would move heaven and earth
to protect her....**

A haunting and sensual new story from

Eden Bradley

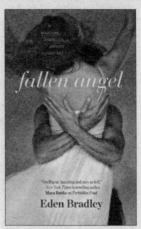

Haunted by a military mission that ended in personal tragedy,
Declan Byrne still bears a soldier's scars. As a park ranger on the
secluded Mendocino coast, he guards his heart while standing ready for
anything. Anything except a beautiful, ethereal woman falling from the
cliffs, badly injured and strangely attired....

fallen angel

Available in stores now.

www.Harlequin.com

PHEB717

New York Times bestselling author
and undisputed master of romance

BERTRICE SMALL

invites you to discover the magical,
sensual realm of Hetar.

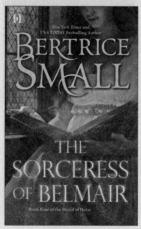

THE
SORCERESS
OF BELMAIR

Available now.

"Small's newest novel is a sexily fantastical romp."
—*Publishers Weekly*

www.Harlequin.com

PHBS690

An angel poised on the brink of destruction.

New York Times **bestselling author**

GENA SHOWALTER

is back with a dark, seductive new series....

Leader of the most powerful army in the heavens, Zacharel has been deemed nearly too dangerous, too ruthless—and if he isn't careful, he'll lose his wings. But this warrior with a heart of ice will not be deterred from his missions at any cost...until a vulnerable human tempts him with a carnal pleasure he's never known before.

Wicked Nights

Available now.

www.Harlequin.com

PHGS698

A heartfelt and classic collection from
#1 *New York Times* bestselling author

NORA ROBERTS

Meet the next generation of the beloved MacGregor family,
as cousins Laura, Gwendolyn and Julia discover that their
busybody grandfather has an unerring instinct for love!

THE MacGREGOR BRIDES

Available now.

www.Harlequin.com

PSNR159

REQUEST YOUR
FREE BOOKS!

2 FREE NOVELS
FROM THE ROMANCE COLLECTION
PLUS 2 FREE GIFTS!

YES! Please send me 2 FREE novels from the Romance Collection and my 2 FREE gifts (gifts are worth about $10). After receiving them, if I don't wish to receive any more books, I can return the shipping statement marked "cancel." If I don't cancel, I will receive 4 brand-new novels every month and be billed just $5.99 per book in the U.S. or $6.49 per book in Canada. That's a saving of at least 25% off the cover price. It's quite a bargain! Shipping and handling is just 50¢ per book in the U.S. and 75¢ per book in Canada.* I understand that accepting the 2 free books and gifts places me under no obligation to buy anything. I can always return a shipment and cancel at any time. Even if I never buy another book, the two free books and gifts are mine to keep forever.

194/394 MDN FELQ

Name	(PLEASE PRINT)	
Address		Apt. #
City	State/Prov.	Zip/Postal Code

Signature (if under 18, a parent or guardian must sign)

Mail to the **Reader Service**:
IN U.S.A.: P.O. Box 1867, Buffalo, NY 14240-1867
IN CANADA: P.O. Box 609, Fort Erie, Ontario L2A 5X3

Not valid for current subscribers to the Romance Collection
or the Romance/Suspense Collection.

Want to try two free books from another line?
Call 1-800-873-8635 or visit www.ReaderService.com.

* Terms and prices subject to change without notice. Prices do not include applicable taxes. Sales tax applicable in N.Y. Canadian residents will be charged applicable taxes. Offer not valid in Quebec. This offer is limited to one order per household. All orders subject to credit approval. Credit or debit balances in a customer's account(s) may be offset by any other outstanding balance owed by or to the customer. Please allow 4 to 6 weeks for delivery. Offer available while quantities last.

Your Privacy—The Reader Service is committed to protecting your privacy. Our Privacy Policy is available online at www.ReaderService.com or upon request from the Reader Service.

We make a portion of our mailing list available to reputable third parties that offer products we believe may interest you. If you prefer that we not exchange your name with third parties, or if you wish to clarify or modify your communication preferences, please visit us at www.ReaderService.com/consumerchoice or write to us at Reader Service Preference Service, P.O. Box 9062, Buffalo, NY 14269. Include your complete name and address.

**Temptation and danger collide in a daring
new historical tale from**

CHARLOTTE
FEATHERSTONE

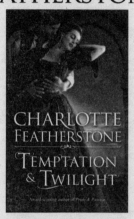

CHARLOTTE
FEATHERSTONE

TEMPTATION
& TWILIGHT

Award-winning author of Pride & Passion

Iain Sinclair thinks there's a special place in hell for people like him.
The Marquis of Alynwick and an unrepentant rake, he holds nothing
sacred—except for the beautiful Elizabeth York, the woman
he loved so well, and treated so badly.

When Elizabeth, the blind daughter of a duke, discovers an
ancestor's ancient diary, she longs to uncover the identity of the
unnamed lover within and hesitantly enlists Alynwick to help. But
a centuries-old secret will lead them to a present-day danger....

TEMPTATION
& TWILIGHT

Available now!

HARLEQUIN® HQN™
www.Harlequin.com

PHCF662

Wo Ko

VICTORIA DAHL

77609 REAL MEN WILL	___ $7.99 U.S.	___ $9.99 CAN.
77602 BAD BOYS DO	___ $7.99 U.S.	___ $9.99 CAN.
77595 GOOD GIRLS DON'T	___ $7.99 U.S.	___ $9.99 CAN.

(limited quantities available)

TOTAL AMOUNT	$ _____
POSTAGE & HANDLING	$ _____
($1.00 FOR 1 BOOK, 50¢ for each additional)	
APPLICABLE TAXES*	$ _____
TOTAL PAYABLE	$ _____

(check or money order—please do not send cash)

To order, complete this form and send it, along with a check or money order for the total above, payable to HQN Books, to: **In the U.S.:** 3010 Walden Avenue, P.O. Box 9077, Buffalo, NY 14269-9077; **In Canada:** P.O. Box 636, Fort Erie, Ontario, L2A 5X3.

Name: _____
Address: _____ City: _____
State/Prov.: _____ Zip/Postal Code: _____
Account Number (if applicable): _____

075 CSAS

*New York residents remit applicable sales taxes.
*Canadian residents remit applicable GST and provincial taxes.

HARLEQUIN® HQN™
www.Harlequin.com

PHVD0712BL